THE
DOWRY BLADE

CHERRY POTTS

ARACHNE PRESS

First published in UK 2016 by Arachne Press Limited
100 Grierson Road, London SE23 1NX
www.arachnepress.com
© Cherry Potts 2016
ISBN: 978-1-909208-20-9
The moral rights of the author have been asserted
Printed on wood free paper in the UK by TJ International, Padstow.
Thanks to Muireann Grealy for her attention to detail on proofing, and to many, many people for reading drafts - especially Johnny and Katie.

THE
DOWRY BLADE

For Alix,
everything, always.

For Ghil,
who introduced me to women warriors
at an impressionable age.

Chapter One

The way down the hill was steep, the track slippery in the rain. The horses scattered stones from beneath their hooves; the warriors blinked water from their eyes and slid in the mud, anxious as much for what might be out in the blinding rain as for their footing.

The noise of the rain and of the new-born stream running down the path, deadened their hearing. They knew that if they were attacked, they would not hear their assailants coming, and with the litter bearing their injured leader to hamper two of the horses, there would be no question of running.

They had removed their identifying badges, their banners. Rain darkened, their clothes merged with the landscape – but the horses would be noticeable from a distance; and in this place even so few horses meant only one thing, and so they were as conspicuous as if they rode in full battle gear, glittering and loud with banners.

Brede slid on mud and gravel, her breath coming in hard painful gasps that did not know how to let the air out again. She fell, scraping hand, knee, elbow, face. Rolling herself tight against the vast roots of a fallen tree, she pressed herself to the dead bark, fingers digging for purchase in the mossy growth between the reaching limbs. The harsh gasps stilled sufficiently that the hissing of breath would scarce be distinguished from the rain. She closed her eyes, as though that could make her less visible, and prayed to anything that was listening and kindly disposed, that this new band of warriors had not seen her as she careered round the edge of the hill, away from the much larger company she had already avoided.

What were they all doing, still skulking about up here? The battle had been miles away and days ago, and there was no telling which side was which, not that it would mean much, no one was exactly a friend anymore, the Marshes had been disputed land for far too long for that.

Breath slowing, but her heart still painful in it dipping and pounding, Brede listened for any hint of pursuit, and heard voices – indistinct, but quite close. She didn't dare raise her head to check, simply praying that the mud and rain would disguise her sufficiently that the riders would pass her by. She shivered, cold, wet and afraid, and wondered whether she would ever get down from the hill and back to where Adair would be watching, and her mother would be pretending she was not terrified by an absence of nearly two days.

Involuntarily, Brede remembered the rebellious sheep she had been tracking, the ewe and her adolescent lamb, bent on adventure at the worst possible time. She had found them, or what was left, after some marauding group of warriors had made a supper of them. That was the way things were, and had been for years. Brede hugged the ground even closer as a horse knocked a shod hoof against the far side of the great tree, and her heart pounded in response.

Maeve pushed wet hair out of her eyes and then dropped her hand to steady the litter hung between the horses stumbling on the path down to the marshy valley, where perhaps there was a village. She watched Corla riding slowly back up the barely discernible trail, silently willing her to bring good news. Almost without thinking she checked her limping band of warriors; Cei moving up to ride at her shoulder, ready to take his turn on foot; Balin and Inir slightly ahead, Riordan a way behind, watchful of the horizon. She looked with more deliberation at Tegan, white-faced and still, within the tight wrapping of the makeshift litter. She listened hard, trying to hear Tegan's breathing over the roar of rain, watching for movement, her intent gaze noting the water pooling once more in Tegan's eyes. She reached to wipe it away, and Tegan, woken from her uneasy sleep, reached out a hand and tangled her fingers into Maeve's.

'Your hands are freezing,' Maeve said, worried that Tegan could still feel icy to her own hands, which were numb with cold. She glanced up anxiously as Corla's horse crowded her.

'There must be a village,' Corla insisted. 'This is a track that leads somewhere, and I can smell smoke.'

'Another burnt village?' Cei muttered sourly. Maeve glanced up at him, angry that he voiced her own fear. Corla offered Cei the battered leather hat with which she had so far protected her thin pale hair.

'No,' she said, patiently, 'cooking.'

Cei grinned. 'You must be sure, if you're willing to giving up your most treasured protection.'

Tegan loosened her hold on Maeve and reached out.

'I'll have that, then Maeve can stop waking me to mop my eyes.' Tegan's voice was faint in the roar of the rain, and Cei had to strain to hear her next words; 'Corla will be right.'

'So there's a village. That doesn't mean there's a welcome, we don't know if we're over the border yet,' Cei insisted.

'We need a village,' Tegan said tersely, 'and a welcome, and somewhere warm – a healer would be – a good idea.'

Maeve looked at her sharply, and slowed the lead horse to a gentler pace.

Brede tried to untangle the sounds of hooves, how many were there? Five? Six? Moving on, thank the Goddess; she could hear the bridles, even though they had done their best to muffle them. She lay and waited until she could hear nothing but rain, and lay a few minutes more to be sure, then slowly lifted her head and stared down the hill, at the group of warriors heading straight for her home.

Brede counted the horses. This group was too small for an army, too closed up for a scouting party, too slow for a group of messengers. She turned quickly and started down the slope, heading for a way only someone on foot would risk, one that in this weather she would prefer not to have to try. She cursed the warriors for their instinct for the landscape.

The gatekeeper waved urgently to attract Brede's attention as she hesitated at the brink of the mud stirred water – the river had risen alarmingly since she went out. Brede blinked water from her eyes and followed his exaggerated arm waving. Despite Adair's attempts she was soaked to the waist by the time she was across to the gate.

'You look as though you've something to report,' Adair said cheerfully.

Brede shuddered at the clinging weight of her clothes.

'Warriors – only about seven as far as I could tell, but definitely headed here.'

'They won't get across the river now,' Adair said, gauging the strength of the flood eating away at the far bank.

'Oh, they will. They've got horses.' Brede stared at the wider branch of the river, on the far side of the village, trying to judge how swollen that reach had become. Adair followed her gaze.

'They'll not get that far, not unless their horses were bred of giants.' He grimaced, and started towards the gate. Brede made to follow and help but he waved her away. 'Get yourself dry. I can manage.'

Adair closed the gate, and pulled the extra bars into place, his mind on Brede, not the work in hand.

Corla was first to glimpse the smoke she had smelt. She slowed, trying to work out what lay ahead. She felt a presence at her shoulder and looked up at Balin. His bulk sheltered her for a moment. He turned his eyes down the hill towards the swollen turn of the river.

'Is that a village?' he asked. Corla raised her shoulder, the sodden woollen coat sticking to her back, cold against her flesh.

'It looks like a fort.' Balin persisted, and Corla bit her lip as his words solidified her anxious uncertainty into ramparts and walls, that had been uncertain blur until now.

'Marsh dwellers don't like outsiders,' she said.

'It's not just that, surely. Those walls mean business.'

'But there are fields look, someone's been growing crops – and there are too many sheep to just be provisioning a fort – this is a settlement not an outpost.'

Balin sighed.

'I wish I knew whether that was a good thing.'

Maeve rode up behind them.

'What now?'

'Walls – and a gate and a guard.' Balin hesitated. 'Only one guard.'

'Then why are we waiting?'

'They'll not let us in, Maeve.'

Maeve eased her tense shoulders, and looked back up the hill, to the stand of trees that could have been their shelter for the night. She stared at the uncertain plain beyond the village.

'We didn't come this way before, this valley doesn't look as though there's been a battle here – not recently.'

Corla and Balin waited for her decision, pretending not to hear the uncertainty in her voice.

'If we go on, we have to cross the far branch of the river tonight.' Inir offered, resting his hand on the shuddering neck of Corla's horse. 'We'll not manage it. The water looks high, the horses are exhausted, and there's Tegan –'

Maeve's eyes flickered to Tegan, asleep, or unconscious. She looked again at the steep rise of the hill, and flexed a knee that was complaining at the cold and the damp and the incline.

'We have to risk the village,' she said quietly.

There was no welcome for the bedraggled group of mercenaries at the gate.

Maeve twisted her gloved hands about her sword hilt, lower lip caught between her teeth. She stood over Tegan, willing her back into consciousness.

Tegan sighed, and turned her head. She focused on the tall palisade beyond Maeve's tense shoulder.

'You're not dragging me back up that hill,' she said weakly. 'We'll make camp out of reach of any archers and wait.'

'For what?'

'For curiosity to bring them out to us.'

Tegan shivering with bone-deep cold. Maeve reached within the tightly wrapped oilcloth, seeking any sign of warmth in her shuddering body. Tegan clenched her teeth at the effort it cost her to still the trembling; hating the fear in Maeve's face.

'I've no intention of dying out in the rain,' she said.

With no way of keeping a fire alight, the warriors huddled together, horses tethered close outside their leaky canvas shelters, protecting and warming them slightly with their animal bulk. They spent a miserable, wakeful night, and by morning would almost have been glad at the sight of a hillside bright with enemy banners. They would sooner have fought again than spend any longer shivering in the rain.

The village paths resembled a mire. The only fire that belched warmth with any success was in the forge. The smith kept her apprentice hard at work all morning, making up for her truancy of the previous days. It was not until the rain died out at noon that Faine finally sent Brede out to the camp by the gates to find out why the warriors were still there.

Faine followed Brede as far as the gate, and stood close beside Adair as he pulled the bars free. She glanced out at the bedraggled shelters on the edge of the rapidly rising river as Brede shouldered her way through the meagre gap Adair allowed her.

'Lock it.' Faine said firmly, refusing to allow her anxiety for Brede to show.

Brede didn't hesitate when she heard the gate's locking bars pushed back into place behind her. She strolled down from the raised ground of the village's defences, to the three dripping shelters ringed by wretched looking horses. She ignored the man on guard and ran her hand down the shoulder of the nearest horse. It barely flicked an ear in response to her touch. She waited for the guard to challenge her, but he stood unmoving between her and the shelter.

'What are you doing here?' she asked, looking up at last. Riordan shrugged.

Brede tried again.

'Why do you want to come into the village?'

Riordan shrugged again.

'You've been told not to speak to me then?' Silence. Brede lost patience and pushed past and under the dripping shelter.

She blinked, trying to adjust her eyes to the dimness of the light within. She took in two crouching figures, and one lying, and to either side of her, crowding the space, and settling her hackles up, a giant, and another man. Someone missing, she registered, without quite realising it.

'Is there anyone here who is willing to talk to me, or shall I go back to my mistress without knowing what you want?'

One of the crouching figures rose to her full height. She was a little taller than Brede, and Brede was tall. The warrior's head grazed the damp cloth of the shelter, setting a soft trickle of water across her shoulder.

'We need someone who knows something about healing. We need somewhere warm for our injured companion. We won't ask for anything else.'

Brede measured out the words, listening to the tight control in the woman's voice, balancing need against ask, and wondering how much might be taken without need, without asking.

'This village has a wall for a reason. Will it be rebels, foreigners, or the government next at our gate, demanding retribution for any help we give you?'

The woman shrugged. Brede glanced at the sword strapped at her back, out of her way, but very much to hand if need be, and at the recumbent figure, and the woman crouched at her side. She nodded.

'I'll ask.'

Brede took another look at the horses as she passed – she missed horses.

Brede warmed her chilled bones at the forge and watched the smith work, and Faine allowed her to keep silent, while she concentrated on her hammer work, each content to let the moment drag.

Faine finished the repair she had been working on and plunged the hot metal into the trough. The steam curled thickly into the air. She put down her tongs, wiped her hands on a rag and turned to Brede, breaking in on her reverie.

'Tell me then.'

'One of them is injured; they want aid and warmth, nothing else.'

'Trust them?'

'Probably, but they don't look after their horses.'

'And you didn't tell them how to treat them better? All right, I'll speak to Keenan – finish this for me.' Faine indicated the work she wanted Brede to do, and strode away in search of her fellow Elder.

Brede bent her back to the work, wielding her hammer with almost as much skill as her mistress. She had been nine years in the learning. Today those nine years shouted at her. Perhaps it was the horses. The village had a team of oxen for their ploughing; twelve score sheep and assorted dogs, but there had been no horses since a raiding party stole Brede's one remaining beast.

The sparks flew from the rough metal. The ore belonged to Finley, but it wasn't Finley's pattern that Brede's mind followed as she hammered, and cooled, and heated, and hammered again; refining the metal, and with it, thought.

Brede welcomed the heat of the fire, the sweat building on her skin.

Nine years, she hissed, suddenly angry where she had been content, bending the metal to her will. Nine years in one place, never travelling, only setting foot out of the village for her self-imposed scouting after danger; playing the obedient daughter, wasting her youth.

Brede was her father's daughter, a nomadic impulse was in her blood. She longed for open spaces, speed and noise; but that need was incomprehensible to her Marsh kinsfolk.

Brede cooled the metal once more, and inspected it critically. She wasn't satisfied with her work, and returned the piece to the fire, seeking yet more heat. She worked the bellows rhythmically, patiently.

The warriors at the gate unsettled her. It was months since they had seen so much as a smudge of smoke from the war that ran its course somewhere out beyond their valley. Every incursion smelt of another life, a life she longed for. The sorry group of horses raised ghosts for her, and brought into sharp focus the lack of movement her life had taken on since she came to the Marsh.

Brede hit the metal a touch too hard. She swore, brought back to the matter in hand. She inspected the barely formed blade, sighed, and continued.

She had been pretending to herself that she didn't care what happened to the strangers, but she did care.

She wiped the sweat from her eyes. She breathed in the smell of hot iron, harsh on her tongue, a smell she had learned to enjoy. She took up the metal, holding it just above the surface of the water in the trough. The heat forced the water into hissing movement before the metal touched it. She slid the piece into the water, gently, letting the liquid caress the metal. The steam, rising, dampened her face, setting a light sheen on her skin, prickling. The metal darkened, the water quietened. Brede put down the tongs and stretched her cramped back. The anvil wasn't the right height for her. Faine was shorter than her apprentice and it was Faine's forge.

Faine kept her words to Keenan as brief as Brede's and paced impatiently while he considered.

'Send Adair out to bring their leader in to talk.' He said at last.

Faine frowned, and nodded to Darcie, lurking in the corner of his father's hut, eyes aglow with excitement.

'Go to it,' she said sharply. 'You take gate duty – keep the gate barred until they are ready and only the one comes in, mind.'

Darcie scampered away.

Faine returned to her pacing. Darcie was gone longer than she had anticipated, and she was beginning to think he had misunderstood the message, when he returned, towing a tall slender woman by the hand.

'Where's Adair?' Keenan asked.

'Out with my people,' the woman replied. Keenan sat more upright and let his glare travel from her to Darcie.

'Who is at the gate?'

'Rhian.'

Keenan huffed through his moustache. 'All right then.' His gaze returned to the warrior. 'Tell me properly what you're after.'

'We have a wounded companion; we need a healer to take a look at her. We'd be grateful for somewhere warm for the night.'

'And in return?'

'We can pay.'

Keenan shook his head impatiently. 'There's nothing much we need money for.'

'Information then?'

'Possibly. Depending what it is. Start by telling me what you're doing here, and where the rest of your force is.'

Maeve hesitated.

'We do have a healer,' Faine put in, encouragingly.

Maeve nodded quickly.

Keenan tilted his head expectantly, and Maeve took a settling breath.

'There's been a big battle, way south of here, almost a week ago now. I don't know who won, exactly; the weather drove us all off eventually. As far as I'm aware everyone but us is long gone, having Tegan slowed us down, and we've seen no one for more than four days.'

'Now there's a lie already,' Keenan said. 'Brede came across a larger group than yours not an hour before she spotted you.'

'She did? Then we were lucky not to have encountered them ourselves. We didn't see them and I thank the Goddess for it. I can be sure they weren't ours.'

'And who was fighting?'

'Phelan, and Ailbhe.'

'And which side are you?'

'We are mercenaries.' Maeve said, deliberately obscuring. Keenan nodded, he wasn't going to trust her whichever side she said she was, and he didn't much care, really.

'Do you think they've done for the winter?'

'Yes, I'm sure of that.'

Keenan smoothed his moustache.

'All right then, you can come in, you'll get your healer.'

Faine pushed through the leather-curtained doorway.

Brede watched her, schooling her face to patience. Faine glanced at the faint stirring of steam still rising from the trough. She peered in, and her easy smile creased her face.

'I see you already know the answer,' Faine said, fishing with the tongs for the still warm metal. She pulled out the piece Brede had been working on. She squinted down its length.

'A good edge that will have, true and straight, but the length's a little strange, and there won't be enough strength in it. What have you been told about planning your work?'

'They're staying then?' Brede asked, ignoring Faine's words.

Faine shook her head slightly, and let the long knife that Brede had made slip back into the water. Brede moved out of her way, restless for the answer.

'The injured one will stay. Her name is Tegan. The others will go tomorrow. I have agreed that they can come here to get warm and dry. They will eat, they will sleep, and they will go.' Faine crossed her arms, her hands gripping above her elbows. 'What, Brede? You want me to keep the whole band of them fed all winter just so you have someone to talk to?'

'I'm not sure I want any of them here,' Brede said.

'It's as well no one is asking you for a decision then.'

'The injured one,' Brede said, feeling a way through Faine's amusement, wanting a serious response, 'will she die?'

Faine frowned.

'That depends on Edra – and on you.'

'Me?'

'I told Keenan you'd care for her, once Edra has done everything she can. We don't want a stranger taking too much of our healer's attention.' Brede shook her head slowly, confused. Faine said, 'They're leaving her horse, you can nurse that too.'

Brede laughed.

'The black gelding?'

'No; nothing showy for her. She has that ugly speckled one with the white streak on its rump. It's called Guida.'

'That old nag?' Brede said crossly, but a grin spread across her face. The horse might be old, even ugly, but she had been, and could again be a magnificent animal. As a consolation for the desertion of the remaining mercenaries, the horse was adequate. Faine shook her head.

'Get rid of that excuse for a weapon you've made from Finley's metal. There will be no more of this work today. Clear up in here, dismantle the bellows, we need space. And when you've done that, find somewhere for those horses. Ask Darcie if they can go in with the oxen – failing that, use your initiative.'

Brede nodded, rising to her feet. She took her not-quite-sword blade from the trough, giving it an experimental whirl. *Not bad.* She stashed it carefully in one of the baskets lodged in the rafters above her head.

Chapter Two

Maeve moved swiftly out from the gate, her skin prickling with relief. She nodded to Riordan and within moments the camp was dismantled and her small band of mercenaries were headed for the village, Cei pushing a bound Adair before him, Maeve keeping up a steady murmur of instruction and warning.

As they stumbled in through the gate, Cei let Adair loose. The gatekeeper glared and straightened his clothes as he caught his father's eye. Keenan nodded carefully, and Adair walked over to cuff Darcie not overly gently about the shoulder. Darcie's lip trembled, then Adair grinned at him, forgiving him for his incompetence, and his own brief captivity. Adair straightened and caught Brede watching, he nodded to her, an unconscious echo of his father. Brede lowered her head and followed the mercenaries to the forge.

There was scarcely room for them all in the building, but the warmth of the forge fire was wonderful. Maeve basked as steam rose from her clothes, but she did not drop her guard.

Tegan was equally grateful for the warmth and for the woman who examined her wound.

'You'll live, providing you stay still and warm,' Edra said at last, and began to rebind the deep sword wound; 'the blade went deep, but you are lucky. There's no serious damage. Infection and exhaustion are the dangers here.' Tegan nodded, silent in the face of that warning. Edra turned to Faine. 'Are we keeping her then?'

Faine gave Tegan a long look, aware of the tension in all those about her, waiting for her final decision. Then she nodded firmly. Tegan let out her held breath. But for Faine's word, infection and exhaustion would be her fate.

Corla eyed the healer resentfully, absently making a sign against witchcraft.

Maeve returned to her minute inspection of their temporary lodging.

Tegan met Edra's eyes in silent apology, uncomfortable with her own vulnerability and with her welfare utterly in Edra's hands. She snagged Maeve's hand as she passed, tugging her down.

'I'll be safe here,' she whispered.

Maeve put aside the temptation to shake her into caution.

'We may have no choice but to leave you here,' she said steadily, 'but we are still in enemy territory.'

Brede, lounging in the doorway, was more diffident on her own ground than she had been in the warrior's camp at the gate, but she was indignant at Maeve's careful searching. 'If we wished you harm,' she said, 'we'd have left you where you were. The river would have swept you away by morning.'

Maeve bowed slightly in acknowledgement of Brede's comment, and reached down the basket containing Brede's half-made weapon. Brede flinched, but Maeve merely frowned at the blade and returned it to its perch. She nodded silently at her companions. They stripped away their outermost garments spreading them in dripping curtains wherever they could find space.

Brede drank in newness, strangeness; variety. A smooth faced giant, who moved with an agility startling in one so solidly made; a thin silent man who turned immediately to care of his weapons; a woman with hair so fine and pale that rain flattened, she looked almost bald. All of them had a hungry look about them, faces sharper than they should be. Brede tried to stop categorising them, but she was giddy with newness. Maeve was the most striking. She was tall, and not as slight as she at first appeared, more wiry than slender. Brede could see now, as her unbraided hair started to dry and the colour lightened, that she was red-haired. Her skin was unnaturally pale, freckled, giving an impression of constantly moving sunlight on her face. She was difficult to look at, full of movement and sharp angles.

Trouble, Brede decided, shifting her gaze away. The young guard resembled Maeve, as though he might be her brother. He was scarcely out of boyhood. Brede looked again, guessing that Maeve must be at least five years younger than herself.

Maeve glanced up, and caught Brede's eye upon her.

Trouble, she thought wearily. She frowned, distracted. She was afraid for Tegan and would miss her; miss her assurance, her good sense, her warmth at night. Maeve twisted her thoughts away from that temporary loneliness. At least she could hope she wouldn't lose Tegan this way, as she might have, *would* have, if they had continued to struggle eastward through uncertain territory in ever worsening conditions.

Brede pressed warm bread into Maeve's hand. Maeve took it, observing her thoughtfully, noting a strength of feature which Brede did not share with her kin. She had a bright defiant expression and a carelessness about her; dark hair tied into a loose braid that did not serve to keep her eyes clear. Maeve wanted to call it a lack of discipline, but it was more than that: she was alive with curiosity, dangerous with it. Maeve made a small adjustment in her assumptions about Marsh dwellers, and remembered what the smith said when Tegan thanked her for her hospitality.

I'm not doing this for you.

Brede's keen dark eyes made her uncomfortable – darting about – following every movement. She was relieved when Faine came to beckon her away.

Brede went reluctantly, unwilling to settle back into her established routine. She allowed herself another check on the horses. Perhaps her mother would like to see them? Brede considered, and rejected the possibility. Leal wouldn't want to be reminded that she had once been entranced by movement and uncertainty, by the wind patterns on the tall grasses of the plains, that she had once lost her heart to a Plains rider.

And this was no time to be thinking of Devnet.

Brede returned home, intending to be a gracious and dutiful daughter, but her gentle kiss went unacknowledged, her greeting unanswered. She settled the other side of the smoky fire; her eyes smarting, and delved into the pot of stew hung over the flames.

Leal watched her daughter and was afraid for the first time since returning to the safety of her birthplace. She wanted to scream at her daughter,

You know what happens when you go. Something terrible always happens. Don't leave me again.

Thoughts of that terrible time brought Leal to thoughts of Devnet, and Leal's anxiety spilt into accusation.

'I suppose you find one of these mercenaries attractive?'

Brede put her bowl aside, her stomach tightening into revolt.

Dear Goddess, she thought, *I don't believe we're going to fight about this now.*

'In what way?' she asked, scrupulously neutral.

'Like Devnet.'

Brede considered. She was tempted to agree, to say –

Yes, Leal, there's a stunning redhead.

'They are leaving tomorrow,' she said instead.

'And what will you do?'

'What the Elders ask of me.' Leal snorted and struck out again.

'Why aren't you more like your sister?'

'Falda is *dead*,' Brede said, her voice barely under control.

Leal recoiled, then went on: 'Why couldn't you have hand-fast and had babies? Why couldn't you be a *real* daughter?'

'I take after my father,' Brede snapped, a phrase often used to cover what made her different from her mother, a disappointment, a problem.

She unfolded her legs, and went out into the cold night air.

Leal regretted her temper at once and she was out into the rain almost as swiftly as Brede. There was no sign of her daughter, and her anxiety took her to her sister, Faine.

'I've been expecting you,' the smith said gently, beckoning Leal in.

Leal raised her hands in a gesture of helplessness.

'Tomorrow, when the mercenaries go, Brede will go.'

Faine sighed. 'You may be right. You know Brede can't settle, Leal. You should never have expected it.'

'It's been almost ten years, that should have been long enough. She should have found herself a hand-mate by now.'

'It's a small village, in difficult times, there aren't many for her to choose from.'

'Oh Faine, you know that isn't it. She thinks she's too good for the likes of us, just as her father did. She despises us – she despises me.'

'No,' Faine hesitated, trying to find words for her partial understanding of Brede. 'She has nomad blood, yes. That's why she finds it so hard. She's like – like a river that has been dammed.'

'She has no more conscience than a river.'

'Conscience? She's stayed all this time, Leal. I never thought she would. What more d'you want of her?'

'I want her to stay. I want her safe,' Leal shook her head. 'Brede is all I have left in the world.'

Faine snorted.

'Your world needs expanding then.' She caught Leal's expression. 'I've no sympathy to offer you. She's a grown woman. She'll do as she pleases, just as you did at her age.'

'But I was *wrong*.'

Faine caught at Leal's hands.

'How can you say that? You loved Ahern. How could that be wrong?'

Leal looked at the hands about her fingers, and said nothing.

Brede, out in the rainy darkness, stood in the forge doorway, watching.

Maeve sat cross-legged beside her leader, her hair still loose on her shoulders, polishing the sword laid across her knees. The edge of her mail sleeve caught the metal with a soft ringing. Her head was bent to her work and she was oblivious to Brede's silent watchfulness.

Brede glanced around. Three of the men were missing. The others seemed to be asleep, except Tegan, who watched Maeve as carefully as Brede.

Maeve finished one side of the sword and turned it over. Tegan reached to catch her hand. Maeve turned her head, and the curtain of her loosened hair covered her face as she leant to kiss Tegan softly, putting aside the sword.

Brede turned quietly away, ashamed to be standing in the rain, watching where she had no business to watch. She walked back through the cluster of huts, noticing, as she did so, the silent movement of Maeve's scouts returning to the forge. Brede stood where she was, letting them see her, letting them know that she had seen and was unconcerned. In their place, she too would be checking her surroundings in preference to sleep. She watched them slip past in the darkness, listening to their breath, the slap of feet in mud, and knew abruptly that she wasn't going to sleep any time soon. She turned and set off towards the gate, thinking to talk to Adair. She glanced up at his habitual post, and saw, not the familiar welcome bulk of his wolf-skin cloak, but Rhian in his mass of cloaks and scarves. She could tell even from a distance that he was shivering. She sighed, and turned away, heading now for the ox-stall. There were horses that would be glad to be groomed properly for once in their wretched lives. In the darkness she could pretend they were hers, pretend they were well bred, pretend that at any moment Devnet would come to stand at her shoulder, or that tall sun-lit Maeve would find her in the morning and suggest that she join the mercenaries. Anything, anything, but stay here for the rest of her life.

Brede knew that any thought of joining the mercenaries was insanity. She put away the brushes, and stumbled out into the depth of night, back to her bed. She lay and watched the darkness and felt again the probing of Maeve's grey eyes, the distrust and prejudice of Corla's ice blue gaze. She forced her thoughts away, turning instead to horses, remembering animals that she had bred: the feel of hot horse skin beneath her hands, the sound of a particular young stallion's breathing at full gallop, harsh and regular. At last she lost herself in that remembered sound, and drifted into fitful dreaming.

She dreamt of Devnet, of lying in semi-darkness flushed with the residual heat of the enormous gather-fire and one too many cups of brew, and the afterglow of an afternoon spent riding and dealing and lovemaking. The soft comfortable murmur of many voices engaged in their own affairs, the gentle rumble of someone making rhythms from a stretched skin, the shrieks and giggles of the child-herd about their usual nonsense, just far enough away to not be annoying.

Brede dreamt belonging, acceptance.

Someone was singing; his voice was muffled, but Brede knew the tune well enough to fill in the words for herself. She reached up and pulled Devnet close for a kiss. Devnet threading heron feathers into Brede's hair.

Brede dreamt darkness, waiting, and Devnet – face outlined in the firelight, brow, nose, cheekbone, chin; eyes cast deep into shadow, and tightly curling hair bronzed and flickering. The line of Devnet's neck and collarbone sharp and glorious and her own hands reaching up to touch.

Brede dreamt feathers in her hair, and a rich, searching, passionate kiss, laughter and the illusion of privacy, and a warning; and Devnet still with that look, hungry, purposeful, playful.

Brede dreamt herself travel-stained and sweaty in Devnet's tent, and not enough trading to justify the Gather … and woke with hot tears running into her ears, and her heart pumping with the old anger, the anger that had grown between Devnet and herself, as sharp as a thicket of thorns, so that every time they tried to reach across it they tore themselves.

Chapter Three

Morning: Brede forced herself from her bed, anxious lest the mercenaries had already gone. She threw clothes on, her head aching from her restless night.

But they had not gone. The horses still crowded the ox stall.

Brede slowed her scurry and checked whether the animals had been fed. They hadn't, and she saw to it. The closeness of so many horses brought back the comfort and certainty of childhood, although her father would never have allowed his beasts to be ridden so hard, nor starved of food. She rubbed the forehead of the black gelding and left the makeshift stable for the forge.

The building smelt strange, of food and bodies. The warriors were ready to leave, their cloaks dry, their swords belted about them. Brede ducked back out of the doorway to look for Faine, and nearly fell over her. Faine cursed good-naturedly.

'What are you doing here? I've been looking for you. Go and get the horses, and take them to the gate.'

Brede loped back to the ox stall, calling softly to the horses as she approached, telling them in Plains language that she was the one who had fed and groomed them, that they would not shy from her and that they would follow her where she led. She tightened their girths, loosened their tethers, and led out the flashy black gelding. Brede glanced back at the string of horses following her lead, and breathed in the morning air as though the world had been made over during the night. She tucked the gelding's lead rein into the saddle and talked companionably to the horse as he willingly followed her to the gate.

Change, she sang to herself in her throat, happy with weak morning sun, and the sound of hooves, a sound she had missed for so long she had forgotten she missed it.

The warriors came to the gate, keeping close together, their intimacy with change making them careful. Brede glanced about trying to see her familiar surroundings as the mercenaries must see them. The village appeared deserted. Brede knew this was Marsh dwellers at their most stubborn, ignoring anything that displeased them; but to the warriors it meant danger.

Maeve took the gelding's reins, tugging slightly harder than she needed to, discomfited by the silent village, disconcerted by Brede's talent for horses, out of place in this Marsh village. She frowned her uncertainty, and Brede knew again that she could neither ask, nor be asked, to join the group of warriors.

The mercenaries claimed their horses and waited for Maeve to give them the order to mount, still watching each other's backs, waiting for the gate to be opened. Adair was up on the wall, staring out at the mist-smeared landscape. He glanced down and raised his chin in a nod. Brede did not wait for him to climb down, but went to lift the great bars herself, wanting them gone swiftly. Adair would have something to say later, but for now she didn't care. She liked to see the tension leave the warriors' shoulders, and know that she was responsible; knowing that she shared their relief.

Maeve was refreshed by her warm, dry, night, but she did not want to leave Tegan. She gave a curt nod to her band of fighters, and they settled into saddles that someone had dried and cleaned and waxed – Brede perhaps. Maeve regretted her earlier sourness and smiled at the apprentice. Not her problem, praise the Goddess. She saluted the smith, and led the warriors out of the village.

The river had risen, sweeping through their abandoned camp site, tearing away the few bushes growing at the foot of the ramparts. Maeve reviewed her last words from Tegan. *If I do not come to you within three weeks of the spring thaw, come and find my body.*

She had felt a cold hand of fear at her heart, but she had promised, casually, as though there was no doubt. Balin turned in his saddle to look at Maeve, then nodded silently at the raging river. Maeve returned his look, inclining her head slightly. She did not think Tegan would die.

Brede climbed up to stand beside Adair, watching the mercenaries head swiftly north along the river which was too swollen to cross safely now. Adair caught the trembling in her limbs, which had nothing to do with cold, and grimaced to himself.

Faine called up, forcing Brede from her reverie with sharp words.

'There's work to do. Finley's still waiting for a mattock that should have been finished yesterday and I'm sure our guest's horse could do with a new set of shoes; why don't you ask her?'

Brede shook herself, and walked back to the forge, knowing perfectly well that the horse needed to be shod.

The forge seemed unusually bare and spacious after the crowding of the night before. Brede glanced around uncertainly, trying to remember where she had put everything. She reached down the baskets from the rafters, and came across her embryonic sword. She squinted at it angrily, what was the point of a sword she would never use?

'Can I see?'

Brede looked down at Tegan in surprise. She had been lying so still and quiet that Brede had assumed she was asleep. Brede handed the sword to her, and made her first intent inspection of her charge. Tegan was a small woman, not as short as Faine, but not so broad either. She propped herself awkwardly on one elbow, and ran a careful hand over the weapon, finding its point of balance. Her concentration was all for the knife. In the ruddy glow of the forge, Brede couldn't decide the colour of the thick springy hair, nor of the eyes that suddenly flickered back to her face.

'You make many swords?'

Brede laughed.

'No one in this village is prepared to choose sides outside the gate. Why would I need to make swords?' She expected that to be an end to the conversation, but Tegan had other ideas.

'That would explain the length. How do you plan to use it? It's a bit like the double daggers assassins use.'

Tegan was breathless. It hurt to prop herself up, but now that she had done so, she didn't know how to lie back down with any dignity. Brede sat beside the wounded mercenary.

'I wasn't planning to use it. It was a mistake that I was making the best of. Do you think it worth persisting?'

'Yes. But you need two, a matching pair. Can you fight two-handed?' Brede shook her head impatiently.

'I can't fight at all; well, don't fight, rather.'

Tegan looked up from the sword, gazing levelly into Brede's eyes.

'Time to start.' She said, half in earnest, loose-tongued with pain.

Brede moved to protest, but her ears picked up the sound of Faine's return and she quickly changed the subject.

'Smith Faine asks if you wish your horse to be re-shod,' she said formally.

Tegan replied with equal formality,

'I do wish Smith Faine to shoe my horse. I also ask Smith Faine's apprentice to keep my horse exercised. You can ride can't you?'

Brede heard Faine at her back, and bit her tongue on fierce agreement, merely nodding. She rose to her feet and went to find some metal to make into the mattock that Finley had wanted.

The smith stood over her guest, who was trying to hide the sword from her. Faine put her foot on it.

'I am not trying to tempt your apprentice away,' Tegan said, swiftly.

'Yes you are,' Faine said quietly, 'and if you succeed, I will be glad for her.'

It took Brede most of the day to finish her work. It was strange to have Tegan constantly in the forge, a silent observer. Mostly Tegan slept, but Brede was aware of her, moving restlessly in her dreams. Faine came and went, fidgeting in a most un-Faine-like manner. She stood over Tegan, watching that painful sleep then turned abruptly to Brede.

'Do you think she's feverish?' she asked.

Brede shrugged. 'I'm not a healer.'

Faine sucked air through her teeth and frowned at Brede.

'Not a healer, no, but you've had to heal from an infected wound, you remember what that was like, I suppose?'

Brede put her tools to one side, pulling her hair into a tighter braid, thinking.

'Actually, no. I remember almost nothing.'

She moved closer to Faine, standing at her shoulder, considering Tegan.

'She makes reasonable sense when she's awake. I don't think her fever's strong.' Brede glanced at Faine, then back to Tegan. 'On the other hand, she does look flushed, and she doesn't rest easy.'

'Do you think you can keep her alive?' Faine asked.

Brede shrugged again, turning back to the anvil. Faine sighed and went to ask Edra's advice.

When she found Tegan awake on her fourth visit, the smith settled beside her to talk. Brede glanced at the two of them; heads close, an intimate murmur of conversation already in steady flow, and took herself off to fetch the horse.

As soon as Brede was out of earshot, Tegan asked, 'Where did you find her? She's not Marsh bred.'

'Marsh bred, yes. Marsh reared, no. She is my sister's daughter, but her father was of the Horse Clans.'

'And she is here because...?'

'Her father was killed, ambushed by some mercenaries.' Faine considered Tegan. 'She was at the Gather, she got home to find her father dead, her mother nearly so, and Brede wasn't in much better state herself. They had nowhere else to go.'

Brede returned with Tegan's horse, and Faine turned to a different subject.

Tegan kept the smith talking, gleaning anything that might keep her alive in this uncertain safety, saying anything she could think of to bolster Faine's liking and confidence in her guest. She set about fascinating Faine, drawing her in with confidences and subtle, clever, questions. Even the loud hammering of the horseshoes and the irritable stamping of the horse did nothing to break the contact between the smith and her guest.

When she had finished fitting new shoes to Tegan's horse, Brede took her back to the ox stall, saddled her with slow pleasure, and led her to the gate, trying to keep the tremor of anticipation from her knees.

Adair barely glanced at Brede as he opened the gate for her, but he was uneasy at the sight of her with a horse once more.

Once Brede was through the gate she mounted, gathered up the reins and urged the beast forward, along the bank of the river. The mare was no longer in the prime of youth, and had been ridden hard and poorly cared for recently. Brede did not want to push her too far too soon, but it felt so good to be astride a horse again. Her muscles settled into old patterns, and she felt the pulling that spoke of years without riding. All the more reason to go only a short distance, she told herself; but in her mind, she saw this horse in peak condition, bearing her across the vast expanse of the plains.

Adair watched her go, and his disquiet settled into an unhappy conviction of trouble to come.

Brede went upstream, following the slight rise of the land, seeing familiar landscapes from a different angle, appreciating them anew, hungering for yet more difference, more change. A roar of thunder muttered across the hills. Brede glanced anxiously upward, but the rain clouds were still miles away. She gauged the height of the sun and how long she had until dark. She let the horse choose the pace and headed for the woodland on the upper slopes of the hill, hoping to find some late berries for her mother.

As she passed around the shoulder of the hill into the next valley, Brede caught a flash of light on the opposite ridge. She reined the horse in to watch. Again – the flash of brightness.

The fading autumn sun was reflecting off metal. There was someone wearing armour on the far ridge; perhaps many warriors were there.

Slowly, Brede eased herself out of the saddle and to the ground, and pulled the horse into a cautious walk, taking the most direct route into the cover of the trees. At least she had no bright bridle irons to catch the light. A horse in this country meant only one thing, a warrior, and she did not want attention drawn to the village. Brede snorted to herself; it wasn't the village she was protecting, but Tegan.

Brede crept back toward the trees, drawing the horse after her, eyes on the opposite ridge and that continued flashing of metal, ears straining to hear anything above the cacophonous arguments of the birds in the trees. She wondered, briefly, whether the birds on the farther ridge were complaining, or had fled from the disturbance. Under cover of the trees she moved more quickly, pulling the horse into the undergrowth, to hide the tell-tale white rump. She tied the beast securely, and slunk back to the edge of the woodland.

A small group of horses wound slowly down the slope heading roughly in her direction. Five of them, in full armour, with banners unfurled. The rashness of showing their colours when they were such a small band staggered her. Then Brede saw the rest of them.

Massing on the ridge above, there was an army. Even though they couldn't possibly see her, Brede crouched lower, scratching her face in the brambles. She had never seen so many riders even at horse fairs. Now that she could see them, Brede registered the ominous clattering rumble that the movement of that army made. Her mind told her that she had been hearing that noise since entering the valley, and that there had been a strange, many-throated roar that had reached her ears even before that.

Thunder. Brede cursed her lack of caution. She ought to have known better, even if the ways of rain were no more than a muddled childhood memory. And what could have caused that anguished, thunderous cry? It was like an animal in pain – or enraged triumph.

With a stab of anxiety Brede wondered whether she had been seen before she recognised that flash of sun on armour, whether the five riders moving ahead of the main body of the army were coming for her. She couldn't risk returning to the village now.

Brede searched the valley before her, trying to see what might have sent this group down from the ridge. They might be following some trail, looking for someone else, or merely seeking out a good camping ground. She glanced back at the main army. They weren't waiting for their scouts, moving slowly, along the ridge. Not camping then. The scouts weren't moving fast enough to be chasing her, so what were they doing?

The sun was nearly down. The valley curved away to run west, and at this time of year the sun seemed to set just where valley closed back into hill. The army travelled towards the sun; the scouts reached the bottom of the valley. Brede could no longer see them. There were still warriors directly opposite her, still the dragon's tail trailed along the ridge. Brede backed carefully into the wood, untied the horse, and led her cautiously through the trees, in the same direction as the army travelled.

When darkness closed, and there was still no sign of her daughter, Leal went looking for her. She found Faine in the forge, deep in conversation with the mercenary. Leal sneered at the stranger. This might be one of the very band of murderers who had killed her hand-mate, or one of the vast raiding party that had slaughtered Cloud Clan and scattered Wing Clan, losing her elder daughter for her. She did not, would not, trust Tegan.

'Where is Brede?' Leal asked, without preamble.

Faine started at the unexpected sound of her voice. She glanced about her. 'Did she not take the horse to exercise it?' she asked.

Tegan nodded agreement.

'Wherever the horse is, there Brede will be.'

Leal shrugged impatiently.

'And where is your horse?' she asked, angry at their complacency, suddenly sure that Brede had stolen the horse and gone. Faine sucked at her teeth thoughtfully.

'She has been gone a long time, but there's no telling where.'

'I can tell you,' Leal said, 'she's gone after the mercenaries.'

'If she has, you'll not see her again,' Tegan said.

It wasn't until it was full dark that Brede saw the scouts returning to the main army. She saw because they carried torches. They must consider this home territory. Until now, Brede had no idea which side currently claimed the Marsh as theirs, leave alone the westerly valleys and hills, but those banners were red. They were heading west, which suggested that they weren't the same side as Tegan's mercenaries, but Brede did not know what colour Maeve's carefully hidden banners bore.

Brede waited for the last of the soldiers to disappear from sight, for the faint clamour of armour to die. At last she led the horse out into the open and rode down into the westerly valley.

The floor of the valley was completely dark, the moon obscured by the rain clouds that had rolled resolutely back across the shoulder of the western ridge. Brede had not been into this place before; it was too far on foot. The horse placed her feet hesitantly, uncertain of the footing.

Brede listened anxiously, but there was only the rush of the river, and the harsh cries of night birds, too familiar to be threatening. There was a more solid darkness that must be a building. Low, hunched against the shoulder of the river. An offering place. Brede wasn't convinced that an army would send five warriors down the side of the valley to leave an offering at a perfectly ordinary shrine. She slid from the horse's back, feeling for the even darker darkness that was the entrance, wishing for the moon to strike through the low clouds, and light her way. She had never been one for these lowland shrines. She did not talk much to the Goddess and rarely made offerings. When Brede spoke to that one, it was with wind in her hair and change stirring her blood; there had been little conversation between them since she left the plains. So she hesitated at the darkness of the shrine, listening. Nothing stirred within the building. She feared enclosed spaces; she imagined how ordinary the mud hut would appear in daylight – she should come back at dawn – but she knew that she would not. If she was to enter this place of airless dark, it must be at once.

Brede took in her breath and stepped into the close darkness of the shrine, bowing her head under the low lintel. She did not like the grave-smell of the place. She felt for the flint and taper that should be on the shelf to the left of the door. Brede struck and raised the meagre light.

There was the usual bowl shaped depression in the earth, as wide as the average person might spread their arms, scattered with desiccated offerings of fruit, flowers, and locks of hair; but across the bowl of earth lay a length of metal, darkly gleaming. A sword.

Brede let out her breath sharply. Had some great warrior died, that this sword should be left here? Or was this deliberate sacrilege? Her skin crawled.

Brede crouched to place a cautious finger to the blade, wanting to remove the sword. There was a slight groove in the centre of the blade, and one finger came away sticky. The sword was still covered in drying blood. She wiped her hand quickly on her trouser leg. She wedged the taper into a crack in the wall, and skirted the offering bowl, until she knelt where she could take the hilt in her two hands, and lift it from the earth. The balance was wrong for her, too heavy. She lifted it with difficulty, trying not to disturb the offerings already laid on the earth. She circled back to the entrance, and backed out into the air, grateful for the moon that had at last cleared the cloud bank. She headed straight to the river, and all but dropped the blade in her haste to get it into the water. Brede left the sword where it lay, and went upstream to cup clear water from the river to carry back to the shrine as an offering of her own, a cleansing.

She walked carefully so as not to spill the liquid and when she came to the offering place, at first thought she had misplaced her steps. She walked cautiously to and fro, but there was no entrance to the mound of earth before her.

Brede let her hands fall and gazed at the mound, water dripping from her fingers. She stepped back, half expecting the sword to be gone; but it was still there, lying half in and half out of the water. She took up the sword and an unexpected quietness settled within her, and about her, as though she was completely at one with her surroundings, as though she had stepped for a few seconds, not upon the earth, but within it.

Chapter Four

The rain struck again just as Brede reached the closed gate. She whistled, a sharp sound that cut through the faint murmur of the village. Brede smiled to herself, knowing everyone would have heard, and that Rhian would have to open the gate promptly or answer, at the least, to her mother.

However she wasn't prepared for how swiftly the gate opened. Brede ducked low and rode through while it was still swinging open, crowding Adair, as he struggled to close the great door again. Adair ought to be asleep, not gatekeeping, that wasn't promising. She headed for stabling and privacy.

Safe from prying eyes in the ox stall, Brede slipped from the horse and thrust the sword into a manger, scuffing hay over it. She turned quickly to loosen the girth as Faine appeared at the entrance.

'You were only meant to be exercising the horse, not wearing it out. Where have you been? Your mother thought you'd run off to join the mercenaries.'

'There was an army on Westerly ridge. Red banners; thousands of them. I had to wait before I could come back, in case they saw the horse and followed. Do you think I should tell Keenan?'

'Which way were they going?'

'West.'

Faine nodded.

'I will tell him by all means, but no need to get him out of bed if they were going away.'

Faine leant back against the doorpost and picked her teeth; studying Brede's turned back.

'Were I you, I would make peace with your mother.'

'How?' Brede asked.

Faine shrugged in response, and was gone.

Brede glanced swiftly to make sure her prize was properly hidden, and then finished removing the gear from the horse. She took more time over the grooming than she had taken when she had all the horses there to attend to. Running her hand over the horse's neck, under the mane, Brede felt the slight ridging of a tattoo and made a mental note to look in the light of morning. She had delayed long enough. Brede slapped the horse gently and brushed down her clothes to remove the mud, dust and loose horsehair. She stepped out of the ox stall and into Adair's arms.

'Not a word – gone all that time and not a *word* to me.'

Brede tried to extricate herself, but he stepped closer, blocking her way.

'Your mother thought you'd gone after the warriors.'

'What did you think?'

'I think you can't be trusted with a horse.'

'What is that supposed to mean?'

'I got to thinking you weren't coming back.'

'Well you were both wrong. Here I am.'

Adair stepped back, and nodded.

'Here you are. Yes.'

'Here, and tired and hungry – and in trouble with my mother – and with you, apparently.'

'No.'

Brede smiled. 'Sure?'

'Yes.'

'Good. Just Leal to apologise to, then. So go get your sleep and let me get at it.'

Adair threw his arms up in capitulation. Brede laughed, and after a moment he joined in.

'I was scared,' he admitted. 'I worry.'

'Me too,' Brede said softly, as she squeezed his arm and pushed past.

Leal did not scold as she had intended, she burst into a torrent of weeping. Brede settled beside her and put her arms about her mother, rocking her tenderly until Leal hiccupped into silence.

Leal laughed unsteadily, pushing her away. Brede sat back on her heels, watching her mother mop the tears from her face with her sleeve.

'I thought I'd lost you. I thought you'd stolen that horse and run away.'

'I'm here, I'm safe. There's no need to worry.'

'I always worry about you. Always. Something always happens.'

Brede sighed and hugged her mother again.

'Nothing happened this time.'

They spent the remains of the evening in close companionable silence, and it wasn't until the morning that Brede felt she could leave her mother, collect her new sword, and take it to the safety of the forge.

Wiping the dust carefully from the blade, Brede was reminded that she wanted to check the horse's tattoo. She rested the sword against the wall, and lifted the horse's mane. The tattoo was a folded wing. Brede caught her breath. Not just Wing Clan's mark; but Falda's name mark. The irony of that naming struck her, *Folded Wing*, never meant to take flight with the rest of her kin.

Brede rubbed her finger along the mark, to make sure she wasn't seeing things, trying to remember whether Falda had a mare like this at that last Gather. The mark hadn't been cancelled to show the beast was sold, so, she had been stolen. Brede took a ragged breath, caught up the sword, scarcely noticing the weight in her haste, and went to speak to the current owner of that horse.

Tegan was awake, feverish and disturbed. Her wound did not allow her to sleep long, the slightest movement brought pain, and with it, wakefulness. For all she was awake, she thought she was dreaming when she saw a tall woman bearing a greatsword enter the forge. She opened her eyes wider, wondering if she had died, and this was the Battle Maiden, come to guide her soul through the Gate. Then the apparition stumbled, and used the sword to hold her balance. Tegan let out her held breath in a short laugh.

'Where did you get that monstrosity?'

Brede laid the sword beside Tegan.

'I found it.'

'Found? No one would leave that lying about to be picked up by a village apprentice.'

Brede smarted under the implied slight.

'It was in the hands of the Goddess,' she replied, deliberately ambiguous.

'Meaning?'

'I found it in an offering place, all covered with blood. I took it away to clean it, and when I went back, the entrance to the offering place was no longer there.' She waited for Tegan to sneer disbelievingly. Tegan dragged her eyes from the blade, and considered Brede.

'What are you going to do with it?'

'Learn to use it.'

Tegan shook her head.

'It's too big for you. That thing was made for someone a good four inches taller than you and plenty broader. It would unbalance you every time you swung it. Stick to the double knives.'

'The Goddess gave it to me. She must have had a reason.'

Tegan frowned, raising herself cautiously onto one elbow. The effort set sweat running across her skin, and her arm shook under her weight. She leant carefully into the rooftree, trying not to let Brede see her weakness.

'You don't strike me as fanciful, Brede. It's just a sword, a sword *she* didn't want. The most mysterious thing about it is why anyone thought she would.' Tegan stopped, her head spinning. She swallowed carefully, willing solidity into the ground beneath her. 'Melt it down. Turn it into something you can use. It's good metal, use it to pay off your bond, but don't imagine the Goddess wants you as a holy slayer, people don't go in for that sort of thing anymore.'

Brede answered angrily, listening to only half of what Tegan said.

'I'm not bonded. Faine gave me the apprenticeship as a favour. I can go any time I please.'

'Then for pity's sake, why haven't you?'

'I choose to stay – my mother needs me.'

'No,' Tegan agreed, shifting to lie on her back; suddenly exhausted. 'No amount of metal will buy off that bond.'

Brede shrugged away Tegan's words, uncomfortable with the truth and turned the subject back to the sword.

'I can't melt this down, it would be a waste. Look how well it's made – I couldn't make anything half so fine.'

'It's no use to you as it is. It's probably a liability. It will make you conspicuous and you'll never master it. If this were my blade, I would not part from it willingly, and I would know it again if I saw it in another's hand, and want to know how it came to be there.' As she said it Tegan looked again at the blade, a prickling under her skin making her wonder.

Brede's eyes narrowed: a cold, wintry look. Tegan suddenly felt vulnerable, lying there beneath that icy regard.

'That is a question I'd like you to answer. You have in your possession a horse with a distinctive breeder's mark. Where did you get that horse?'

Tegan shifted uneasily under the tone of Brede's voice.

'She came to me at a Gather, I couldn't resist her.'

'Which year?' Brede asked.

Tegan considered the bearing of the woman sitting beside her. She wished Brede were really a Marsh-dwelling smith to whom it would matter not at all where she had got her horse. And since she was not, since she was a survivor of the worst mistake Tegan had even been party to, there was some truth needed.

'The last year. The year there was the trouble,' she answered.

'Do you remember the man you bought her from?'

'I don't remember anything special about him, no.'

Brede slammed her hand flat against the sword hilt and glared at Tegan; her teeth bared as she struggled to control herself, to spit out the next words.

'You were one of the raiders. If you had bought that horse, you would remember my sister. Perhaps it was you who rode her down, or one of your friends who sold her into slavery?'

Tegan's blood raced painfully and her wound tore at her, making breathing hard. She forced her eyes from the fingers curling about the hilt of that sword.

'I was there, yes.'

Tegan said no more, staring levelly at Brede, waiting for her response.

Brede made no move to use the blade that lay between them.

'That is all you have to say?'

'I've already told you, being a warrior is a job. I go where I am sent.'

'And kill whomever you are told to kill.'

Tegan sighed.

'Yes. If my orders include a specific death, then that is what I will do, either that or end my contract and starve when I get a reputation for refusing work.' Tegan did not take her eyes from Brede's face, but she was acutely aware of the hand that still touched the sword lying between them. 'Now, I tell you,' she said, with slow emphasis, 'this horse came to me of her own free will, after the skirmish. I found her wandering, lame. I did not cut her tether, I did not kill or enslave anyone to gain her, and I do not know what became of your sister. Believe me or not, as you wish.'

Tegan stopped abruptly.

Brede listened to the unsteady breath she drew. She could see the sheen of sweat on Tegan's face; she found it hard to ask her next question.

'Did you take prisoners? Did you make slaves of my kin?'

'No.'

Brede sneered disbelievingly.

'I don't take prisoners.' Tegan said carefully.

'Oh? And I suppose you'll tell me now that you killed no one that night?' Brede wanted Tegan to deny it, to lie, so that she would know she had been lying all along.

'No, I'd be lying if I told you that.' Tegan said, very quietly.

'How many?'

'Four, I think.'

'*You think?*'

'You don't stop to check you've killed someone, not in a battle.'

Brede's glance dropped to the sword, and her hand resting against the hilt. 'Teach me to use this sword.'

Tegan took a careful breath, tension beginning to ebb into trembling. Brede's hand no longer rested on the hilt of the sword.

'So that you can kill me with it?' Tegan whispered.

Brede tried to smile but the movement went awry.

If not you, then someone else, she thought; *I am owed a life.*

'No, so I can be a holy slayer, what do you think? It's a skill; it may come in useful sometime. We've all winter. When you are well enough you'll need to practise, I can partner you.'

'Brede, have you ever seen a real fight? Blows struck in anger?'

'Oh yes. I've seen – I was there that night, at the Gather. I saw – I *felt*.'

Brede rubbed her face; uncomfortable with the rage that made her fingers ache to hurt someone. 'I know what I'm asking,' she said, 'and why. This is no idle fancy.'

'I didn't think that.'

'Yes you did. I have another question for you. What colour is the banner in your pack?'

Tegan gave Brede a sharp look.

'Surely you know if you were at the Gather.'

'And you know, since you were at the Gather, that the raiders wore no colours, and I stayed out half the night to keep from leading an army here so I'd like to know whether I need have bothered.'

Tegan nodded, and forcing her curiosity down, pointed at the rough leather sack that held her belongings.

'Help yourself. It's wrapped in the mail shirt.'

'You could just tell me.'

'But would you believe me?'

Brede shrugged and pulled the pack towards her. She loosened the neck and extracted the shirt. Unfolding it carefully, she found the banner. It was green. Running her fingers lightly over the coarse cloth, trying to soothe remembered pain; Brede sighed. She was about to thrust the shirt back into the pack, when she saw the condition it was in. There was a large tear in the leather, and many of the rings of metal were broken. Brede spread the armour out, inspecting the rings closely. Tegan watched uneasily. Brede turned the leather, stiff with dried blood, and looked from it to Tegan.

'That was a blow that meant to kill.'

'I am fortunate to be alive,' Tegan agreed. 'Do you think the mail can be mended?'

Brede raised an eyebrow, and forced the shirt back into the leather sack. She kept the banner across her knee, slowly folding it into as small a space as she could, and did not answer Tegan's question.

'Why?' she asked at last, holding out the government colours.

'The horses,' Tegan said, 'they wanted the horses.'

Brede choked on a laugh.

'They made a poor bargain there. No Clans, no horses. Did they think we'd ever deal with them again after that?'

'It was a mistake. Most of the Clans are dealing with the rebels now.'

'Which rebels?'

Tegan narrowed her eyes thoughtfully.

'Now should I tell you that?'

'You think I'm going to go riding after the red riders to tell them something they already know? They had plenty of horses.'

'Red? It was them yesterday? How many?'

'Thousands. I don't know. It took them a long time to go away. West, before you ask.'

Tegan's face twisted with anxiety.

'They could have seen –'

Brede considered.

'They were on the next ridge south and west, not the one you came down, so they wouldn't have been into the valley.'

'Maeve would stick to high ground.'

'Further north though, as she wanted to get across the river.'

'I don't know.' Tegan's voice was thick with worry, 'I don't think she was sure where we were, or where to go next.'

'Not sure, no, but with wit enough to ask. I saw them heading off north. And they would have been going fast, and under cover of trees.'

'Yes –'

'Yes. And the red banners had other things on their mind. They left the sword, I think.'

Tegan pulls the sword closer to her, grateful for a distraction.

'Why do you think that?'

'I saw five of them go down into the valley and then rejoin the rest.'

'You said it was bloody.'

Brede nodded, puzzled. Tegan fingered the blade, admiring the quality of the forging. It was a very fine sword. She could never afford a sword that fine.

'It can't be a ritual sword, it's too well used, or perhaps I mean ill-used,' Tegan said, without taking her eyes from the blade, 'look at the state of the edge. Why would they leave a blooded sword in an offering circle?'

'I thought perhaps someone important had died,' Brede offered, thinking of that roar of voices, and doubting the memory. Perhaps that strange sound had only been thunder after all.

'Yes, perhaps they would leave the sword as a promise of revenge. If this was the weapon that struck him down.' Tegan's fingers flexed, stroking the smooth flat of the blade, finding the subtle indentation at the centre, failing to find a hint of a maker's name.

'Him?'

'Just a thought. If they didn't know who was responsible – why not ask the Goddess for a sign as to the culprit?'

'But the blood was still sticky. They had to know – they had to have *done* it. And I took it away.'

'Perhaps she's on our side then.'

'*Our* side? I don't understand.'

'Not yet, perhaps, but you will.'

Tegan ran a hand down the blade again; restless to be up and away, to let her friends know this news. She coveted that sword.

'You'd best put that thing away before Faine sees it, or she'll have you turning it into a pitchfork.'

Brede nodded, and started wrapping the blade in Tegan's green banner.

'What are you doing?'

'Faine would expect you to have more than one weapon. She won't even notice it if it's with your belongings.'

Tegan didn't argue. Brede's simple logic was faultless.

Chapter Five

The stranger at the forge caused more of a stir in the village than anyone was prepared to admit. Individually, many people sought out the smith, full of questions, motivated by fear and curiosity; for the most part unfriendly. Leal, brandishing her suspicions, demanded progress reports from Faine.

'I want to know what that woman says, especially what she says to Brede.'

Faine shook her head.

'If you tell me what Brede says to you, I'll tell if it's true, and I might tell you some of what she leaves out – but you shouldn't intrude on her privacy, Leal.'

'Don't presume to tell me how to manage my daughter.'

'Then don't ask favours of me. And it was *not* managing her that I meant.'

'She's my daughter.'

'She's my apprentice. I don't want to lose her any more than you do, but she has a life of her own to lead.'

Leal's eyes narrowed in frustration, and Faine recognised the look as one that Brede offered her regularly. She laughed.

'Don't worry so. If there is anything amiss, I'll tell you.'

'I'm afraid for Brede. There is something wrong between them already Faine, you must have seen it; Brede has become – silent. She is hiding something from me. She's awake half the night, and she looks at me sometimes, as though she wants to tell me something and can't bring herself to it.'

Faine frowned uncertainly, reluctant to admit that she had noticed that hesitant silence herself.

Often, when she went to the forge of a morning, Faine would find Brede already there, dressing Tegan's wound, while Tegan talked, and Brede kept uncharacteristically quiet. But she noticed that although Brede carried out her nursing duties without comment and with very little consideration, she did not shirk her duties, and that she frequently stayed long after her work was finished, idling over unnecessary tasks. Faine resented Brede's presence at those times, wanting the unnecessary tasks for herself, appreciating Tegan's efforts, where Brede seemed oblivious. Faine listened to Tegan and answered readily, embarrassed by Brede's hostility. She was forced to accept Leal's assessment: there was something not right, and she began to regret her first impulse, which had led to the enforced intimacy between these two.

Tegan was persuasive, witty, charming and challenging. She used every skill she had to get Brede to unbend. Brede listened, and said nothing. It was lonely. Tegan had exhausted everything she could remember about the summer campaign before Brede responded.

'You've not always been a soldier.'

Tegan considered before she answered.

'I was brought up on a farm, but that failed quickly when the drought came – I don't think it was ever exactly fertile soil my parents worked, and they were quick to abandon it. We moved to the city, I – got into bad company. *Interesting* bad company mind you, I moved in some very illustrious circles.' Brede snorted disbelievingly. 'You can mock. I have shared a bottle of the best with our present monarch before she ever thought she might be in line for the crown, and with our then monarch's half-brother.'

'You? A dirt poor farmer's daughter and *Queen Grainne* drank together?'

'I was a lot younger than Grainne, she and Phelan used to enjoy rowdying, she took a liking to me, and I was of an age with Phelan. He got me my first posting. As a scout. Being little has its uses.' Tegan fell into a memory, not an entirely happy one; of the rather dubious uses Phelan had put her skills to in the early days, before there was a purpose to his tirelessness. 'I made myself useful, and when Grainne became queen, she made sure I got a proper commission in a group of mercenaries, I was pretty good with a sword by then. I've fought under Phelan's command many times since then; he's a great soldier – and quite the politician too, when he bothers.'

'So important! Who'd have thought that a tiny band like yours would be so significant?'

Brede's voice strove for innocence and failed. Tegan felt needled and let it show.

'I command over forty swords.'

'And where are they now?'

'At winter quarters.'

'And who's commanding them?'

'Chad.'

Brede quirked an eyebrow.

'Not Maeve?'

'No. She chose to stay with me, so she lost the chance. She could have had the command, but it was her choice, and I'm glad she made it.'

Faine walked into the forge, and glanced at the two of them, Brede, blood encrusted bandages still in one hand, Tegan, still with her shirt unlaced. Brede threw the bandages into the fire; Tegan laced her shirt, and wondered how long Faine had been listening, whether she had heard what had been said about

Tegan's allegiance. Brede handed a length of iron to Faine, and turned to the bellows.

'So what about the rest of them, how did they end up soldiers?' she asked, as she settled to her task.

Tegan gazed thoughtfully at Brede, wondering why she was at last taking an interest in this.

'Soldiering is a profession of last resort for most people. The drought has brought many to it who would never have thought of themselves as warriors. No one would choose to put their life at risk so regularly unless they had a considerable ability and very little choice. Very few people are born into it. One or two, I suppose, if their parents were soldiers; but birthing and raising children as a warrior is something of a struggle. Maeve's an exception. She and Riordan had a mercenary captain for a father and an archer for a mother.' Tegan paused and grinned. 'Maeve was amazing even as a stripling. She's the fastest thing I've ever seen, she knows absolutely what she is doing with a blade, no matter what kind it is.' Tegan's happy recollection waned in the face of absence and she was silent. At last she shook herself and started again.

'Inir, now, he started as a scout, same as me; but I think his parents ran a water mill. He's better at it than I ever was. He's good with the landscape as well as with people – he really knows how to melt into the scenery.'

Brede tried to remember Inir, and failed. She remembered noticing that someone was missing when she had confronted Maeve outside the village gate; that must have been Inir.

'When you say 'scout' do you mean 'spy'?' she asked.

Tegan took a sharp breath and shot Faine a look. Faine refused to intervene.

'In some contexts, that is certainly what I've done, and Inir; but Corla's a genuine scout: what she can't work out from the landscape isn't worth knowing. And she's a healer of course. Her parents were healers.'

Brede nodded, she well believed Corla knew how to work the landscape; she'd not have found a way down to the valley else. Tegan continued her list.

'Cei – Goddess knows where Cei came from, or why; but he's a tactician – or would be if he weren't so given to believing the worst of every situation. I sometimes think he tried his hand as an assassin, but found it too lonely.'

Faine and Brede stared at her aghast, and then laughed, Faine because she found it funny, Brede in spite of herself. Faine, pulled gently on Brede's braid, and said,

'No smiths, then?'

Brede shook her off.

'What about Balin?'

'Balin started life as a sailor, but he was always getting picked on, and learnt to defend himself. Having someone that big around helps to win us contracts. Merchants are impressed by size, but –'

Tegan stopped herself. Brede glanced sideways at Faine, who chose to ignore the blatant veering away from something dangerous. She knew she had taken a risk sheltering Tegan, she was happy to not know how great a risk it might turn out to be.

Brede was profoundly uncomfortable with the idea of handling Tegan's body in the course of her nursing. She coped by being as impersonal as she could. She did not want to be close; she did not want to have this intimate knowledge of Tegan's body. She tried to tell Edra that she couldn't do it, a muttered comment as Edra was leaving the forge.

Edra turned back and stared at Tegan's huddled form, not caring whether she heard or not.

'Then let her die.'

Brede backed away. Edra went out into the first fall of snow, impatient with Tegan and with her unwilling assistant.

Tegan covered her face with her arm. Brede stood above her, silent and uneasy. At last Tegan uncovered her face, and looked up at her, unable to make out her expression.

'There's a knife within arm's reach. I'd rather you finished me quickly than be left with this wound festering from my own filth until fever takes me.'

'No.'

'No to which?'

'No, I'll not cut your throat. No, I'll not leave your wound to fester.'

Tegan took a deep, steadying breath.

'Why not?'

'It would be harder than the alternatives.'

'Then why did you say you would no longer look after me? If it's not my death you want?'

'I don't want to be the one who allows you back out there to kill more of my people. But I can't take a step to prevent you either.'

'That is not a weakness, Brede.'

'Of course it is. Stop being so reasonable, I can't match it.'

Tegan was abruptly reminded of Maeve.

Brede pulled her day's work down from the rafters. She set the bellows, and began the slow process of building the heat in the fire to the temperature she wanted. She fetched more charcoal, sorted her tools and put the ones she needed within reach. Tegan followed her movements, trying to see her face, waiting for the frozen immobility to soften. It was a long time before she dared speak again. Brede was standing over the fierce heat of the fire, watching the metal bar change from darkness to red heat, when Tegan at last broke the silence.

'Maeve has never liked my attempts at reason. She always fights to have her way. But you don't do that. If your wants are not met, you pretend they don't exist. I don't understand. If you hunger you eat; if you are tired you sleep. Why pretend any other need is less important?'

Brede clenched her hands into fists.

'If your needs injure others, do you still follow them? If satisfying your hunger took food from the mouths of your loved ones, would you still eat?'

'Ah, philosophy.'

'No. Reality. This village hasn't starved, through twenty years of drought and bad harvest, through as many years of war, although we've come close. Now the rains have finally come, they have washed away what little there was. We don't help our starving neighbours; we congratulate ourselves on the quality of the grain we have stored, and the fact that we got our harvest in on time.'

Tegan flinched, aware that her position in such a culture was precarious.

'I was thinking of less basic needs,' she said, wondering what Brede might say if the dam of her silence truly broke.

'Such as?'

'Companionship. You've not hand-fast, have you?'

Brede turned back to the fire, and took the metal bar from the heat. She steadied the metal against the anvil, and took up the hammer.

Tegan studied Brede's profile, sharply defined in the firelight. She was beginning to appreciate the curve of Brede's nose; it fit well under her broad brow, and balanced the width of her mouth. In profile it was almost elegant.

'Well, I won't ask,' she said into Brede's half mocking silence, 'but you can't tell me you aren't lonely.'

Brede brought down the hammer, a light touch.

'There was someone, once. Not here.' She smiled and set the metal ringing under a volley of blows that prevented Tegan from saying more. She rested for a moment. 'Now you'll tell me that I'm wasted here, or you'll start telling me how perfect Maeve is, again.'

Tegan's laughter became gasping, choking. Brede waited for it to pass, but it continued. She abandoned the hammer, and went to Tegan's side, helping her to sit up. The choking continued. Brede supported Tegan, holding her, helpless to do more than wait for the spasms to pass. At last Tegan could breathe easily again. She leant against Brede, and wiped tears from her face, exhausted. She felt Brede's breath against the side of her cheek, and made an effort to move away, discomfited by their closeness. She glanced up at Brede's face, which was once more closed and distant.

'How often do I say that, then?' she asked, her voice a mere thread of rasping breath.

'I've lost count.'

Tegan tried to focus on Brede: too close for comfort – kissing distance. Tegan was shocked at the thought, more so as Brede's hands probed beneath her shirt, checking the dressing over her wound, brushing against her breast as she did so.

'I think you'll live,' Brede said, careful to keep any emotion from her voice, 'but if talking about Maeve has this effect, perhaps...'

'...I miss her,' Tegan replied, her voice stronger. 'Talking about her helps.'

'Are you hand-fast to Maeve then?' Brede asked abruptly.

'No.'

'No? You surprise me. Had I such a paragon at my side and in my bed, I'd not leave her loose to find other partners.'

Tegan stirred restlessly within the circle of Brede's arm.

'Maeve wouldn't agree. I was her first lover, but I don't expect to be her only, nor her last. What am I saying? I know I'm not.'

'Not so perfect after all,' Brede said, loosening her support, moving away from Tegan. 'So again, if your need hurts others, do you sate it?'

She went back to the anvil, thrust the cold metal back into the fire, and was not surprised when Tegan did not answer.

Brede spent more time than she should with the horse; she wanted the beast in good condition, just in case – but in case of what, she was not precisely sure. By the time the snow had fallen deep enough to cut the village off, the horse was strong once more, growing sleek in the stall. With no hope of travelling, Brede fell back into her old routines. She rose early and took a warmed cup of ale up onto the wooden palisade that surrounded the village to watch the sunrise, to watch the first flight of birds, to see which way the wind blew.

Sitting so, for the first time in more than a month, huddled into her warmest cloak, she felt a momentary contentment. As Adair shuffled up beside her, she glanced up and smiled.

'Not seen you for a while,' he said in quiet accusation.

Brede offered him the cooling ale as he settled beside her, feet braced against the rough wood.

'I've been busy,' she said, shrugging.

Adair took the beaker from her, and took a sip, turning to look out across the Marsh at the first red streak of day.

'So, which way is the wind blowing?' he asked her, as he had asked so many times before.

'Today, north by west. But not for long.'

'And how long before the wind is strong enough to carry you away?'

'Not as long –' Brede stopped, her usual *'as it will take to grow the wings to ride it,'* silenced.

Adair frowned. This wasn't part of their joking ritual. His eyes strayed away from the Marsh and he focused on the way the wind played with Brede's hair, teasing it loose from her inadequate bindings.

'Grown your wings, have you?'

'Maybe.' She sighed. 'Perhaps I should have gone back to Wing Clan as soon as I had recovered from the fever; it gets harder to leave the longer I stay.'

Adair stood abruptly, almost overbalancing.

'You spend too much time with –' he could find no words.

Brede froze, her hand half extended to steady him.

'Faine's guest?' she asked, her heart suddenly pounding.

'Her.'

'I do only what I have been asked to do by the elders.' Brede said gently.

'Many would have refused. No one would have blamed you. Why should we nurse one of those killers back to health? We're only storing trouble for later.'

'I know that. I've said that. But I've thought it through. I chose to do this. And I have far more reason for distrust than you.'

'But? Say what's on your mind.'

'Since when do you have the right to know my mind?'

Adair stepped away, his frown deepening.

'I've not found you untruthful,' he said, puzzled at her sharpness. Brede nodded, regretting her irritation.

'Well, the truth –'

'You should not have agreed,' Adair burst out. 'You should shun her as we all do.'

'All? I see no sign of that from Faine, nor Edra. They aren't afraid of a helpless wounded stranger. Why are you afraid?'

'I'm not afraid of her.'

'No, well neither am I. I like her.'

Adair leant forward, and hauled Brede sharply to her feet.

'You should not *like* her,' he said forcefully. Brede closed her hand over his, prising his grip away one finger at a time.

'The footing is uncertain up here,' she said, her voice very quiet. 'This is no place for fooling about.'

'I'm not fooling. I'm warning you, Brede; we don't want you with her.'

Brede scowled, judging the distance to the ladder, the narrow footing, and Adair's bulk between her and safety.

'Let me by.'

'Not until you promise.'

'For pity's sake, Adair.'

'Promise.'

Brede shook her head, preferring even Tegan's known wrongdoing to this unexpected aggression.

'I thought we were by way of being friends,' she said.

'I thought we could be more, but you're after riding the wind, aren't you?'

Brede considered Adair's hurt pride.

'Wherever it takes me,' she said, and stepped quickly away from Adair's angry lunge. Too quickly. She missed her footing, and measured her length in the snow. Adair's movement after her turned from anger to concern in half a thought, and he grabbed a handful of clothes, preventing her from falling headlong to the ground below. Brede writhed free of his grip, shunting herself out of reach. Adair straightened, and sighed.

'You're not so good at flying yet. There's time to tame you.' He leant and stroked her ankle, the only part still within reach. 'Still time,' he said wistfully, and strode back to the ladder, and out of her view.

Brede lay where she was. When she was sure he had gone, she struggled up, and limped, wet and bedraggled, to the forge.

'What have you been doing?' Tegan asked as melted snow dripped onto her hand. She wiped her fingers clean.

'Wrestling with my conscience,' Brede said, flinging her cloak across a low beam, and turning at once to the fire to warm her shivers.

'Who won?' Tegan asked.

Brede stopped rubbing her stiff knee and thought about that one. She smiled to herself.

'I think you did.'

Tegan frowned, puzzled. Brede laughed at her expression, and turned to setting her bellows for the day's work, but her mind was not on the metal. Adair's harshness, his *you should not like her,* sank into her heart and festered there. Her own admission of that liking made her uneasy and she turned to watch Tegan. A burst of reddened light fell across Tegan's upturned face and Brede asked suddenly:

'Have you ever faced ambush?' she reached with her foot to stir the blanket around Tegan's shoulders. 'Ever found arrows in your fire when you're wrapped in your blankets?'

Tegan pulled the blanket out of her reach and considered that sudden change from laughter to grimness.

'No.'

'No; but you were prepared to put us through that, weren't you. One moment, we're idling over a jug of wine, singing of horses and fine riders, and the next –'

Brede turned back to her bellows, forcing air through the charcoal, and firelight into her face, lighting the set brooding anger on her features. She tried to quell the memory that made her muscles jump and her teeth ache, but words spilt from her.

'All our horses,' Brede waved a hand and the dancing light became those horses, hurtling through the darkness. Her hand dropped suddenly, she hardly knew if she made sense, '– arrows, spears, swords –'

Tegan settled her blanket about her shoulders more tightly in a sudden gust of cold wind from the forge's doorway. She glanced up at Faine, who shook snow from her clothes.

'I was scared half to death, but Devnet was amazing,' Brede said, a half smile on her face. Her hand rose suddenly, grasping an imaginary mane, 'I thought she would fall and be trampled, but not her.'

Brede's smile faded and the hand strayed to her shoulder. 'Falda was somewhere in that turmoil –' she wiped sweat off her face, stamping once more on the bellows, '– eight months pregnant.' She sent sharp yellow light across the forge, harsh as the bitterness in her voice.

'Devnet was so concerned for her horses. She barely stopped for me, and she wouldn't listen, wouldn't hear until they were safe, too late.' Brede shivered. She glanced at Tegan's grim-faced silence, and found more coherent accusation: 'Cloud Clan and most of Wing Clan were destroyed by that raid. We went back to search, to help collect the dead, to aid the wounded, but there was no trace of Falda.'

'I'm sorry,' Tegan said quietly.

'Sorry?' Brede raised her hands in futile anger. 'We were not armed.'

Faine laid a light hand on Brede's shoulder.

'It's ancient history,' she said gently.

Brede started away from her touch, and pushed past, out into the snow.

'Is it?' Tegan asked Faine bleakly, burrowing into her blanket a little more. Faine stared down at Tegan.

'She's blaming you,' she said at last. 'Is she right to?'

Tegan's silence gave sufficient answer. Faine began mechanically clearing the forge, putting the tools away safely, smothering the fire and then she went in search of Brede. She did not find her with Leal, and cut short Leal's enquiry. She set off toward the ox stall, half expecting to find the horse gone. Brede was there, grooming the beast with slow, considered strokes, murmuring in the Plains tongue. Faine stood in the doorway, and waited for Brede to notice her.

At last Brede turned away from the horse, cursing softly. She started at the sight of Faine, and turned away again, trying to hide her tear-streaked face.

'Brede –'

Faine did not know how to broach it.

Brede leant her head against Guida's neck, and waited for whatever it was Faine had to say.

'Brede, if I had known what she was, I'd not have –'

The smith stepped closer, resting her hand on the horse's shoulder, not yet daring to touch Brede.

Brede focussed on Faine's hand in preference to her face.

'I don't want you to tell anyone.'

Faine's hand made a convulsive movement, and the horse jerked her head, forcing Brede to step away.

'How did you find out?'

Brede quietened the horse, moving her hand under her mane, feeling the tattoo. She pulled Faine's hand across to feel the ridges.

'This is an uncancelled breeder's mark.' Brede's voice sank to a disbelieving thread of breath. 'This horse was bred by Falda.'

'Then she is dead.' Faine pulled her hand away.

'Do not tell Leal,' Brede begged. 'Tegan says she doesn't know what became of Falda.'

'And you believe her? Brede, how can you stand to – ? I should throw her out.'

'And have a frozen corpse at our gate? This isn't a village matter. I won't endanger you all for the sake of a revenge that is not yours.'

'You are one of us, and Falda was my niece too. I know I never met her, but – she was kin – of course this is ours.'

'Not this.'

Faine reached out and pulled Brede's hand away from its obsessive movement across the tattoo. Brede shuddered. Faine caught her into her arms, hugging her fiercely.

'What do you want to do?'

Brede laughed; a bewildered sound.

'I want to believe her. I want to think she's not to blame, I really do. I want to be free of hating her, but I can't.'

'Why should you? If you don't want revenge, you let her recover. What difference does it make whether you believe her? She'll be gone as soon as the thaw reaches us. *Gone*, Brede.'

Brede shook her head.

'I don't want her gone.'

Faine stepped back, to get a better look at Brede's down-turned eyes.

'What a mess.'

'You mustn't say anything to Leal.'

'No. I wouldn't begin to know how – but – does Tegan know – ?'

'I hope not.'

'And does she – ?'

'She talks of Maeve constantly.'

'That's something.' Faine frowned at Brede. 'I can't tell you how responsible I feel.'

Brede stared at Faine, mystified.

'None of this is your fault. And as you say, by the thaw, she'll be gone.'

Chapter Six

Edra's final visit to the forge and her unwelcome patient coincided with Brede's completion of her second knife.

Tegan had healed enough to offer help in sharpening the edges and polishing the knives, but she made slow progress. She was alarmed at how quickly she tired; her wound seemed healed, but she was still unpleasantly weak.

Edra made no comment as the blades were shuffled out of her way. She stood above Tegan, her eyes narrowed, waiting for Brede to stop crowding her.

'You're healed,' she said finally. 'What you need now is exercise, or you'll favour those muscles and grow into bad habits.'

She turned away from the look of relief in Tegan's eyes, and caught Brede's mirroring expression.

'You are well suited,' she said, 'as well matched as those sorry excuses for knives you've been working on. Faine must be mad to countenance such a wanton waste of good metal.'

When Edra had gone, Brede got the knives from their hiding place, and inspected them critically.

'If only it were good metal.'

Tegan pulled herself up to look, wincing at the aching of muscles weakened by long inactivity. 'Edra's right.'

Brede frowned.

'Not the knives, the exercise. Those match reasonably well, considering that wasn't the plan when you started, but the proof of the forging is in the use. And the proof of the healing is in the use too.'

'You shouldn't let Edra see you're frightened of her, it's insulting.'

Tegan raised an eyebrow.

'I'm to take lessons from you on courtesy, am I?'

Brede opened her mouth to answer, but Tegan cut her off.

'Or prejudice perhaps? You know as well as I do that Edra could have done more to heal me swiftly; she chose not to. What is that but prejudice?'

Brede tried again.

'I meant that since you owe her your life, you could show your gratitude.'

'No. I'll not be grateful for that. I'd need to be grateful to you too, and you wouldn't bear with it.'

'Grateful to me for what?'

'If you had told anyone about that horse, I would be long dead.'

'Faine knows. She has kept her own counsel.'

'Why has she?' Tegan asked, challenging.

'Because I asked it of her.' Brede admitted.

'And why did you ask her?'

Brede tossed the knives into their basket.

'It is between you and me.'

Tegan glowered. *And always will be*, she thought.

As soon as she was able to walk so far, Tegan went to the ox stall to look at the horse. She was tempted to blame the animal. Once again she sorted through her memories of that night, trying to persuade herself that she would remember if she had seen a heavily pregnant woman taken up by any of her comrades. But her mind was a blank. She remembered the four people she had killed – she always remembered those. She remembered helping a man blinded by one of the stones the Plains folk were so expert with; she remembered finding the horse, limping and frightened when the worst of it was over; she remembered the string of prisoners, many of them women, but pregnant? No. She remembered swearing at the general in charge of the chaos. Tegan's face creased into a travesty of a smile at that memory, not one she intended to share with Brede.

She rubbed her thumb over the tattoo, and regretted ever taking the beast. She was aware of the edgy hostility of the villagers. Only Faine's protection kept them from making outright threats. Tegan had seen the way their eyes skittered away from her. Even Faine, now. The smith's initial openness had stilled into suspicious scowls and long doubting looks. Tegan needed Brede's trust. Reluctantly, she decided that she must teach the apprentice how to use her knives, and run the risk of finding one of them between her ribs.

Brede came into the forge to find Tegan leaning precariously against one of the rooftrees. In each hand she held one of Brede's knives.

'You want to learn how to use these vipers,' Tegan said, without moving from her position, 'but first you must learn to protect yourself from them.'

She flicked one of the knives into the air, and caught it again. Brede waited, keeping her stance as relaxed as she could. These were not throwing knives, too long in the blade for that. Nonetheless, Tegan threw one, not at Brede, but to her. The weight of the hilt dragged it down, and Brede caught the knife awkwardly. It felt strange in her hand.

'Wrong hand,' Tegan said, 'Which means I have the advantage. You have to decide whether you have time to change hands before I attack you. This time, because it's me, and you know I can't move fast, you have time. Did you know which knife I was throwing?'

Brede shook her head, already beginning to be confused. She changed hands and felt better. Tegan threw the other knife, faster, lower. Brede caught it, instinctively changing her grip to accommodate the angle.

Tegan gazed at her thoughtfully, then motioned for Brede to throw the knives back. She threw them, again, and again, and Brede couldn't help but notice that Tegan caught them more easily each time, and she did not.

'Better,' Tegan commented at last. 'You made those knives to fit your hands, not mine, and you made one to fit each. You need to know which is which, or change them so you can use either.' There was still a half question in her eyes.

'You didn't tell me that when I was moulding the hilts.'

'You didn't ask.'

Brede hated the knives for a moment.

'I'll change them,' she said reluctantly, 'if you tell me before I make a mistake next time.'

'No bargains. I won't always be there to tell you. You have to learn by your mistakes or die from them,' Tegan answered irritably; hoping Brede was taking in what she said. She hesitated a moment longer, then said softly, 'You favour your right arm. You need to work on that.'

Brede straightened her back, and worked her shoulder thoughtfully. *Still?* There was a persistent pulling across her shoulder blade, a heat in the muscle, a coldness in the bone.

Tegan was feeling the restlessness of a slow convalescence, and she began to plan and prepare. She begged new leather and the loan of tools from Faine, and set to repairing her mail shirt. Brede sat opposite her, watching her struggle with the intricate links of metal, and made no move to help. At last Tegan could stand no more of Brede's silent disapproval.

'What ails you?' Tegan asked, testily.

Brede raised a shoulder in a slow shrug.

'What did not protect once will not protect again,' she said, lowering the shoulder once more.

Tegan inspected her handiwork, vaguely aware that out beyond the forge there was music playing.

'It's better than nothing,' she said, trying to place the source of the music.

'You intend to continue as a soldier?' Brede asked.

'I can't do anything else.'

'And so you'll keep killing until your armour fails you once more and there's no one to help you?'

Tegan frowned, and put aside the pliers she had been using to bend the rings back into shape.

'I don't expect to make old bones.' It was not something she had thought about for some time, not even when she felt that blade in her flesh. Now, Tegan shivered under Brede's steady, questioning gaze.

'If that is the sort of question you ask yourself,' Tegan said, 'why are you so keen to learn my way of life? It won't suit you.'

'I know that,' Brede said irritably. 'I have to do something. I can't go back to the Clans and claim Clan-right without a horse, preferably a whole string of horses.'

'You're a smith.'

'Can you name me anywhere you've been that was short of a smith?'

Tegan shook her head.

'You'll not stay here?'

Brede folded her arms and leant back against the rooftree.

'I've stayed long enough.'

Tegan laughed, feeling a sudden affection for Brede.

'Are you staying away from the festivities out of preference for my company?' she asked, inclining her head toward the sound.

Brede smiled her agreement.

'I was invited,' she said casually, 'but it's not because of you I'm staying away. I'll go and dance later. If you think you're spoiling my chances with some local lad, be easy about it.'

'Adair, for instance?'

Brede smiled, tilting her face into the firelight.

'Adair is young, he has eyes and a mind; I can't prevent him using them. I don't want what he hopes to offer.'

Tegan wondered if she read those words aright, and hesitated before she asked her next question.

'And Faine?'

'It's Faine's party,' Brede said. 'It's her son's hand-fasting.'

Tegan laughed as she considered Brede's response, trying to divine how much truth she was being offered.

'I'd have thought you would want to be at the party, that you would miss the companionship of the Clans.'

Brede raised an eyebrow, and took the pliers up, opening and closing them aimlessly.

'Companionship? At Gathers, maybe, but the rest of the time I was almost completely alone. We weren't a typical Clan family. My parents compromise between their Clans: breed horses but stay still. I got used to it. It was a mistake of course. It made them a target for the horse raiders.' She raised her eyes to Tegan, an unspoken question between them. 'We lost everything. My father was killed. We weren't welcome with the Clan, and Leal would never have been able to live like that. There was nowhere to go that was safe, apart from here. The Marsh folk aren't overly fond of me. I don't really fit into this way of life.' She glanced at the pliers, surprised to find them in her hand. 'Did you think Faine would ask you to the hand-fasting?' Brede asked, suddenly divining a different cause for Tegan's questioning.

'Ah no, Brede, she has more sense than to ruin her son's hand-fasting by antagonising the entire village.' Tegan considered Brede's face, flushed with the heat of the fire.

'She'd have invited me if she didn't know – wouldn't she?'

'She would.'

'And knowing what you think you know; you'd still have invited me?'

Brede nodded.

'They'll never learn that you are not to be feared if they hide from you.'

'And am I not to be feared?'

Brede frowned, not pleased to be caught out in this way. 'Not by them.'

Tegan decided not to risk asking what Brede meant.

'So you're different, you choose to hide and let them think ill of you?' Tegan watched Brede's face close, and changed tack: 'you don't fit?'

Brede glanced at her.

'I don't care a damn for their land obsessions, and I don't want a hand-mate, not the way they understand it. That makes it difficult.'

Brede fidgeted with the pliers once more.

'But there was someone once?'

'Devnet.' Brede frowned, sighed, a memory conjured: Devnet, sudden and silent at her shoulder, one arm around her waist in a not to be argued with embrace of welcome.

'And Faine?' Tegan asked again.

'Faine protects us. Without her word for me, the elders would have thrown me out long ago,' Brede flung the pliers down. 'I wish they had.'

'Because then your mother couldn't blame you.'

Brede lifted a miserable shoulder.

'She needed me at first – we needed each other – and now she is used to me. It will hurt her when I go; she may even hate me – if she doesn't already.' She glanced at Tegan's expression, and got to her feet, moving restlessly about.

'I do try. They need someone to keep watch on the hill? I do it. They need someone to guard the sheep on the higher pasture? I'm a nomad, I know about herd animals.' Brede laughed, 'Sheep. I've scarcely been living all this time, they don't understand what moves me, what makes me who I am. Oh and they try, I know that – Faine's son prefers farming to ironwork? Brede's tough, why not ask her? And I'm grateful, I am, we had nowhere else to go, but you've seen the walls. That's how their minds work. They've been lucky – the Marsh survives drought better than most places, and it makes them too certain of themselves. And – there's – there's no movement.'

Tegan laughed, a rich, full laughter that surprised her – for the first time laughter was free from pain.

'Very well,' Tegan said softly, 'if it's movement you crave, and there's to be no dancing yet, there is time for another lesson.'

Tegan put aside the mail shirt, and reached once more for Brede's knives.

As she did so there was a sound of scuffling at the door to the forge. Brede turned incurious eyes towards the sound, but Tegan froze. The suddenness of the sound suggested that up until that moment the person out there had been more careful, more secretive in their approach. Her hand tightened about the hilt of the knife.

'Brede –' she said softly, sliding the other knife towards her. Brede's face registered alarm, and then understanding, and then something approaching panic. Her hand leapt away from the hilt of the knife as though it had bitten her. Tegan closed her eyes in furious frustration. 'Brede – *use it.*'

Three men stumbled into the forge. Tegan tucked her legs up, trying to get them beneath her so that she could stand if she had to. Brede grabbed up the knife and put herself between the men and Tegan, her skin cold, and then prickling with heat. Adair and Darcie and Rhian. She blinked rapidly, nervous, and kept the knife at her side, out of sight. They kept close to the doorway, slightly huddled, each apparently unwilling to be the first to make a move. They held lengths of wood, large enough to do damage. They stank of ale and fear.

'How's the party going?' Brede asked.

Adair looked startled. Not the question he was expecting. Brede grinned, running her free hand through her hair.

'You come to set something up for the blushing hand-mates?'

Darcie laughed uncertainly.

'No?' Brede persisted, aware of a rivulet of sweat coursing down her back. 'Orla will be expecting something; we don't want to disappoint her.' She looked from Darcie back to Adair, trying to work out who the ringleader was. Normally it would be Rhian, but Adair was more committed to whatever they had planned. She didn't like the firm grip he had on his weapon. Darcie held his club awkwardly, almost hiding it; Rhian's grip was slack, and he swayed, confused by too much ale. Perhaps Rhian was the one to work on.

'Who got gate duty tonight then?' she asked lightly.

52

'Why guard the gate when the enemy is in here?' Rhian said scornfully.

'What enemy?'

'This one.' Adair stepped forward waving his club in Tegan's direction. Brede stepped sideways, putting herself in the way once more. The branch grazed her thigh as Adair swung back to rest the rough-hewn end against the ground.

'Are you neglecting your duty, Rhian? Keenan will be angry.'

Tegan braced her hand against the rooftree; ready to use it to push off from, but not sure she had enough strength in her legs.

'Keenan won't care.' Rhian replied, a grin spreading slowly across his face.

Brede glanced at Adair, wondering whether she could still make an ally of him. She laughed, and reached out, touching Adair gently on his sleeve,

'Adair, you should take your brother home, he's very drunk if he thinks that.'

'We're all very drunk,' Adair agreed, but it was not a compliant agreement. A tremor of anxiety ran down Brede's arm and she withdrew her fingers from his wrist quickly, afraid he would notice.

'You might have brought me some ale,' she said sulkily, and then, as though it had only just occurred to her, 'You could have come alone.' She let her closed fist rest against her hip, suggesting irritation, disappointment, scorn – 'But if you want to play with your friends, don't come looking to me for –'

'For what?' Adair interrupted softly, and Brede wondered if he was not perhaps drunk at all.

'Company. Or support when Keenan finds out Rhian isn't where he should be, and that you got him drunk. You did get him drunk, didn't you?'

Adair grinned.

'Company?'

Brede edged closer to Adair.

'Send them back to the party, Adair. You're sober enough to guard a gate, so long as someone is there to keep you awake.'

'And you'd do that?'

'Done it before,' she said softly, unfolding her fist. Adair watched that hand opening out of anger into potential pleasure; 'If it will keep you all from getting in trouble with Keenan, I might do it again.'

Adair winked slowly.

'Wouldn't want to get in trouble.' He turned slowly to his brother. 'Go'n tell Keenan me and Brede are gate-keeping so's you'n join the party.'

Rhian shook his head and giggled.

'Gate-keeping,' he said, and the giggle turned into a guffaw.

'Keenan will understand,' Brede said, 'Don't you think Darcie? Your father will understand that you wanted Rhian to enjoy the party, and that Adair and I agreed to cover for him?'

Darcie nodded, confused that what had started out as something deeply frightening was turning into a trick played on his father, and that Rhian seemed to be in trouble, and that Adair seemed to be finally getting somewhere with ice-maiden Brede. He pulled insistently at Rhian's arm, dragging him out into the snow, not wanting Rhian in trouble with his father, wanting not to crowd Adair. He didn't trust Rhian to fully understand how precarious the balance was between Adair and Brede; they couldn't afford to spoil Adair's chances.

Brede listened to their scuffling withdrawal. She looked curiously at Adair, wondering whether he believed what she had been saying. He was swaying. She pulled the club out of his hand. He barely resisted.

'Thank you for bringing more firewood,' she said, tossing it onto the fire.

Adair frowned at his empty hand, then found better use for it, clasping Brede to him, a tight embrace that sought to bring every inch of his body into contact with some part of her. Brede wrapped her arms about him, keeping her knife arm free of his engulfing hug, and let him kiss her – a deep, forceful kiss. Her heart pounded in panic, her whole body seemed to reverberate with the force of her blood. A wonder they couldn't hear it above the row of partying. She wished someone would hear. Adair remembered to breathe and she pulled away slightly.

'I meant it about the gate-keeping,' she said lightly. Adair shuddered, and returned to kissing her, moving away from her mouth to run his tongue across her throat, and up around her ear. Brede laughed, trying to writhe out of his embrace, not quite managing it.

Tegan turned her head away, her eyes smarting with the hot firelight and the sight of the embrace silhouetted against the flames. Why in hell Brede didn't just stick the knife in him and have done – she knew damn well why not. Protecting her. Tegan listened to the urgent scuffling of loosening clothes, flesh against flesh, Brede's breath getting troubled, Adair grunting. Tegan caught her lip between her teeth, biting hard, to keep from intervening. *Goddess.* Tegan covered her eyes, trying to block her ears in the same movement.

Silence – and not the silence of muffled hearing. An incoherent gasp, a soft, heavy thud. Brede, against the light, her hands tangled in Adair's clothing, bent over as she let his body gently down to the floor. A huddle of fallen limbs, her face unreadable, her breathing uneven.

'Tie him up. I'm going for Faine.'

'It's her son's hand-fasting.'

'That's right, and I'm her apprentice.'

'What did you do to him?'

Brede shrugged her clothes into order, pulling her belt unnecessarily tight.

'Clan secret. For dealing with horses that won't be told. I've never tried it on a person. Check I haven't killed him?'

And then she was gone – out into the snow. Tegan crawled over to Adair, still not trusting her legs. He was breathing. There was nothing obvious to tie him with, so she made use of his already loosened belt, binding his hands as tightly as she could. She thought about kicking him while she was about it, but she hadn't the strength, and she wasn't sure how Brede's choice of explanation would sit with broken ribs.

Brede's choice was to be light-hearted until she had Faine on her own. Then she told her mistress everything.

Faine pulled her round so that her face was in the light.

'Are you all right?'

Brede nodded, letting her hair fall back over her face.

'How far did you let him get?'

Brede pushed her fingers through her tangled hair, dragging braid and binding apart.

'Not far.'

Faine shook her head.

'Come.' She glanced about the gathering, looking for someone halfway sober. Her eye fell on Edra, who was watching with undisguised curiosity. Faine lifted her hand slightly in invitation. Edra rose and came quietly to join them.

'Adair has had far too much to drink and got beyond himself. I need help to put him to bed, or to guard the gate. Are you willing?'

Edra glanced at Brede's dishevelled appearance.

'I'll mind the gate, but find someone to relieve me soon; I'm ready for my bed too.'

Faine nodded, and taking Brede by the elbow waved to her son and headed off to the forge.

'Are you really all right?' she asked again.

'Yes.'

'And Tegan?'

'Upset.'

'Do you want to take this to Keenan?'

'No. They were very drunk. I doubt they will remember in the morning, and I burnt most of the evidence. If we make something of this, it can only mean more trouble.'

'And the other?'

'Adair believes I invited him. I hope he will think he imagined the whole thing in the morning. I don't want him trying to build on false foundations.'

Faine pushed through the leather curtain at the forge doorway. She glanced from Adair, beginning to stir, but not yet aware of his bindings, to Tegan, sitting with her back to the rooftree, knife in hand.

'I hope you will forgive my kin's behaviour. It seems they can't hold their drink.'

Tegan stared up at Faine and said nothing.

'Well,' Faine said, 'let's get this idiot to his bed.'

Between them, she and Brede got Adair to his feet. Faine made a grab for his breeches just in time. He swayed between them, muttering incoherently.

'You could help us by holding up your own trews,' Faine said irritably. Brede pivoted him about and almost dragged him through the doorway.

'Where we going?' Adair asked as the cold air stirred him to greater sense.

'Bed.' Brede said, and then wished she hadn't. 'You, your bed, alone.'

Adair kept silent, concentrating on his feet. Faine toppled him in at his door and rolled him into his bedding, only then loosening the belt about his hands.

'Where you going?' Adair asked, sensing the movement about and above him.

'To gate-keep.' Brede said angrily, yanking his wolfskin off the peg it always hung on.

'You don't have to,' Faine said.

'It's what Rhian and Darcie think I'm doing. Let's not muddy the water any more than we have to.'

Faine walked with Brede to the gate, and watched her up the ladder. Edra was down the rungs swiftly. She turned as she reached Faine, and looked up at Brede, hunched against the palisade.

'She's crying,' she said quietly.

'Adair's a bastard when he's drunk,' Faine said savagely. Edra raised an eyebrow.

'I didn't think she cared.'

'Oh, I don't know.' Faine sighed. 'I can't work her out at all.'

Edra nodded and waved vaguely as she headed for home.

Faine stood in the darkness, but the gathering held no charm now, it was deteriorating into a younger person's evening. She retraced her steps to the forge.

Tegan looked up as Faine entered, and laid the knife on the floor. Faine stood above her unwelcome guest.

'What are you trying to do to Brede?' she asked at last.

Tegan frowned.

'Get her to trust me.'

'How are you going to do that?'

'Teach her to use her knives.'

Faine hissed air through her teeth.

'Obviously you trust her already.'

Tegan hesitated, then slowly nodded.

'I think so.'

Rhian struggled out into the dawn, nursing a split boulder for a head. He had a confused idea that he and Adair had split their shifts to allow them both to spend time at the gather, but there was a nervous anxiety that there would be no one at the gate. He was relieved to see Adair, wrapped in his treasured wolf skin, staring out at the brightening horizon.

'Quiet night?' he asked genially.

Adair turned, and was not Adair after all.

Brede unwrapped herself from the wolf skin and held it out to Rhian.

'Eventually,' she said.

Rhian took the fur and stood wordless as she slid down the ladder, landing with a soft explosion of loose snow. He watched her stride away, her shoulders hunched against the cold, and a confusion of memories from the night ambushed him. His heart sank.

Brede went home.

Leal met her, hope warring with an urge to scold.

'Adair was here looking for you.' She left an expectant silence. Brede did not answer. She shrugged out of her tunic and dragged on a warmer garment then huddled beside the fire, her fingers knit tight about her knees.

Leal gazed at her daughter, silent and withdrawn, and reflected that Adair had not looked like an eager nor triumphant suitor. He had seemed uneasy.

'Brede?'

Brede shook her head. Leal sighed and sat beside her, reaching to stroke hair out of her eyes.

'He's a good lad, really.' Leal said.

Brede pulled away from her mother's touch.

'He's a violent, drunken, lecherous idiot.'

'Ah.'

Brede looked at her mother; hand still raised to caress, if she would allow it. She smiled wearily, and leant into the offered embrace.

'Is there any mending it?' Leal asked softly. Brede shook her head. Leal put her arms about her daughter, pulling her close.

'Was there anything to break?' she asked.

Brede sighed.

'A friendship, nothing more. A friendship. I don't want to speak to him, not yet. Not if he were to crawl naked through the snow to beg for forgiveness.'

Leal's breath jerked between laughter and disapproval. Brede grinned.

'I might enjoy him doing that, though.'

'I'll mention it when he comes back.'

'When?'

'He's only gone to the forge to look for you.'

'He forgot I was gate-keeping then?'

'Gate-keeping?'

'I told you, he was drunk.'

Leal shook her head in disgusted despair.

'I thought better of him. Rhian said he'd offered to relieve him, but that is irresponsible.'

'I dealt with it.'

'But –'

'Leave the poor sot alone, mother. I plan to punish him quite sufficiently. He doesn't need Keenan as well.'

'So he hasn't lost your favour completely?'

'Despising his weakness and pitying his folly isn't what I call favour.'

'You are a harsh judge.'

Brede pulled away from her mother and stood up.

'You don't know the crime.' She groaned, stretched the last of cold-cramp from her back. 'I've work to do.'

Leal watched her daughter go in silence, wondering what Adair had done or said to wreck his chances so thoroughly.

Chapter Seven

Tegan's reach had become limited, her speed slowed, her reactions dulled. She couldn't bear the weight of her newly mended mail, and knew that she wasn't pushing Brede as she should. She was afraid that she would not be able to do that pushing, that she could no longer use her own sword with sufficient skill.

She exercised relentlessly, trying to force the speed and suppleness back into her reluctant body; but she still accommodated her lack of reach, the lack of power behind her blow, and saw those adjustments mirrored in Brede's movements. She shouted her frustration at Brede, who was bewildered to be told that she was wrong, when her actions seemed identical to Tegan's.

They had been working within the confines of the forge, but now Tegan came to a decision. If Brede wanted to learn to use the knives properly she needed space to work and a variety of blades to work against.

Tegan bundled up her swords and knives, including Brede's ridiculously long greatsword, and carried them to the ox stall. The weight of the metal tired her. She laboured over Guida's saddle and reins, wearily tightening the last buckle. She heaved the bundle of weapons onto the horse's back and was trying to balance them when Leal appeared beside her.

'Leaving us?' Leal asked hopefully.

Tegan tried to hide her breathlessness, wondering suddenly whether Faine had really kept what she knew to herself.

'No. I need to practise my trade, to get fit again. I can't do that here, so I must find somewhere with space to swing a greatsword. Your daughter has agreed to partner me.'

'If Brede wishes to learn from you, I've no objection; there's no need for half-truths. If I'd known how to use a sword, her father might still be alive.'

Tegan smiled. Leal did not.

Meeting her daughter on the way back to her hut, Leal gave her a piercing look, which stopped Brede in her tracks.

'What is it?' she asked.

Leal shook her head slightly.

'Your lesson is to take place somewhere with room to swing a greatsword, according to your tutor. There's a good clearing up by the cress stream where you won't get an audience.'

Brede gave Leal a careless hug, and went in search of Tegan.

Leal was right about the clearing by the stream. The snow was unbroken except where a fox had been through.

Brede slipped from the horse's back, and took the heavy bundle of weaponry from Tegan.

The older woman dismounted stiffly, it was the first time she had ridden her horse since the rebel sword had found its way under her ribs. Tegan felt the scarring pull as she reached for the ground.

Brede watched Tegan's awkward descent from the horse and frowned. She had already noticed the pallor of Tegan's face, even the sharp wind failing to bring colour to her cheeks. Now she looked almost grey. Brede's fierce gaze penetrated Tegan's weakness, but she did not know how to stop Tegan from pushing herself on. Tegan turned to meet that gaze. Now that she was here, she did not feel able to provide Brede with the opponent she needed. She cleared a fallen tree of snow and sat.

'Pick a blade,' she told Brede. The younger woman unrolled the heavy bundle, and immediately reached for the greatsword. Tegan frowned impatiently, but bit back her comment. Let her learn by her mistakes. In this snow, the sword would overbalance her in no time.

'Take your time,' she said, 'find its balance, and use the weight if you can.'

Tegan watched Brede's first tentative passes, swinging the sword two-handed, stiffly. Unable to make much use of her wrists because of the weight, she slashed from the elbow, swung from the shoulder, drove with her whole body; all wrong, but there was no other way to use such a heavy sword. The weight pulled against her so that she was using some of her strength to hold it back, leaving her less able to follow each move through, and there was that persistent imbalance that Tegan couldn't account for.

Tegan shifted impatiently, waiting for Brede to realise the sword was useless to her. Despite herself, she had to acknowledge that given the limitations, Brede was making a reasonable pass at it.

'Stop now,' she suggested. Brede let the point drop into the snow, breathing hard.

'Do you see why it is no use to you? That sword was built for someone like Balin, with the strength and height and reach to master it. By all means dance with your sword, but it should be an extension of you, not a partner that you have to balance.'

Brede laughed.

'It wouldn't be my first choice, but if I had no choices, I'd want to know how to make the best of it.'

She wiped sweat out of her eyes, and flung the sword beside the rest. Tegan nodded as Brede picked out a lighter sword, one that she could use one-handed if she had to. Brede made a face; there was no hiding the poor quality of the metal, nor of its forging. Tegan relented.

'It is a pity you can't make use of that monstrous blade, it's beautifully made. If you were in a position where that was the only sword to hand and you were attacked, how would you use it?'

Brede hesitated, and picked up the longer weapon again. She swung it, letting it carry her body in a slow arc. She rested the point in the snow again.

'I'd end up scything my friends as well as my enemies.'

'That, and leave your guard wide open. It's not practical. The idea is to stay alive with the least amount of effort on your part. You have only to put your enemy out of action, no need to slice them in half.'

Brede nodded reluctantly, and picked up a more practical weapon, but as she straightened her eyes narrowed.

Tegan waited, recognising this now.

'And putting the enemy out of action includes enslaving children does it?'

Tegan ran her hand across her face, gauging the space between them, and the slipperiness of the snow. If she needed to get to a sword, she would have to move fast and she was sure of neither her strength nor the footing.

'I'm talking about my rules of combat.'

'And those include ambush?'

'Sometimes,' Tegan admitted, 'but I was not in charge of that raid. And it didn't go according to plan.'

'It seemed pretty successful to me.'

Tegan stood abruptly, testing Brede's mood.

'Do you want to talk about this rationally or do you want to fight?'

'I want to fight – I'll try rationality – for a while.' Tegan listened to the jerky way Brede's words came out, chopped and fierce. Definitely fighting. She walked towards her, as steadily as she could manage.

'Put the sword down.'

'No.'

'Then I'll have one too.' Tegan snatched up the longsword, and winced at the weight, heavier than she remembered. She glanced at Brede and leant on the sword, using it for support. 'It was a disaster from the start. We were late starting out, we got lost, we were nearly too late for the Gather.'

Brede nodded.

'That's why it was only us left.'

'Yes. We caught up with Cloud –'

'We were waiting for them.'

'Yes, once we knew that, we played on it. We hoped you'd think we were them.'

'We did –' Brede raised her free hand to stop Tegan from continuing, struggling for the rationality she had promised; '– even after the first few horses. Cloud were coming for a hand-fasting, there's a tradition that the woman's Clan drive off a few horses to state their intentions, a game – you let them –' Brede's breath deserted her, '– and the man goes after to get them back, and brings the rustler back with him – Ivo – he was hand-fasting with Luce of Cloud. We thought that it was Luce – until you killed Ivo.'

Tegan dragged together what she thought was safe to say, wondering whether she should stop, hardly daring to.

'We were expecting the horses to all be together, we thought we could get them all in one go: fast, clean.'

'We drive them together, but it's not like that at a Gather. We're trading then, as individuals. We keep our own string close at hand.'

'So, little pockets of horses, lots of people, plan gone wrong.'

'And that's your justification?'

'What do you want? For me to say the intention was to wipe out two Clans and fill our coffers with slave-silver? Because it wasn't, Brede.'

Brede glared at the sword in her hand.

'I can't do this.' She let it drop into the snow. 'Not now.'

Tegan let the longsword fall.

They had stayed out in the cold too long. By the time they returned through the gate under Adair's scowling regard, Brede was exhausted, and Tegan was shivering with cold. Brede thought of the work waiting for her in the forge with distaste, feeling the strain in her shoulder muscles from the greatsword. She had hoped to stand up to it better given her work at the anvil. Tegan stumbled dismounting from the horse; Brede raised an arm and caught her without thinking. Tegan leant into Brede's encircling arm, grateful, but afraid to need that support. She looked Brede in the eye, making a question of that glance. Brede returned her gaze and Tegan turned her head away fighting to recover her poise. This close, Brede could see that Tegan's hair wasn't the light brown she had imagined, but a darker brown, well threaded with grey.

What does that change? she asked herself severely, but still, it changed something. Brede withdrew her hand from Tegan's elbow and stepped away.

'I'll see to your horse,' Brede said, 'then I'll bring the swords. Go and rest.'

Tegan walked away almost blind with weariness. Brede turned to the horse, fire burning in her cheeks. She told herself it was anger, but it was not. She wondered if Tegan noticed the *your* horse. Probably not.

As she reached for brush and cloth her eye caught movement outside. Brede put the brush back, and made a long stretch for the leather curtain. Adair stepped back sharply. Brede held the curtain wider open, and tilted her head in question. Adair ducked under the low lintel to join her. Brede picked up the brush and gave a slow, steady swipe to Guida's coat.

'Swords, now?' Adair asked.

Brede nodded. Another steady sweep along Guida's mane.

Adair said nothing for a long time, watching her hands moving in the semi-darkness. She wouldn't meet his eyes.

'Brede, tell me what is happening.'

Brede stopped to worry a snarl from Guida's coat.

'I don't know myself.' She looked up finally. 'I can't tell you.'

'You'll leave with her when she goes?' Brede rubbed dust off her face, and frowned.

'Will I?' she asked. Adair frowned in turn, puzzled at the tone of Brede's question.

'I think so.'

Brede went back to the snarl in the horse's mane.

'If you say so. I hadn't thought of it.'

Adair snorted in disbelief. 'No Brede, don't play games.'

Brede shook her head slowly.

'You know I can't stay. Not now.'

'What has changed?'

'Everything.'

Adair, watching her doubtfully, saw her fight tears. He reached, and when she did not step away, brushed the dampness from her face. Brede wrapped her arms about herself, protective, restraining, stopping herself from weakening into his concern. She bit hard on her lip, and blinked quickly.

'If I'm to be a warrior, I have to learn to stand without comfort.'

'Are your wings strong enough?'

Brede laughed a damp, doubt-drenched laugh.

'I don't know how strong they need to be.'

Adair shook his head, rubbing her tears into his fingers. He walked away, head down, fingers still tracing the touch of her.

Chapter Eight

Tegan practised with sword and dagger, grim and silent and alone; night after night. She couldn't allow her weakness to overcome her. She must be ready to leave with the thaw. To do that, she must be able to get as far as the cress stream unaided, and be ready and able to partner Brede's embryonic sword-skill. It was more than a week of ferocious effort before she could do it.

Brede's body grew used to the new demands she made of it; a subtly different set of muscles grew into an understanding of their work. Her feet became swifter and more agile; even in snow. She learnt how to breathe with her strokes, learnt strength and accuracy and force. Tegan was quietly satisfied with Brede's expanding physical ability, but there was a nagging doubt.

'Do you want to die?' Tegan asked abruptly, as she once more pulled short her stroke, turning her blade so that the flat of it thumped into Brede's ribs.

Brede recoiled from the blow, glanced at Tegan's stance, and did not lower her sword.

'No,' she said simply, waiting for Tegan to explain herself.

Tegan scooped a handful of snow and threw it at Brede.

'You are still favouring your right side; it is weak, surprisingly weak, you should work on that.'

Brede flicked her head out of the way of the cold spray, and stepped deliberately away, indication that she was ending the bout, but Tegan would not drop it.

'What would you be willing to die for? What are you willing to kill for?' Tegan asked, as she stepped forward, knocking Brede's blade upward. Brede altered her grip slightly, forced Tegan's sword away and stepped back into the bout. Tegan's dagger tangled into Brede's; too close to avoid a rip across the knuckles. But then, Tegan close enough for a blow that would kill her. Brede tapped her gently above her heart with the hilt of her dagger.

'You're dead. Again.'

'Who are you willing to kill?' Tegan countered. Brede pushed her away.

'Is this a game you play with all your recruits?'

Tegan blinked. 'In fact it is, but I want to know where you stand – you leave yourself open to attack. You think about how to reach your opponent, you think of their vulnerability, but you ignore your own.'

64

Brede looked at Tegan blankly.

'Is that really what I'm doing?'

Tegan slowly repeated each move of the last encounter.

'You see? That weakness on the right – if this were for real, you'd have been dead long before you got that dagger into my heart. There is no point in dying for the sake of a sure blow at your opponent.'

Brede frowned, thinking hard.

'And you think too much. You are measuring and planning, and hesitating when you should be reacting. It doesn't matter what I might do in response to your blow; if your blow is sufficiently effective I won't do anything. It's not a game of strategy.'

Brede winced, recognising the truth there, but not agreeing with Tegan. Tegan saw the change of expression and pounced, pushing her advantage.

'So, who do you want to kill so much that you'd risk dying for it?'

Brede pulled at the lacing of her jerkin and dragged it off, her dagger tangled into the cloth. She wrenched her shirt clear of her shoulder and turned her back, letting Tegan see the livid scar.

'That's the 'weakness' you're so concerned at. If I were to want to kill someone, it might be whoever did that.' She pulled the shirt straight, and reached for her jerkin. Her face was hidden when she spoke again, hair falling over her eyes. 'I don't know who it was, so I don't want to kill anyone,' she said swiftly, without emphasis. Tegan sighed.

'Then learn to defend yourself,' she said briskly, stepping once more into the attack, just as Brede collected up the dagger.

The winter passed, the snows began to thaw, and Tegan began to think of her place with her companions, of duty, and of moving on. It was hard to think of those things here, in the slowness of the water lands, despite her steady work towards making herself ready for the journey.

Walking with Brede from the village to the now familiar cress stream, Tegan said, 'I must leave soon.'

Brede was instantly alert.

'I don't believe I'll ever be strong enough to lead anyone into battle. I would be a danger to my friends.'

Tegan's voice shook. She had said many things to Brede over the winter, many things that she found hard to say out loud to anyone, but this was the most painful truth she had forced into the open.

'I am never going to fully recover from this wound,' Tegan said into the waiting silence, 'and if I do not, I'm afraid I will lose Maeve.'

The silence stretched, and Brede must say something, for Tegan had stopped walking, and was staring at her, breathing in that cautious, shallow way she had when the air was cold.

'Maeve either loves you or she doesn't,' Brede said with abrupt irritation.

Tegan pulled her ragged breath into her lungs and followed after Brede's stiff striding. She took silent note of the shift in the way Brede held her shoulders; it was only a moment's distraction, but Tegan's feet went from under her, slipping in melted snow. Brede was there, a hand under her arm. Tegan shook her off, cursing silently,

Too quick, damn you. She couldn't afford to depend on Brede.

Brede stepped back and left Tegan to herself, walking briskly ahead through the slush.

'I have to leave,' Tegan said through her teeth. Brede did not turn, did not hear.

'I have to leave *you*,' Tegan muttered, as she struggled up the hill, her throat tight with misery.

'Leal's been asking about you again,' Brede said casually, as she rested on her sword hilt. 'She and Faine seem to do nothing but gossip about you these days. Whatever answer I give her, she always says: *Faine doesn't see it that way.*'

'Leal has changed out of all recognition,' Tegan agreed.

'She has,' Brede said thoughtfully. 'I've never felt so close to her. But she never stops her questions. It's as though she wants to know everything I've done or thought. It frightens me.'

'Curiosity's healthy,' Tegan said. Brede shrugged. Some of those questions had been intended to challenge, and to wound – questions about Brede's relationship with Tegan.

Brede hadn't responded to those half accusations, not knowing the answer. Now, she watched Tegan with the latest of Leal's snide remarks in her mind, and despaired at the unsteady and distressing happiness that suffused her. She tamped it down; forced herself to remember that nightmare of flying arrows and blood, to remember Falda, and Tegan's part in her disappearance.

'It's only the novelty,' Brede said, thinking of the frightening strength of her desire, but determined to put away those emotions, to make what use she could of Tegan's presence and to learn from her.

'Yes,' Tegan said, briskly, partly aware that Brede hadn't spoken in answer to her comment about Leal. At least Brede had said something.

The grass was beginning to recover from the frosts; the river was in spate with melted snow. The air was full of change, migrant birds were beginning to pass; soon, the farmers that remained would be back to casting seed on their fields, the armies would be back to their killing. It was time to move.

'So,' Brede said, resting her sword point in the slippery mud, 'when do we leave?'

Here it was then. Tegan looked uneasily about the clearing, regretting that Brede had chosen to ask that question with a sword in her hand. She glanced at the blade in her own grasp and tightened her grip slightly.

'The thaw comes earlier in the east,' she said. 'I am expected back within three weeks of that.'

'How long will the journey take?'

Tegan shrugged. Brede waited, a breath of unease stirring her.

'It should take me about nine days.'

'But we'd be slower together; we should be leaving in the next few days.'

Tegan gazed steadily at Brede.

'I shall be travelling alone.'

She saw Brede's eyes flicker and waited for her response.

Brede gazed at Tegan. She took a difficult breath, anger closing her lungs.

'You owe me,' she said finally. 'You owe me a life. You, and all your kind.'

Tegan wasn't expecting this – not after all this time. She had thought they had resolved this long since.

Damn that horse, she thought, despairingly.

The point of Brede's sword came to rest on her collarbone. A light, controlled touch.

'I think it is time we settled this,' Brede said.

Tegan frowned, angry at allowing herself to be so misled. She had been training Brede in how to cut her throat, after all.

Stupid. She allowed her eyes to measure the length of the blade against her neck, the steadiness of Brede's hand, the anger in Brede's eyes. She stared at Brede's troubled face, not yet afraid, and saw that it wasn't just anger that had that metal against her flesh.

Having started this, Brede wasn't sure how to continue. The anger was not sufficient to allow her to simply turn the edge of the sword against Tegan. Hurting, she wished Tegan to hurt, but that did not answer her anger.

Tegan registered Brede's hesitation, and dismissed regret from her mind. Her own responses gathered in the face of Brede's challenge, but she would not allow her instincts to have full rein yet, there was still a remote chance –

'There is nothing to settle. We've talked this into the ground. I did not kill your sister. You don't even know that she is dead. If you want to leave here, there is nothing to prevent you. You don't need me. Go back to the Horse Clans. Go back to Devnet.'

Brede sighed.

'Go horseless to Wing Clan?' she asked quietly.

Tegan felt the contempt that quivered down the length of the sword. She tried again, beginning after all to be afraid – to feel that she had underestimated Brede.

'If I'm not back when I'm expected Maeve will come looking.'

Brede shrugged.

'Let her come.'

'I have not raised my sword against you,' Tegan observed.

The hilt still filled her hand, the point still rested in the mud. It would take only a flick of her wrist to have Brede's guts spilt on that churned earth.

'I know,' Brede said – she had been wondering why that sword had stayed motionless; she had been aware of the involuntary tightening of her muscles, flinching away from the vulnerability of her position. Her arm was beginning to ache.

'This isn't a matter for swords,' Tegan said.

Brede would have liked to agree with her, but some part of her, the part that was feeling hurt and angry and disappointed, some part of her that had kept silent for months, was now roaring for vengeance. She would have liked to force that roaring back to rational silence; she would have liked to be able to let the sword drop, and to say, *This is only jealousy, this is only hurt pride; it will pass;*

She would have liked to be able to say, *I think I am going mad; give me a reason to back down.*

Brede said none of these things, but she listened to the tightening of her muscles and to the rational tone that Tegan used, and knew that it was a cover – that Tegan had decided to kill her.

Tegan had taught her well, but Brede was fighting that training. She did not push her advantage, her blade against Tegan's bare neck. She sensed the clenching of Tegan's muscles, and stepped swiftly away, just out of reach of the upward slicing sword.

There is no point in dying for the sake of a sure blow at your opponent.

So: now they faced one another in earnest, and something in the dynamic had changed, it was no longer Brede's initiative. Tegan had been a warrior for a long time; she had learned to separate her mind and sword from her heart. This was nothing to her now, but a meeting of metal, but they were more evenly matched than Tegan cared to admit.

Tegan made the first move, swiftly in under Brede's guard and back, but the blow missed. Brede's eyes narrowed. Tegan lunged again, and again Brede wasn't quite where she had been.

The ground was slippery underfoot, already churned from their earlier practise, but now this was real. Brede couldn't concentrate, she found herself questioning – not attacking – exactly as Tegan had predicted.

Brede was not afraid, she did not think that she would be killed; she believed she could keep out of trouble. What she questioned was whether she was willing to kill Tegan to prevent her leaving. There was no logic to it, but there was still that roaring, raging bitterness, that wanted blood. Brede gave in to the rage, allowing it to guide her to seek weakness, to take advantage of Tegan's pain, her shortened reach, her difficult breathing. So she kept Tegan moving, kept her stretching, kept her slipping in the mud, and made no move to strike at her.

Tegan saw that cold calculation – the almost casual way that Brede forced her to the moves that were so hard for her. She also saw the many hesitations, the uncertainties. Tegan changed her tactics, making no more swift darting movements, she moved in close, forcing Brede to defend herself, not by slipping away, but by using the sword. Brede did so correctly, but with no great instinct for the skill needed. She managed to keep Tegan occupied, until she was forced to break away, to return to her circling, trying to catch her breath. Neither had yet drawn blood.

Tegan saw another of those flickering uncertainties cross Brede's face, and leapt back into close contact, still breathing hard and short from the last bout. She caught Brede a glancing blow, scarcely a scratch; a wasted opportunity. Tegan kicked out. Brede stumbled, slipped in the mud, and went down on one arm – not her sword arm. Tegan jumped away from the swift arc of metal that threatened to take her legs off. She waited for Brede to get back to her feet.

Now Brede was angry with all of her being, not just the part that already raged. Her hands were slippery with a mixture of mud and blood. Her braid was coming undone, and hair was beginning to fall into her eyes. Tegan was waiting for her; *waiting*, as though this was still a lesson; she was about to learn something about waiting. Brede moved. She moved so fast that Tegan, weak as she still was, did not have time to dodge the blow, nor to parry it.

Chapter Nine

Brede groaned in despair. She threw the sword down and crouched beside the discarded blade, her arms clasped to her body as though it was her own flesh she had torn. Her lungs did not want to co-operate, determined to wrench her body with sobs of misery. When at last she could breathe easily, Brede wiped her face, smearing bloody mud into her skin. She pulled the tie out of her hair, and rebraided it, ruthlessly tight. For the first time she realised that she was bleeding. She pulled the remains of her sleeve apart, using the ruined cloth to bind the long tear in her flesh.

She shook with misery and the sudden release of tension. She whistled Guida to her and began loading the swords into the saddle pack, putting off the inevitable decision – where to go. Her half-formed plan to search for Falda in the city faded to foolishness, and she couldn't imagine what her Wing Clan kin would say if she went to them bearing a sword.

Brede leant her head against the horse's shoulder, abruptly unable to continue. After a moment she forced herself away from the warmth of Guida's skin and walked back to where she had left Tegan sprawled in the mud. She stared at the bloody tangle of Tegan's hair, feeling again the force with which the sword hit Tegan's body, hearing the impact of Tegan's bones on winter-hard earth. Such finality that sound had. Brede hardly dared touch her – hardly dared *not* touch her. She stood uneasily over Tegan, then knelt and turned her face to the light, straightening her limbs; gentle now. Her hands shook. She narrowed her eyes against that trembling and forced herself to wipe the mud from Tegan's face. Cold skin, unnaturally pale beneath the smearing of earth and blood – and the faintest flutter of a pulse at her neck.

Brede blinked, startled, thinking that perhaps she had felt only her own tremor of exhaustion against Tegan's skin.

Tegan's eyelids flickered. She opened eyes that were unfocussed and confused. Her seeking gaze fell on Brede, and she watched a long silent moment.

'Not going to finish me off?' she asked at last, barely a whisper, her words not as jaunty as she had hoped – she sounded old and afraid.

Brede sat back on her heels, flooded with relief.

'No,' she said, and waited to see what Tegan would do.

Tegan put a cautious hand to her head, feeling the bruise rising on her skull. Slowly she raised herself on one elbow. Not good – the trees swam in and out of focus, and her hearing was equally unreliable. Brede was saying something, but Tegan couldn't make out what it was, losing the words in a roar of blood. Bile rose in her throat and Tegan forced herself more upright, afraid of choking. She was barely conscious of Brede's arms, supporting her as she retched.

Tegan took a shuddering breath, and unravelled herself from Brede's arms. She squinted at the younger woman, still struggling to find a horizon to hang the sky on, still fighting to make sense of noise and movement.

'Is cracking my skull sufficient? Are you done?' she asked wearily, her voice still no more than dry rasping, she wasn't sure that her words made sense outside the ringing roaring cacophony of her skull. Brede did not answer, wandering away from her, out of range of Tegan's willingness to focus. She curled herself back onto the earth, hugging her aching body, trying to gauge her hurts, her ability to stand, whether it might not be better to close her eyes and give in to the whirl of darkness that sought to swallow her.

Out of nowhere Brede's voice, harsh in her wounded hearing, water against her lips, cold against the angry ridge of bruising under her hairline. The familiar feel of Brede's hands, seeking out her needs – Tegan tangled her hands in Brede's, pushing her away. She forced her eyes to focus, barely able to open one of them.

'What was this about?' she asked.

Brede wouldn't meet her gaze. Tegan forced her body more upright, and leant unsteadily towards Brede. She reached to rub the dried blood from Brede's cheek. 'I think we have misunderstood something important,' Tegan said softly.

Brede sighed. It seemed pointless. She resisted the temptation to catch Tegan's hand and hold it against her face. She glanced sideways at Tegan, and wondered how to say the words. It would make her look a fool, it would make her vulnerable, and it would change nothing. She pulled away from Tegan's touch and shook her head.

Tegan cursed. *Stupid stubborn* – 'What has this resolved?'

Brede stood abruptly, walked away. She whistled the horse to her, and pushed the last sword into the pack.

Tegan watched Brede, knowing what she wanted. She thought about what she felt about that possibility an hour ago, and what she thought about it now. All that separated those responses was anger. She struggled to her feet.

'Damn you,' she said under her breath, furious with Brede for her silences.

Brede settled herself into the saddle. She walked the horse across the clearing to Tegan.

'That's my horse,' Tegan said aggressively, suddenly afraid that Brede was going to leave her here, virtually helpless.

Brede ignored her words and said stonily, 'Are you coming?'

'Where?'

'You tell me. East, to begin with. I wouldn't want Maeve to have a wasted journey.'

'How can I trust you?' Tegan asked. For answer, Brede reached into the saddle pack, and wrenched free one of her knives. She flicked it into the earth at Tegan's feet.

'If you get up behind me, you can put that between my ribs, if you're so minded. Or you can walk home, and defend yourself against every footpad and army deserter you meet. Or you can trust me. Decide.'

Tegan picked up the knife, a slow cautious stoop; careful of the ocean of confusion her brain swam against. She was grateful for the smooth feel of the hilt in her hand, it was the sort of trust Tegan recognised. As an answer, it sufficed. She pulled herself up behind Brede. She held the knife and seriously considered thrusting it into Brede's side. Tegan changed her grip, pushing the knife into her belt. Brede tried not to wince from the feeling of the hard metal of the hilt pressing into her back. Tegan shifted her position slightly, and the pressure was gone.

'Have you left anything behind that you'll need?' Brede asked.

Tegan thought about that. She had most of her belongings on the horse. She said so. Brede nodded.

'What about food?' Tegan asked.

'I have supplies hidden up in the shepherd's hut. I wasn't sure we wouldn't have to make a run for it.'

'You thought Adair might turn ugly again?'

'Him, or one of the others.'

'And your mother?' she asked.

Brede snarled.

'What do you care about my mother? What is she to you, but a woman whose daughter you killed?'

'You owe her a goodbye. She'll think you are dead.'

'No she won't. She'll think I'm a heartless bitch who doesn't deserve to be called her daughter, the same she would have thought it if you had killed me just now. I don't imagine you'd have taken my corpse back to her?'

'No, I would not,' Tegan answered fiercely. 'But you are live enough to carry yourself back, and you care enough about your mother not to let her suffer, or you wouldn't have stayed with her so long.'

Brede said nothing, but she pulled the reins sharply and kicked the horse into motion, back down to the village.

Brede did not dismount at the gate – she did not trust Tegan alone with the horse.

As they reached the forge, Faine stepped out from the doorway. She halted abruptly at the sight of the horse, and at the look on Brede's face.

'We're leaving,' Brede said.

'So I see.' Faine rested her fists on her hips and gazed up at Brede.

'Will Leal be all right?' Brede asked.

'I think so.' Faine leant in through her doorway, and called out 'Leal, come say goodbye to your daughter.'

Leal pushed aside the leather curtain. Her hands found her hips in unconscious echo of her sister.

'You've decided then.'

'Yes.'

Leal gazed up at her daughter, trying to imprint her image in her mind.

'I've a mind to say goodbye properly, Brede; get off that blasted horse and come here.'

Brede laughed uncertainly, then unravelled the reins from her fingers, and slipped to the ground. She refused to even glance behind her, willing the horse to stay where she was. She heard Tegan shift forward on the saddle, the leather creaking slightly under her weight.

Leal hugged her daughter fiercely, pulling her head down so that she could speak privately to her.

'There's blood on your sleeve.'

Brede tried to nod, but Leal had too tight a grip of her.

'It will be all right,' she whispered.

'How can it be? Dear Goddess – how can you trust her?'

'I don't know. I do, that's all.'

Leal glanced beyond Brede at Tegan for a second, taking in her battered exhaustion. She wasn't sure what it meant.

'Good.' Leal released her tight hold at last. She smiled wryly. 'Which way does the wind blow?'

'Towards the future,' Brede responded; and for the first time in nearly ten years it was the correct response.

'Follow,' Leal said.

Brede clasped her mother to her, briefly burying her face in her hair. She turned swiftly away, to catch Faine into an embrace.

Faine pushed her away gently.

'Be strong,' she said clearly, including Tegan in her farewell, 'stay safe.'

Tegan laughed weakly, acknowledging Faine's use of the ancient warrior's valediction. She walked Guida a few steps forward, offering a hand to Brede, to help her up. Brede rejected the offer, a feral grin softening the rebuff, and sprang up behind Tegan in a smooth Clan move.

At the gate Adair stood, his back pressed against the bars, arms crossed, brow creased. Guida danced under the combined confusing tensions of her riders, trained to battle but not sure who was asking what of her.

Brede couldn't think what to say.

'I'm not going to ride you down, Gate-keeper.' Tegan said keeping her voice light and cheerful. 'You wanted me gone and I'm going, so open the gate and let me by.'

Adair shook his head. He fixed his eyes on Brede and lifted his chin – half command, half pleading. Brede sighed. She slid from the horse and stalked over to him.

'Well?' she asked.

Adair closed his arms about her, a suffocating, intimate embrace, which made her shudder. She kept her arms rigidly by her sides and turned her face sharply away from his seeking mouth.

'What do you think you're doing?' she asked, evenly.

'Checking for wings. I can't find any.'

Brede shrugged him off and pushed sharply at his chest. Adair was no match for her forge-strong, sword-swift energy. His back thudded into the gate.

'You can't stop the wind from blowing, Adair, and you'll not stop me following it.'

'You aren't even a little sorry, are you?'

Brede watched the expression on his face, gauging what was safe to say.

'I am sorry for the friendship we might have had if you could have been content with friendship. I'm sorry that you are hurt.'

Adair shook his head, a loose weak movement.

'You don't understand me. I'm still your friend. I'm trying to protect you.'

'From what?'

Adair focussed beyond her shoulder.

'From being hurt.'

'She's done her worst already. We've both survived it.'

'She'll never let you close. I know; I recognise the signs.'

Brede stared intently at the ground between them, and then raised her head to nod. Adair sighed, a huge, anguished letting go of tension and hopes.

'Go then.'

He turned and threw the bars to the ground, yanking forcefully on the gate so that it fell open in a great sweep of light from darkness.

Change was not the passionate whirl Brede had imagined, it was a drudgery of days spent walking through a landscape that changed only slightly, a landscape unpeopled, barren from old disasters, silent of voices, save those of

Marsh birds, complaining at their presence. Tegan admitted to no knowledge of the best route, the last days of her journey into the Marsh were only a vague memory of endurance; she had no idea which way they had wandered following Corla's lead. In the absence of more than a direction to travel, Brede kept to the uncertain ground of the Marshes, where no army would risk their horses. Let them keep the high ground, Brede could find a route safe for their one beast, even if it meant walking the entire way, prodding the ground ahead with rational caution.

Emerging suddenly from a screen of willows, Brede startled a heron. She watched the great sweep of wings as the bird took flight, so close she could have reached out and touched the slate sheen of its wing tip. At her shoulder, Tegan half raised a hand, the same thought in her mind.

Brede glanced at her, with laughter in her throat, but she silenced it, waiting for Tegan to speak.

Tegan's hand dropped. 'Which way does the wind blow?'

Brede lifted her hand after the heron; flying into a wide grey sky full of possibility. Suddenly she flung the other arm up, and spun on her heel, laughing.

'Well?' Tegan asked, unconsciously kneading the fierce agonising tension in her neck. Brede saw that movement, and silently acknowledged the pain Tegan was enduring. She relived that second when metal sang in her hands, keening her anger, seeking to slake her despair in blood. She remembered an earlier time, and Tegan's half-laughing protest,

Don't imagine the Goddess wants you for a holy slayer.

She clenched her fingers against memory.

And why was there a blade in my hand? Brede asked herself, recalling the effort it took to turn the blade, to pull back the strength and speed behind the blow. She recognised the split second when she found herself launched into killing. She was sick to her core with fear of that moment, not sure that she would have the strength to resist that singing arc of murder again.

'I should not have tried to force your hand,' she said. 'I'm sorry for it.'

Tegan shrugged. 'Bruises fade.'

Chapter Ten

Two days on, and into the well-wooded landscape of the hills to the east, they crouched in undergrowth, waiting for the sound of horses to fade. Tegan was tight-lipped and uneasy.

'It's too early for this; soldiers shouldn't be on the road so soon.'

'We should have kept to the Marsh,' Brede breathed.

'No.' Tegan gathered the reins, leading Guida back onto the track; 'Speed is even more vital now.'

Then, three days later, they came across the remains of a skirmish. No attempt had been made to bury the corpses, although some had been laid out, as though prepared for some rite that had been interrupted by something more urgent.

Tegan stood amongst the slain, trying to judge what had happened. She followed the trampled marks in the soft earth; restless to know where any danger might lie. The parties had come from the north and west, at speed, and the victors had moved on, equally swiftly, in a direction uncomfortably close to Tegan's planned route.

Green cloth told her who these losers were. None among them were friends of hers, but she felt a wrench at leaving them lying, at putting her own safety first.

Tegan turned, intending to speak to Brede, but found her no longer at her shoulder. She hadn't gone far. Standing with her back firmly to the carnage, she worked imaginary snarls from Guida's mane. Tegan sighed and put a hand on Brede's shoulder. Brede recoiled from the sudden touch, and turned to Tegan, her eyes blazing.

'You can't allow this sort of thing to distress you,' Tegan said, with more kindness than she had intended.

'The last time I saw *this sort of thing* I –' Brede closed her mouth, covered her face, fighting to get control of her emotions.

'The last time you saw something like this, you were looking for your sister among the Clans' folk *we* had slain,' Tegan said for her, drawing away, and folding her offending hand into the crook of her arm.

Brede drove her fingers into her hair, trying to find a way to say what she needed to, without forcing yet another confrontation. She glanced sideways at Tegan's folded arms, her bowed head, her frown.

Let it go, she told herself, but the anger stayed firmly rooted, and couldn't be shaken away.

Tegan's head came up abruptly, as though she had reached a decision. She winced as she did so. Brede met her gaze, and realised how tired Tegan looked behind the curtain of her hair, beneath the livid bruising covering half her face. Brede turned back to the horse, caught up the trailing reins.

'You should ride,' Brede said, undermining her irritation.

Tegan raised an eyebrow, and took the reins from her without comment.

The dark night and the cautious lack of a fire did nothing to ease Tegan's anxiety, nor the continuing rictus of pain in her neck. When at last she slept, she stirred and called out from her dreams. Brede shifted closer, pulling the tail of her cloak over Tegan to warm her, so that she would settle back into silence. Brede rested her arm along Tegan's back. Half aware of the encircling arm, Tegan turned in her sleep and tangled herself more firmly into the cloak and arms, so that Brede must lie beside her, or lose her cloak, or strangle on it.

When Tegan woke, she was wrapped tightly in Brede's arms, her head cushioned against her breast. She started up, alarmed that they had both slept.

'Hush,' Brede said softly, 'I've not closed my eyes.' She untangled herself from Tegan and stood stiffly.

'Have I slept all night, then?' Tegan asked.

'Yes.'

'And have you held me against the cold all night too?'

Brede shrugged, and began to rebraid her hair.

'Most of it. You had me fairly caught.' Brede smiled cautiously through her hair. Tegan tried to work the stiffness from her shoulders, then took the end of Brede's plait and fastened the tie for her.

'You should have woken me for my watch.'

'You needed to sleep; besides I quite enjoyed the warmth of you.'

Tegan handed Brede the end of her plait.

'It was dangerous.'

Brede shrugged her cloak straight.

'We survived,' she said softly.

Tegan made anxious use of every vantage point, but on the eighth day of their journey, despite her caution, they heard fighting before they saw the warning signs.

Tegan's every instinct was to give the battle a wide berth, and travel on, but the risk of having a war party travelling on her trail was too great, and there was the chance that she would be able to help another outnumbered, beleaguered company bearing green banners. She did not consult Brede. She dismounted and led the horse through the densest cover, Brede at her shoulder.

At first there was only utter confusion, but as Tegan watched, it became clearer. A small band of green cloaks, a number of red banners. An uneven match. Tegan loosened the buckle that held her sword across her back so that it dropped to her hip and caught up the reins. She found a restraining hand at her elbow.

'She's my horse. You do not ride her into danger.'

Tegan sighed in exasperation.

'Then I'll walk.'

'It's not your fight. How many times have you said to me, do only what's necessary?'

Tegan smiled in spite of herself.

'If you look down there, oh wise one, you may see a horse or two that you recognise. That's Maeve. It is my fight. It may not be yours, but will you join me?'

Brede grabbed hold of Tegan's mail shirt, deliberately forcing her fingers into the damaged rings, holding her still. Tegan glanced down at that hand, laid so precisely across the scar beneath the leather. She raised her gaze, sweeping over Brede's woollen coat. She lifted her eyes a fraction more.

'I shouldn't ask you, should I?'

Brede shook her head, and pulled her fingers loose of the mail.

'Go,' she said.

Tegan did not step away immediately; she gazed at Brede for perhaps another three seconds, and then startled her with a swift embrace and a cold kiss on her cheek.

'I can take care of myself,' Tegan said, then set off down the wooded slope, at a steady, easy run. Brede noted that ease, as she led the horse after.

Brede watched from the shadowed edge of the trees. Tegan's friends were not seriously outnumbered, and were holding their own for now.

Tegan was tiring, the wound still weakened her, she should pull back, but she would not.

Brede sighed impatiently for Tegan's stubbornness, stepping further back into the trees, as the confusion of warriors surged in her direction.

Her movement drew the eye of one of the red-clad swordsmen, who was no longer intimately involved in a life and death struggle, having just withdrawn his sword from a sheath of flesh. Brede saw the look on his face and she reached for the sword that protruded most readily from the saddle pack: the greatsword. As her hands gripped the hilt she faltered, but there was no time to think, she pulled the blade free and turned into the attack.

Of course, Tegan was right about the sword; it made her balance awkward, especially among the trees, where there was so little space. It was hard to get close, to manage more than a feinting and dodging weave. Had she picked one of the knives, he might already be dead.

Not dead, Brede told herself fiercely; *there need be no death*. The man was unduly cautious of the reach of her blade, and did not come near, waiting for the weight of it to tire her, as it must.

So, when at last the warrior closed, he was careless, he underestimated her, and he watched the wavering, glistening blade, not the eyes of the woman who held it. He did not parry the awkward, tired thrust Brede made until it was too late.

It was not how she had imagined. This was no stabbing sword, and even if it had been, this was not the same as stabbing at a sack of straw. Brede knew the instant she felt the vibration in the metal, that she would never forget that tremor of bone grating on blade. She watched, blank-eyed, as the fallen warrior gagged and gasped through the spilling of his life's blood, and she had not the wit to finish him quickly, nor to watch her back.

It was only a glancing blow; the killing impetus behind it drained by death. Brede felt the blade slide across her back, catching on her hip, tearing cloth and skin, but no more than that; then the body hit her, knocking her to the ground. She struggled out from under her lifeless attacker, and found Maeve standing over her, ready for another attack. Scarcely glancing at Brede, she kicked a fallen weapon to within reach of her hand, and was away again.

Brede snatched up the blade, got to her feet, and followed.

This blade was easier to handle, and she made use of it only when she must turn aside the blades of those who attacked her or the green-coated warriors about her, resisting the sense of power and vulnerability that a sword in her hand gave her, fearful of what she might do. She did not notice how many times Maeve or Tegan must parry a blow meant for her.

An uncertain shifting and the fading away of enemies. Brede glanced around anxiously, to be sure that the only red coats remaining were wounded or dead. Abruptly she felt completely alone, completely a stranger, and would have taken Guida and gone, but the chance slipped away from her.

Tegan and Maeve faced each other in considering silence, Maeve raised her hand to the bruising on Tegan's face; a wounded man raised his red-sleeved arm and gathered up a lost sword to slash at Tegan's unprotected legs. Brede couldn't get her brain to formulate the words needed for a warning. She flung her borrowed sword in the direction of that reaching arm and knocked his blade aside. There was little strength behind his blow, and Brede's intervention was enough. Tegan flinched away from the unexpected clash of metal so close, and narrowly missed both blades. She stared down at the fallen enemy. He lay limply now, his eyes beginning to lose their understanding. Tegan stepped away, leaving him to die in his own time. She raised her eyes to meet Brede's.

'Protecting me again?' she asked.

Brede shrugged, and Tegan turned swiftly away, joining the huddle of warriors about an injured comrade. Brede followed hesitantly. The confusion of strangers resolved itself. Corla, supporting a heavy-set man Brede remembered from the Marshes. She dredged a name from her memory: Balin. He leant back against Corla's shoulder, barely conscious. His coat was dark with blood, slick and glistening. His breathing was harsh and thick, loud in the waiting silence of the warriors about him. Brede glanced at the intense expression on Corla's face, at the blood pumping from beneath her protecting hands. Abruptly one of the other men snatched her hands away.

'Let him be, Corla – let him go,' he said, his voice wretched. He cradled Balin against him, hunching his back against the others. There was a hesitation, then they stood and left Inir to his private leave-taking. Corla staggered as she walked away, and the young boy, Riordan, caught at her elbow, supporting her. Still that silence, waiting for Balin to die.

Tegan was short of breath, her head and neck were a fire of tension and her older wound ached miserably. She looked around for Brede, beckoned her close, welcoming the touch of her hand, and needing support. She missed the suspicious look Maeve shot her.

'So, the apprentice has broken her bond, and come to join the mercenaries?' Maeve asked, her voice low, in deference to Inir's quiet sobbing.

Brede eased out from under Tegan's arm. Brede met Maeve's gaze, but Tegan answered for her.

'She kept me alive all winter. I've taught her to use a sword.'

Maeve snorted.

'She'll have to do better than that. I've had to guard her back today. I don't want to have to do so again. If you can't train her to do that, she can't be a fighter in my band.'

'Yours?' Tegan asked softly.

Maeve flushed but she continued to meet Tegan's gaze, to challenge her, for the sake of the fear in her heart.

'You've fallen out with Chad, haven't you.' Tegan said, no longer questioning, but unwilling to discover the details just yet. 'Well, I can't lead you. My wound will not heal as it should; I am too old for this. If you want the command, you may have it. I shall work out the year of my contract and then I shall retire gracefully.'

'But I've got us a new contract,' Maeve said, warily.

'Doing what?' Tegan asked, puzzled.

Maeve grinned.

'Household guard to Grainne.'

Tegan raised a disbelieving eyebrow, until she caught the wan grin on Riordan's face.

'In that case, I won't retire. I think I could manage some ceremonial marching.' She saw Maeve begin to relax and added sharply, 'But you keep the command.'

'It's you Grainne wants.'

'Was that what she said?'

'Her exact words were: *I remember Tegan. I will trust the people she trusts at her back, but most of all I trust her eyes. If she lives, I would welcome her eyes into my service.*'

Tegan laughed, and blushed.

'Is there something we should know?' Maeve asked.

'No,' Tegan said firmly, 'my eyes she can have and gladly, but I am a liability now, I can't put you at risk. You'll have to keep the command, Maeve, like it or not.'

Maeve nodded reluctantly, but her eyes drifted back to Brede, an unspoken suspicion still festering.

'If our new contract is to sit about in the capital, what are you doing here?' Tegan asked.

'Short term contract, special orders. Find you and bring you back in one piece,' Maeve grinned. 'Grainne was eager to have us, but I don't think she's especially happy with Chad's crew, and since it's you she wants really, it was best to come get you. Ailbhe's spawn are out early, we thought you might run into trouble – there are a lot of odd rumours about.'

'What sort of rumours?'

'A ritual bloodletting?'

'The rain, you mean?'

Maeve nodded. 'Rumour has it that Ailbhe has lost his head.'

Something stirred in the back of Tegan's mind and she glanced sideways at Brede, to see if the same thought had occurred to her.

'And did rumour suggest the whereabouts of the sword needed for that?'

'Of course. *Allegedly* it isn't where it belongs, so *naturally* it is imagined to be somewhere in the region of the decapitated monarch.'

Maeve caught the look that passed once more between Tegan and the Marsh woman, and her voice trailed off. Tegan looked up sharply, caught out.

'You sound like Chad,' she said.

Maeve nodded.

'I was quoting him.'

Maeve scowled at Brede's uneasy look, and changed the subject. 'You had better look after the horses until we've taught you how to fight properly.'

Brede turned away to collect Guida from the trees where she had left her.

'Not now,' Maeve said, amused. 'You're bleeding. Care for yourself first.'

Brede glanced down. Apart from the glancing blow across her back, she had a scratch across her thigh and a deeper wound above her elbow. The wound on her forearm where Tegan had cut her had barely started to heal. It would help if she had mail like the others, but then, she was not going to be a fighter, she was to care for the horses. Brede had never felt so grateful to be under-rated in her life. With a quiet contract in the capital, the mercenaries wouldn't be seeing much fighting; with luck, she wouldn't need to draw a blade against anyone. And, there was the possibility of finding Falda.

Corla had made good use of the enforced idleness of the winter, and was considerably more confident in her treatment of the wounded than she had been, but losing Balin had shaken her, and there were other injuries to her comrades. She watched Inir anxiously, dwarfed as he was by the body of his friend, still holding him, still weeping helpless angry tears. Corla forced herself to look away from that anger and found the Marsh woman under her regard. Her hands trembled as she helped Brede bind her wounds. She unwound the binding of Brede's wrist, and frowned over the angry edges of the cut. She discarded the tattered rag that had served as bandage.

'Surely, between you and Tegan, better work could have been made of this?'

Brede flexed her hand carefully.

'That is Tegan's work.'

Corla poured a tincture of herbs over the cut. Brede winced.

'Wounds heal better if they are cleaned before you bind them,' Corla said sternly, and then Brede's words sank fully into her mind. She glanced at Tegan and Maeve, stiff with one another, as they had never been before, and wondered. 'And that crack Tegan has taken to her skull? Is that your work? I've often wanted to knock her head against a wall, her and Maeve; but I wouldn't stand between those two, were I you,' Corla offered, as she tied off the bandage. She caught Brede's wary expression and shrugged. She pulled Brede about to inspect her back, and exclaimed sharply at the scars beneath the new wound. 'That one should have killed you.'

Brede turned her head, frowning and confused. Corla traced the line in her flesh, absently probing.

'It's a mess, this old one. You don't heal well, do you?'

Brede shook her head, and tried not to wince as Corla dealt with the new cut. Corla glanced beyond Brede at Maeve and lowered her voice, to murmur directly into Brede's ear, 'They argue all the time. You could get caught up and used as a weapon – by either of them.'

Corla caught the furtive look Brede shot towards Tegan, and was almost sorry for her.

'We don't take sides,' she whispered. 'We just wait for the dust to settle.'

Brede nodded her thanks for the warning, and went in search of her horse.

The red-coated warriors still lay at Guida's feet. The bloody sword lay abandoned near the man Brede had killed.

Brede gazed at the sword, thinking about Ailbhe, and how a king might come to lose his head, and what she might have done with the sword once the deed were done. A valuable sword – one that might be bartered for information – or used to buy her sister's freedom, if she still lived. Brede heard steps behind her and swiftly wrapped the sword in the man's red cloak and thrust it into the saddle roll. Maeve stepped past her, and turned the other body over, automatically searching the pockets. Brede flinched from the staring eyes of a woman scarcely out of her teens. She remembered the weight of that body striking her back. She turned back then, to look at the man she had killed. He looked younger in death than he had any right to.

I did that, Brede thought, panicked bile rising in her throat. She looked from the one body to the other, and Tegan's words rose in her mind. *Anything you are willing to die for?* Maeve glanced up from her task.

'What's the matter? Have you not seen a dead body before?'

'Not one I killed.'

Maeve grimaced.

'Pray the Goddess you never get used to it,' she said.

She inspected the small handful of valuables she had stripped from the corpse, and pocketed them with slow deliberation. She stood, abruptly grim, and wiped her hands against her breeches, angry with Brede.

'No one should get used to killing,' she said, and walked away, her head lowered.

Brede soothed the horses, including a lame beast with a red saddlecloth, fed and watered them, cleaned and brushed their flanks. She worked methodically, scarcely thinking, comforted by the normality of her task. The abandoned horse was too lame to go any distance, even unloaded. She was still trying to persuade it to put weight on its injured foot, when Tegan arrived at her side.

'Is that horse going to be any good?' she asked.

Brede shook her head.

'We'll have to leave it then. When we get to the capital, the first thing you're going to do is find me a new horse; that is, if you are coming?'

'I can keep Guida then?' Brede asked.

'She's your horse,' Tegan said firmly. 'I'll have to ride Balin's monster for now, if I can reach to get up to his back.'

Brede grinned. Her horse, then; and Tegan her friend once more.

'So, are you coming with us?'

Brede glanced beyond Tegan to Maeve.

'I can't be a fighter.'

'You could,' Tegan said, 'if you would only –'

Brede shook her head.

'When I have a sword in my hand – I become someone I don't like. It isn't fear; it's – I don't trust myself. I don't want to be a killer.'

Tegan smiled wistfully, part of her glad to hear that unwillingness, part of her wanting to shake Brede into some kind of sense.

'This is war, Brede. You may not get a choice. If you want to take Guida and go, I'll not stop you, but this is no time to walk alone.'

Brede hesitated.

'No,' she said at last, 'I've a sister to find, and a horse to choose for you. I'll come with you to the city, then I'll decide. I've been without my Clan for years; I can wait a while longer.'

Tegan nodded and touched Brede lightly on the shoulder, intending to encourage her, but finding her hand resting longer than necessary, trying to find a way to say goodbye.

She pulled the torn edges of Brede's ruined jerkin together, and laid her hand over the wound beneath, as Brede had done to her no more than three hours before. Brede waited for whatever it was Tegan wanted to say. She felt the blood pounding against the restriction of the bandage, and her skin prickled with sudden heat.

'You need some mail,' Tegan said at last, 'and some new clothes, there's no mending this.'

Brede moved away from Tegan's touch. She turned to face her, trying to control a smile.

'Tegan, enough; I'll manage.' She glanced beyond Tegan, observing the furtively watching Corla, and the un-furtive glare of Maeve.

Maeve caught her gaze and held it, then deliberately turned her back, scorning to give her notice. She gave some signal that Brede missed, and the warriors mounted. Tegan got some looks as she mounted Balin's horse. Inir in particular watched her longer than the movement warranted. Brede scrambled for Guida, caught out and slow, and followed after the swiftly retreating group.

They did not travel far, just far enough to put some distance between them and the site of the battle, and find a safe place to camp. A stream and a clearing, some screening brush and trees between them and the road; a subdued gathering of firewood and cooking of food, carried out in near silence.

Brede's offer to take a watch was rejected. The mercenaries studiously ignored her, waiting to see how the dust settled. Even Corla spared Brede no more than the briefest nod, as she settled into Riordan's arms. Maeve's brother, Brede reminded herself, acutely aware of the tangle of alliances about her, and that she did not fit the pattern. She pulled her cloak tight about her, shuddering with cold, and tried not to let her eyes drift to Tegan, missing the light pressure of her body against her back, pretending that was all she missed.

When Brede woke, it was to find Maeve standing over her.

'You have a lot to learn,' Maeve said, 'and very little time to learn it. The first lesson is not how to use a sword, but how to avoid using it. That includes how you sleep, and how you wake. You should know where you are and who and what is about you, before you open your eyes; before you think about opening your eyes. You have a few days to learn that. This is enemy territory; treat it as such. I could have been one of Ailbhe's spawn, with a knife at your throat.'

Maeve stepped away and Brede sat up, resentful of her words, and tone, but silently in agreement. Maeve was as like to slit her throat as any of Ailbhe's warriors.

Maeve met Tegan's gaze sheepishly, but she wasn't going to give ground.

'All winter, and you haven't taught her that?' she asked.

'We were not sleeping under the same roof,' Tegan said softly. 'I've not had the opportunity.'

Maeve's anxieties hardened into fears. There were many things she needed to hear from Tegan, so many questions.

'This Marsh woman is special to you, is she?' she asked.

'I am in her debt.'

'Meaning what?'

Tegan shrugged, wary of Maeve's easy anger, trying to dredge a safe answer from the confusion of what she thought about Brede.

'I owe her my life.'

'Is that all?' Maeve asked. Tegan laughed.

'*All*? Isn't it enough?'

Maeve remembered thinking that Brede was trouble when she first saw her, chafing under the yoke of her apprenticeship. She remembered being glad that Brede wasn't her problem.

'Barely.' Another thought overtook the trouble that Brede might be. 'That sword – did she make it?'

'Sword?' Tegan knew which sword.

'The long one. It's hard to miss. If she made it, I'll keep her as armourer-smith.'

'No, it isn't of Brede's making.'

'So I'm to do what with her? She's no warrior. You shouldn't have made her promises.'

'I didn't, beyond getting to the city. We can lose her there.'

'Shame about the sword. I'd like a sword like that.'

Tegan thought, briefly, to tell Maeve what she suspected about the sword. She hesitated, and the moment was gone.

Chapter Eleven

Chad stood in the doorway of Grainne's tower and counted Tegan's crew in. The numbers were right, but something about them was wrong, something beyond the harried expressions and the sweating horses. Concern took him down the steps into the courtyard, starting an automatic pairing into relationships and alliances – *Balin*. The lack should have been more obvious. Balin had been a substantial figure among the slightly-built fighters Tegan favoured. His eyes raked over the new girl. Good shoulders, sloppy unsuitable clothing, lousy attitude. Chad nodded his sympathy to Inir, the most comment he could muster, and the most Inir would be likely to accept. Tegan was at Chad's shoulder.

'– right under the walls.'

'What's that?'

'Aibhe.' Tegan repeated sharply.

Chad nodded.

'I'm not surprised,' he said, fuelling her outrage. 'If you have criticisms, Tegan, take them elsewhere. My instructions have not included any sorties beyond the walls.'

'And why not?' Tegan asked frostily.

'Our duties are within the city; I've been answering directly to the Queen. If she wanted me out beyond her pale she'd have told me so.'

'But you're not surprised that Ailbhe's troops are so near and so early?'

Chad shrugged. Tegan pondered his choice of words. *Elsewhere*: A warning? Tegan shrugged in her turn; she was used to fighting, within the army as well as with more obvious enemies.

'And on that subject,' Chad said sharply, 'you can come and see the Queen now, if you're so sure you can do better.'

'Fine. Let's go.'

Tegan watched Chad's expression but she couldn't tell if he was bluffing.

The Queen could hear voices, fierce with subdued argument, just outside her door. The door opened and Oran ducked his head round the edge to announce her visitors.

'I know who it is.' Grainne said and the muttered argument fell into silence. She smiled thinly and nodded to Oran. The door was pushed further open and Chad's bulk loomed familiarly over the threshold.

'See who I found idling about the gateway,' Chad said cheerfully.

'Tegan.' Grainne held out a hand that shook very slightly. 'It's good to see you back. Are you recovered?'

Tegan bowed. As she straightened she got a good look at Grainne. This was a woman she had met off and on over the last twenty years and thought she knew. She barely recognised her. Tegan gazed in silence, all thought of accusation gone.

'Considerably.' She said at last. 'Ready to take over whenever you want me.'

Grainne considered Tegan: travel-stained, bruised, dishevelled; badly repaired mail covering a body that was out of condition and half starved. Her eyes slid to Chad's glossy good health and immaculate armour.

'Your eagerness need not have led to neglecting your own wellbeing.'

Tegan glanced down at herself. She grinned.

'I'll stay down-wind until I've time to wash.'

Tegan flicked her eyes about the room, letting the darkness and staleness impinge on her for the first time. No audience chamber this, more of a sick room: a bed in the shadowy corner, a sticky residue of some kind of physic in the deep glass beside Grainne. Tegan sniffed gently, but could not tell what the herbs were. Corla might have recognised them. Grainne smiled wanly.

'Chad will advise you on anything you need to know, which of his team he can offer you and so on. You'll have friends who you want to see, you'll need to order provisions – and new armour, *better* armour, Tegan, please. Come back when you're ready. Chad will suffice for now.'

Tegan bowed again, and as she straightened, felt Grainne's eye on her, doubting her, and for a moment she felt another gaze, raising hairs on her arms. She glanced about the room again, sure there was someone else there. No one that she could see. She crooked an eyebrow at Chad, and strode out onto the stairs, nodding briefly at Oran as she went by. As the door closed she turned back to Chad and hissed angrily.

'Why didn't you warn me?'

Chad's mouth thinned to an angry line.

'I assumed you knew. I thought Maeve would have mentioned it.'

Grainne listened to the receding sound of dissent and leant her head against the chair back and closed her eyes. She sat still, listening to a different voice, a different tone, a different message, dragging breath and strength back into her body. She turned towards the woman standing motionless in the shadows cast by the bed curtain.

'They had no idea you were there.'

'You're wrong. Tegan knew something; but she couldn't find me. You are right about her; she has a knack for seeing. She saw right through you.'

'Chad is easier to fool. He's afraid of me, so all he sees is temper or haughtiness. Tegan knows me.'

'A winter in the Marshes doesn't seem to have done her much good. It's as well you have Maeve also.'

'Yes, Maeve. I suppose Tegan trusts her –'

The woman beside the bed leant forward slightly and started to sing, a soft lilting song that insinuated itself into Grainne's muscles, easing pain, bolstering confidence.

'Sorcha,' Grainne said gratefully.

'Mmm?'

'I think this could work – but I need someone up here. Not Maeve, someone I can be sure of.'

'So I'll have to do something about that.'

'How?'

Sorcha lifted a shoulder and came to sit at Grainne's feet, her long dark curls a cloak. Grainne lifted a handful of curls and spread them over her knee; smoothing the curls straight and letting them spring back against her palm.

'Tell me,' she said at last.

'I'm not sure, but I have an instinct for people.'

'Like your instinct for riding?'

'I can ride.'

'I've never seen you.'

'There are lots of things you've not seen. Take it on trust.' Sorcha leant her head against Grainne's knee and gazed up at her. Grainne shook her head, burying her fingers in the mass of hair in her lap.

'Not trust then.' Sorcha said. 'I will buy a horse, then you can watch me ride it. No – when you are stronger, you can ride with me.'

'I didn't think your kind needed horses.'

Sorcha pulled her head clear of Grainne's hand, twisting to face her.

'My kind?' she asked softly, her expression masklike.

Grainne found her heart beating fast, and pain winding back into her limbs.

'Sorry,' she whispered, 'that was foolish.'

The mask slipped and Sorcha sank back to the floor.

'Well, so we don't need horses for transport. I still need exercise. Besides, I like the way horse minds work.'

'And how's that?'

'Not like yours.' Sorcha said firmly. She stood, shaking out the myriad pleats of her skirt. Grainne smiled.

'I missed you.'

'It's been too long,' Sorcha agreed.

'I've been lonely without you, and vulnerable.'

'Vulnerable, yes. Lonely? You? As I remember it, I used to have to fight for a share of your time.'

'That was before Aeron died.'

'It wasn't just Aeron I had to compete with.'

'Everything changed when she died.'

Sorcha checked her rejoinder, searching Grainne's face.

'If you needed me, you had only to ask.'

'I did ask.'

'A week ago. I'm talking about twenty-two years, Grainne. Are you telling me you've been lonely for twenty-two years?'

'People find it hard to be intimate with their Queen. Only Phelan stayed the same towards me, and even he – Aeron's death maimed him.'

'Well Phelan –' Sorcha grinned. 'Has he asked you to hand-fast recently?'

'Not since last summer.'

'He must be losing interest finally.'

'He never did cope well with rejection.'

'Hardly surprising. I'm not fond of it myself.'

Grainne frowned.

'I never rejected you.'

Sorcha wandered to the shuttered balcony, her hands tucked defensively into her long sleeves.

'I didn't give you an opportunity to put it into words, Grainne. I'm not keen on humiliation. I could see the way the wind was blowing.'

She pretended not to hear the gasp of protest and peered through the slats of the shutter. The angle of vision was poor. She glanced at Grainne and walked into the side chamber, which offered a better view of the courtyard. The windows here were very high but if she got onto the deep sill and braced herself against the side, she had a reasonable view. She wasn't sure what it was about the courtyard that was drawing her out there. She jumped back to the floor and gathered up a small stone jar. She took the jar back to Grainne.

'You should lie down. If you need it, here's the drug. You know how to mix it. I'm going for a walk.'

Grainne opened her mouth to protest, but Sorcha was gone, only a slight disturbance in the air to show where she had been standing.

Tegan retired from the meeting with Grainne and the argument with Chad in an ill humour, which she took out on the first person she encountered, who happened to be Maeve.

Maeve heard her out in silence.

'Fine.' She looked around for Corla, couldn't find her and settled instead on Inir. He could use something to keep him occupied.

'We're not in charge yet, find one of Chad's and negotiate barrack space.' Her eyes strayed over the yard and lit on Brede, fidgeting with the reins of Corla's horse. 'Take the Marsh woman round to Eachan, but sort out the billets first. We'll be down on the corner when you're ready.'

Maeve shook her head at Tegan's protest.

'You're not on duty. You need a drink,' she grabbed Tegan's arm and walked her firmly down the narrow street to the inn at the corner. Tegan allowed her first resistance to fade. An inn was a good place to learn what was happening, and she was restless with nothing official to do.

The inn was crowded, as it always was, and smelt of sour beer and stale sweat. Tegan hesitated on the threshold, overwhelmed by a wave of nostalgia. It had been a long winter.

She loosened Maeve's grip on her elbow, and put her arm about her waist. Maeve grinned, and guided them both through the crush of bodies to the row of barrels at the rear of the building.

Settled into a corner, Tegan relaxed for the first time in months. She drank long of her beer and sighed contentedly. Maeve sank onto the arm of Tegan's chair and shifted against her to aid her balance. She rested her elbow on Tegan's head, creating the illusion of private space. Tegan wished Maeve had chosen somewhere more genuinely private and caught her hand, pulling her arm around her. Maeve laughed and leant in close, seeking a kiss. Their lips had barely touched when Maeve unbalanced and they tangled into a precarious closeness that had Maeve's ale slopping across Tegan's shoulder. Maeve righted herself.

'Missed you,' she said quietly, and leant forward to force her tankard onto the crowded table. Her movement caught the eye of a man at a table near the centre of the room, who called her name with some urgency. Maeve hesitated, glanced at Tegan, then recovered her drink and wove her way through the maze of stools and outstretched legs.

'Missed me?' Tegan muttered, glaring at Killan's arm about Maeve. She shrugged him off quickly enough, but – Tegan never trusted Killan. She mopped at the spilt ale on her sleeve.

A solid looking woman, one of Chad's lieutenants, took Maeve's place at her side. Tegan shifted slightly to make more room for her.

'Well, Tegan?' Ula asked, planting a kiss on her forehead.

'Passable,' Tegan said, taking her hand; 'worried.'

Ula glanced across at Maeve.

'About that?'

'No,' a lie. And then, 'about Ailbhe.' The truth.

'Chad said you were being over-scrupulous.'

'Over-scrupulous? I left him minutes ago. He's in a damn hurry to spread his opinion of me. What does he mean by it?'

'What do we care how someone else does their job?'

'I care when it puts me and mine at risk; I care when the woman paying me cares.'

Ula raised her shoulder awkwardly.

'I think you might have more need to worry about Maeve and Killan.' She twisted awkwardly and waved to Murdo, at the barrels. His mouth widened into a grin at the sight of Tegan, and he struggled through the throng to loom over them both.

'Tegan! Alive after all. You have no idea how glad we are you're back. Maeve and Chad have been fighting so badly it's a wonder we still have a contract.'

'So I've heard. How did we get it in the first place? Who had it before and why have they gone?'

Murdo laughed.

'Tegan, the Queen changes her household guard like other people change their underclothes. We'll need to be very good to keep this contract, regardless of Chad's bickering. But I hear Grainne likes you?'

He looked expectant. Tegan smiled at the memory of Grainne's liking.

'More than she likes Chad, anyway. If we split the team, which way will you go?'

'Split it? Why?' Ula asked anxiously.

Tegan sighed.

'I'm not sure I really want to get into this yet, I haven't had a chance to talk to Chad.'

'No, just to argue with him yourself!'

Tegan laughed. Murdo poured ale into her cup and frowned at her in mock severity.

'You're back, Tegan, that's all that matters; you can control them both.'

Tegan shook her head, feeling exhausted.

'I don't think I can, and I'm not going to try. I'm giving Maeve the lead, and I doubt Chad will agree to serve under her. I know that your first loyalty is to Chad, but would you consider staying with Maeve?'

Ula and Murdo looked at one another. Tegan watching them sharply, saw a *yes* forming in Ula's smile and a *no* in Murdo's grimace. She waited. Ula won the silent argument. She turned briskly to Tegan.

'Wherever you are, we are, you know that Tegan. You're the best thing to happen to Chad, and if he's too much a fool to know it, I'm not.'

Tegan hugged Ula.

'Give me a chance to talk to Chad, won't you, before you talk to anyone else? I'm glad you want to stay.'

Ula flushed, but nodded. Tegan glanced over at Maeve, still engrossed in whatever tall tale Killan was spinning. Ula once more followed her gaze.

'I'd make sure Killan goes with Chad,' she admitted softly, not entirely sure whether it was kindness or malice that prompted her words.

Tegan nodded.

'I need to go and get clean, I think. Tell Maeve where to find me when she surfaces.'

Tegan drained her mug, hugged Ula again, and for good measure hugged Murdo, grinning at his surprise; and forced her way to the entrance. She stopped then and turned to survey the crowd, not looking for Maeve, but watching her back. She shook her head at her own uneasiness; this inn was the closest thing she had to a home, these people were her chosen family. Her eyes drifted to Killan; one did not always love one's family.

Inir dispatched his duty regarding sleeping quarters swiftly. The mercenaries dropped their packs onto their allotted beds and began searching for clean clothing and money belts, disappearing in ones and twos to the bath house. Inir turned uncertainly to Brede.

'You need new clothes. You'd better have mail, whatever Maeve thinks.'

Brede tilted her head in enquiry. Inir smiled, or it could have been a sneer. He eyed her, measuring. Brede stood taller under his regard, uneasy with it. Abruptly he turned and tore into a pack on his bed, not his pack – Brede winced: Balin's pack. Inir held up a sleeveless jerkin.

'With a belt?' he asked. Brede reached out a reluctant hand. The wool was good quality, but the jerkin, meant to reach to mid-thigh, came to her knees. Brede caught Inir's glance, an awkward moment between pain and laughter. Laughter won. Inir rubbed tears out of his eyes and took the jerkin back.

'We'll barter these for something that will fit better.'

'I don't want you to part with anything that matters to you on my account.' Brede said nervously.

Inir shrugged.

'They are just clothes. Borrow something of mine for now; you can't even look after horses in those rags.'

Inir flicked breeches and tunic at her, and wandered away, giving her a semblance of privacy while she whipped one set of clothing off and a fresh set on. Inir returned from his slow circuit of their quarters and eyed the transformation.

He returned to his pack, and came back with a sleeve band of green cloth. He held it out silently; unable to voice just how foreign Brede now looked, dressed in his own clothes. Brede took the band and worked it up her arm to where it wouldn't slip.

'Don't take that off,' Inir said, his voice suddenly husky with doubt. 'It wouldn't be safe.'

He shook himself. 'So now we do the grand tour. Pay attention, you need to know where things are and who is who; it's dangerous else.'

Brede clenched her hand into her belt, *not safe* and *dangerous* swimming about her mind and her pulse beginning to skip and dive in anxiety.

Inir was an excellent guide, keeping his explanations and cautions to a low murmur, his introductions clear and brief. To everyone they met he said the same.

'This is Brede; she kept Tegan alive this winter. She's good with horses, when I find Eachan, we'll see if she's good enough.'

About everyone they met he told Brede, name, associations, how long she could expect them to be about.

Brede watched. She observed and wondered and doubted. Of each person she met she asked herself: *Is this one, at least, too young to have been at the last gather?* She couldn't ask. She was reasonably certain of Maeve, Corla and Riordan; unless they were let loose in battle as children, none of them could possibly have been there. But Cei and Inir were certainly of an age to have been there with Tegan. And she couldn't ask Inir about himself, so couldn't ask about anyone else. Who to trust?

She walked restlessly around the yards, pretending an interest in the architecture, allowing Inir to think her some easily impressed simpleton gawping in wonder. She developed a swift dislike for the arrogant stone towers about her. They stopped at a gate. Beyond it stretched manicured gardens and smaller, lower, but equally brutal stone buildings.

'What's that?' Brede asked.

'We don't go there, unless the Queen does,' Inir said, turning his back on the ornate ironwork that bound the heavy boards of the gates together. He caught Brede's expression. 'We make them uneasy.'

'But who would live there if –?'

'Well, they don't exactly live there, that's the guest hall, it's where the people come who want to influence the Queen – the ones who aren't army.'

'Are there any?'

'You'd be surprised. Landowners too old to fight, merchants with more money than sense, the occasional foreign envoy –' Inir moved away from the gate quickly, as though afraid of being overheard; 'They think that by coming here they can sway the Queen's decisions, and I suppose they do when she gives them a chance. It's my belief she hides from them as much as she can.'

Brede laughed, amused by the idea of the Queen hiding from anyone.

Finally, the tour of the barracks brought them to the stables and to Eachan. Inir's introduction changed subtly.

'This is Brede. She's a friend of Tegan's. Maeve thinks you can make use of her.'

Brede considered the man before her. He was much older than anyone else she had yet met, his hair grey and thinning. He had a scar across one side of his face, the eyelid puckered out of shape, the eye beneath it clouded and blind. He looked her up and down, and his eyebrows drew together. He nodded at Inir.

'I'll let you know.' Inir grinned and turned to go. Brede gazed after him, uneasy at being left alone with this stranger.

Eachan flexed his fingers thoughtfully, and turned his sideways gaze to inspect the woman before him.

'There are no new horses in Maeve's string.'

'Tegan's given me Guida.'

'Given?'

'Given.' Brede did not think Eachan would be patient with long explanations.

Eachan nodded slowly. Guida was not a horse he would have parted from.

'What's Tegan doing about another?'

'I'm to help choose.'

Eachan laughed at that.

'I wish you joy. Show me what you can do. There's a stable full of horses out there. Take a look, and bring me out the three best, and the worst. Only the one worst, mind. You can take your time. I'll go fetch us some food.'

Brede started towards the stable. She was going to like Eachan, she could tell; but he might have been at the gather, and the first thing she did once he was out of sight was to check the tattoos on every horse in the stables. She found only one more stolen beast, and few Plains bred animals at all.

Eachan returned with two deep bowls of mutton stew. He held one out to Brede, and let his gaze drift across the line of horses she had tethered outside the stable. One of them was Guida.

Brede took the stew and shovelled up a hot spoonful. Eachan leant on the corral fence and chewed thoughtfully.

'You're quick to judgement.'

'I know horses.'

'Why these?'

Brede chewed her way through a tough bit of mutton.

'Breeding. The piebald is in lousy condition, and has a cranky temperament, but he can be brought back, because he's well-built and strong in the heart. Guida's one of the best horses I've seen. The grey colt has potential to be stunning.'

'And your reject?'

'Should have been put out of her misery years ago. It's cruel to ride a horse with a back like that. And her lungs are shot.'

Eachan nodded, wiped out his bowl and held out his hand for Brede's.

'Then you know enough to pick Tegan's new horse. Show me how well you ride. Bareback.'

Brede grinned and walked towards Guida.

'Not her,' Eachan said fiercely, 'You're used to her. The colt.'

'He's too young to be ridden yet.'

'So you'll argue with an order?'

'If it'll hurt the horse.'

'Good. The other then.'

Brede approached the piebald stallion. He rolled an eye at her. Brede glanced back at Eachan, and she worked the bridle buckles loose and pulled it over the horse's head so that he was loose and untrammelled by bit or rein. He stepped away from her, shaking his head so that his mane lashed about. Brede took a firm step forward, one hand to his neck, a steady sweep of palm against the arch of muscles, making sure he knew where she was, then hand into the mane, a twisting kick away from the ground and she was on his back. Brede settled herself, thinking her muscles into concert with the creature beneath her.

Eachan watched as the stranger brought his most tiresome horse under swift control and took him through his paces, reminding him of battle training he'd long forgotten, jumping him across the corral fence almost at Eachan's shoulder. When she slid from the horse and persuaded him back into his halter, Eachan came to stand by the horse, his blind eye to Brede. The horse was blowing hard, but its ears were at a more cheerful angle than they had been for a while. Eachan listened to the huff of the horse's breathing, and tuned his ear to Brede's breathing – fast, but soft, regular and deep. He smiled to himself. If Brede had ears like a horse, they too would now be at a better angle than they were when she walked into the stable yard.

'Go and find Tegan. If I approve what she brings back, you have a job.'

Brede coincided with Tegan as she returned from a long soak in the bathhouse.

'Come on, we're due at the horse market.'

Tegan tried to dampen Brede's urgency.

'Have you been introduced to the master of the Queen's horses yet?'

'Eachan? I have: He'll take me on as a stable-hand if I pick a good enough horse for you. I think he wanted to come too, so he could disapprove my choice.'

'You've made a friend then.'

Brede grinned, not believing that Eachan could be so easily won, uneasy with the thought of another uncertain friendship.

'Very well,' Tegan continued, 'but we don't step outside the gate unarmed.'

'I'm the probationary stable-hand.'

'You are at risk.'

Brede looked doubtfully at Tegan, then nodded and loped back to the barracks. She was back almost at once, strapping her double knives about her.

Out in the street her stride lengthened and Tegan had to make an effort to keep up.

'Slow up, girl.'

'Sorry – glad to be out of the tower.'

'Why?'

'All that stone – towers make me uneasy.'

Tegan eyed Brede doubtfully; there was a tone to her voice that was at odds with her words, a haste that Tegan did not trust.

'Are you lying to me?' she asked.

Brede halted abruptly.

'There is nothing here I recognise, nothing I can trust.'

Tegan nodded slowly, and gathered Brede by the arm. She pushed gently until Brede was walking once more, but at a more leisurely pace.

'Tell me.'

'You tell me,' Brede said softly. 'I need to know who was there.' There was no need to be more precise. Tegan sighed.

'Chad. Inir – and Balin. Killan. Ula, Murdo. Eachan. Cei. A group of Maeve's friends you've not met yet, Oran's their leader; all of them were there. Maeve of course.'

'Maeve?'

'She started young, I told you all this. I suppose you weren't listening?' Brede shook her head. 'Maeve turned up here when she was barely sixteen, with her father's sword and her baby brother in tow. Riordan was nine, and she was all there was between him and death. And all she had to earn a living with was the sword. Maeve's a fast learner. That was her first real battle, although it wasn't meant to be, I wouldn't have taken her if I'd known how it would turn out.'

Brede glanced at Tegan, her face marred by a half frown.

'Did you really tell me that already?'

'Yes. More than once I shouldn't wonder.' Tegan focussed beyond Brede, her eye caught by something, and then refocused her gaze on Brede. 'Turn slowly and look at the man in the doorway to the left, keep turning so you don't obviously look at him.'

Brede did as she was told, noting a tall bony man in dark green, with a staff.

'Yes?' she asked quietly.

'Town guard,' Tegan said softly, 'most likely to question a Plains woman without a collar, most likely to see no problem with locking her up and finding someone to claim she had a collar once.'

'This is the sort of place Grainne creates, is it Tegan? Are you sure you want this contract?'

'Won't be out in the town much. At least – you won't.'

'I will, Tegan, I'll be out looking for Plains women, with collars or without.'

'Better get you a good green cloak then.'

Brede shook her head at Tegan, bemused and starting to be angry. She started downhill and steered towards the horse market, heading for the far end of the merchant quarter, near the river. Her confidence had Tegan wondering.

'Have you been here before?'

'No. I've only ever been to one city horse market, and it wasn't this one. We always preferred to let the city merchants come to us, but it's obvious where it would be. Besides, there's the smell.'

Tegan looked at her blankly. She couldn't smell anything.

Chapter Twelve

Brede led the way to the rings, grateful for something in which she was the expert and revelling in the warm, welcome smell of massed horses that spoke of childhood, and raised her spirits.

She watched the horse rings for some time, conscious that she was not only looking for a horse for Tegan, but also for horses she recognised – horses she herself had bred – amongst the animals being led around the rings. She didn't see any; but this wasn't the horse market Brede had been expecting: there were no freshly trained horses here to be snapped up by eager merchants, or people like herself and Tegan, looking for something a little special, not trusting a merchant to find it for them.

'This is a depressing spot,' Tegan observed.

Brede rubbed her face, trying to erase the gloom that sat across her brow, heavy with disappointment. She glanced at Tegan.

'This won't be easy. Not now that the Horse Clans refuse to trade with the cities, I should have known.'

Tegan glanced about anxiously, and caught a dark-haired woman watching them with thinly disguised interest. She tugged Brede's elbow, pulling her away from the ring, leading her towards the strings, where the brood mares were tethered.

Sorcha, her attention caught, followed after; although she couldn't fathom what it was about this pair that had caught her interest. Was it only that she recognised Tegan, or had the soft lilt of Brede's accent trapped her ready ear? It was an accent she recognised, and she was curious.

'I don't approve of taking brood mares into battle,' Brede protested.

'What do you think I've been doing with Guida all this time?' Tegan asked irritably. 'She's not been with foal the whole time I've had her. If it's the only way to get a good horse, I'll give it serious thought. And keep your voice lower, girl; Plains folk in this place usually wear a bond collar. If we attract any attention, *that*' she flicked a finger against the green band on Brede's sleeve, 'may not be enough to protect you.'

Brede pulled her arm out of Tegan's grasp.

'Don't remind me,' she warned.

Sorcha slowed her walk, dropping back to give herself space to think what it was that drew her after the fierce looking woman with the mellow voice.

The brood strings weren't quite so depressing, but many of the mares were past their prime for breeding, and therefore cheap. Too cheap.

Brede turned away again, leaving Tegan absently scratching between the ears of the only mare with much potential.

'There must be something wrong with that beast,' she cautioned. 'She probably bites.'

Tegan moved slightly away from the horse, eyeing her thoughtfully.

'I shouldn't think so, she looks mild enough to me.'

Tegan glanced at Brede, who was shifting restlessly from foot to foot.

'You didn't come here just to look for horses.'

Brede shook her head, and glanced along the line.

'Merchants, perhaps even a breeder I know.'

'Hoping for word of your sister?'

Brede nodded.

'I can look at horses on my own. I'll find you if I want your opinion.'

Brede nodded again, failing to put into words how she felt about Tegan's understanding.

Brede walked around the ring, keeping a watchful eye on the traders, but still seeing no one she knew. Her thoughts strayed back to the horses. The stallions were a more promising proposition. The prices seemed high, but she reminded herself she hadn't been into a market for so many years that this might be the norm now. Mostly they were showy beasts, and of uncertain temperament. At least there was some hope of a beast not past its prime, one that could still be worked on.

Brede was aware of someone at her shoulder, looking with feigned interest at the bay, which was probably the only decent beast amongst them. She glanced around. The woman smiled politely and returned to looking at the horse. Now that she had taken a good look, Brede was fairly sure the woman had been following her around the market. She continued to stare, until the woman met her gaze.

'What do you think?' The woman asked.

'I think you – you're following me.'

Sorcha didn't answer immediately, still trying to understand what it was about Brede that had drawn her eye. She didn't deny Brede's accusation, saying only, 'You seem to know something about horses. I need a good horse.' Brede looked her up and down, irritated by her tone. She took in the rich dark blue of the woman's gown: an expensive colour and the dress itself was not suitable for a day at the market, far too – designed to be looked at. Brede wrenched her eyes away from the dizzying pleats, forcing them back to the woman's face.

'My advice is generally paid for.'

'Not just your advice?' Sorcha asked, her eyes sliding across Brede's knife belt, taking in the two long knives. There was something intrinsically wrong about those weapons, at odds with the sense she had of Brede.

'Not for hire,' Brede said firmly. She turned, but found that she did not actually want to walk away. Brede heard the woman behind her sigh, a strange almost musical tone.

'And your advice?'

Brede looked once more at the ridiculous dress, at the heavy snakes of dark hair caught up at the nape of her neck with silver combs. Brede decided that she liked what she saw – somewhere behind the cosmetics, and the flat grey animal-blankness of her eyes there was a spark of humour that almost made up for the ostentation.

'My advice is to ask someone else,' she said, softening her refusal.

Sorcha masked her disappointment and irritation, thinking that she had been wrong; but still there was a feeling in the air between them to which she longed to give a name.

'Very well,' she said, and turned away.

Brede felt the abruptness of that turn shut her out from some potential pleasure. Caught up in her thoughts, she didn't hear the commotion further up the lines at first. When she emerged from her thoughts enough to hear, she ran.

Shouting, screaming, both horse and human – it was too reminiscent of that last Gather for comfort. Brede caught at the rail around the show ring to regain her balance, searching for the source of the screaming that rose above the exclamations of the anxious and excitable crowd.

Out in the ring, a horse reared, screaming in fury. One of the showy stallions loose – no, *not* loose – the child who was leading the enraged animal still clung, terrified, to the lead rein. All the shouting was making the animal more confused, more enraged; he struck out with those raised hooves, trying to free himself of the child. Brede pushed through the little knot of shouting people and ducked under the rail into the ring. As she did so, she felt someone brush against her, forcing a way through the crowd with as much purpose as Brede herself. The woman beside her continued towards the rearing horse, and Brede heard something she was not expecting: three sharp notes, followed by a falling trill, just as she herself had planned to use to calm the horse.

The stallion jerked his head suddenly, as though he had received a blow, then placed his front feet to the ground, delicately, carefully, well clear of the sobbing child. Brede made a grab for the reins, to pull the horse away, and saw why the child had not let go. The lead rein was caught about her wrist, the leather pulled tight by the horse's rearing. The child's hand was swollen and bloody. Brede cut the rein through. The child clasped her injured hand to her chest, the sobbing becoming a mere gulping of air; she was too shocked to cry any longer.

The horse stood stock still, sweat standing on his skin, muscles twitching as though he would be back in motion. He bared his teeth and rolled his eyes, but did not move. Brede rested her hand against his quivering neck and he flinched, but didn't turn to bite nor move away. She pulled his ears gently, cursing him in the language of the Horse Clans. His ears flickered under her touch; the panicked breathing seemed to ease a fraction. Almost without thinking, Brede ran her fingers under his mane, and found a tattoo. She bit her lip. She parted the long hair and squinted at the raised lines. Cloud – uncancelled. Brede's breath tightened and she did some quick calculations. The horse was probably too young to have been fully broken when he was stolen at the Gather. That explained some of the temper.

Brede spared a glance for the child, still huddled at her feet. The woman, the same woman, Brede now saw, who had asked her advice, held the child in her arms, crooning gently to her; but it was not the meaningless noise a mother might use to quieten a frightened child. In amongst that murmuring there were words of command. Brede heard them, but it was as though her hearing was at fault. She was not intended to hear. Those words were for the child alone; not even for the child perhaps, but for her body. Over and over, softly persuading the body that it was not, after all, as injured as it believed. The woman's face was closed, her concentration solely for the child, her hair loose of its combs, falling in a cascade that completely hid the child's face from Brede.

Brede let go of the horse, convinced he wouldn't move. She picked up a fallen comb. The child was quiet now; her injured hand was no longer swollen.

'You're a witch,' Brede said, surprised.

Without thinking, she still used the language of the Clans. Sorcha blinked, adjusting to the unfamiliar tones of the language.

'And you are of the plains,' she said calmly, her eyes flickered across Brede's knife belt again, 'or you were.'

Her words were half criticism, half question: she would like to know which Clan, but she could guess – that knife belt told her enough. Now the witch understood the contradictory message Brede sent out, but she still couldn't place the reason for her fascination, strangely like greed.

It had been a long time since Brede had heard anyone speak in that language. It softened the criticism. She still thought of it as a language for love, spoken so rarely now, and when it had been spoken, most often to those she loved; to her father and sister, to her horses, to Devnet. And now she had spoken it to a stranger, and been answered.

'Which Clan?' Brede asked the woman. She was sure that this stranger must be a Clan member, despite being a witch. She had used Clan whistles to steady the horse.

'No Clan,' Sorcha said, barely a whisper, almost a warning.

The witch got to her feet, aware of the approach of others, now that they could see that the danger was over. It was not good for her skills to be discovered; it had been a stupid risk to aid the child. She had acted without thinking, still confused by Brede.

'But the horse?' Brede asked.

Sorcha whispered a soft lilting phrase. The horse backed away a few steps, released from her thrall. Brede grabbed the rein, and hissed at the beast to be still. He bowed his head slightly, crest-fallen. Brede held out the comb. Sorcha took it, her fingers grazing Brede's in passing. The witch glanced down at her dress: there was a tear in the hem, and there was a large sodden stain across her knees, where she had knelt beside the child. She grimaced, and pulled her hair back into the control of her combs.

'I think I'll buy this horse,' she said. 'We have an understanding, he and I.'

Brede thought about warning her that the horse was stolen, but said nothing, distracted by the way the light fell across the woman's face, and a fleeting scent of herbs. She recognised the smell, could feel the flavour on her tongue, but couldn't name the plant, nor remember where she had smelt it before. She smiled and handed the reins to the witch, bowing slightly. Sorcha smiled, and Brede felt a strange sensation in the pit of her stomach, dizzying, wrenching; frighteningly powerful. She turned abruptly, and walked back to the fence around the ring, finding Tegan there. Seeing Tegan, she recognised that feeling, and measured the intensity against how she felt for Tegan. She smiled, nervous of the tangle she had herself in.

'There's a decent bay I want you to look at,' she said, surprised at how calm her voice was. Tegan nodded, her glance sliding past Brede to Sorcha.

'I've already seen her,' she said, recognising the look on Brede's face. Feeling cut out of Brede's regard, she hid an unexpected loneliness behind teasing.

Brede shook her head.

'A horse,' she said, 'I'm talking about your new horse.'

Brede looked back at Sorcha, who still stood in the ring, the stallion docile at her shoulder.

'Where is this horse?' Tegan asked, resigned to Brede's lack of attention. Brede gave instructions without taking her gaze from the witch, who was negotiating the price of her steed with the trader. Tegan followed her gaze, and frowned. She slapped her gloves uneasily against Brede's shoulder, and got no more than a flicker of response.

'You're bewitched, girl,' she said, and turned away. Brede nodded, unaware that Tegan had gone.

'Probably,' she said.

Sorcha bought the difficult stallion for a greatly reduced price, partly because his show of temper made him difficult to sell, partly because the trader's daughter, still nursing bruises, insisted she be given a good price. With the deal successfully negotiated, she led the horse out of the ring. A Horse Clan assassin waited for her. She bowed her head in acknowledgement of Brede's silent greeting.

'Will you walk back into the city with me?' Sorcha asked.

Brede nodded, and fell in step.

'I've never met a witch before,' she said, and wished she hadn't. It sounded so – naïve.

The witch laughed.

'I am called Sorcha. And I have known very few Plains women – certainly not any who dressed as assassins. Can you use those knives?'

Brede shook her head.

'After a fashion.'

'Why the disguise then?' Brede was silent, wondering if she had really hidden herself and if that was what she had intended.

'Why your disguise?' she returned, unwilling to broach the complications of an answer.

Sorcha was surprised.

'My disguise?'

Brede nodded sharply.

'You know better than to come here dressed like that.'

As she spoke, the witch's face changed subtly: bare of cosmetics, sharper, clearer. Her eyes darkened and deepened and her mouth widened. Brede grinned.

'That's what I thought,' she said, welcoming the honesty of the face Sorcha turned toward her. 'I thought you would be beautiful.'

Sorcha frowned, disturbed.

'And how do you know which is the true face?' she asked.

Brede shrugged.

'You dress in a way that means people will remember only the woman in the silly blue dress, not who you might actually be. And you should look the way you sound.' She wasn't sure what she meant, groping after words for the way her mind was reeling, trying to find safe ground, and failing to do so; yet discovering a strange delight in the danger so evident in this exchange.

I'm talking to a witch, she reminded herself, trying to find some modicum of caution, and finding instead, a rash delight.

Sorcha slowed her walk and nodded.

'As should you,' she said, casting a curious eye over the weapons once more. She caught the look on Brede's face and responded to that delighted smile without thinking. Suddenly she frowned and cursed to herself.

'I must leave you now,' she said suddenly, and swung onto the back of her newly purchased stallion. The horse did no more than blink at the weight settling onto his unsaddled back. Before Brede had a chance to recover from the sudden change of mood, the witch was gone.

Brede stood aimlessly for a while and suddenly remembered all the *not safe* and *dangerous* that both Inir and Tegan had told her that day. She turned, and retraced her steps, hugging the thought of the witch's smile to her heart, a most successful foil for her sudden disappointment.

Tegan waited patiently beside her new horse. She cast about her hopefully, wondering what had become of Brede, mildly anxious at her desertion.

'What will you call him?' Brede asked from an unexpected direction. Tegan frowned.

'Something to encourage reliability.'

Brede loosened the tether, whilst considering the horse.

'Colm?' she asked.

'For a war horse?' Tegan said scornfully.

'Devlin?'

'No. I knew a thief called that once.'

Brede shrugged, pulling the horse's head up to get a good look at him.

'I know what I'd call him.'

'What?'

'Donal.'

'I can't call my horse *sweetheart*.'

'I don't see why not. He's bound to respond to it. I don't imagine he's had much affection up 'til now.'

Tegan frowned at the horse.

'Donal?' she asked. The ears flickered and he turned a sceptical eye upon her. She shrugged. 'Maybe. I'll see what else he answers to. What was your bay called?'

Brede was not amused at Tegan's persistent joke.

'The lady was called Sorcha.'

'Lady? Have you set your sights so high?'

Brede pulled a face. 'She's a witch.'

'Really?' Tegan was oddly pleased to hear it. Some justification for the slight of Brede's sudden change of heart.

'Why that tone of voice?'

'I wouldn't mess with a witch. They're all trouble.'

Brede wrapped the tether round her hand, wondering whether to persist. There were things she needed to know that perhaps Tegan could tell her.

'I've not met a witch before. Hardly even heard of one. All I've heard has been bad.'

'Exactly,' Tegan said, wanting Brede to be cautious. Then her natural fairness made her add, 'But you have met a witch before.'

Brede frowned.

'I have?'

'Yes. Edra.'

'That's different, I'm talking real power, not just healing.'

Tegan wasn't about to underestimate Edra's powers, not when she owed her life to her healing knowledge. Brede's dismissal of those skills irritated her and she said so. Brede shrugged.

'Eachan is going to judge me on this horse,' Brede said.

Tegan hooked her fingers into the bridle, forcing the horse's head round so that they were eye to eye.

'Behave when uncle Eachan speaks to you.'

Brede laughed. 'Not like that.'

'How then?'

'You'll see.'

Tegan watched as Brede fidgeted needlessly with the bridle. Brede suddenly looked up, and it seemed to Tegan that they were too close.

'How does it work?'

The too-close-ness became a chasm. Tegan sighed, knowing perfectly well what Brede was asking.

'I'm not an expert. Song mostly, but don't ask me why or how. Not everyone who can sing is a witch.'

'And would you be able to tell if you were being spelled by a song?'

'Of course. Unless the witch was very skilled.'

'How skilled?'

'Better than any I've ever met. I don't really think you've been bewitched, Brede. I shouldn't have said it.'

'I'd rather I had. There'd be some excuse then.'

'Excuse for what?' Tegan asked, anxiously.

Brede shook her head thoughtfully, and did not answer.

Chapter Thirteen

Riding the horse back up through the city, Sorcha laughed to herself. She was still smiling when she reached the rooms she shared with the ruler of the country.

Seeing the happiness on her friend's face, much of Grainne's anxiety disappeared. Sorcha was no longer angry with her.

'What causes such a smile?' she asked.

Sorcha didn't answer immediately, settling beside her friend's bed, singing softly, partly to herself, partly to ease the pain in Grainne's joints and lungs. When she could see that Grainne's suffering was lessened, she said,

'I've bought a horse, and I think I've found us a solution; and I think I like her very much.'

Grainne considered her.

'When I sent to the Songspinner for a healer, I never expected you;' she said, caught up in memory. Sorcha raised an eyebrow, and hugged her knees to herself.

'Are you sorry?'

'I asked for secrecy, and they sent the one person who might be recognised here.'

'You have secrecy. You didn't recognise me, how could anyone else?'

Grainne nodded. 'You have changed,' she said thoughtfully, 'I would have expected you to be the same rebellious girl.'

'But I am, really, and so are you.'

'I don't think so. I am a ruler, and you –' Grainne searched for the words to describe Sorcha. 'You are so disciplined, so confident, so – alarming.'

Sorcha laughed.

'Alarming?'

'You have so much power, so much control.'

'Of course. I spent years training to get that control, I'm glad you can see the benefit.'

Grainne shook her head.

'I still don't recognise you.'

'Grainne,' Sorcha said, holding out a hand. 'Grainne,' softening what she had been about to say, feeling the weakness of her grip, 'when you wrote to me, did you think I'd send anyone else?'

'I wrote to the Songspinner.'

'I *am* the Songspinner.'

'I was afraid you were. Why are you here? Surely there are more important things for you to do?'

'Rebellion, Grainne. I may be the strongest of my kin, but I'm not in charge, I have no skill for leadership. I get asked to do a great many things that I wouldn't choose to do. This I chose.'

'And do your kin know that you made that choice?'

'You asked for secrecy.'

Grainne frowned, but she felt secure now, more alive – she even felt brave.

'I do not deserve you.'

'You think not? Then you should put right all your failings, until you do.' Sorcha said, pulling away to walk restlessly about the room.

Grainne watched, not at all sure Sorcha was teasing. She recognised that restlessness as something that ought to worry her, but she could not find any corner of her mind that was willing to doubt.

'I'm glad you found a horse. You need to work out some of that tension,' she said, almost severely. 'You were going to tell me more about your trip to the horse market?'

Sorcha returned to her perch on the bed.

'I found a horse for me and a guard for you. Congratulate me.'

Grainne didn't think it was the horse that caused Sorcha's delight.

'So,' she said, softly, 'are you in love so suddenly, sorcerer?'

Sorcha frowned.

'Not yet,' she said, suddenly cautious. 'It takes more than a common interest in horses to make me fall in love.'

'I won't be jealous,' Grainne said, 'I'll even try not to get in the way. I do realise that it is difficult for you to have a private life, cooped up in here night and day.'

Sorcha leant over and kissed her gently on the brow.

'You needn't worry. I plan to make it exceedingly pleasant to be cooped up here. You said you need a new guard, one not sullied by the arguments here. She's perfect – one of Maeve's I suppose, – she was with Tegan – that will make it easier – straight from the provinces, dresses as an assassin, moves like a dancer. She looks mean, but I don't think she is, I don't think she knows the meaning of the word.'

Sorcha hugged herself. Grainne rested a hand against her knee.

'No problems at all?'

Sorcha's eyes strayed into the darkness.

'She knows what I am.'

'Perceptive.'

'Hardly.' Sorcha sighed, and explained about the horse, and the plains" woman.

'You know which Clan she'll be, don't you?' Grainne said quietly.

Sorcha nodded sadly.

'So where is this paragon? What's her name?' Grainne asked.

Sorcha felt suddenly foolish.

'I forgot to ask,' she said; 'but I could find out.'

Grainne nodded, momentary exhaustion catching her unawares.

'You'd best do that.' She lifted her hand from Sorcha's knee, and sniffed it experimentally. She recognised the smell. 'You're taking getting to know your horse a little seriously, aren't you?'

Sorcha laughed, and started unlacing her dress.

'It was a foolish notion, wearing such easily damaged cloth to a horse market.' She pulled the dress over her head and flung it into a corner. Grainne wondered what had possessed her to imagine that rebellious streak had been quashed.

Eachan watched Tegan and Brede walk into the stable yard, laughing together like old friends. He had already caught up with Inir and asked several questions, none of which Inir could answer – nothing but Balin's death had stayed with him from the last week. No more than Eachan should have expected. Eachan scratched his chin and wondered how Maeve felt about this so-called Marshlander. He walked towards the women, and focussed his attention on the horse Tegan led by the halter.

Brede looked up as he approached and glanced nervously at her choice. Eachan nodded slowly, reaching to sweep the mane to one side. He turned his head so that he could see Brede properly, and raised a joking eyebrow.

'Not Plains bred, then. That isn't particularly promising. Talk me through your choice.' Brede took the halter from Tegan, and considered the horse, doubt hitting her a body blow.

'The others were useless,' she said shortly.

'I dare say they were. You could have waited and traded with one of the private stables.' Brede gave him a sharp look.

'Private stables?' she asked. Eachan didn't answer, noticing that Tegan stiffened and shot a look at Brede.

Nothing to do with horses, that look.

Eachan nodded.

'So, given the poor choice, why didn't you wait? Tegan could have gone on riding Balin's horse if she had to.'

'Sweet tempered.' Brede said cautiously. 'Strong in the neck and shoulder.

Deep-chested, reasonable back, about the right size for Tegan. Sound feet. No obvious bad habits.'

'Nothing special?'

'He smiled at me.'

Eachan roared with laughter.

'He did what?'

'You know what I mean. I can train a horse that asks me to buy him.'

'And one that didn't?'

'That too, but why put myself to the effort if there's no need?'

Eachan turned the horse about, judging him against Brede's criteria. She was right; he did have an amiable expression.

'Name?' he asked.

Tegan and Brede exchanged a glance.

'Donal.' Tegan said, as though owning up to an embarrassing secret.

Eachan's hand strayed to his blind eye, and he massaged the scar that puckered his eyelid gently.

'A real lady's horse.'

'No,' Brede said patiently, 'biddable yes, but I can train him to war craft.'

'All right. I bet you were as good at selling your horses as breeding and training them.'

'I was.' Brede said shortly, clamping her arms protectively across her chest. Eachan glanced at the knives in her belt and sighed.

'So what sort of contract do you want? Are you independent of Maeve, or will you want to be away with her lot if they go off?'

'Independent.' Brede said firmly, her eyes on Tegan.

'Fine.' Eachan thrust his hand into his money belt. 'Here: first month in advance. Go and get yourself some respectable clothes. As you are a part of the household your food and lodging is covered, and one green cloak or coat, state-your-preference, from the quartermaster. I'd advise you to buy your own mail – and don't get it from the armourer here, she overcharges. And unless you particularly want to sleep in the barracks, I'll want you sleeping here, above the stables.'

'The stables, definitely,' Brede said absentmindedly as she pulled the slip of paper from the pile of coins in her hand. She waved it at Tegan. 'He had this ready. He knew I'd pick you a good horse.'

'Of course he did,' Tegan said amiably.

'Of course I did,' Eachan echoed indignantly. Brede grinned at him.

'When do I start?'

'When you've got your provisions sorted. Now go and get on with it.'

Maeve, at last, had control of the household guard. She was anxious at Grainne's insistence that there be no guard at the inner door to her chamber, and that the guard on the stair should be different each day; it smelt of a lack of trust. Tegan wasn't surprised by those precautions, and took comfort from them. She was content to leave Maeve to guard Grainne, whilst she used her eyes, as Grainne wished. Maeve was satisfied with Chad's superfluous men, Oran's team in particular; apart from Ula, Tegan was not. Tegan bit her lip against any comment. She had handed control to Maeve, and must live with her choices.

Silently, Tegan started a routine of walking the city watching for trouble. The first trouble she found was personal. When Chad left with those who chose to go with him, he left Killan behind; but Maeve had not chosen him to work with her team; she had been to talk to the Queen, and Grainne had been quite clear as to which of Chad's people she would tolerate, Killan wasn't one of them.

Tegan watched Killan sloping off down into the town, bedroll over his shoulder, leading his horse on a halter, and she wondered. She couldn't honestly tell what she feared more, Killan's influence on Maeve, or the possibility that he might have been left behind for a purpose.

Maeve watched Tegan's scouting with anxiety, only partly aware of its cause – Tegan was sharing neither her concerns nor her findings. Silence grew between them, and Maeve sought out other companions, and found herself back in Killan's company when she was not on duty, even though she had promised herself she would not seek him out. Somehow, he seemed to be there, at the inn when she went there with Ula or Inir, three times in a row. There was no denying Killan's charm, he was good company, he made her laugh; he lit something in her that was damped down most of the time. Inir liked him too, and Killan took some of the burden of weaning Inir out of his grief from her, and Maeve was grateful for that lessened burden. She was not good at helping Inir, she had no idea how to do it, she didn't know when it was right to be light, when to be intense, when to be silent; Killan had a gift for it.

The fourth time Killan slipped into the seat beside her and poached her ale, her silent acquiescence was sufficient. Inir and Ula feigned interest in some arm-wrestling at the next table. Killan's hand found hers, and she felt the heat of his thigh against hers, and her heart skipped, the way it did before a battle. Her fingers twined with his and gripped tightly. She took the drink from him and downed what he had left. They stood as one, and wove their way out into the coolness of the night. He led the way back to his room in a house just within the walls. At the foot of the ladder Maeve pulled back slightly. Killan turned, his fingers still between hers, and raised their joined hands to his mouth, kissing between her fingers. His eyes met hers across their knuckles. He smiled, and she pushed him before her up the steps. He led her, feeling behind him for the rungs, his eyes locked on hers. Their hands did not loosen one from the other until she lay beside him on his bed.

'I wasn't going to do this again,' she said at last.

'I was,' he replied.

Sorcha spent much of her time at the high window that overlooked the barracks, watching Brede, wanting to know more about her, but not trusting anyone to tell her the truth. She listened to the idle gossip of the barracks, standing almost invisible in doorways, singing a gentle discouragement to any eyes that turned her way. Mostly, the gossip was silent on the subject of Brede, but when she was spoken of, it was in relation to Tegan and Maeve, and there was much speculation, and laughter. Following Brede on her apparently aimless wanderings through the city, listening for word of her, Sorcha gained a disturbing impression of the mood of the city, which she did not confide to Grainne.

Brede forced herself to check the tattoo on any new horse in the tower stables, grateful to find only one more stolen horse; a black stallion that she recognised.

'Whose horse is this?' she asked Eachan casually.

The stable master glared at the beast, and leant against the wall.

'Damned if I can remember,' he said, a look of puzzlement on his face. 'Nasty beast he is, I'd have a care of him, were I you.'

Brede drew her own conclusions as to his unusual failure of memory. Eachan was not from the plains, and to an extent, Brede resisted his authority because of it. Racial pride prevented her from believing he could be as skilled as the least of her tribe; but for all that, he had a tight hold on his work, it was unlike him not to know who rode a horse in his care.

Eachan found Brede's refusal to acknowledge his mastery amusing. He admired her skill with the horses and her care of them. He learnt from her and called her ferocity stubbornness, not quite understanding her reasons; and slowly wore down her reticence.

Brede returned again and again to the horse market, searching for anything that might lead her to Falda. It became a ritual, part of testing the wind each morning. She grew familiar with the city, walking the main streets, the back lanes, the alleys and snickets. She discovered the many markets: livestock, meat, vegetables, leather, silver – slaves. Brede forced herself to spend time at the slave market, watching for the sharp profile and dark skin of Plains folk, trying to understand. While she searched, giving close attention to the many women wearing a bondservant's collar, and grateful for the overt protection of her green cloak, Brede searched for the witch; although she scarcely realised that she was doing so.

She saw a great many children sold. She followed those children to the homes of their new owners, furtive, horrified, dreading now that she might after all find Falda.

Returning from one of many visits to the horse market, Brede was accosted by a man whose face she recognised. For a split second her heart lurched with unforgivable hope, as quickly extinguished as she recognised him: one of Chad's lieutenants, one of Maeve's drinking companions.

Brede returned the man's greeting, keeping her eyes down, hoping she hadn't betrayed the kindling of hope. He fell in step with her and walked in silence for several minutes. Brede eyed him carefully, wondering what he wanted. At last he spoke, as though making casual enquiry.

'What is it that draws you down to the market with such regularity?'

Brede shrugged.

'I like horses.'

'Aren't there enough horses in the Queen's stable for you?'

Brede laughed, and shook her head impatiently.

'Not made arrangements to meet someone?'

'Arrangements?' Brede asked; her mind full of the possibility of arranging a meeting with the witch.

'You haven't many friends.'

'Nor enemies,' Brede said pointedly, quickening her pace, 'and I've no interest in gaining either.'

'You're getting a reputation –'

'I'm not interested in reputations. I came here for my own purposes, and I've no intention of being pulled into whatever petty rivalry is going on in this – ant nest.'

'Petty?' Killan asked softly, a detaining hand on her arm.

Brede shook him off, letting her hand fall to the hilt of her long dagger. His eyes flickered from the hand to her face and he backed away one step.

'You might want to think about having more friends,' he called after her, as she walked away. 'The Queen's horse master might not prove enough to protect you.'

Tegan, who had been following Killan, hurried to catch Brede up.

'What did Killan want?' she asked.

'I wasn't sufficiently interested to find out.'

Tegan nodded slowly, but her frown deepened as Brede's eyes became anxious under her regard. She tugged at her gloves trying to find something to say; wanting to ask after Brede's search for her sister, but the failure of that search was self-evident. She allowed her gaze to drift after her quarry, and by the time she turned back to speak to Brede, she had lost patience and walked on.

Maeve observed Brede's return to the barracks and settled down to see how long it would take for Tegan to follow her. Tegan was through the gate only a few minutes later and Maeve drew her own conclusions. She shifted from her post and walked away, Tegan's greeting unanswered.

Journey after journey proved fruitless. Brede abandoned searching and tried to lose herself in her work.

Eachan noticed the change in the quality of Brede's attention, no longer concerned with proving her skill, merely cloaking her misery in effort. Tegan's new horse was learning some particularly vicious fighting skills, and he didn't want Brede to spoil Donal's famous amiability. Impatiently, he cornered her.

'So, girl, what ails you? Are you in love? What?'

Brede glared at him, insulted, although she could see that her long absences and deep gloom suggested just that. She said nothing.

Eachan tried again.

'Pining for the Plains?'

Brede flinched from that.

'You can't imagine I don't know you're Horse Clan?'

Brede shook her head, wondering where this was leading.

'There are no secrets here, girl. I know that horse of yours used to be Tegan's, I know an uncancelled breeder's mark when I see one. I've met other Plains folk searching the city for something they won't find. What are you searching for?'

Brede considered Eachan.

'Were you part of the raiding party at the last Gather?' she asked, already knowing the answer, curious as to whether he would admit it.

Eachan rubbed the blind side of his face.

'Where do you think I lost this eye?'

Brede nodded. *Well then.*

'I lost a sister there. We never found a body.'

'There are a lot of bondservants in this city,' Eachan said cautiously.

'Yes,' Brede said impatiently, 'But where? Where do I look?'

'You'll have found the slave markets.'

Brede nodded impatiently.

'If you're looking for a Plains woman, try the big houses with their own stables. It's a long time though – she might have bought herself free, or pined away, like you're doing.'

'I am not pining,' Brede said irritably, 'compared to the Marshes this is paradise.'

Eachan raised an eyebrow.

'I've met Marsh dwellers,' he said, and walked away, leaving Brede to her restlessness.

Eachan's casual saunter took him to Maeve.

'Your wild woman from the Marshes is here under false pretences,' he said.

Maeve gave him her full attention. Eachan rubbed at the scar beneath his blind eye, not entirely sure why he was talking to Maeve about this.

'You surely never thought Marsh folk know anything about horses?'

'What are you telling me?'

'Horse Clan.'

'I should have guessed.'

'No, Tegan should have told you.'

'You mean that she knows?'

'She must.'

'Yes,' Maeve's voice was tight with anger, 'she must.'

She nodded her thanks to Eachan and went to find Tegan.

'So,' she said, without any greeting, 'Brede is a Plains woman.'

Tegan was taken aback.

'Yes, you knew that didn't you?'

'No. You forgot to tell me.'

Tegan shrugged.

'What does it matter? Brede hasn't ridden with the Clans for almost a decade; she is hardly a security risk.'

'Not ridden with them?' Maeve remembered that somewhere she had known this; something had been said in passing, that night in the Marshes, and her rage intensified at the thought that she had missed the import of it all this time. 'Tegan – which Clan is she?'

'Wing Clan.'

Maeve thumped the wall beside Tegan's head.

'Wing Clan? And you think she's not a security risk? Are you out of your mind? She'll have to go.'

'No.' Tegan caught Maeve's arm.

'No?' Maeve asked coldly.

'I owe her my life. I take full responsibility for her.'

'For pity's sake, Tegan, think. If you do that I may end up hanging you.'

Tegan raised an eyebrow, and let Maeve's arm drop.

'I do not think that Brede will give you cause,' she said.

Maeve considered the likelihood of Brede causing the sort of trouble she feared. She hadn't forgiven Brede for coming between herself and Tegan and she was furious with her for being trouble after all.

'Right.' Maeve spared another glance at Tegan's face. 'I'll deal with this my way.'

Maeve glanced about; satisfied that she had something by way of an audience. She set off across the yard, yelling for Brede.

Brede came out of the stables blinking at the sunlight. Her enquiry as to what was wanted went unanswered.

'I don't willingly have Plains women under my command, so if you're staying you'll prove your worth. Go get a sword.'

Brede had not been expecting this, was not entirely sure what this was. Maeve reminded her of Devnet. Not a good thing, not worth the risk.

'I did not think I was under your command. I am content with the horses,' she said, giving Eachan cause to laugh, 'I do not wish to learn to be a warrior.'

Brede's mind raced. *Tegan? Wing Clan?* Which was it that Maeve wanted to hit her for?

Maeve had worked herself to a fever of anger, and Brede's refusal to be a part of the scenario she had planned tipped the balance. What had been anger was now something else. She saw Brede's scowling face; the arms crossed over her chest, in a defensive, half threatening pose. She remembered that posture from the first time they met. Brede glanced about, bitterly angry at Maeve's determination to make a fool of her publicly. She felt eyes upon her, saw the rank curiosity and delight in spectacle that rippled through the crowd of onlookers. *No*, she would not allow Maeve to goad her into fighting.

'I am not under your command,' she said again. 'Eachan pays me, and it is an arrangement that suits me well.'

Very deliberately, Brede unfolded her arms, and turned away, collecting up a feed sack to take to the stables.

Maeve's fist caught Brede a blow on her shoulder, knocking her slightly off balance. Brede dropped the sack, her breath tightened. She gritted her teeth, but refused to turn.

Tegan grabbed Maeve's arm preventing another blow.

'Stay out of this.' Maeve said. Tegan let go, stepped back. She had never heard that tone in Maeve's voice before. At least Maeve did not aim another blow at Brede's unprotected back. Eachan pulled Brede to one side, muttering swiftly, 'Maeve has a temper, like one of those horses of yours. When the horse challenges, you meet on its terms, on its own ground, and you show that you know better. This should be no different. Go and get ready.'

Brede looked at Eachan's calm brown eyes, the one sightless from that old wound; she saw the scars and lines of age on his craggy face. A warrior first and foremost, he knew Maeve as well, or better, than he knew his horses. Brede forced her anger back to a steady flicker, a safe level. She handed Eachan the sack, and met Maeve's glare. She nodded once, careful that it didn't look like submission, and went to choose a sword from the rack in the practice yard.

Other eyes, high above the yard, watched the preparations. Sorcha turned from her high window to Grainne, having to adjust to relative darkness.

'I think this might be a good opportunity for you to see this woman,' she said. 'Can you manage the stairs?'

Sorcha grasped the hand Grainne raised to her, she took a steadying breath, and began a low singing, that wound into Grainne's shaking limbs, giving her the strength to force movement from her ravaged muscles.

Grainne closed her hand over Sorcha's in silent acknowledgement, and they began the slow, agonising descent of the stairs.

Brede belted her long knives about her and took her chosen blade onto the practice ground, holding the sword as though she had never touched a blade before. Tegan's sharp eyes approved the choice of weapons, but she despaired at the expression on Brede's face. Brede felt the cold of the metal leeching through the binding leather of the hilt, drawing the warmth from her hand, and remembered the tremor of death running up the length of a blade. She glanced furtively at Tegan, but couldn't tell what she was thinking.

Maeve waited impatiently, swinging the shorter blade that she favoured from one hand to the other. Brede considered the antagonism that brought her here to face Maeve with a weapon in her hand, and for a moment her nerve failed her completely. Maeve wanted this confrontation, and that made her dangerous. Brede straightened her shoulders, and forced the tremor of fear from her arm; she had not the slightest intention of harming Maeve.

What Maeve proposed was another matter.

Chapter Fourteen

The two women entering the practice yard hesitated as they heard the ugly mutter of the over-eager crowd. They glanced at one another. Grainne shrugged and continued her careful walking, leaning heavily on her companion. Her hand as she gripped the guardrail was white-knuckled with effort; but she would not permit anyone to make her decisions for her, least of all one on which her life might depend.

The Queen's entrance had gone unnoticed. All attention was on the two women in the ring.

They fought hard, underhand, and brutal.

Grainne turned to her companion, a half-angry, half-puzzled frown on her face. This was not what she expected of warriors in her pay.

'Find me someone who knows what is happening here,' she demanded.

Sorcha scanned the many watchers leaning against the rail. She considered for a short while, reviewing what she knew of Tegan, whose slouch attempted to cover a tension that Sorcha saw clearly.

'Tegan,' she called quietly.

Tegan raised her head and glanced along the rail. The slouch vanished and she left Eachan's side with undignified haste. Sorcha grabbed her arm to prevent her from saluting the Queen.

'Not here,' she said shortly.

Tegan hesitated between standing to attention and pretending that these were two friends casually met on the grounds. She decided on the latter since Grainne had not come attended. Tegan leant against the rail once more, no longer watching the fight between her pupil and her lover. Her back flinched at being turned to the harsh sounds of combat. Grainne nodded at the pair in the ring.

'What is this?' she asked, giving Tegan permission to turn once more to face the conflict.

Tegan sighed, rubbing her face. *Jealousy,* she wanted to say.

'Maeve seeks to undo my teaching. She wishes Brede to learn how to fight for her life. She has had to cover her back in battle. And now she wants Brede to learn to kill, and step away ready for the next assailant; to learn that there is no time for grief at every blow struck. At least, that is what she would say if she was asked. Mostly she is just angry.'

Grainne leant more of her weight against the rail, knowing that she couldn't sustain this for long.

'And Maeve is willing to kill her to make this clear?'

Tegan's breath caught, and she watched the way Maeve was holding herself.

'So it seems,' she admitted, her voice weak at the thought.

Sorcha's quiet murmur increased in intensity, giving Grainne the strength to remove one hand from the rail. She pointed at the dark-haired woman.

'This Brede,' she questioned, 'you trained her?'

Tegan nodded, not sure that she was proud to own it.

'She is quick,' Grainne said, 'but this is not her kind of fighting, her heart isn't in it.'

Tegan struggled to hold back a smile, remembering Brede's speed when her heart was engaged with her blade.

Grainne saw Tegan's expression.

'What makes you smile?' she asked.

Tegan shook her head slightly, but then remembered who asked the question.

'I have trained that woman,' she said cautiously, 'and I've seen her in battle; but I have only once seen her raise her sword in anger. Then her heart was with her blade, and only then was she dangerous. She doesn't have the breeding to be a killer, she doesn't understand how not to care – and so she will only strike to kill in defence or if she is angry.'

'And what was it made her angry?'

Tegan hesitated before answering.

'I did.'

'And yet you are not dead.' Grainne frowned at Tegan, and Tegan lowered her eyes, uncomfortable with having piqued the Queen's curiosity.

'What else?' Grainne asked, and Tegan heard a tone she recognised in her voice, a tone from a long time ago. This was not the Queen asking, but the woman, Grainne.

'She won't protect herself when she is angry. There is only – this –' a gesture at the ring, 'or all out insanity.'

'And yet, you are not dead.' Grainne said again, forcing Tegan to think hard about the why of Grainne's questioning, and the why behind what she was trying to explain about Brede.

'She was – protecting me?' Tegan's uncertainty turned the statement into a question part way through, and her eyes focussed once more on Brede. Grainne sighed and followed her gaze. Sorcha's song sank to a murmur.

Sorcha watched the fighting, watched the level of skill and judgement behind each movement. She saw that Brede had made no effort to overcome

Maeve, who was trying to force her into a mistake. She saw that she held back the spark that would make her dangerous; she defended herself, but no more than that. She saw that Brede was tiring, and that Maeve was not. As she watched, a scuffling exchange brought the sparring pair about so that Maeve was facing her. Just for a second, Maeve glanced in their direction. Brede made no use of that slender advantage and Maeve lunged swiftly under her guard, knocking a knife away with her left fist, catching the falling blade before it struck the earth. Sorcha winced, and turned away from Maeve's contemptuous skill. She didn't want to see Brede humiliated.

'Don't make her angry,' she said.

Tegan began to understand why Grainne was here. She bit her lip, doubtful, wanting to say that Brede was no warrior, was only permitted to stay because she was good with the horses; wanting to say that Brede couldn't be trusted. She wasn't sure that any of these things were true, and could not say them. The Queen straightened her back and stepped away from the rail.

'When Maeve has finished, send the other one to me,' she said, having no doubt that Maeve would win, and having won, would not choose to kill Brede.

She had no strength for more. She needed Sorcha's arm as well as her song to hold her up. Tegan inclined her head and turned away, so that the Queen could pretend she hadn't seen her weakness.

Tegan leant once more against the rail, and watched the swift whirl of Maeve's two-knifed dance end, trying to dull the disquiet in her brain. The hilt of Maeve's left knife crashed down on Brede's wrist, numbing her hand so that she dropped her remaining knife. Maeve threw all her strength into her raised arm and the other hilt thudded into Brede's back, throwing her forward, to sprawl in the dust. Maeve's foot landed on Brede's blade so that she couldn't reach it.

Brede rolled hastily away and fought to get her knees beneath her. She'd had enough, beaten with her own weapons. She moved her shoulders cautiously trying to ease the paralysing pain knifing from between her shoulder blades into her neck, her shoulders, and her legs, briefly preventing further movement. She fought pain, and a wrenching fear that Maeve might not, after all, stop with humiliation. She staggered to her feet, head spinning, and limbs barely under control. She was determined that she would not be on her knees when the blow came.

A hush fell on the watching crowd, not one of them sure that Maeve would stop now, each wondering what that meant for them, under her command. Tegan felt that moment drag; aware of Eachan slowly drawing himself up straight beside her, his hands gripping the rail tightly, twisting about the pole in unconscious anxiety, willing Maeve to stop. Tegan's mind was empty of future; there was only the space between Maeve's anger and Brede's painful fear.

Maeve held her tension to herself, tempted, no question but she was tempted. She caught the look in Brede's dark eyes, and nodded abruptly, allowing Brede to end the bout. If she had really wanted to kill Brede it would not have been the hilt of the knife that she used. Maeve tossed the knife down and wiped the sweat from her face with her scarf. Brede's face lost its closed, frightened expression and she blinked, getting her ragged breathing back under control. She flexed her hands and found they would obey her, just, although she still shook. She gathered her knives back into their sheaths and picked up the discarded longswords aware of the buzz and murmur of the watchers, trying to disguise the way her body was barely under her control. She carried the weapons back to the racks, checking for new nicks and scores as she walked.

Tegan met her at the racks. Brede scowled at her, self-conscious. Tegan barely noticed, shaken by what had just occurred, uneasy with knowledge.

'You've attracted some interest,' she said tersely.

'Whose?' Brede asked, instantly alert.

'The Queen. She has asked to see you.'

Brede stiffened, recognising the cause of Maeve's abrupt skill – *showing off for Grainne* – and then the full meaning hit her.

'Must I go?' she asked.

Tegan laughed, incredulous.

'Of course you must. It wasn't a casual request.'

'How should I be, what must I do?'

Brede fiddled with the swords, sorting them unnecessarily to size, concentrating her thoughts on making her body do what she wanted of it without shaking too much. Tegan began to relax. This was the Brede she was used to, not the fighter she had been watching on the practise grounds.

'Wash;' she suggested and Brede laughed despite herself.

Tegan thought, giving serious consideration to how best Brede should present herself.

'Be honest,' she said, 'be yourself. If that isn't what she wants, you'll be back out here fast enough and none the worse for it. If you are what she needs, you'll be glad you have no boasts to live up to. And don't stand on ceremony; she hasn't the strength for it.'

'It's true then, that she's dying?'

Tegan drew in her breath.

'Never say that out loud. No, I do not think it is true. She looks better than the last time I saw her. She has some witch in attendance; she seems to be doing some good.'

Tegan didn't mention that she recognised that witch, and had drawn her own conclusions. Brede must sort that for herself. Brede pulled a face.

'For all I care she can wither away.'

Tegan cast a sharp look at Brede.

'If that is how you feel you'd best not go. Grainne won't thank you for that association.'

'I don't mean that I believe the superstitious nonsense they talk in the inns. I don't think that she can be crushed by war or starved by famine; I doubt she cares enough for the trouble out here to bother her.'

'Well, but you've not met her. You don't know what you're talking about.'

'Do I not? And haven't I been a beneficiary of Grainne's *concern* for people who are none of hers?'

Tegan shook Brede's arm gently.

'Peace. If you can make a friend of me, can you not make an employer of Grainne?'

Brede frowned, considering Tegan, and friendship.

'But you don't trust me, Tegan, friend or no, or you wouldn't be talking to me like this, you'd have stopped with the advice to wash.' Brede stopped for breath, now that the fear was gone. 'So why should Grainne trust me? Why did you let her think she could? And why would she want to speak to a raw recruit who isn't even contracted to her guard, who is permitted to do no more than tend the horses and make use of the practice yard – one she has just seen *humiliated?*'

Tegan shrugged unhappily.

'She didn't stay to watch, they didn't see.'

'They?' Brede asked blankly, and then she remembered. 'A witch?' she asked thoughtfully, and a fleeting smile crossed her face, smoothing the anxious scowl. Tegan sighed, recognising that expression for what it was and cuffed Brede across the shoulder.

'I'd worry about that, were I you, not smile like a love-struck goose.'

Brede's smile broadened, and she became abruptly aware of the warmth of the sun on her bruised and protesting back. She turned her face into the sun, drinking in the light, her eyes closed.

'Are you listening?' Tegan asked.

'Oh yes,' Brede said, loosening her collar, conscious of the cooling sweat in her hair, 'but I've never known a goose smile.'

Tegan shook her head in mock despair.

'There is no hope for you,' she said, moving out of the sunlight, back into the deep shadow of Grainne's tower. 'No hope at all.'

Brede idled away to the bathhouse, stripping away her borrowed leather guards, piling them together in the outer room. She glanced around, seeing that Maeve's guards also lay on the bench. She slid resignedly onto the wooden slats and worked off her boots, wincing at the pain in her back and wrist as she tried too hard to get the tight boots free. She could hear faint splashing from within. Brede would have preferred not to speak with Maeve for now. She would have much preferred to wash away the sweat and dust and aches in comfortable silence. She needed time to think how to speak to a ruler she did not acknowledge as her liege, who held the lands of her ancestors, and ordered the destruction of her kin; who had bought her allegiance with money. For the space of a heartbeat, Brede couldn't remember why she was in this city, closed in by walls, choking on alien dust. She swallowed her need for open space, for movement. Grainne was only a woman; Brede could only speak to her as she would to anyone else – like Maeve, perhaps?

Corla glanced in through the door and grinned sympathetically.

'Here,' she said and threw a bundle of herbs to her; 'put that in your water and mash it up a bit, it'll help the bruising.'

Brede gathered the bundle to her and sniffed. There was that smell again, it reminded her of something, but she couldn't place what.

'Thank you, Corla,' she said softly, but Corla had already gone.

Brede pulled the ties out of her hair and ran her fingers through, forcing her braid apart. She sighed; she couldn't afford to wait. She pushed through the leather curtain, glancing swiftly at Maeve, and then away, busying herself with the cisterns of water filling the tub as hot as she could bear, throwing in Corla's herbs, pulling bits of clothing off as she went, her back and shoulders protesting at every jug of water, and thanking the Goddess that she was permitted to ignore Maeve's rank in the bath house.

Maeve watched her in silence, noting the awkward way Brede was moving, and her determination not to acknowledge her presence. She inspected the spreading bruise on Brede's back furtively. An inch or so further to the left and she might have paralysed or killed her. Maeve sank lower in the water, so that Brede was out of her line of vision. She had made a fool of herself, insisting on a public display of her disapproval. She had not sated her anger, nor had she forced Brede to recognise the errors she was making in the way she fought, which was so subtly different from what Tegan had tried to teach her. And, it seemed, humiliation didn't work with Brede. Perhaps she should have killed her. She listened to the slop of water as Brede lowered herself into the tub, the involuntary groan of relief as the hot water cradled her aching body. Maeve frowned at Brede's apparent indifference; still smarting from the way Tegan had gone straight to Brede after the bout.

They lay in far-from-companionable silence; the only sounds the slosh and slap of water in the tubs, dripping from one of the cisterns. Maeve stared at the ceiling, at the curls of steam dissipating in a stream of sunlight, and sighed. The water was getting cold. She got her feet under her, forcing herself upright against the drag of the water. Brede glanced in her direction, and continued the slow washing of her hair.

Maeve wrapped a towel securely about her, and turned to up end the tub, emptying the water into the runnels in the stone floor. Not really thinking about what she was doing, her grip was not as secure as it could be, and she let the tub fall.

Brede heard the curse, and the sodden thud, and grinned to herself, as water slopped over the edge of the tub, soaking Maeve's towel.

'Leave it,' she said, 'I'll empty it when I've done.'

Maeve rounded on her, anger rekindled.

'You think you can manage that?' she said, scornfully.

'Yes, despite your best efforts to maim me. I've not lost the strength that nine years at an anvil gave me,' Brede said, biting down on her own swift anger. 'I told you I don't want to be a warrior. I know my limits. Why do you want to make me into something I'm not?'

Maeve glared at Brede, white with anger, then abruptly shook her head, and laughed, unwilling to compound her earlier misjudgement. She pulled another towel from the pile between the tubs, discarding the wet one. She was about to turn away when Brede spoke again.

'Did you see Grainne watching us?'

Maeve nodded, feeling again the abrupt surge of conceit, which had made her force the pace so dangerously. It had worked against Brede, but against a more experienced opponent it would have been rank idiocy. Not that Brede knew that. Maeve sank slowly onto the edge of the tub.

'Did you?' she asked, wondering that Brede could have divided her attention from the fight.

'No. Tegan told me. Grainne wants to see me. Can you think why?'

Maeve frowned.

'Are you asking me what service she wants of you, or why she chose you?'

'Both.'

'I don't know. If she asked me, I would tell her not to trust you; but she won't ask. You are a no more than competent fighter but also eminently expendable, which might be the reason she chose you – so whatever it is she wants you for is likely to be dangerous, or secret – so don't tell me what it is when you find out.'

Brede nodded slowly, recognising the lukewarm praise in Maeve's terse words. She started to pull herself from the water, and gasped as her back locked and refused to let her up.

Maeve laughed.

'I don't think you are going to be emptying any tubs, Brede, not when you need help to get out.' She hesitated, wondering whether she could bring herself to help, watching Brede try to get a purchase on the edge of the tub with arms that would not take her weight. 'Can you get your feet under you?'

The tub was narrow and awkward. Brede scrabbled until she had one knee under her. Her back eased. Carefully she got her other foot flat to the bottom of the tub. She pushed up slowly and steadily until she could sit on the rim.

'Ahh, Goddess,' she gasped, past caring what Maeve thought of her.

Maeve draped a towel over her shoulders, shrugging away Brede's muttered thanks. She retired to her own tub and emptied it carefully, giving Brede time to clamber out with a semblance of dignity. They viewed each other with wary curiosity.

'There's something you could tell me,' Maeve said cautiously.

'What would that be?'

'What is there between you and Tegan?'

Brede stared at her, wondering how to tell her the truth.

'A death,' she said.

'Tegan says she is indebted to you for her life.'

'She would say that. It's not how I… but you don't want to know what there is between us. You want to know what there has not been between us. We haven't been lovers, Maeve, if that is what has been causing you pain. We could never be that.'

Maeve would like to know why Brede was so adamant, but the trembling in Brede's hand, where it held the towel close, warned her not to ask. She had pushed too far, words would make Brede dangerous, in a way that no other threat could. She saw, in that trembling, the spark that she had hoped to see on the practice ground. It made her uneasy. Maeve left Brede to empty her tub, if she could, and went in search of cleaner clothes, and what she hoped would be an honest conversation with Tegan.

Chapter Fifteen

Tegan walked slowly, loose limbed with released tension, towards the barracks. Eachan had given her one sharp glance and vanished towards the stables, his opinion of Maeve unvoiced. And Tegan's opinion of Maeve? She hardly knew, but future was finding room in her brain again. She stopped at the bottom of the steps. Her breath came in short angry gasps. She leant against the wall, wondering what she had sent Brede into. With her breathing easier, she dragged her heavy limbs up the steps and into the darkness of the barrack block. No one was around except Inir, sitting silent and brooding in the darkest corner. He glanced up as she came in, saw who it was, and subsided back into his shadows. Another problem. She was not equal to his grief. She nodded to him, and climbed the ladder to the upper floor, trying not to let her weariness show.

Tegan sank onto her bed, and lay on her back staring at the low vault of the ceiling, measuring the depth of the darkness and the play of light from the slit of window at the end of the room. She closed her eyes, but nothing could block out her thoughts. Up again to pace across the small room, from one stone wall to the other. Her wound was pulling; she concentrated on that; anything rather than the look on Maeve's face earlier. Gently Tegan stretched her arm above her head, grazing the ceiling with her fingers. It hurt. She was almost glad. She located her pack, and the salve Corla had made for her.

Maeve took the steps up to the barracks two at a time. Her wet hair was loose on her shoulders, her shirt and jacket unlaced; she carried her guards bundled under her arm. She strode into the darkness without a glance, making straight for the ladder. She stopped at the bottom, her head raised, listening for sound from above. Her sharp hearing caught a faint rustle. She put her foot to the first rung, and climbed the ladder as though scaling an enemy wall in the dark. Not so much as a creak from the wood to betray her presence.

Inir watched, and was uneasy at the sudden change from bustle to stealth. He edged off his bed, and crept forward. As he reached the bottom of the ladder he heard Maeve's voice above him, astonished into laughter.

'What on earth are you doing?'

Inir's mouth twisted into a smile. He patted the ladder gently, scooped up his money belt, and went out into the sunlight.

Tegan pulled her shirt together. She held out the little pot of salve. Maeve dropped her guards, and came to sit on the floor in front of Tegan. She crossed her legs, and straightened her back, flicking wet strands of hair back behind her ear. She took the salve, and sniffed it.

'Ugh.'

'It's not meant to be a perfume.'

Maeve dipped her fingers into the salve and offered her hand. Tegan frowned, then pulled her shirt up so that Maeve could smear the greasy mess onto the shiny ridge of new skin.

Maeve hesitated, her fingers not quite touching Tegan's flesh. She took a good look at the wound, then put her hand lightly over it, letting her fingers slip to and fro, feeling the thickness of the ridge, probing gently for the edges of the pain. Her expression softened, and she let her hand lie against Tegan's ribs, warming her with the light pressure of her palm.

Tegan looked down into Maeve's face, into an expression molten with loneliness and relief and desire. She placed her own hand over Maeve's. Maeve shifted her eyes upwards, meeting Tegan's gaze.

'You are angry with me.'

Tegan nodded. Maeve frowned.

'I did not kill her.'

'Why not?' Tegan asked.

Maeve slipped her hand out from under Tegan's. Tegan let her go, massaging the stiff skin herself; and waited while Maeve worked out what to say.

'I didn't want to enough.' Maeve glanced away, finding her soiled shirt an adequate place to wipe the remaining salve from her fingers. She shifted onto her knees, meaning to stand, but couldn't summon enough will. She sank back onto her heels, and looked up at Tegan. Her eyes focussed on the curve of Tegan's breast, above the still circling fingers against the scar tissue. She bit her lip.

'Tegan.'

The fingers stopped moving.

'Maeve?'

'I've talked to Brede.'

'About me?'

Maeve nodded. Tegan wondered what Brede would have found to say about this, after an entire winter of saying nothing.

'I'm sorry.' Maeve said quietly.

'You didn't trust me.'

'No.'

'You were right not to.'

Maeve flinched. She reached and pulled Tegan's hand into her own.

'What do you mean? Brede said… '

'And it was the truth. And I would never have asked her, but if she had…'

'Why didn't she? Not because she didn't want you. Any idiot can see she worships the ground you walk on.'

Tegan laughed.

'Not anymore she doesn't. No, that wasn't it. Think about it, Maeve. She's Wing Clan. Why do you think I let her have Guida?'

Maeve's hand tightened convulsively about Tegan's.

'Ah. And she still made sure you lived.'

'Touch and go.' Tegan pulled her hair back, revealing the ghost of bruising.

Maeve reached to caress that bruise.

'So, that is all there is to tell. I can't despise a heart that can throw all that at me and still have the sense not to sleep with me. So you were right not to trust me, Maeve, but you can trust Brede. Killing any woman I look at will do you no good, if I am the cause of the trouble.'

Maeve listened to the tone of Tegan's words, and caught a tremor of regret, or pain. She looked away. Tegan worked her fingers free of her grasp, and ran her hand over Maeve's wet hair.

'So now you tell me about Killan.'

Maeve's breathing jumped suddenly. Tegan laughed.

'I'm not stupid, and I'm not as jealous as you, but you aren't going to sit there making me tear my heart out for you to inspect and get away with it. Come on, I've seen you together.'

'You can't be jealous of Killan?'

'Can't I?'

'There's nothing to it.'

'Meaning you don't sleep with him? I don't believe that. Killan isn't a patient man. If he wasn't getting what he wanted he'd have gone with Chad, not slunk off to some back alley.'

Maeve leant both her forearms across Tegan's knees.

'Do you remember how old I am?'

Tegan frowned slightly.

'Twenty-five. What does that have to do with it?'

'There has been nothing but training, fighting – and Riordan – all my life.'

'And me.'

Maeve smiled, a deep, loving smile.

'And you.' She leant her head into her arms, so that her words were addressed to Tegan's knees, muffled, hot against her skin.

'I've had no childhood, no adolescence. This winter was torment. Not knowing if you were alive, so afraid for you, so alone. And I had the command…

Everyone but me had a partner – Corla has started sleeping with Riordan – I needed you to talk to. And then Killan – he's silly, he's brash, but he's funny. He makes me laugh. And he's surprisingly perceptive, under all that teasing.' Maeve struggled to explain the why of it, trying to see how Tegan was taking her explanation, but Tegan's face was in shadow. She continued less confidently. 'He can stand on his own, he wasn't my – he didn't expect – I didn't have to be – responsible for him.'

'And you liked that?'

Maeve frowned, rubbing her brow against her arms, not sure what the answer to that was.

'Not exactly, but once I'd given up being responsible it was impossible to start again, with him at least. It was easier not being. There were no decisions.'

Tegan buried her fingers in Maeve's hair, a convulsive movement. Maeve glanced up, hoping to find understanding in Tegan's eyes, finding misery.

'Every action is a decision.' Tegan said, her words jerky with withheld emotion. A tear spilled from her eye, splashing Maeve's hand.

'Don't.' Maeve reached up, cradling Tegan gently, 'Please, Tegan, don't.'

Tegan sobbed and dragged her hands free of Maeve, to hide the rictus of anguish that her mouth was twisting into, despite her best efforts. She took a deep breath, then another, shrugging Maeve away. She went to the window.

'I resisted – something that meant – Goddess knows what it might have become. You gave in to something that meant nothing? What does that say about us, Maeve?'

Maeve pushed herself upright, beginning to find anger again. She strode to Tegan, dragging her about to face her.

'It says that my body is my own to bestow where I please, and that my heart is yours and not free to be purloined by the first – what? – *enemy*? who offers me something other than a knife's edge. It says that you can't tell the difference, and that you value my heart at very little worth.'

Tegan shuddered, watching Maeve's face, convulsed with anger and pain, with truth.

'Maeve.' She reached a shaking hand to Maeve's face, stroking tender fingers across the frowning brow. 'Maeve.'

Maeve turned her lips into Tegan's hand, kissing her palm at first gently, then catching a tiny fold of skin between her teeth, desperate to be understood. Another hand closed about the other side of her face. Maeve closed her eyes, standing passively, feeling every inch of her skin awakening to Tegan's gentle touch against her neck, the pressure of lips against her collarbone. She let go a held breath and gathered Tegan against her.

'Missed you,' she whispered. 'Goddess, I missed you.'

Chapter Sixteen

Brede made herself as presentable as she could. She did not know how to approach this meeting. Should she go armed? She decided not. She dawdled about making sure her belt was hanging straight, that her hair was neat, putting off the time she must commit herself to the stairs that led to Grainne's private quarters.

She tried not to think about what she was doing or where she was going. She strolled casually as far as it was safe to stroll. The stairs then. She was allowed through the guard at the bottom with scarcely a glance. They knew she was expected. Corla watched her hesitant progress up the steps with amusement.

The stairs were still a wonder, so permanent, such an arrogant use of stone. Standing now, surrounded by stone that had stood for four generations already, Brede wondered once more why she was here, why she was not riding the plains, leaving nothing but the occasional footprint to be destroyed by the next gust of wind.

As she reached the top of the stairs Cei nodded her through a half-opened door and closed it behind her. Beyond that, another open door, unguarded. She hesitated. Should she wait, or knock, or walk in? Tegan's advice surfaced.

Be yourself.

Brede had never knocked on a door in her life. She pushed the door further open and cleared her throat. That was as polite as she could manage.

She stood in the second doorway, looking down at the two women seated in front of the fire. There should be no need of a fire; the weather had been fine and warm for a week. The room was unbearably hot; the tall shutters at the balcony window were tightly closed. Brede waited. The younger woman, who sat at the feet of the other, looked up and beckoned her in. She had been half expecting this, but it still threw her off balance.

'Close the door,' Grainne said.

The Queen gestured to a seat. Brede was surprised. Perhaps Grainne did not care to be towered over. She sat, grateful not to be kept standing in the unexpected heat, and waited to be told why she was there.

Grainne felt the comfort of Sorcha's touch against her knee, the faint hum of song that only she could hear, keeping her alive. She glanced at the warrior, who was so out of place here, covering her discomfort with a show of indifference. She liked her for it. She saw a woman in her prime, strong, awkward. She saw dark hair, sharp features, long limbs and those restless hands, unconsciously tracing the grain of wood.

Brede returned Grainne's stare. She saw an old woman, a worn, sickly face; a thin body wrapped in too many clothes, hands that shook. She saw power, sickness, fear, and pride.

'What do you know of the war?' Grainne asked at last, mesmerised by the constant restless movement of Brede's hands – not the question she had planned. Brede was jolted by the unexpected question, and had to dredge deep beyond her prepared speeches for an answer. Her hands stilled, curled about the arms of the chair.

'It has lasted too long. I've lost family and friends to it, not always to those you call your enemies,' she said; and then, 'your majesty.'

Grainne wondered how to get to her original intent now, with that bald statement lying between them.

'Where were you born?' she tried.

Brede shrugged.

'The place of my birth hardly matters. I am born out of Wing Clan. I am daughter to Ahern, who was murdered by warriors; possibly yours. I am daughter to Leal, of the Marshes beyond the western forest, land currently held by your enemies.'

'Wing Clan?' Grainne asked thoughtfully, her worst fears on that count confirmed.

And it being Wing Clan, she wondered what the woman was doing here. She touched the back of Sorcha's head. Sorcha looked up, frowning slightly.

'Why are you with Tegan's mercenaries?' she asked.

Now there was a question. Brede considered it, struggling with her sense of the stone about her, longing for a breath of wind to stir the staleness of the air. Her fingers resumed their tense exploration of the smooth wood of the chair arms. Tegan's advice drifted back into her mind.

Be honest.

'I look after their horses,' Brede glanced at Grainne and saw from her frown that this would not do. 'They offered me a way out from the Marshes. I took it.' Honesty of a sort.

'Do you consider them to be your friends?' Sorcha asked, interested for her own sake as well as Grainne's.

'No, I wouldn't say that.' Brede kept her answer short, unsure of how far she herself believed what she said.

'Then where are your loyalties?' Grainne asked, beginning to tire.

Brede again considered. She couldn't answer, as she would like, that loyalty was a concept to match the permanence of the stone about them. An uneasy memory of Leal stirred in her mind. She didn't trust loyalty; it made unreasoned demands.

'I don't know. I've yet to find them.'

Grainne nodded. The fight she saw earlier confirmed Brede's reservations about committing herself to either friendship or loyalty for her warrior companions. So far at least, the woman had been truthful.

The ache returned to Grainne's limbs, and she knew that she must leave the rest of the questioning to Sorcha. She rested her hand once more on Sorcha's hair.

Sorcha got to her feet. Brede stood without thinking. She glanced at the white-faced woman sitting beside the fire, noticing the sudden care with which she breathed. Sorcha opened another door and beckoned Brede out of the room, into a smaller chamber.

'Wait there,' she said, and closed the door.

Brede was glad to be out of the heat. She pulled her scarf loose and flicked her braid out to lie free of her collar. She could hear movement in the next room, faint voices. A swift, unexpected drawing in of breath. Brede winced, tuning her ear away from it.

She wandered to the window, and peered out of the narrow opening. She could just see the exercise yard, chequered by sunlight and deep shadows. The height made her uneasy, but she appreciated the vantage point. Brede wondered how long she had been watched, and what it was that Grainne wanted of her. She stepped quickly down from the window as the door opened once more, twisting awkwardly; her bruised back making her gasp.

Sorcha saw that abrupt backward step, heard the gasp of pain. She ignored it, shutting the door firmly behind her. She gave Brede her full attention for the first time, freed of her constant support of Grainne for the while. She liked what she saw.

Brede was taller than Sorcha; she seemed strong, if awkward. Sorcha reminded herself of the fight she had seen, of the occasional almost-beauty of Brede's movements. Not always awkward. Sorcha smiled, as she had not intended to.

Brede returning her appraising look, smiled in response. She reminded herself that this woman was a witch, and her smile faded. Sorcha moved forward and sat in one of the low-backed seats. Brede joined her.

'Who knows that you are here?' Sorcha asked.

'Tegan and Maeve. The guards on the stairs – Corla, Oran, Cei.'

'And what did Tegan and Maeve say?'

Brede sighed at that.

'Tegan said to be honest with Grainne, and not to stand on ceremony.

Maeve said I was wanted for something secret, and likely dangerous, and not to tell her what it was.'

Sorcha nodded.

'You listen to advice then?'

'To Tegan's.'

'Why hers?'

'She is usually right,' Brede said, which was only part of the answer.

'Why do you think you are here?' Sorcha asked.

Brede shrugged, and winced as her bruised back caught her again.

Sorcha took a breath. There were more questions she could ask to test the ground before committing herself, but she didn't believe she needed to.

'You know that Grainne is dying?'

Brede gazed at her, a considering, watchful look. The question lay between them. Sorcha felt a strange release at having finally said it out loud, to someone other than Grainne, and having been offered no surprise or outrage.

'Is it true then?' Brede asked, remembering her snarled conversation with Tegan, feeling guilty. 'I thought it was superstition.'

Sorcha shook her head.

'It has nothing to do with the famine. She has been poisoned, slowly and systematically, by someone she trusts, and she does not yet know who it is.'

Brede stirred disbelievingly. Sorcha gave her a considering look, reading that movement correctly.

'She has been ill a little over three years. People forget quickly what they do not wish to remember. The myth about the Queen as a symbol of the earth is a convenient propaganda tool for Grainne's enemies. It is an excuse for Ailbhe to march his red-bannered monster onto our lands, to claim them for his own.'

Our lands? Brede questioned silently.

'I heard a rumour that Ailbhe was dead,' Brede suggested, taking the opportunity to confirm the warrior's gossip that had so disturbed her.

Sorcha nodded in agreement. She had heard that.

'Back at the edge of winter, when the rain began, they started saying the earth had been watered with blood, that the ritual sword was missing from its place, and that Ailbhe had parted company with his head.' She shrugged. 'It did rain, the sword is gone, Ailbhe is dead, and I don't know the cause of his death. If there is a connection, I am not aware of it, are you?'

Brede almost answered that, but caution kept her silent. She remembered a line of red-bannered warriors on a hill, and a blooded sword, a sword now in her keeping. And Ailbhe *was* dead.

'And my part in this?' Brede asked to cover her momentary lapse.

'Grainne finds it hard to trust anyone when there may be poison in everything she touches. She has no bodyguard because she can't afford the risk that intimacy would bring from someone implicated in that poison. You'll have heard rumour and counter-rumour; you'll know that there are factions and disagreements in every corner of the city. You've not been here long enough to have drawn up your battle lines. You've not taken sides.'

'I've taken Grainne's pay,' Brede said hesitantly.

'Spoken like a true mercenary.'

Brede perceived a touch of scorn in Sorcha's words and hit back.

'And you *aren't* paid for your services?'

Sorcha laughed aloud.

'I am paid, yes. But it is in my interests to keep Grainne alive.'

'Is that what she wants?' Brede asked.

'For now it is,' Sorcha said – too swiftly – wanting to believe it. 'Grainne wants an end to this war,' she continued, 'Ailbhe's death has complicated that. The rumour that she ordered it makes it harder. If she dies, those who are loyal to her would take the war to the borders.

'No one wants Ailbhe's boy, Lorcan, a fourteen-year-old, to rule two countries. And with us firmly committed to war with Lorcan, the rebels would take the opportunity lent them by our weakness; the Horse Clans among them.' Sorcha's eyes searched Brede's face, and she shook her head. 'Those loyal to Ailbhe would want vengeance; those loyal to Grainne would fight for her memory. Somewhere this has to end, and her death won't resolve it.' Sorcha wondering what Brede was making of this. 'Grainne wants all the factions drawn together. She *wants* to talk peace. You half believe that she brought the famine on us by refusing to marry Ailbhe. Yet it is raining, the sun is out; the crops are beginning to grow. We have to remind people of that. She must stay alive. That is my task, but those who don't trust her, will not trust me. If they see a witch at her elbow, they will be suspicious, the more so if they see no bodyguards. You have to be that guard. You have to be visible and you have to be alone.'

Sorcha glanced at Brede's impassive face. She hadn't yet given any indication of her feelings. Sorcha kept talking. 'We don't know who has been poisoning Grainne. They are not yet aware of my presence. I want to trick them into the open. You are unknown, you may tempt them out of hiding.'

'One guard isn't enough. I have to sleep. You must have asked others.'

'No.'

'Just me? You've seen me fight. So, perhaps, has your poisoner. And every one of Maeve's warriors knows that there is no guard at that door, and they know me. I'm the *stable-hand* –' Brede shrugged. 'How can you expect me to do this alone?'

'You don't believe that fiction of Maeve's, do you? You're exactly what we need. You do not allow yourself to get carried away. You were a model of control out in that yard today; you didn't even care that Maeve beat you in front of everyone. I doubt I could be so controlled.'

Brede shook her head.

'I cared.'

Sorcha inclined her head, inviting further comment.

'I hated it.'

'But you didn't let your anger get the better of you.'

'*This* time.'

Sorcha shifted awkwardly, under Brede's dark brooding gaze. If she wanted she could discover what Brede meant, but this was not the moment.

'If anyone does attack Grainne she will want them living to be questioned, not some bloody corpse that can't answer for its actions. You control yourself; you will not kill out of hand, nor out of misplaced loyalty. You treat your sword as what it is, a necessary tool, not a lover.' Sorcha took a breath, steadying herself, sure now that she had Brede's attention, that something she had said struck a chord. 'So no, you're not an inspired fighter. You do not need to be. It is only Maeve who sees a problem. You're wasted looking after the horses.'

Brede opened her mouth to protest. The horses needed her. Her eyes met Sorcha's, and the protest went unspoken.

'I know,' Sorcha said, almost patiently, 'Wing Clan. Horses. I remember. But you are needed here. Eachan can see to the horses without your help, he can't do this for us. You are to be the visible guard. When Grainne must be in public, she must have a guard; that will be you. In private, who is to know?'

'Your argument is flawed. I would notice. Many people will notice. Anyone planning to attack Grainne would see me, a barely competent guardswoman, living on insufficient sleep, and be certain they could overcome me. The uncertainty of there being no guard at all would keep them away better. You have to have more than one guard or your feint is pointless.'

'If we tempt them into an open attack, all to the good.'

Brede clasped her hands tightly together. She shook her head, and allowed some of her anger to show.

'Maeve said that I was asked because I am expendable. I see she is right.'

'And you have such good cause to believe Maeve.'

Brede's brows drew together, considering.

'She's not lied to me. All you have said so far has been about deceit – you can't hope to stay hidden. Since it is not yet known that you're here, you could pass as a soldier?' Brede asked. If she was to bait a trap, she would do it in company.

'I suppose I could.' Sorcha said, intrigued by the idea.

'Tegan knows about you. You could pass for part of her crew.'

'Yes.'

'So is she to be included in this?'

Sorcha was distracted.

'What is there between Tegan and yourself?' she asked. 'I sense something – difficult.'

Brede sighed, and instead of telling Sorcha to mind her business, answered, 'A stolen horse. We've come to an agreement. I won't kill her; she will not kill me. I won't make demands that she can't meet, she will not ask the impossible of me. I won't say that I love her, she will not insist I leave.'

Brede stopped suddenly, shocked at the force of the depression that sank into her bones as she spoke. She hadn't intended to say so much, she wasn't even sure that she had known what the agreement was, until Sorcha asked. She glared, listening for the hum of song. There was a noticeable silence. Sorcha looked away, caught out; and regretting forcing that confidence from Brede.

'And do you love her?' Sorcha asked, simply, without any subtle strain of song for persuasion.

Brede had not asked herself that for some time, it had been too painful. She felt cautiously for that thought.

'Yes,' she said, 'I do; but it doesn't seem so – all consuming – now that I no longer hate her.'

It was an unexpected revelation; a relief.

'Why should you hate her?'

'Wing Clan,' Brede said. 'There is a death between us.'

Even that pain seemed dulled, away from her mother and despite her constant, fruitless search for Falda. And what would become of that search, should she accept this post?

'Wing Clan,' Sorcha said, as though that was all the explanation that was required. But then, it being Wing Clan, 'If Wing Clan can cause you to hate Tegan, what of Grainne?'

Brede shrugged, and the pain in her back flared once more. She recovered quickly, but Sorcha saw: not a woman who knew how to lie convincingly. She waited for Brede's answer with a curiosity that was about more than danger to Grainne.

'If I can accept Tegan, I can accept Grainne. I kept Tegan alive all winter, I suppose I can keep Grainne alive if that is what she wants; it is not so very different.'

'So, daughter of Leal,' Sorcha asked, 'are you willing?'

Brede thought of the isolation that the task would inflict, and the restrictions it would place upon her. There would be no riding the plains; she would be alone, yet again.

Sorcha waited, smothering the questions that she wanted to ask, letting Brede find her way through her objections.

'This place is – to be here all the time would be –'

Brede had been going to say *torture*, but she realised that wasn't true. In the face of Grainne's pain how could it be? She replaced the word in her mind: *lonely*. And even that was no longer true.

'I came here partly because of Tegan, but mostly in search of change.' She hesitated; she couldn't mention Falda –

'Change is an uncertain mistress.' Sorcha said, sensing Brede was holding something back.

'This is not the change I had planned,' Brede agreed.

She thought of the closeness of this woman, within the cold stone, and wondered if there was enough warmth in the witch to keep the cold out of her soul. She looked at Sorcha with a pleasure not yet fully acknowledged. Acting on that half recognised feeling, she risked a different vein of personal comment.

'You'll have to cut your hair if you're to pass for a warrior,' she said.

Sorcha smiled cautiously.

'Is that an agreement?'

'I'm not sure that it is. How long...?'

Sorcha groaned. 'How long? Would that I knew. Would that Grainne had some way of knowing. I can't answer that.'

'And how will these peace talks come about?' Brede asked, divining flaw after flaw; 'Who is to speak for Grainne, and to whom should they send? To Ailbhe, who is probably dead? To Lorcan? And who among the rebels is the acknowledged leader? Who speaks for the Clans?'

'I don't know.' Sorcha was not used to uncertainty. She glanced at Brede, waiting for a response. Brede didn't believe that Grainne could live so long.

'Refusal will do me no good, will it? Grainne has been honest with me, and honesty breeds assassination in this place.' Brede assessed the waiting tension in Sorcha's silence.

'Very well,' she said at last, and saw that tension vanish.

'Good,' Sorcha changed the subject swiftly, relieved to have crossed that vital and dangerous bridge. 'So, Grainne will sleep for a while. Show me what to do with my hair, and tell me more about Wing Clan, and what is so dreadful about the Marshes, and this stolen horse – ?'

'Why would you want to know about Wing Clan?' Brede asked, suspicious.

'I want to understand you.'

Sorcha watched Brede hesitate. She pulled the combs from her hair, shaking it out to its full length.

Brede eyed Sorcha's black curls, falling beyond her shoulders, well down her back. No warrior would risk hair so long. Besides, she wanted to see what the witch's face was like, when it wasn't hidden behind the weight of that hair.

'I've not brought a knife with me,' Brede said.

Sorcha reached into the top of her boot, and pulled a knife from the leather. She placed the hilt into Brede's outstretched hand without hesitation or comment.

Brede stepped behind Sorcha and gathered up a handful of her hair, pulling clear of her shoulder. Brede's back spasmed suddenly, objecting to the angle of her arm. Brede let her hands drop, remembering Tegan, mounting Guida with Brede's knife in her hand. She took a steadying breath and tried again. The weight of Sorcha's hair lay across her hand, and then Sorcha felt the sudden brush of loose ends against her back, the uneven weight. Involuntarily she put her hand up to feel, and tangled with Brede's hand, reaching for the next hank.

Thinking that she was regretting her hair, or perhaps sharing that momentary fear, Brede hesitated.

'Changed your mind?' she asked.

'Too late for that,' Sorcha said, letting go of her hand.

Three more flicks of the knife, and Brede gathered the not particularly even ends together, and began to make a plait. Her hand grazed the back of Sorcha's neck as she did so and her fingers found a row of beads threaded into her hair, behind her ear.

'Do you want these?' she asked, Sorcha's hand once more met hers, tangling around the beads in a convulsive movement. She couldn't believe she had forgotten them.

'They are not for adornment,' she said hesitantly. 'That has always been the safest place for them.'

Brede shrugged, and worked a tie loose from her cuff.

'They will still be safe,' she said, tying the braid tightly.

She stepped back to survey her work.

'Better,' she said, absent-mindedly rolling her cuff up to stop it flapping against her wrist.

Sorcha looked at that wrist. Bony: with the tail end of a scar disappearing under the rolled cuff. Somewhat to her surprise, she had a momentary urge to run her finger along that line of raised flesh, to see where it led her. She ran her hands over her hair instead, checking that the Singer stones were secure and out of sight.

Brede gathered the cut lengths of hair together, and handed them to Sorcha.

'What will you do with that?' she asked.

Sorcha shrugged.

'Stuff a cushion perhaps,' she considered. 'Two cushions.'

She had no intention of doing anything of the kind. She saw the thick strand that Brede was twining between her fingers and had to dampen a flicker of superstitious anxiety.

'You were going to tell me about Wing Clan,' she said.

Brede lowered herself into a chair, and began to explain about the Horse Clans and her father's Clan in particular. She had not spoken in this way since the winter, when she had tried to make Tegan understand what it was that had been destroyed by that raid. Then, anger and loss had motivated her, wanting to make Tegan feel guilty. Now, she told the witch more honestly, more objectively about life on the plains, and about the horror of the last gathering of the Clans, her lost horses, and her lost Clan.

Sorcha listened with only half her attention for the words. The rest of her was concentrating on how Brede held herself as she relaxed, forgot herself in her telling. She took in everything she heard, to be analysed later; it was far more important to her to drink in the sound of Brede's voice, the range of emotion she betrayed, husky one moment, harsh the next. She regarded the sharp curves of Brede's face, that trailing scar on her wrist as she raised her hand to describe something – the quick glance of those black eyes, as Brede's voice faded to silence. Sorcha held her gaze for perhaps two breaths. Brede stood, stretched cautiously against the stiffening in her back.

'When am I wanted for – this?'

'At once.'

'And am I truly to say nothing to anyone, not even to pass the time of day with my friends?'

'For now.'

'What do I tell Tegan?'

'Bring her back with you. Tegan needs to know what to say when she is asked about me.'

Brede nodded. She turned to the door.

'Wait,' Sorcha said, not sure why she said it, only wanting to detain her a while longer. Brede laughed.

'I am coming back,' she said. 'I'll be gone an hour at the most.'

Sorcha lowered her head, feeling foolish. When she looked up, Brede was gone.

Chapter Seventeen

Brede's legs shook as she walked down the short flight of stairs from the Queen's quarters.

Too fast, this – too much change all at once. She wondered if the witch had charmed her with an unheard song, if she had been rushed into this decision by magic. She did not think so, and yet, Sorcha had charmed her. She grinned to herself. She was out of the habit of being desired, of being flirted with. It was pleasant, and dangerous.

She went first to the stables. Guida hadn't been exercised yet, and there would be little enough time for the horses now. That was something she would have to negotiate – she needed the horses, they were her lifeblood, and she would not willingly abandon them, most especially Guida.

Brede saddled Guida and walked her out of the warrior's quarter, down to the riverbank, where she rode as though there were demons at her heels, grateful for the wind in her face and the dazzle of sunlight off the water.

The river wound round and under Grainne's tower. Brede glanced up at the balcony, with its long window still firmly shuttered. It occurred to her that she was being asked to give up her freedom; that she was being asked to share that confinement with a witch and a monarch.

With Guida safely returned to her stable, groomed and watered, Brede went to find Tegan in the barracks.

The lower floor of the block was deserted, but she could hear voices above, from Tegan's quarters. Mindful of Sorcha's instructions, she set her foot to the bottom rung of the ladder, but this close, she could hear the quality of those voices, the intimacy of Maeve's sudden laugh. Brede backed away, and bolted before her presence could be detected.

Brede found Eachan asleep in a corner of the stables, beside a mare that was due to foal. She edged past the twitching animal to shake his shoulder.

Eachan's eye opened before she had quite touched him, his one pupil boring into her. Brede backed away slightly.

'You're away then?' Eachan asked, then laughed at her surprise. 'I have one good eye in my head,' he said reproachfully. 'I can see the woman who pays me when she comes into my yard.'

'And you know what she wanted?'

'I don't need to know more than that she found it. Be careful what you say, girl, and what you hear. Have you told Tegan?'

'She's – otherwise occupied.'

'Maeve tracked her down then?'

Brede nodded. Eachan settled back into his mound of straw.

'I'll tell her. You've not time to help this mare, I suppose?'

Brede was jolted by his change of tack. She didn't have time, but his invitation was a balm to her uneasiness.

'Grainne can wait a while longer,' she responded, settling into the straw beside him, suddenly comfortable with the idea of setting her own rules.

When she at last returned to the tower, Brede met Sorcha's anger levelly.

'I was needed,' she said calmly, 'and Tegan was not available. She can keep her mouth shut without being told, she's no fool.'

'I am disappointed,' Sorcha said.

'Yes, but it isn't you who pays me.' Brede glanced at Sorcha's change of clothes, green jerkin and darker breeches, and a sword belt. She nodded at the sword. 'You and I are of equal standing in this matter, two novice guards in the Queen's household.'

'I have underestimated you,' Sorcha said.

'So,' Brede said cautiously, 'I have something to show you that may be of interest to Grainne.'

Brede held out a long, heavy bundle, wrapped in a red cloak. Sorcha could sense the strength of it, even before she took it into her hands and felt the cold of metal through the cloth. She flicked the cloak to one side, uncovering the hilt of the sword.

'What is this?' she asked, already half guessing.

'If I'm right, it's the sword that ended Ailbhe's life.'

'And how did you come by it?'

Brede thought about her answer to that question, and answered as she had when Tegan asked the same.

'I had it from the hands of the Goddess.'

Sorcha nodded, unsurprised. She could still feel the resonance of the places this sword had lain, singing within its core. She could feel the blood it had spilt.

'The *Dowry* blade – Grainne must see this,' she said, 'but she must be prepared for it. To bring *any* unsheathed sword into her presence without warning would put unnecessary strain on her.'

'Then it is the same blade?'

Sorcha glanced from the sword to Brede.

'Did you ever really doubt it?'

Brede shook her head, and took the sword back into her arms, cradling it against her, aware of its weight as her back and shoulders protested. She touched the simple, unadorned hilt.

'What is so special about this sword?'

'It is a symbol – like the crown. Without it, Ailbhe cannot become king as he hopes. Without it, Grainne is not entitled to rule alone. She will want to know how you came by this, and riddles won't suffice for her. Be ready to say exactly where you found this blade.'

'I'll wait,' Brede said, daunted by Sorcha's seriousness.

Brede could hear the murmur of voices, and the sharp intake of breath, as Grainne understood the import of Sorcha's message. She didn't need prompting to take the sword through to Grainne's chamber.

She laid the sword across the arms of Grainne's chair so that she need not take the weight. Grainne fingered the red cloth, before pulling it away to examine the sword. She gazed at it in silence, engaged in a detailed scrutiny, her fingers resting lightly against a small nick in the edge.

'Then it is true. Ailbhe brought us rain with his blood.'

She covered the sword again, but kept her hand upon it. She searched Brede's face, not finding was she was looking for. Her eyes strayed to Sorcha.

'Did you know about this?'

Sorcha shook her head.

'I felt something – I did not think it was –' she shook her head again. 'No, I had no idea.'

Grainne focused on Brede once more, her gaze intent, full of doubt.

'And you didn't know what you had.' He voice was harsh with disbelief.

'I think Tegan guessed. But I'd not heard of this blade when I found it.'

'And when did you find it?'

Not where or how, but *when*. Brede suddenly understood that look, recognising it from Tegan's face, the first time she saw the sword.

'Just as the fighting stopped for the winter. Tegan or Maeve can tell you when exactly. I met Ailbhe's army heading westerly out from the Marshes, with this sword left at an offering place. The blood was still sticky.'

Grainne sighed. It had been raining for weeks then. If Ailbhe did not die to bring rain, then her illness couldn't be tied to the failing of her land, and she need not search Brede's face expecting to find the Scavenger of Souls there.

Brede shifted uncomfortably under Grainne's searching gaze and was grateful when Sorcha reached for the Queen's arm, distracting her.

'Ailbhe's force went back to their winter quarters calmly; hostilities started early. Someone is in control of that army.'

Grainne sighed for her hoped-for peace. 'Poison was never Ailbhe's weapon. As soon as Lorcan was old enough to go into battle and earned the right to be considered his father's successor, he started his challenge. In the eyes of some, including at least one person I trust, he has earned the right to be considered the successor to my throne too.' She looked at Brede, then Sorcha; she did not find them sufficient to her need. She longed for her niece, dead these many years; for Aeron, who once held the world together for her.

Grainne gave the sword a slight push, indicating that she wanted it gone.

Brede gathered the sword's weight to her, wondering what she should do with it. As though reading her thoughts, Grainne answered her.

'Keep it, and keep silent. If that blade stays lost, it can't be used to harm me. And I may yet find a use for it,' Grainne leant forward to rest her fingers against the blade, disturbed by it.

'You must know the value of this blade, and of your news – I am greatly in your debt. Ask me for anything, and if it in my gift, you may have it.'

Brede shook her head.

'Not yet, but there may come a time – if I may wait?'

Brede took the sword away. Sorcha hesitated to follow, looking at Grainne closely, trying to judge whether the pain in her friend's face was anything that she could ease. Grainne intercepted the look and shook her head.

'Even you can do nothing about the death of my niece, nor the fact that her offspring is male, and a power grabbing fool, like his father. I do not think you can ease that for me. Go and talk to your – friend – scrape together some pleasure for yourself.' Grainne shook her head slightly. 'Do you believe she didn't know what she had? Do you suppose that *we* are being offered *her* trust?'

Sorcha leant close to Grainne, so that she could hear her whispered answer. 'Never. No trust, not for you, my sweet.' She kissed Grainne lightly, and followed Brede from the room.

'How much did you hear?' Sorcha asked, as she closed the door. Brede shrugged, not sure whether Sorcha meant what Grainne had to say about her family, or what Sorcha had to say about trust.

Sorcha sat beside the empty fireplace, rocking slightly and chewing her knuckle. She glanced at Brede, and doubted the usefulness of explaining to her, but she needed to talk to someone. Brede recognised that look.

'Try me,' she said. 'There is no one else to talk to, unless you plan to risk Tegan or Maeve.'

'Those two again, what is it about them?'

Brede didn't answer. It was, to her, a foolish question. Sorcha smiled.

'Very well. You do not have to answer me.'

Brede made an irritated noise.

'Tegan has offered me nothing but honesty, a rare thing, I've since discovered. She made me believe it was possible to trust anyone, even an enemy.'

'Oh? And Maeve?'

'Maeve taught me to trust no-one, not even a friend.'

Sorcha laughed. 'Useful lessons. Where do you place me? A trustworthy enemy or an untrustworthy friend?'

'I've yet to discover. All I know is that you expect truth from me, but you have not, so far, offered much honesty in return. You lie. I can trust you to do that.'

Sorcha's face froze a fraction.

'I've underestimated you again.'

'Yes.' Brede shrugged, watching Sorcha's turned face, waiting for her to thaw. 'There is something wrong in all this,' Brede said cautiously. 'If I understand you, Lorcan should have kept hold of that sword. Why leave it in an offering place?'

Sorcha frowned.

'I hadn't thought of that. It's as well that he did, since we now have it safe, but you're right. There may be another faction of whom we know nothing, working against Lorcan, but not with us. Another unknown.' Sorcha covered her face. 'I don't see a way through this. It is too complicated. I do not know what I should do.'

Brede watched Sorcha struggle with her anxiety.

'Why is it your responsibility?' she asked.

Sorcha stayed silent, brought up short once again by Brede's ignorance. She shrugged, deciding to lie.

'I am forgetting myself. A small part of the great design, thinking I can change the world. It is only that I care for Grainne, what matters to her, matters to me.'

'You care for her a great deal.'

Sorcha smiled, secure in the depth of her affection for Grainne, but uncertain of Brede.

'She has been more to me, been closer to me than anyone else until now.'

'And now?' Brede asked, hardly believing she had summoned the courage to ask.

'Now – now she is a Queen, and I – am in her service.' Sorcha turned her face away, uncomfortable with that service for the first time.

Brede watched the worried frown darken Sorcha's face once more and levered herself from the chair for a restless circuit of the room. She hesitated near the door to Grainne's chamber.

'She looks well, considering,' Brede said, determinedly changing the subject.

'Yes. She doesn't need me for a while.'

'Can she stay well?'

Sorcha shrugged.

'A while, perhaps; enough to consult with her generals and advisors, enough to see that the war is well conducted.'

Brede nodded, more at the bitterness in Sorcha's voice than at what she said. She was hesitant to offer her meagre resources, lest they prove insufficient, but she thought she might like Sorcha, she enjoyed her teasing and her swings between honesty and artifice. She appreciated her wanting change, and believing she could influence a war. And so, she reached out a hesitant hand to the witch.

Sorcha pulled her gently down to sit beside her. Brede felt the softness of that hand clasping hers. Strange, and inappropriate: not a warrior's hand.

'If you are to be a guard,' she said, 'keep your hands covered.'

Sorcha looked at the smoothness of her fingers against the rough darkness of Brede's skin, callused, scarred and bruised. She said nothing for a while; cradling Brede's hand in her lap, pursuing a thought that was not directly connected with Brede's words. Almost without thinking, she whispered a thread of song, and the bruising on the wrist faded.

Brede watched wordlessly, and tried not to think about that fading bruise. She tried not to pull away from Sorcha's touch, which sent strange tremors through her, which were nothing to do with the healing.

Sorcha ran a finger along the scar on Brede's outer wrist, finding its end under the loosened cuff of her sleeve. Not a particularly long cut, nor deep. It shouldn't have left a scar. Sorcha did not look into Brede's face when she spoke.

'You don't heal easily, do you?'

Brede gave in to the uneasiness that trembled through her and tried to withdraw her hand, sensing more than words, but Sorcha's grip was firm. She twisted round to look at Brede, and there was none of the teasing laughter about her eyes.

'Where did you get this scar?' she asked.

'Tegan,' Brede replied without wishing to.

'Of course,' Sorcha rubbed her finger along the scar again. She raised her head, staring at Brede, measuring. Her hand slipped up Brede's arm to her shoulder and she rose slowly, and ran her hands across Brede's back. 'And this one is Maeve,' she said laying her palms gently across the bruising beside Brede's spine. Brede tried to sit more upright, but Sorcha murmured a denial and sang a half breath of words and the pain lifted out of Brede's muscles as simply as breaking a spider's web. The sudden easing of tension and pain had Brede breathless and adrift. She felt the warmth of Sorcha's hands exploring further, up to her shoulder, and the fierce scar that still weakened her sword arm.

'It is too late to heal this properly,' she said. 'It has set into the pattern of its choice and can't be torn apart and made new.'

She inspected Brede's face, and gathered her hand up once more.

'It doesn't trouble me,' Brede replied, swiftly, untruthful and frightened.

'You trouble me,' Sorcha said quietly, speaking sudden truth out of the depths of her worry. She let Brede's hand loose, waiting for her to withdraw.

Brede did not choose to do so. She laced her fingers into Sorcha's.

'Yes,' she said, 'I had noticed.'

Sorcha didn't answer immediately, but when she did, it was not with words.

Brede was not surprised by the kiss, nor its urgency, nor its completeness. Relief flooded through her. She had not been imagining this attraction between them; she had not, after all, made a fool of herself. And so a second kiss, and a third, and – voices on the stair.

Sorcha drew away, smiling wryly.

'Time to be Queen's Bodyguard,' she said.

Brede kicked the sword under a chest, and took her double knives from her pack. Sorcha was already making a convincing show of being an aware and responsible guard. Brede went to the door, and schooled her face to impassive responsibility, just as the two men reach the top of the stair.

The men looked in confusion at Sorcha, not recognising her, and surprised to find themselves challenged. Sorcha gazed back, without stepping from their path. She knew full well who they were, and knew, although she had temporarily forgotten, that they were expected; but they could meet the requirements of a password as well as any, be they generals or no.

Phelan accepted her passive insistence on protocol, and stated his name and business, and that of his companion. Sorcha let them by, and nodded to Brede. Brede didn't know what was expected of her as guard, but instinctively, she left the door ajar behind them, and stood in full view of them. Grainne shot her a questioning look, not expecting her to take this position.

'Your guests bear arms, lady,' Brede announced.

Phelan raised an amused eyebrow.

'Your stable-hand has opinions?' he enquired.

Rumour of Grainne's extraordinary choice of guard had reached him, as she knew it would. She registered the slight start that made Brede stand more stiffly at attention.

'My personal guard has bested the finest fighter within my ward, General,' Grainne replied, drawing a veil over the nature and reasons for that unexpected victory; giving Phelan the courtesy of his title, a courtesy he had not yet shown to her, trading on their kinship.

Brede wondered how Grainne knew about Tegan. She looked a half question at her charge.

Grainne nodded to Brede, giving permission for her to stay. Phelan shrugged, and turned to his business.

'You wanted someone to take word to the Horse Clans.'

Grainne inclined her head.

'Madoc here has offered his services.'

Brede's attention intensified. Madoc hardly seemed likely to win the confidence of the Clans. Brede suppressed the temptation to show her disdain. Grainne noted the stiffening of Brede's stance, and recognised what she believed to be the cause, although she hadn't expected Brede to know who Madoc was.

'No,' she said firmly. 'Not Madoc. He could never have any standing with the Clans. As the leader of the raid on the Horse Gather, it would be insanity to send him as my ambassador.'

She spoke clearly; making sure that Brede understood that she would hide nothing, even this, from her bodyguard. Brede couldn't believe what she had heard.

Phelan frowned, and tapped his fingers against his sword hilt. Grainne was tiring, the numbing pain beginning to grip her again. She waited for Phelan to respond, but he did not.

'I will not have him,' she said, firmly.

'I was acting on your command,' Madoc said, seeing to his own defence in the face of his sponsor's silence.

'You exceeded my commands. Had I known the outcome of your disobedience to my word, had I known the trouble that would spring from your doing, I should have hanged you – I may yet. *Leave.*'

Grainne turned her face away, ignoring Madoc's existence. When he was slow to move, Brede took a step towards him. She would have liked an excuse to handle him roughly. He didn't give her the pleasure.

Phelan cast an eye after his protégé.

'You are unfair. He knows a lot about the Clans; he knows their routines, their patterns, and their language. Without him, you'll never track them down.'

Grainne shrugged.

'I'll find some other way,' she said, not letting her eyes flicker to Brede, not trusting Phelan with an admission of the desperation that set a member of Wing Clan as her guard. The rest of the interview was an uphill struggle against the rising tide of pain, and Phelan's stubborn refusal to understand her. At last Phelan's voice trailed into silence. Grainne looked up guiltily, aware that she hadn't responded to a question. Phelan smiled sadly.

'You are not well, Next-kin. You shouldn't have let me tire you.' He stood abruptly, shaking his head at her denial. 'You shouldn't let me bully you like that. Forgive me.'

'Always.'

His smile softened almost to indulgence. He took Grainne's hand and kissed her fingertips.

'Sleep, my dear, solves everything; so my dogs assure me.'

'You take advice from your dogs?'

'About the need for food and sleep, yes. They are far more regular in their habits than you or I.'

Grainne lifted her hand to his face, caressing his chin.

'I will take your canine advice. Goodnight, Phelan.' She raised her face to him, and he kissed her gently on the brow, before turning and striding out of the chamber.

Grainne waited until Phelan's hurried steps could no longer be heard. She reached for Sorcha, trembling with exhaustion.

'Help me.'

'Sleep?'

Grainne nodded wearily.

'Sleep, sleep.'

Chapter Eighteen

'You knew, didn't you,' Sorcha said. 'I saw your face when you caught sight of Madoc.'

Brede shook her head, wearily.

'Grainne said he was not acting on her orders. If that is so, why does he still have the favour of her closest advisor?'

'He is Phelan's friend. Others think less well of him. I suppose Phelan is trying to – to rehabilitate him.'

Brede shrugged that away.

'He is a poor judge of character to keep Madoc close.'

'Yes.' Sorcha frowned. 'But what does that matter?'

'It matters to me. It says that the Clans are still not safe – my people – so, I don't think I believe Grainne. If what she says is true, Madoc would not still be welcome within her garth. If I am to believe her, then she should not trust Madoc, nor Phelan if that is the kind of friend he chooses.'

'Madoc hasn't had her favour for many years, and you saw how she dismissed him. But she won't do the same for Phelan, he's her most valued general and he is kin.'

Brede scowled.

'If I understand it, her next-kin has murdered his father and is trying to win her lands from her. So much for kin.'

'Yes, but Phelan is – well – Phelan. They love each other. They truly do. I've known Phelan since he was born. He'd hand-fast with Grainne if she'd let him, which really shows he's no judge of character, but he'd never put Grainne in danger.'

'And Madoc? Can you claim great knowledge of his boyhood too?'

'You are very sharp of a sudden.'

'I'm out of my depth. I came to this city looking for a sister taken into captivity, and now that I'm in no position to continue my search, I find the man responsible. I do not know what I'm doing here.'

'Do you think Grainne is doing more than groping after answers in the dark? When have you done more than follow where the wind leads you? Why this urgent need to know?'

'Nomads may follow the wind, or run before it, but that doesn't stop us knowing where we are when we get there. I don't know where I am. The wind is still blowing.'

'You aren't a nomad. You've never travelled with the Clans.'

'It is in my blood,' Brede snapped. Sorcha took a breath, then shook her head sharply.

'We are both tired,' she said.

Brede shook her head.

'You aren't listening to me. You are listening for what you need from me.'

'And what is that?'

'Compliance.'

'And what should I have been listening to?'

Brede couldn't speak. She shook her head again, numb with anger.

Sorcha stood abruptly, laying her sword across the chair and went to the outer door. She bolted it, and placing her hands to either side of the frame, sang a few words. She went to each window in turn and did the same. When she had done, she scooped up the sword once more, put it beside her couch, and began to undress. Brede stayed where she was, stiff with unspilt words.

'I don't know what to say to you,' Sorcha said at last, lying on the couch and untangling blankets. 'I don't know why you are here either, with a sister to search for.'

Brede started and Sorcha smiled sadly. 'I was listening, you see? What I heard is pain, Brede, and loss. Is there more? Have I missed anything else? If you want to tell me again so that I hear you, I will listen.'

'Why are you here, Sorcha?'

Sorcha looked up, puzzled at the question.

'I'm being paid.'

'No. The wind didn't carry you here. You have a reason, outside of Grainne's purpose.'

'Grainne trusts me; can you not do the same?'

'Loyalty?' Brede asked.

'No,' Sorcha answered her. 'No, not loyalty, something much more difficult than that. Grainne and I grew up together; we have been friends for – more than thirty years. We have shared happiness and loss, we have helped each other with harsh decisions; we know where we stand. We can each say when we think the other is wrong – or we used to.' Sorcha hesitated, no longer sure it would be safe to challenge Grainne. 'Would you call that loyalty?'

'No. So, I came to this city looking for a sister –'

'– taken into captivity, and now you believe Madoc to be the key to your search, but you feel trapped by your obligation to Grainne?'

'She is my sister –'

'– and she may have been dead these nine years.'

'I need to know.'

'Of course.'

'Of course what?'

'Come here, Brede. I understand: I'll help, if I can.'

Brede sat on the couch within the curve of Sorcha's body.

'How?' she asked baldly.

Sorcha lifted her shoulder awkwardly.

'I have spies.' Her eyes glinted and Brede wasn't sure whether to take her seriously. 'I can ask questions with greater freedom, and in places that you could never go. I have no sisters, Brede, but I've lost friends. I know that it isn't the same, but I can imagine.'

'If I ask, will Grainne truly give me anything? If my sister lives, if her child lives, I want them freed. Will she do that?'

Sorcha nodded.

'Of course.'

Brede's head came up and her smile faded into a cold glare.

'And even if they are alive and freed, I will be wanting Madoc's head, will Grainne give me that I wonder?'

Sorcha shook her head very slightly.

'No, perhaps not that, not officially, nor with a ribbon in his hair, but she might not choose to investigate some unexplained death in a tavern brawl. You know she doesn't value him. There might be others who'd be more – concerned – should he die.' She cast her eyes down, then fixed them on Brede's face. 'I have a question. You never said until now, even when I asked you – persuasively – what you were doing here, you gave no indication.'

'I did not lie.'

'I know that, but so strong a reason, I should have known, I should have been able to convince you to confide in me. So it seems you are able to resist me;' Sorcha caught a grin on Brede's face, and laughed, 'Yes, it is a rare occurrence, but if I ask you something now, will you tell me the whole truth, not just enough to satisfy me?'

'Perhaps.'

Sorcha leant her weight gently against Brede, curving an arm about her, feeling the tension in the rope of muscles beside her spine.

'What keeps you here, with a sister to pull you away?'

'You know the answer to that.'

'No.'

Brede grinned.

'There was a woman at the horse fair, in a silly dress and silver combs.'

Sorcha rested her hand against Brede's back; the rope was loosening. 'And what was it about this woman that attracted you?'

'I don't know, but it wasn't the dress or the combs. She distracted me so far from my path I don't know if I'll ever find a way back.'

'Not without help.'

'No. And you are offering?'

'Yes –'

Brede sensed that Sorcha might say more, but the faintest sound came from the inner room, and Sorcha was on her feet and gone.

Sound carried in these rooms, Brede noticed; she could hear Sorcha soothing Grainne's distress. She wondered that the spell did not affect her too, but Sorcha's song was a skein of notes and meaningless words to her. She wondered if Grainne had been conscious long, whether she had been listening.

And Sorcha, what of her? There was a link between her and Grainne that Brede couldn't quite fathom: thirty years shared. She thought of the way Sorcha's mouth felt against hers, and wondered if Sorcha had ever kissed Grainne that way. She wished, and did not wish, to hold Sorcha in her arms. She wanted to be out of Grainne's hearing.

Sorcha leant against the door, her bare feet flinching from the cold floor.

'Is she asleep?' Brede asked.

Sorcha shook her head. She moved across the room, gathering her blankets from the couch.

'Not sleeping, nor likely to. I will have to stay close by her tonight. The sword has disturbed her. She needs me more than she needs drugs or my songs. I'm sorry.'

Brede shrugged.

'I can sleep anywhere. Nomad blood, remember?'

The uneasy frown slipped from Sorcha's face.

'Of course,' she said, flicking the edge of the blanket across Brede's face in a playful feint. 'It was just that I was hoping you'd be sleeping with me,' Sorcha said casually, gathering the blanket back up.

'You presume on very short acquaintance.'

'Tell me you would have refused.'

Brede swallowed what she wanted to say, her whole body crying out to say *no*.

'I would have refused.'

Sorcha raises an eyebrow in genuine surprise.

'Why?'

Brede laughed.

'Because I think you've been short on truth again.'

'About what?'

'Grainne. Tell me she has not been your lover.'

Sorcha grimaced. 'A long time ago.'

'And you really want to make love within her hearing?'

'Ah. Now who is presuming? Some people sleep together to keep warm.'

'You are an impossible flirt,' Brede said, suddenly feeling relaxed, certain once more of the ground.

'Yes, it is too warm to share blankets for any other reason. However, I hope you will understand me if I tell you that I'm going to share Grainne's blankets tonight, because she is cold – cold to her soul.'

Brede blinked, the teasing had vanished again, replaced with the weight of all of Grainne's pain and fear. Sorcha was visibly trembling with the effort it had already cost her to cope with Grainne's poisoned frame.

'I understand you,' Brede said, quietly, lapsing into her native tongue. 'You'd best go to her.'

Sorcha lit more candles, and spread the extra blankets over Grainne's bed. She finished undressing, and climbed in beside her friend.

'You did hear, I suppose?' she asked.

'Yes,' Grainne said. 'It won't be easy.'

'That is the least of our problems,' Sorcha said tersely, feeling raw to that suggestion.

'Ah, but it is one with a solution. I want you to be happy, my sorcerer.'

'I've not told you this before, Grainne, Lady, most worthy liege; I can't stand it when you call me sorcerer.'

'Well then, that is something I can put right. If you are going to spit liege at me, I will call you Songspinner.'

'You will not. Sound travels, remember?'

Grainne nodded.

'Brede has made that point adequately.' she dropped her voice to the merest breath. 'Hold me,' she said. 'I am so cold.'

Sorcha edged closer, encircling Grainne's trembling body with her arms; knowing that her very touch brought pain, but that even the pain was better than the fear which had roused Grainne despite drug and spell, to stare into the darkness watching for the Scavenger to come claim her soul.

Brede listened to the murmur of voices from the next room, and watched the fingers of light across the ceiling, from the many candles that Sorcha had lit, trying to drive the shadows from Grainne's night. For a long time she turned over Sorcha's few words about Grainne. Her thoughts stuck on those thirty years. She drifted into sleep at last, Sorcha's changing face before her eyes, first the unremarkable face she offered the world, and then the fierce brightness of the face she turned to Brede, and to Grainne.

Brede woke to the sound of ash being scraped from the fire. She glanced round for Sorcha and realised who was clearing the fire in the adjoining room. No wonder she was constantly tired.

Brede shrugged into her clothes, and joined Sorcha over the embers of the fire. She took the shovel from her, and finished cleaning the fireplace. Sorcha folded herself into a chair, pulling her knees up to her chin, in exhausted acceptance of Brede's presence.

Brede glanced at Grainne's unmoving form.

'Do you cook her food too?' she asked.

'No. I go to the common kitchen, and I take food from the common pot. The Queen eats what we all eat.'

'When did she sleep?'

'Not above two hours ago,' Sorcha responded, 'but she'll not sleep long.'

'Can you rest?'

Sorcha grimaced.

'I could try.'

She dragged herself out of the chair and wavered through to Brede's rumpled couch, asleep before she had completely laid herself down. Brede pulled the blankets from beneath her, and tossed them carelessly over her huddled body. She gazed down at Sorcha, wondering how Grainne had inspired such devotion.

Brede returned to the inner room, and laid more wood on the fire, one piece at a time, slowly, careful of making noise. Before she had finished the task, she was aware of Grainne's wakeful stirring. She went to the end of the bed, wondering what, if anything, she could do for Grainne.

The Queen's wandering gaze lit on the shadowy figure at the end of her bed.

'Where is Sorcha?' she asked.

'Asleep,' Brede said quietly. Grainne nodded.

'That is good. Come and sit beside me, Ahern's daughter.'

Brede hesitated at this unexpected command, and Grainne beckoned her forward. There was nowhere to sit but the edge of the bed. Brede placed herself cautiously, so as not to jolt Grainne's frailty.

'So,' Grainne hesitated, finding words to fit the strangeness of the occasion, 'we hear each other too well, Plains woman.'

'Yes.'

'You and Sorcha deserve some quiet time together. I promise you shall have your time, when I can spare Sorcha.'

Brede didn't respond.

'Talk to me, daughter of Wing Clan. It seems you have thoughts to share.' Grainne suggested.

Brede tilted her head, questioningly.

'You have Sorcha firmly influenced,' Grainne persisted. 'What can you persuade me to?' Grainne reached out and touched the braided hair Brede had tied about her wrist. 'Sorcha hasn't cut her hair before. A passing remark from you, and a lifetime's growth was on the fire.'

'She did that for you, not me.'

'Yes, she told me. And that is what she believes.' Grainne shifted herself slightly towards sitting, trying to make the movement look easy.

'Before Aeron died, when I did not expect to rule, I did what I liked. And what I liked included Sorcha.' Grainne smiled, in easy reminiscence, an infectious smile. 'I was not always as you see me, Brede. I had a youth – a happy, misspent, wild youth. A lifetime ago; but now, Sorcha takes your suggestions. The question is: should she trust you?'

'I do not believe that she does. What is it that you and she are afraid of?'

Grainne shrugged slightly.

'Sorcha has her own secrets. She'll tell you or not as she pleases, it is not for me to tell.' Grainne tugged gently on the hair bracelet. 'I need to be sure of you. I know what you think of my choice, I certainly know what Phelan thinks of it. I also know why you accepted my offer. You believe I would have you killed if you refused.'

'Would you not?'

'Who would I ask to carry out that order? I can't trust many people.'

'Maeve.'

Grainne laughed.

'Yes, for that task, I think I might trust Maeve.' Grainne peered hard at Brede, trying to see her expression in the half-light.

'If you want to go, you may.'

Brede's eyes locked with Grainne's, startled.

'But if you go it must be now, before we grow dependent upon you. Take your horse, and go back to Wing Clan, tell them who was responsible for the last Gather. Tell them what really happened. Tell them we want an end to this.'

Brede waited to see if Grainne would regret those words. They gazed wordlessly at each other for several seconds.

'Why now? Why not five years ago? Why not nine? When did it become important to you that Wing Clan forget their injury at your hand?'

'Ailbhe is dead, that changes everything. Lorcan is a child; his army will be weak. Now is our chance to force them to a peace.'

'And this is your greatest need, Grainne?' Brede asked quietly. 'The Clans back under your control?'

'No. I want the Clans at peace, with me and with my heir. There is no point in continuing the war. I want peace.'

'What about the rest? The Clans are not the only alienated peoples to have taken up arms against you.'

'They'll come to terms if I am not fighting Lorcan, they are taking advantage of the fact that we can't fight so many enemies at once. The Clans are different. They have better cause to fight.'

'And what of the one who is poisoning you? Will that one be satisfied with Lorcan as liege? Will you live long enough to bring this about?'

'I must.'

'So what is of most use to you, Grainne; my presence as guard, or my absence as emissary? I can't do both.'

'Which do you want to do?' Grainne asked, curious despite herself.

Brede sighed, and walked to the shuttered window, peering through the slats at the faint tinge of dawn.

'If I'd wanted to go back to the Clans I'd have done so before now.'

'And what keeps you here, when the threat of a knife between the ribs is not part of your decision?' Brede's hand slipped on the window ledge, hearing an echo of Sorcha's words.

'Sorcha, potentially. Is that why you want me gone?'

Grainne looked away, considering whether she would really risk her own safety rather than see Sorcha with another woman. At last she smiled.

'Yes,' she said, waiting for Brede to respond.

'Is that knife back?'

Grainne had to think about that too.

'No.'

'So, what is this war about? What was so important that it lasted thirteen years, only to be dropped now?'

Grainne considered Brede's sudden change of direction. She supposed that Brede was refusing to see her as anything but the Queen. And being Queen, she pulled her thoughts together and tried to explain.

'Ailbhe always wanted the power for himself, he was never content to be Aeron's consort.'

'So you think he killed Aeron. And she was your – sister? Cousin?'

'Niece.'

Brede nodded. 'Reason enough for war.'

'More complicated than that. When she died with no daughter, I was her heir. Ailbhe and his kin would've had me hand-fast with him, so that he could keep the throne. I could not, when I suspected him of a hand in her death. And he wouldn't have been satisfied to be my consort either. I've no doubt I'd have died before I could've had a daughter.'

'So there was no way for Ailbhe to gain by Aeron's death?'

'Of course there was, but not once I refused him. He misjudged my resolve, my loyalty. But once I am gone, a male relative who is blood of her blood can succeed.'

Brede watched Grainne thoughtfully, wanting to say *You've really flown in the face of the wind, haven't you?*

Grainne turned restlessly away from Brede's gaze.

'So,' she said softly, 'I was forced to be the ruler I never wanted to be, to stand between Ailbhe and his ambition. And I did it, for the country, for Aeron's memory, out of duty. And I thought I was right to do so. And now someone I trust is trying to poison me. When I find out who that trusted someone is...'

Brede shook her head. 'And then what?' she asked.

Grainne had not looked beyond her final proof, her justice, if she could have it.

'Then Ailbhe will have lost.'

'He is already dead,' Brede reminded her gently.

Grainne rubbed her temples. 'At the hand of my Aeron's son. I can't believe she spawned him. I must make peace of some sort with that viper. If I do not, the war could last forever.'

'Is it still within your control to end this?' Brede asked.

Grainne sighed, bemused by her memories, and her anger and resentment at fourteen years of her life wasted and ruined.

'Barely in my control, but it is my responsibility. The second that I allowed that circle of metal to touch my brow, it became my war, my fault. Perhaps even before, when Aeron died, it became my task.'

'There was no war then,' Brede protested.

'You think not? No battles perhaps, but war, yes. You have handled that sword; can you tell me that you do not understand the way you can be drawn into the scheme of things, until you can no longer find a way out, until your own needs and wants mean nothing? Haven't you heard Sorcha? There has always been a war; I didn't choose this, it chose me, but it is mine for all that. Even when I don't wear that crown, I can feel it pressing against my head, burning into me.'

Brede took a breath to interrupt, and hesitated. Grainne's eyes focussed on her for the first time in a while. She was trembling with effort, beads of sweat on her brow. Brede laid a steadying hand on Grainne's wrist. Grainne considered the hand resting against her skin, and recovered herself. She had forgotten that this was an ill-educated Plains woman, not Sorcha, to whom she spoke.

'Take your rest,' Grainne whispered. 'I shall sleep again for a while. No one shall disturb us yet.'

Brede returned to her couch, where Sorcha lay, tangled in her blankets. Patiently, she unravelled the coverings from Sorcha's sleep heavy limbs, and worked her way under the covers beside her. The bed was far too narrow for them both, but somehow she managed to get reasonably comfortable, and would have been almost content were it not for the thought of the freedom that she had allowed to slip away from her once more.

Chapter Nineteen

Eachan was aware that it looked strange, to have the master of the Queen's horse going from gate to gate, garth to garth, asking after horses of Plains breeding. It helped nothing that he did not know what he was looking for, beyond a woman a little older than Brede, a child, gender unknown, aged around nine; and a particular breeder's mark. Nonetheless, he judged it safer that he go than Brede. The owners of the private stables would be curious about him, but they would as like as not set the town guard onto Brede.

So, when Eachan walked in at Doran's gate his mind was on horses, and his own dignity, so he did not at first recognise the man standing in the shade of the long porch running the length of the building. He had no reason to recognise the woman, and it wasn't the owners of the house he particularly wished to speak to, so he turned his blind eye to them, looking for a servant. Even so, as he waited for the child to find the stable mistress, there was something about the way the man held himself that impinged. He stepped into another shady corner and watched as Killan detached himself with many backward glances for the woman on the porch. Doran's wife, or his daughter, Eachan supposed, but it was too far away to tell which. He wondered if Killan had spotted him.

Just as Killan sauntered through the gate, the child returned to say that the stable mistress was not within the garth, and offering to take a message. Eachan pressed a scrap of paper into her hand with a rough sketch of Falda's mark on it.

'Tell her I would talk to her about any horse she has with this mark, and whether she knows the whereabouts of the woman who bred them.'

The child nodded, and smiled happily when the sketch was followed by a heavy copper coin.

'I know this mark,' the child said, 'I'll tell her what you say.'

Eachan turned out into the street, his brief glimpse of Killan forgotten.

Sorcha's yet more discreet enquiries took her places even Eachan would hesitate to search. Sorcha could walk where she pleased, unchallenged, unseen if she so chose, and she walked into many private lodgings, and even into Grainne's guest hall, where even Grainne went only when it could not be avoided. She found entire households accommodated there, and retinues of bondservants, and some fine horses, many Plains bred, but there was not a hint of Brede's sister, and she returned dispirited and thoughtful, and would not tell Grainne where she had been.

As she wandered quietly about the halls and garths, Sorcha could not help but notice that there was a certain atmosphere that all these places shared, a feeling that they were waiting for something, that breath was being held. What was being awaited, and why, she could not yet fathom, but she felt it even within Grainne's walls, even in the courts of the barracks. She felt it from the mercenaries under Maeve's command, and wished she could ask Maeve what she had noticed, but there was no telling what Maeve's involvement in that collective held breath might be. Sorcha did not trust Maeve. She could not put her finger on why, but there was something about the gossip in the inn on the corner of the square and the groups that formed and reformed there that made her uneasy. She found herself watching the liaisons and groupings, the pairing and bonding with a fascination that was not solely for the danger they might offer. She saw that she was not the only one watching. She saw Tegan watching, and Ula. And Ula watching Tegan, and watching Maeve. There was something about Ula, something more observant than was called for, something sharp, but at the same time generous, and Sorcha wondered, and watched more closely, so that it happened she was there to witness the making of a particular wager.

Killan put his arms about Maeve's waist, and kissed the back of her neck. He felt the momentary surprise, then acceptance of her body, moulding itself against his. He sighed, and closed his eyes, drinking the scent of her hair. She twisted about, and pulled out of his arms. He opened his eyes.

There was something about her expression, something cleansed perhaps, as though a threatening cloud had passed. He reached, but didn't touch.

'Ah. I feel surplus to requirements.'

Her eyes widened slightly and shifted away from his face. Guilt: he recognised the signs.

'Tegan –' she began.

He reached out, shaking his head quickly and placing two fingers against her mouth to still her words. 'Tegan,' he said, resignation making his voice atypically dull. When he was certain she wouldn't try to explain, his hand found somewhere to hide inside his sleeves, as he hunched his shoulders, feeling unaccountably forlorn. He was concerned to find he minded. Maeve had been fun. He tried to find something to say, but his wit and tongue seemed to have deserted him.

Maeve looked anxiously into Killan's face and found something between hurt and anger there. He turned away sharply, as though it pained him to look into her eyes. Impatience hit her. Surely he wasn't pretending he cared?

Killan rubbed his chest thoughtfully, then turned his shoulder just sufficiently that they could each pretend they weren't together, not apart, not – his feet took him to the row of barrels. His hand beckoned the keg mistress, found coins, curved about a mug. The sharp fire of the alcohol hit his tongue, the back of his throat, his chest, his stomach, his mind. He glanced about the tightly packed room, focussing on each face in turn, aware, of a sudden, that he was glowering and made a conscious attempt to stop. Shoulders back and down. Brows up and relaxed, hands loose. His eyes rested on a dark-haired woman he could not place. Her eyes met his coolly and she turned slightly away, almost scornful. He shrugged and he forgot her. There was Ula. She raised her head and met his gaze. He shook his head, found a smile he didn't know he possessed and bestowed it on the next face that came into focus.

Inir smiled uncertainly back. *Inir? Well, why not?* Killan shouldered his way to Inir's side, making his walk relaxed, his body open and welcoming, shedding his irritation and disappointment, thinking himself into another mood, consoling, warm, subtly sexual. Yes, Inir would do.

Ula rose abruptly from her comfortable corner, made an excuse to Oran, and wove her way towards Maeve.

Maeve watched Killan, wondering what the opening comment of that conversation would be. Inir was part of her crew – if Killan had unkind things to say, she would rather they were not to one of hers. She was too hot, an uncomfortable flush on her face, her collar suddenly too tight and rough against her skin. She loosened the fastening, and put the cool metal of her mug against her cheek. A hand touched her shoulder and she twisted in the tightly packed crowd to greet Ula.

'Did I see what I think I saw?' Ula asked, with a mischievous smile setting crinkles about her eyes. 'Did you just let Killan loose?'

Maeve's mouth quirked uncomfortably.

'You could put it like that.'

Ula laid a finger gently on the frown that knit Maeve's brow.

'And you feel bad about it?'

'A little.'

'Don't.' Ula sipped her ale. 'He'll have a new victim within half an hour.'

'Victim?'

'A new intimate friend, then.'

Maeve found indignation welling up at Ula's low opinion of Killan, and of the worth of her own affection for him, and the effect upon him of her rejection.

'Nonsense,' she said sharply. Ula grinned.

'Then I wager you a measure of best ale if I'm wrong, against a kiss if I'm right.'

Maeve narrowed her eyes at Ula.

'And I thought you and Oran would grow old together.'

'We will. It's just a kiss. I'm no Killan.'

'You don't care for him much.'

'He's a complete bastard, my love. But he is also a charmer. Everyone loves him, he's all and everything to whoever he's with, and that changes so quickly – about now, I'd say.'

Ula waved her mug in Killan's direction.

Inir bent his head slightly to hear Killan, his hand rising to rest on Killan's back, below his shoulder blade. Killan's hand fell against Inir's neck in something that approached a caress, pulling him into an intimacy that might be secrecy, or something more. Maeve shivered with jealousy, then shook herself out of it – what Killan did wasn't her concern now.

'Inir doesn't count, Killan's been helping him over Balin.'

'There's helping and helping. I give it another ten minutes before they leave together.'

Maeve shook her head.

'Go and buy the beer, Ula.'

Ula grinned and fought her way to the barrels. Before she was back at Maeve's elbow, Inir and Killan had gone.

'You owe me two coppers for the beer,' she said, 'and a kiss.'

Maeve handed over the money, and bent her head to kiss Ula chastely on the side of her mouth. Ula moved her head slightly, meeting the kiss full on. She heard Maeve's intake of breath and pressed slightly harder, feeling Maeve's almost involuntary response and taking full advantage. Maeve drew back, the too hot, uncomfortable feeling about her collar once more. Ula rested her hand on the back of Maeve's neck, keeping her close enough that what they said couldn't be overheard.

'Whatever it is that Killan has, that draws people to him, you have it too.'

Maeve reached and untangled Ula's hand from her hair.

'Tegan is back in my life, I've everything I want.'

Ula stepped away.

'Not you, Maeve.'

Maeve frowned, out of kilter and hoping she was still being teased.

'Don't flirt, Ula, someone might think you mean it.'

Ula shrugged.

'So, I can expect Tegan to be less grumpy can I?'

'Tegan is always grumpy.'

Ula laughed, and Maeve forgot about her rough, too tight collar.

Sorcha moved away, reassured that after all, the complexities of the shifting loyalties of Maeve's mercenaries were just about whose blankets were currently tangled with whose.

Inir walked, loose-limbed at Killan's side, more than slightly drunk. His step seemed too light – his *heart* seemed too light. Somehow this felt like betrayal, but he couldn't quite place why. Not Maeve, that was certain, he knew better than Killan how irrelevant that anxiety should be now. No, it was Balin he was walking away from, each step of greater significance than the effort of muscle, the compact of foot and shoe leather and cobble. It was time, somehow. Time to let go, time to try again, time to have a little pleasure.

Killan's lodging was in a tall house that burrowed into the wall of the city, leant confidingly into the stone, a drunk in a doorway. The stairway was no more than a ladder, dark and awkward. But at the top of the stair, beyond a curtain, they came out into light and space. Inir looked round sharply, blinking and appreciably less inebriated. The shutters at the window were thrown back, and the window itself was near as large as a door. A single chair stood in the way of the window, with a small table beside it, and the rest of the room was a substantial bed, and a welter of clothes and gear in apparently random piles on the floor. The table was meticulously clean and clear of everything except a knife, and on the wall above the table a series of shelves held household wares.

Killan grinned at Inir's survey.

'This isn't what I want you to see,' he said leading the way to the window.

He stepped through, leaning his weight on the open shutter and swinging out of sight. Inir followed cautiously, less certain of the pitch of the roof, and the potentially slippery shingles beneath his feet. As he straightened and got his balance, he gasped.

'Worth seeing,' he agreed. The roof of the house came almost to the top of the city wall, and caught the last of the evening sun. Laid out below them, the city sprawled. The lowest reach of the Tower was almost on a level with their viewpoint. The barracks gate was clearly visible. Inir laughed.

'It feels as though you could step off the roof and be at our gate in a couple of minutes.'

'It takes a bit longer than that,' Killan grinned in false modesty, 'but a lot faster than by road.'

Inir shook his head. 'What? You've taken up flying?'

'No. But it is just about possible to get the whole way up there on the roofs. Or it would be if it weren't for the river.'

'Ah, the river.' Inir searched the view below him. 'I can't see it.'

Killan placed a careful hand on his shoulder, wary of unbalancing him, and pointed.

'The tall building there, that's the mill, it's just beyond.'

'It looks completely different from here, but now you've said it, I can see the wheel, and the weathervane on the inn the other side –' Inir knelt and peered down into the street below. Killan grabbed a handful of sleeve.

'Careful, the roof isn't in good condition.'

Inir moved his hand back quickly, and sat back onto his heels, resting his back against Killan's legs. Killan smiled to himself.

'My eyrie, my kingdom.' Inir glanced up, and Killan offered him his hand, to help him back to his feet. 'The best view in the city, warm in the sun, and not overlooked.'

Inir glanced up at the wall behind the house. Killan shook his head.

'The sentries never quite make it up here. The privy is in that tower,' he pointed to his left, 'and in winter there's a fire, so they don't walk this stretch often, with the river below to keep unwelcome strangers out.'

Inir frowned, trying to work out the geography. The frown smoothed as he fit where he was into his mental picture of the city's defences. He looked at Killan thoughtfully, aware that his hand was still in Killan's.

'Still,' Killan said, 'there's not enough sun left to stay out here long tonight. Shall we go in?'

Inir nodded wordlessly, caressing the base of Killan's thumb with his own. Killan's hand tightened about his.

'Are you staying?' he asked softly. Inir nodded again. Killan turned immediately, and led Inir in through the window.

Ula and Oran stumbled in through the barrack gateway, laughing and rain-soaked, just as the guard changed. Ula caught Cei's cold look and sneered.

'You should get out more, man,' she said, over-loud. 'There's been good sport this evening, even you would have enjoyed it.'

Oran shushed her and pulled her away, still muttering indignantly about people with no talent for enjoyment. They turned sharply in at the doorway to their billet, and found Tegan and Eachan with their heads together. Ula giggled helplessly at the incongruity of what looked like an intimate embrace, and could not be – could it?

'Hands off, Eachan,' she said crisply. 'Tegan's spoken for.'

She reached out and patted Tegan's arm, despite Oran's best effort to intercept.

'Maeve's on her way back,' she said, not entirely sure what motivated her to do it. She knew she was drunk, she knew she was half angry with Maeve, she knew that Tegan distracted was Tegan dangerous, but why she chose to stir in that particular melting pot she couldn't say. Jealousy? But she was jealous of neither Maeve nor Tegan; and she certainly wasn't jealous of Killan. She wagged an uncertain finger in Tegan's face.

'You're a lucky woman, lucky to have Maeve, lucky Killan's so fickle.' Oran divined disaster in the look that shot between Tegan and Eachan. He pulled his hand-mate urgently away, towards their shared bed. She staggered ahead of him, Tegan forgotten. Tegan snaked a detaining hand after Oran and pulled him back.

'Killan?' she asked, Eachan's report of his unexpected sighting foremost in her mind. Oran was nearly as drunk as Ula; he thought very carefully before saying uncertainly, 'Inir?'

Tegan let him go. She turned back to Eachan.

'What's going on?'

Eachan shrugged.

'Killan has a way of causing trouble, but it never seems to stick to him. He reminds me of Phelan when he was younger.'

'Phelan?' Tegan laughed in spite of herself.

'Without the leadership skills.'

'Just as well, Killan with a following is a frightening thought.'

Eachan refused to have his comparison laughed away.

'Same single-mindedness, same decisiveness – same ability to change direction without losing step. He's good with people, knows how to charm, and he's a deadly enemy.'

'Who are you talking about?' Maeve asked, as she walked in, rubbing rain out of her hair.

'Phelan,' Eachan said quickly. Maeve frowned slightly, then shrugged and pulled Tegan into her arms.

'What's your duty for tonight?'

Tegan grinned and kissed her.

'Whatever you choose to ask.'

Eachan cleared his throat and stepped away.

'Goodnight, Tegan – Maeve.'

Tegan twisted out of Maeve's embrace for a moment.

'Should we be watching him?' she asked Eachan.

'I hardly know. Do we have any real cause?'

Tegan resisted a glance at Maeve.

'No.'

'Then, no, unless we find something more. Goodnight.'

'Sleep well, Eachan,' Tegan called softly, as she followed Maeve to the ladder that led up to their private quarters.

Chapter Twenty

Eachan listened to the hurried footsteps out in the stable yard. He did not care to hear urgency. His hand strayed to the hilt of his dagger, but then he heard his name called.

Riordan blinked in the darkness of the stable.

'Eachan, there is a Plains woman at the gate asking to speak to you.'

Eachan put his head on one side considering what that might mean.

'What did she actually say?'

Riordan thought about it.

'*I hear that the Queen's horse-master has been asking after Plains bred horses.*'

Eachan turned sharply into the light, and gestured Riordan away.

'Good. Let us find what she has to say for herself.'

Once in view of the woman waiting beyond the pale, he slowed his walk, suppressing his excitement.

As Eachan reached the gate, he scanned the woman eagerly, taking in the good horse at her shoulder, the dark hair, the height, the hawk-like profile, and the age. Too young, surely? He hid his disappointment, and looked closer. A half-hidden bond-collar, and a tattoo on her right temple. Not entirely what he had hoped for.

The woman waited whilst he inspected her, seeing the disappointment, the assessment of her as a source of information.

'You were asking after Wing Clan. I might know what you seek.'

Eachan listened to the hint of Plains accent.

'You aren't Wing Clan yourself?'

She shook her head.

'I'm just unlucky. Do you want to hear?'

'This isn't for me – tell me the basics, then if it's what I hope for, I'll send for the one who'll know for sure.'

'The mark you were asking after, It's Wing Clan. I assume you knew that? There was one in this city had a Wing Clan woman within his garth. She used that sign.'

'What else do you know of her?'

'Taken at the Gather. She had a child of an age for her to have been carrying her at the time.'

'Did she have a name, this Plains woman?'

'I never heard it. We don't share names with your kind, and I never spoke to her myself.'

'She's dead then?'

The woman lifted her chin.

'Four years at least.'

'And the child?'

'Sold. I don't know where.'

Eachan gazed at the woman, wondering if so little was worth the telling. He shrugged, for all he knew the woman was holding back information that she might share with Brede.

'Riordan, are you messenger today?'

Riordan detached himself from conversation with Inir.

'Find Brede, and say to her – say that there may be news of her sister at the gate. Make sure she hears the *may*.'

Riordan nodded and turned away towards the tower.

Eachan and the Plains woman waited in silence, measuring one another. Eachan's eye strayed to the horse, sure that he had seen it before.

'Whose ...*garth* are you within?' he asked, deliberately mirroring the woman's euphemism.

'Doran.'

Eachan's eye flicked back to the tattoo. She saw that glance and pulled her hair back allowing him to see the mark clearly. Eachan shook his head.

'I saw a man within Doran's garth, when I came asking, who I didn't expect to see there –' he hesitated, not sure whether he should ask this. 'Do you know a man called Killan?' She shook her head, frowning.

'Should I?'

'He seemed to have business with a lady of the house.'

Her expression cleared, and something close to a sneer twisted her lip.

'Emer, probably. Doran's next-kin. A younger sister; she has an eye for a handsome man. I assume he's handsome?'

Eachan shrugged, embarrassed, and aware suddenly of his own lack of anyone to call him handsome. He turned to see what had become of Riordan, and saw Brede standing at the entrance to the tower, motionless and silent.

Brede came towards the gate and the Plains woman stepped forward. Immediately Corla and Cei were between her and the entrance. She stepped back again at once. And since they would not allow her in, Brede went out. They stood in cautious silence for a second, and then Brede gestured for them to walk away from the listening sentries.

The Plains woman watched her furtively, taking in the green badge on her sleeve, the knives at her belt, the absence of collar.

Brede headed down to the water meadow beside the river, the plains"
woman at her elbow, the horse following obediently after. At last, at the waterside,
Brede spoke.

'Wing Clan, my blood.'

'Storm Clan, my birth,' the woman replied.

'I am Brede, daughter of Ahern of Wing Clan.'

The woman hesitated, frowning at Brede's readiness to give her name.

'Jodis, daughter of Ute and Sulien of Storm Clan.'

'So Jodis. You may have news of my sister.'

'There was a woman of your Clan, within the garth of Madoc.'

'Madoc? The general?'

'That one.'

Brede watched the slow moving water, the turning of weed in the current;
Madoc.

'My sister was called Falda.' Brede said, making a question of it.

'I didn't know her name.'

'She's no longer there?'

'She is dead.'

Brede pretended an interest in the roots of the willows along the far side
of the river.

'Which do you want?' Jodis asked. 'A niece, and a sister found but dead,
or a sister not found?'

'A daughter?'

'Sold. I don't know where. Her horses were sold too.'

Jodis waited for Brede to make the connection.

Brede looked at her, then the horse. Jodis nodded.

'That's why I brought him with me. Take a look.'

Brede offered the horse a hand to nuzzle. She ran her other hand along his
neck, feeling under the mane for a tattoo. Her fingers grazed the raised skin, and
she bit her lip, closing her eyes.

She parted the mane and studied the breeder's mark.

'Falda,' she said at last, when she could control her voice.

'The mark is hers?' Jodis asked. Brede nodded, rubbing her hand up and
down the horse's neck, as though she could erase the strange mixture of relief
and sorrow by making patterns in the animal's coat. At last she forced herself
away from the horse, and turned to Jodis.

'Tell me as much as you can. This beast is too young to have been taken at
the Gather, why does he bear Falda's mark?'

Jodis settled onto the ground, cross-legged, the traditional storyteller at
a Gather fire. Brede half smiled, accepting the role Jodis had taken, and settled

beside her, cooled by the shadow of the tower wall.

Jodis pulled her bond-collar out from the scarf she used to conceal it.

'By the rules of this, I am not a slave. If I can earn enough to buy my way free, then free I am. They have to give you a percentage of every penny they make from your labour. But it reverts to your owner should you die. You'll not be surprised if I tell you how many bondservants have fatal accidents just as they've earned a chain. Your sister marked every beast she bred from her own mares, but I doubt that Madoc honoured his bond in her case, for her animals would've bought her free in no time. For the child it would be more complicated. If she was born after the time your sister was chained, then the child is a chattel, not a bondservant. She can't buy herself free, and the master is not obliged to sell. If I'd been your sister I'd have worked up enough to buy the child free.'

'Are you saying that Madoc had my sister killed?'

'No. I think not, she was far too useful. But the few times I saw her, she seemed ill.'

'How long?'

'At least four years. I didn't see her for a long time, and then I was sent to the market to buy as many of her horses as I could get for my master. That's how I knew, but she could have been dead a long time before they sold up. Madoc must have needed a lot of money quickly to sell all those beasts at once.'

'And my niece was sold then too?'

'Yes.'

'But you don't know to whom.'

'My master did not need servants. I didn't go to that market.'

Jodis shuddered, breaking out of her storyteller pose to hug a knee to her.

'Your niece was named Neala, I heard her mother call after her once.'

Brede covered her face. She took a steadying breath.

'Is there only the one child?'

Jodis hesitated, blinking.

'I never saw another.' She ducked her head, puzzling it over. 'I never saw her pregnant – I can't be sure. The first time I saw her with the child, the girl would have been four or five years old, there may have been others.' She risked a look at Brede's face. 'She was ill, perhaps she couldn't –' she tried again. 'Madoc isn't known for keeping women that way. He does no great dealings in that market.' Her voice trailed off.

Brede made an effort.

'I am in your debt.'

Jodis shrugged, and turned slightly away, in so doing pulling her hair away from the tattoo. Brede winced at the sight of it.

'Why are you tattooed?'

'My master's idea of a jest.'

Jodis pulled her hair forward to hide the lightning strike that ran down her temple.

'He treats you as though you were a horse.' Brede said, husky with rage.

Jodis watched Brede through the curtain of her hair.

'He calls me his storm-mare, sometimes his nightmare. He is full of jests is Doran. He breeds from me the same as he breeds from his other mares. Doran does a fine trade in slaves. And my children are chattels because of this,' she yanked at the chain about her neck and narrowed her eyes against tears that threatened to fall. 'I want no more children.'

Brede waited in silence.

'The children are the strongest chain. You should find your sister's daughter, and buy her free if you can, before she is old enough to be caught this way.'

Brede shook her head, bewildered. Jodis cleared her throat and pulled her hair tidy.

'So, Brede, daughter of Wing Clan, how did you come to be here without a bond collar?'

Brede raised a shoulder slightly.

'I was in the Marshes, with my mother's kin. A chance encounter with mercenaries – a stolen horse, Falda's horse – I followed them, joined them, came here searching for her – and now I have found.'

Jodis waited for Brede to fill the flesh of her tale, but she did not.

'What will keep you here now?' she asked.

'Falda's daughter,' Brede answered.

'And beyond that finding? If she can be found?'

Brede's eyes strayed to the tower behind Jodis' shoulder.

'A contract, but I will break that when I'm ready.'

'Something else then.' Jodis said firmly. Brede nodded.

'Hand-fast?' Jodis asked, thinking of Eachan.

'No,' Brede said, half surprised at the idea.

'Heart-fast?' Jodis asked, not really knowing why she went on probing.

Brede ran a finger across her cheekbone, thinking.

'Enough to keep me here?' She met Jodis' gaze, frowning. 'I don't know.'

Jodis jerked her head sharply, embarrassed at having asked something so personal, and stood briskly.

'I should not stay any longer.' But Brede was in no mood to let her go so swiftly.

'You are Storm Clan. How did you end up here?'

Jodis mounted her horse.

'An unscrupulous horse trader took advantage of an inexperienced and ambitious young woman who wouldn't listen to the advice of her kin. A young woman who thought Wing and Cloud Clans had somehow earned their destruction, and that she could tempt fate. Most of the Plains people taken at the Gather are dead now, captivity doesn't suit Wing Clan. But I don't understand how you've not found the few left, they are easy to spot, they all wear a collar – unlike you.'

Brede squinted up at the woman.

'Unlike me.' She agreed. Jodis gathered up her reins and turned away.

'Which ways does the wind blow?' Brede asked her, seeing the wary distance in her eyes. Jodis smiled stiffly.

'Towards the future,' she said. 'But ultimately it is a cold wind, Brede, blowing us all towards death.'

Brede watched her leave, then stood beside the water, stripping the bark from a willow switch, tying the soft wood into knots. At last she threw the mangled mess into the river and walked heavy-footed back to the tower.

Eachan caught sight of her, as she crossed the courtyard, and called out to her. Brede changed direction and went to his side, reaching up to touch the neck of the huge war-horse he was leading.

'Well?' he asked.

'My sister is dead. Madoc had her. He sold her daughter.'

The horse responded to Brede's encouragement, leaning his huge head against her, pushing with his considerable weight, forcing her to step back as he searched her clothing for treats.

'Stay away from Madoc,' Eachan warned. 'He is a first rate sword, and he has powerful friends.'

'Who is Doran?'

'One of Madoc's friends.'

'One of the powerful ones?'

'I doubt it. He is a captain, an archer I think; not someone with much influence.'

'The Plains woman said that Madoc had to sell all his horses suddenly, I got the impression that it was common gossip. Are you telling me that as the Queen's master of horse you did not know the quality of his horses, and didn't buy any?'

'I was not the Queen's horse-master then. I couldn't afford the prices. Nor could my then mistress. I never thought about a woman dead years, when I thought of where you might look. I am sorry for it, I could have saved you a lot of long searching.'

Brede shook her head.

'How much does it cost to buy a slave-child?' she asked.

'More than you have.'

'Well.' Brede looked about her, as though unsure of where she was. 'I should be gone.'

Eachan reached around the bulk of the horse and took her hand. Brede returned the pressure then let go, slapping the horse on the shoulder.

'Well,' she said again, uneasy with the responsibility that turned her feet towards the tower, when her mind turned towards the plains.

At the tower door she collided with Tegan. She stepped back, avoiding contact.

'Brede –' Tegan called after her, but Brede didn't respond. Tegan glanced around for what had caused that withdrawal and found Eachan.

'What's wrong?' she asked.

'The sister's found: dead.'

Tegan sighed.

'I hoped –'

'Foolish hope, Tegan. She'll want watching, that one.'

Tegan glanced up at the blank windows of the Queen's tower and said nothing.

Eachan walked to the gate and saw the Plains woman still out on the street, an uncertain look on her face. She caught him watching and turned to go. He whistled, the whistle the Plains folk used to draw a foal from its mother. She turned back, frowning, and led the horse back to the gate.

'I am Eachan, master of the Queen's horse,' he said.

'I know.'

He nodded, letting his eye slide to the horse.

'You breed horses.'

'My master breeds horses.'

'*You* breed horses,' Eachan reiterated, 'and I'll wager you can breed even better than what you have there.'

Jodis shook her head slightly.

'I'm looking for a horse: something special. Can you supply me?'

'Who's to ride it?' Jodis asked.

Eachan jerked his head toward the tower behind him. Jodis nodded.

'Then yes, I can supply. My master would be honoured.'

'Can you bring back your choosing at once?'

Jodis hesitated, then nodded briskly.

'An hour,' she said. Then smiling hesitantly, 'I am Jodis, of Storm Clan.'

Eachan bowed his head, letting his gratitude for her trust go unspoken.

Brede stumbled blindly up the stairs. Passing Ula without a word, she slipped into the side chamber and pulled the door shut. She pulled the blankets from the beds and then wondered what it was she planned – some vague thought of muffling the door, of creating some barrier against the world that had no sense to it. She laid them carefully back where they belonged, and listened to the faint movement from Grainne's chamber, the sound of voices, Grainne almost cheerful, Sorcha, half-singing, half continuing her conversation.

Brede turned her thoughts away from Sorcha, from Grainne, her mind full of confused images of running in darkness, of unknown children born into chains. Her hand strayed to her throat, and for the first time she fully appreciated how fortunate she was to be here of her own free will, without a length of chain about her neck. She shuddered, and the tremor would not leave her limbs. She watched the emotion quivering through her hands. She couldn't ignore the muscles screaming for movement, couldn't be biddable and still. Couldn't stay.

Chapter Twenty-One

Sorcha stroked Grainne's hair away from her face.

'You are sure you want to do this?'

Grainne smiled, happy, confident, and free of pain.

'Certain. It's time my people saw that I am not at the Gate. How better than to celebrate midsummer with them? When better to announce my intention of proposing peace talks than on the anniversary of my birth?'

'Well then, is the Queen ready to discuss the arrangements with her cousin? Phelan's waiting to see you. And you'll want to talk to Maeve, and to Tegan, perhaps?'

Grainne nodded.

'Phelan now, Maeve and Tegan in an hour. Send to let them know.'

Sorcha smiled, Grainne's sudden energy and enthusiasm were infectious. She went to the door, and called Cei to her. She glanced absently at the closed door of the side chamber, but had no time to investigate Brede's continued absence. Phelan was at the top of the stairs almost at once. He followed her back into Grainne's presence.

'Well, my Lord General,' Grainne asked eagerly, as soon as he was seated, 'who shall we send to Lorcan to talk peace?'

'Peace?' he asked, astonished. 'Why?'

'I do not want to be at war with my heir.'

Phelan hesitated before he responded.

'Are you giving up, cousin?'

'Giving up what?'

Phelan searched her face.

'You look better.'

Grainne laughed at his surprise.

'Giving up what, Phelan? Living? Do you think I am giving in because I acknowledge Lorcan as my heir?'

'Giving up all hope of a female heir.'

'I don't have a consort, I'm past child bearing age. Ailbhe is dead and Lorcan is almost into his majority. There's no point fighting anymore.'

'But we are winning. We should not be suing for peace, we should be dictating terms.'

'What terms? What could I want but that this war ends?'

'Do you want him here? After he cut off his own father's head? Do you value your own life so little? He won't wait, Grainne. Once he is within these walls, he'll have the crown off your head and the head off your shoulders in the same movement.'

'Phelan, don't be so dramatic.'

'I'm utterly serious. Your safety is my constant concern.'

Phelan's eyes flickered to Sorcha as he spoke.

'Where's the stable-hand?' he asked, noticing the absence.

'Are you still serious?' Grainne asked, a touch of edge to her voice. Phelan grinned. He reached to pick up her hand and kissed each knuckle thoughtfully.

'Totally, oh Queen of my heart. If it's peace you want, then peace you shall have. As to who should go, I think I might take that message myself, if that would suit you. I'd like to see his face when he hears that his great-aunt wants him to come home.'

'He's not an errant adolescent who has been out on the town for two nights running, Phelan. He's a boy with ambition.'

'Not a mutually exclusive concept. I remember when you used to keep us all up wondering where you were.'

'I never kept you up. You were only a child when I was going through my wild patch.'

'Your wild patch lasted longer than most. We overlapped on that for a while. Do you remember the time I broke a leg jumping from one roof to another?'

'I remember.'

'You egged me on, my glamorous young aunt. You had a stronger stomach and a more reckless nerve than I.'

'Glamorous?'

'I thought so. I worshipped you.'

'When did you stop?' Grainne asked, and her voice lost its breathy weariness and was vibrant with teasing.

Phelan roared with laughter.

'You know I never stopped. I got distracted, once or twice, but you were always the one for me.'

He sighed, and let Grainne have her hand back.

'You are planning to make this public I suppose?'

'On my birthday.'

'The anniversary of Aeron's death.' A twitch flickered below Phelan's left eye. He rubbed the spot absently. Grainne leant towards him, placing her own hand over his. He turned into her caress, and then pulled away abruptly.

'Things to be done, cousin. Thoughts to be acted upon. Only two days 'til midsummer. You want Lorcan told first, or no?'

'No. I need you with me at midsummer.'

'As you wish. I too, need your company then.'

Phelan stood.

'I will be back in two days, with your midsummer gift.' He quirked an eyebrow at her. Grainne smiled, letting him kiss her cheek. At the door he turned, a half wistful frown on his face. Then he shrugged and was gone.

Sorcha and Grainne exchanged glances.

'You jumped roofs with Phelan?'

'I was drunk.'

'And he needed medical attention, but you didn't.'

'Yes. I suppose I did lead him astray.'

'How old was he?'

'Oh, about nineteen. He was having a hard time adjusting to Aeron's becoming Queen. He'd lost his mother, and then he lost his closest friend when Aeron was crowned. Aeron had to start listening to advisors; she couldn't go climbing roofs anymore, so I went instead.'

'I'm intrigued. You never told me about these escapades.'

'You were Journeying.'

Sorcha laughed.

'Journeying? Hmmm. I suppose I must have been.'

Grainne pulled herself up from her chair, waving Sorcha's help away.

'I've two days to get used to feeling this well. I need to look as though I remember how to walk unaided.' She took a few steady steps, her back straight, head erect. 'Yes, I think I might manage that.'

'Don't forget you'll be wearing robes and the crown.'

'No, I don't forget.' Grainne reached the fireplace and leant against it. She rubbed at her forehead, thinking about the weight of the crown.

'Where is Brede? You'll need to give her some instruction for this. Find her. Maeve and Tegan will be a while yet.'

Sorcha did not find Brede. She did not find Guida. She stood in the darkness of the stables, uncertainty keeping her immobile for several minutes. She turned at the sound of footsteps. Eachan backed up at the sight of her.

'Ah.'

Sorcha looked at him. She couldn't bring herself to ask.

Eachan considered the tension in the way Sorcha held herself. He could smell wrongness, danger. Sorcha controlled her breathing carefully, feeling the danger within her as clearly as Eachan, and equally wary of it.

'Brede?' she asked at last.

'Grieving.' Eachan said, covering all she needed to know in one word. He took a cautious step forward and stared hard, trying to connect Brede to the stranger. Something to do with Grainne – and the black stallion.

Sorcha hid her face in the shadow, not knowing what to do.

'The river,' Eachan said, having forced his mind to the connections despite all Sorcha's undertow of persuasion otherwise. 'She'll be somewhere on the river, probably outside the walls this time, if they let her pass the gate.'

Sorcha winced at his poor choice of words. Eachan's steady single eye met her gaze, and she wondered if the choice was deliberate.

'There is another possibility. I warned her against revenge, but she may not have listened. If you think she'd know how to find the general called Madoc, you might want to start there.'

Sorcha nodded sharply. She walked the length of the stable to where Macsen was tethered. Eachan watched the horse's docility under her hand with a touch of envy. He watched her ride out of the yard with a mixture of relief at her going and anxiety for what she might find.

The river then, and a seeking spell, a calling. Sorcha had no time for niceties.

Brede felt Guida's stride falter. The horse checked her pace, complaining at Brede's swift jerk of heel, resisting her command. Fearing that the horse had sensed some danger that she couldn't see, Brede did not insist. She allowed Guida to set the pace, to slow to a puzzled halt. Guida swung her head to and fro, breathing in gusts of anger, ears back.

'What is the matter, you foolish creature?' Brede asked. Guida flicked an ear. Brede raised her head, scanning the buildings alongside the river, trying to see which of the high-walled yards – which *garth* – had been her sister's prison.

Guida refused to move on. Brede dismounted cautiously. She knew horses well enough to pay attention to Guida's resistance. She listened to the distant sounds of the city, a constant murmur of voices and carts and horses, and – something else. Brede turned her head, trying to separate the sound. Children at the river, making reed pipes; a stray dog barking after its own tail; someone singing. A gentle, hopeful, pleading song; but she had no sense of where the song came from – it seemed to invade her body.

Brede closed her eyes and listened, and felt the song stealing into her mind and her muscles – soothing.

She opened her eyes and looked up at Sorcha in silence.

Sorcha lilted her song to matching stillness.

'Don't use anger as a shield against grief, it doesn't work.'

'It helps me,' Brede said softly, 'but you're not the enemy.' Her eyes strayed to those high walls on the far side of the river.

Sorcha put herself between Brede and the sight of those walls.

'I've thought Falda dead for so long, that finding I was right was – a relief. But her daughter – that's new, and harsh, and I want –' Brede raised her hands. 'I want to make Madoc pay for turning one of mine into a chattel.'

Sorcha pulled Brede to her, hugging her tight. She could feel Brede's resistance, her unwillingness to admit vulnerability.

'You want to find the child.'

'And what if I'm too late? What if she is dead, or so cowed – ?'

'A child of your sister, cowed?'

Brede's eyes strayed back to Sorcha's face. The tremor of anger stilled.

'No. But Jodis is right, children make escape impossible.'

She shrugged out of Sorcha's embrace.

'Escape?' Sorcha asked, keeping her voice unconcerned.

'For Falda, for Jodis, for me, now.'

'Escape?' Sorcha asked again, feeling sick with alarm.

'Not from you,' Brede said, at last understanding Sorcha's anxious expression. 'Never from you.' She reached out, pulling Sorcha into her arms and a kiss that left them breathless. Sorcha pulled away, wide-eyed.

'You were thinking of leaving?'

'I thought of it, yes. Falda dead, I thought – go home. But the child – I have to find her – I must stay until –'

'So, if you find her, you'll go?'

Brede considered.

'I want to be away from here. I want the wind in my face. I want you with me, but –'

'But?'

Brede sighed.

'You were with Grainne, and I couldn't – I could not bear the feeling of stone about me for another second. Grainne always comes first with you.'

'No. For Grainne – Brede stop this. Don't make a balance between you and Grainne. I am Grainne's only for the rest of her life. After that, my life will be my own again, and I shan't make the mistake of choosing this kind of responsibility again.' Brede started in surprise. Sorcha raised her hands, half laughing. She pleaded, 'Stop now, this can wait for later.'

'There never is a later,' Brede observed, catching at Sorcha's hand, and kissing her palm. Sorcha shook her head.

'Eventually, there has to be.' She took a steadying breath and called Macsen to her.

Jodis waited at the gate, once more asking for Eachan of the Queen's horse, once more with a horse at her shoulder. The same young sentry set out to find Eachan, and Jodis paced the same short stretch of road waiting for him to return. This time Eachan brought her into the yard and silently considered the horse she had brought him.

'Will she do?' she asked.

'You know she will,' Eachan said softly, approaching the horse with an outstretched palm and an apple. The mare eyed him thoughtfully and huffed down the apple in a single bite.

'She's a little greedy,' Jodis said confidently.

Eachan laughed.

'She's beautiful, magnificent; she's entitled to her greed. Is she yours?'

Jodis shook her head swiftly.

'You asked for the best. Brede's sister bred this one.' She reached to wipe imagined dust from the mare's neck. Eachan sighed at her wilful refusal to look to her own good.

'Doran is willing to sell?' he asked.

'For the Queen, of course.'

Eachan paid the asked price without argument. As Jodis turned to go, he put a detaining hand on her arm.

'Thank you, Jodis of Storm, for the news you brought earlier today. I'm in your debt.'

Jodis shook her head, patting the money belt at her waist. Eachan shook his head in turn.

'That's nothing,' he said. 'Not my money, and not your profit; so if there is anything I can do for you, let me know it.'

Jodis smiled.

'It's good to have friends,' she said, making it a question.

Eachan nodded, and this time, he let her go.

Tegan couldn't concentrate on what Grainne was asking her. Her eyes kept drifting to Brede, trying to see what she was thinking. She didn't like the way Brede's hands constantly pleated the edge of her cloak. Tegan knew that trick of old. Brede would not meet her glance, did not appear to be taking any part in the discussion, not even listening. Every time Tegan looked in her direction, Brede was looking at Sorcha.

Maeve listened to Grainne, but her mind was on Tegan. Every time she looked in her direction, Tegan was looking at Brede.

Sorcha frowned, her eyes flickering from Tegan to Brede, to Grainne, to Maeve – confused, distracted.

Grainne sighed.

'Are any of you listening to me?' she asked.

Three pairs of eyes focused on her with abrupt guilt. Brede remained oblivious, forcing her mind to the precise feel of the cloth between her fingers, the bulk of three folds, four –

Maeve offered a summary of the conversation so far, and glared at Tegan.

'Good.' Grainne tapped her fingers thoughtfully on the arm of her chair.

'Go away,' she said abruptly. 'I'm sure you can all manage the necessary arrangements without any more interference from me.'

The eagerness with which they departed did not please her. She called Sorcha back.

'What is going on?' she asked.

'With Tegan and Maeve? I've no idea.'

'With Brede. Brede and you, Brede and Tegan: you are all – very –'

'Brede's sister is dead,' Sorcha interjected swiftly. 'She holds Tegan somewhat responsible, and Tegan likes her well enough to mind.'

'A sister? Why did I not know about this?'

'It wasn't relevant.'

'But it is more than relevant to you?'

'I'd like the time to be able to comfort Brede.'

'Does she want your comfort?'

'Yes.' Sorcha said very quietly. Jealousy burnt through Grainne. She shook her head.

'There is no time yet,' she said, shamed by her anger, her jealousy, but unwilling to resist it. 'I should have been told, Sorcha – family is always relevant.'

Tegan tried to catch Brede's eye. Brede refused to see. Maeve caught the longing in Tegan's seeking gaze and snarled under her breath, 'Can't you see she's not interested?'

Tegan turned on her.

'The sister's dead. Can't you find any understanding?'

Maeve considered carefully, first Brede's misery, then Tegan's anxiety.

'No.' she said at last, and set off down the stairs.

Sorcha lay beside Grainne, once more keeping her from the cold, and Brede waited, and waited, not able to sleep, not able to keep her mind from dwelling where she did not wish. Falda whispered into her brain, and Jodis' warning, and the unknown child somewhere in the city, wearing a chain about her neck. Brede kicked off the blankets in a sudden fury and paced about the chamber, then reckless and deeply frowning, hauled open the door, to prowl the outer chamber, her head tilted for sound from Grainne's bedchamber. Round and round she went, cat-footed, but fierce with anger and possessed of a darkness she hadn't known before, that she both feared and welcomed.

Sorcha listened to Brede's circuit of the outer room. She felt the air stir, and raised her head.

Brede stood in the doorway, one hand pressed against the wards. She was shadowy, light catching at the collar and sleeve of her shirt, a tangle of half braided hair across her shoulder.

Sorcha couldn't see her expression but as she turned her head, moonlight carved a momentary curve of chin, neck, shoulder and Sorcha drew in her breath and glanced quickly at Grainne. The Queen's eyes flickered. *Go? Don't go?* Sorcha couldn't tell; she glanced away and Brede was gone from the doorway.

Sorcha threw back the blankets and shrugged into Grainne's discarded mantle. Grainne made no murmur and Sorcha almost scurried to the door.

Brede stood with her back to Grainne's bedchamber, turning her head slowly from side to side, seeking out the breath of movement, the stirring she could sense but not place.

A soft, heavy cloth-on-wood sound, a slight coolness in the stifling heat. She slid her foot forward, there; she could feel a draught on her bared instep. A hanging swayed, the edge caressing the floor in soft movement.

And why should it? Cautiously she pulled the hanging back and found a door, a door with the key in the lock.

Sorcha's breath jolted in her chest. She had forgotten that door existed. Brede swung round, her hand still clenched in the cloth of the hanging.

'Where does this lead?' she asked softly.

'The roof.'

Brede turned the key: not stiff, as she had expected.

'Who has oiled this lock?'

The door opened inward and moonlight cascaded in. Brede blinked.

'I did, when I first got here, and thought I might be short of air once in a while.' Sorcha said softly. 'So short of air I've been, I forgot all about it.'

'Is it secure?'

'There is nothing up there but an empty chamber, and above that the roof to this tower. There is no way down to other parts of the building.'

'So it is unguarded?'

'Completely.'

Sorcha reached an arm about Brede, pulling her close, feeling skin heat through the shirt that was all she wore. Almost without thinking her hands curved and caressed and she bent her head, leaning her mouth to Brede's neck. Brede shivered and turned to meet the questing lips with her own, turned, to reach out, to hold and explore.

Silent, concentrated, Brede heard Grainne stirring in the next room. She pulled away slightly, taking firm hold of Sorcha's wrist and led her through the door, pulling it closed and locking it. Sorcha followed her up the short curving flight of stairs to the outer door, which stood open to the sky. Brede closed it behind them, wondering briefly why it was open. Sorcha once more enfolded her in her arms; hands sliding across the surface of shirt, catching in it, taking it with her fingers, sure swift movements and the hands were touching flesh. Brede pulled away suddenly.

'What are we doing?'

'Making love on the roof?'

Sorcha glanced about her. The roof sloped gently up to its ridge, a narrow walkway separating it from the defensive parapet inset with arrow slits.

There was only the one door, and Brede held the key.

Sorcha positioned herself cautiously, back to the stone tiles of the roof, one knee hitched up to keep balanced.

'I've never been anywhere so uncomfortable,' she said. 'There isn't room to stand or sit or lie.'

Brede stretched awkwardly beside her, and scanned the stars.

Sorcha turned and watched the rise and fall of Brede's chest, sharp fast breaths – the key still gripped tightly in her fist.

She reached and smoothed the half-unbraided hair and followed her fingertips with her mouth. Brede turned her head away. Sorcha tasted hot angry tears, she rolled closer, pressing her body against Brede, wrapping them both in the heavy folds of Grainne's mantle, licking the tears away, tracing the folds of her eyes, lashes, lids, brow, with the tip of her tongue. The rhythm of Brede's breathing changed, no longer harsh and contained, now ragged with open weeping. Sorcha moved her mouth to still the trembling, smother the sobs, catching Brede's lower lip between her teeth briefly. Brede sighed, a deep gust of released tension. Her hands tangled in Sorcha's, holding her still, the key hot metal between their joined palms. She returned the kisses with an urgency and tender seriousness that had Sorcha shamed.

'This isn't a game,' Brede said softly.

'No,' Sorcha agreed. 'I see that.'

'I want you,' Brede said, half amazed at how easy it was to say, 'but you are not free.'

Sorcha moved her head sharply, more protest than denial.

'You are not,' Brede repeated fiercely. 'And I do not know how to be how I feel – if I could take off my skin and wrap it about us both and be one with you, I still wouldn't be close enough, and I know you don't feel the same.'

Sorcha shook her head.

'My skin is wrapped around Grainne, but not – I am not free, but not the way you mean. If I could, I'd be with you, as close as you want, but not like this, not stealing kisses on the stairs, not fumbling like adolescent virgins. I want this to be –'

Sorcha stopped, shocked at the word forming in her mind.

'To be … ?' Brede asked.

'Permanent?' Sorcha whispered. Brede's breath had all but stilled. 'This is all I have to offer for now. If it is not enough, I will understand.'

Brede gripped the key tightly, and couldn't look at her.

'I quite enjoy the fumbling,' she said, but there was no strength behind her attempt at humour. She cleared her throat, 'But no, it isn't enough.'

'So I should let you alone to find someone with more to offer?'

'No.' Brede's denial came fast and anguished.

'What then?'

Brede shook her head, not knowing the answer.

'This is different. With Tegan, I knew how far it could go, how much she would allow me, how committed she was to Maeve; and whether I was prepared to settle for what I could get. I wasn't, so I did not begin. I kept silent, I knew she knew, but so long as I said nothing, did nothing, we were both safe. And she was a way out of the Marshes. It wasn't easy but it was possible. With you I feel like – like I started the second I lay eyes on you, there is no keeping silent, no holding myself separate, it's too late already.'

'What has started?' Sorcha asked, confused, and wanting to understand.

'Knowing, wanting – Goddess, Sorcha, can you really not know? I feel as though – I'm walking the edge of a precipice, following you – and you are dancing along it sure of your footing, and I'm stumbling, learning how to find my balance. I can't live like that.'

She pushed herself up from the tiles, wobbling as she found her balance and turned to the door. She sighed heavily.

'Grainne will have missed you by now.'

Sorcha watched her disappear into the darkness of the stairwell, and lay a few seconds more staring at the velvet glory of the night. Then she scrambled to her feet and followed.

Chapter Twenty-Two

Phelan placed his flask carefully on the table, and pulled off his gloves. He turned to Grainne and grinned.

'Are you ready?' he asked.

'As ready as I can be. You know this can never be an entirely happy anniversary for me.'

'Well, we'll drink to your health, congratulate you on the anniversary of your birth, *and* warm you against the rigours of a day under the eyes of the populace.'

He reached for the flask, breaking the wax seal, and looking about for cups. He raised a questioning eyebrow to Brede. Brede looked anxiously at Grainne,

'Lady? Should you drink?' she asked.

'Certainly. That flask comes direct from my next-kin's own cellar, and the seal has been broken in my presence.'

'Or is it that you think the Queen should go about her most difficult day sober?' Phelan asked. Brede smiled politely, and fetched two glasses from a cupboard. She stepped back, but Phelan shook his head.

'You pour it, since you are so concerned – make sure I have dropped nothing into my cousin's glass.'

Brede took up the flask and poured. The wine smelt wonderful.

'You choose the glass,' Phelan suggested, 'and hand it to – not going to taste it?' he asked as she passed the glass to Grainne.

Brede bit her lip. She glanced questioningly at Sorcha, who was immobile at Grainne's side, whispering a breath of song, and paying very little attention to Phelan. Brede turned to face him.

'Only if you don't.' she said, waiting for Grainne's admonition. Phelan shook his head as Grainne laughed. He lifted his glass and drained it in one mouthful.

'A waste of good wine to drink it like that, especially when it is the Queen's midsummer gift from her next-kin,' he observed, pouring another glass.

Grainne raised the glass to her lips, and took a careful sip. She sighed.

'You can't have much of this left, Phelan, even in your remarkable cellar.'

He shook his head and took a mouthful of the wine, letting it sit on his tongue, testing the fine balance of flavours. At last he swallowed, and replied.

'The best of the vintage from before the drought. That wine was bottled in the year of your birth. I have only two bottles left after this one. What will I have to tempt you with after they are gone?'

'Tempt me?'

Phelan put the glass down beside the flask. His eyes strayed to Brede, then Sorcha. Their presence was of no importance.

He went to Grainne and settled on his knees at her side. He took the glass from her hand and held the tips of her fingers between his palms.

Sorcha stilled her song.

'I am your majesty's loyal servant,' he began.

'Phelan, don't –' Grainne protested.

'I am my aunt's loving next-kin,' he continued, his smile fading, and the twitch beneath his eye once more evident. 'I am yours body and soul to do with as you please, and I beg your Majesty,' he hesitated, and looked up into Grainne's face; 'I beg Her Majesty to consider me her hand-mate and consort.'

Grainne pulled her hand gently from his grasp.

'No Phelan. You know it is impossible.'

'Ailbhe is dead. You said yourself only two days ago that you are beyond child-bearing. You are about to name Lorcan as your heir, what possible harm could there be now?'

Grainne shook her head.

'Every year,' she said wearily. 'Every year since Aeron died you have asked me this. Every year I have refused you. Why do you continue to torture yourself?'

Phelan shook his head and rose. He recovered his wine and passed Grainne hers.

'Drink,' he said, 'drink in memory of my sister the Queen, whose death changed everything. Drink in memory of who we might each have been. Drink in celebration of your birth, Grainne; and in celebration of your fifty-eighth year.'

Grainne drank, and Phelan watched, then tossed off the remains of his glass.

'Well, the festivities are about to commence. Will you permit me to escort you?'

He went to the small table beside Grainne and lifted the crown. He held it, frowning.

'A pretty thing, isn't it?' he said as he gently placed it upon her head.

Grainne reached up for his proffered hand and stood. As she did so, a wave of unexpected giddiness hit her. Her grip tightened, and Phelan's other hand took her weight; a sudden, protective reaction. Sorcha stepped forward. Grainne waved her away.

'You were wise to warn me of the weight of these ceremonial robes. I am well now. The general may escort me down the stairs.'

Sorcha waited until Phelan was a little distant then started up her murmur of song once more, slowing the notes and syllables until no-one, apart from Grainne, would hear anything but a meaningless hum.

Eachan had found a truly magnificent horse for Grainne. Brede approved his choice, and he saw the admiring and envious glance she shot the beast as he helped Grainne to mount. Brede found an excuse to stroke the animal's neck, fingers searching for the tattoo. Eachan saw the furtive movement, and nodded to her. She stepped away, glancing up at Grainne as the Queen gathered the reins together and smiled indulgently at Brede.

'Will she do?' she asked.

'Bred for a Queen,' Brede said softly. 'Jodis has been back then?' she asked Eachan.

'Doran was honoured to sell the best horse in his stable for the Queen's use. Your sister bred him.'

Brede mounted, unaccountably disappointed.

'Had he been one of Jodis' breeding, she might be nearer freedom,' she commented. Eachan sighed.

'I tried. Jodis chose him. I can't force the woman to see to her own.'

'I beg your pardon, Eachan.'

Eachan smiled. Brede laughed.

'I mean it.' She turned her horse and joined the group waiting at the gate.

The horses stirred eagerly at the murmur of an expectant crowd out in the streets. Guida's ears stretched forward in curiosity, the gates swung open, and the murmur swelled into excitement.

Brede was taken aback at the sheer size of the crowd, she had not realised so many people lived in the city. She glanced anxiously at the other riders in the procession, a quick survey of the horses, checking for any adverse reaction. No cause for concern there. Her eyes switched to the crowd. She scanned the faces, uncertain of what she was looking for. Guida settled into the pace, and Brede felt an odd sense of cohesion, as though the horses and riders were an entity, not a group of disparate individuals. It was a feeling that belonged on the plains; that belonged to the herd, to following the wind – not to this artificial, cautious control.

Eachan followed the procession on foot, pushing through the crowd with ease born of the authority in his movements, and the green cloth of his coat. Being no part of the honour guard, nor involved in the guarding of the tower, he felt at leisure, a feeling he did not entirely trust. So Eachan joined the

186

crowd, an onlooker, a listener to the timbre of the murmuring shifting populace of Grainne's city. And what he heard was surprise, and hope. He slowed his purposeful progress and listened more carefully, to be sure; and for the first time was aware of the laughter in the crowd – good-natured banter between neighbours, and sensed a release from tension about him. The crowd was telling him, *all will be well. So*, he thought, *Grainne was right to risk this.* Her presence was a reassurance, they could see for themselves that she was alive, even fit, after so long hidden by rumour and fear. He wondered how the mood would change when Grainne reached the square, and told her citizens what she proposed.

Still, hope was a balm to anxiety, and Eachan was almost happy, out in the sunlight and the cheerful buzzing of a crowd in holiday mood. And so, when he saw a horse he recognised on the edge of the crowd in the square he was pleased. The horse was tethered, its rider nowhere within view. Eachan glanced about, looking for the Plains woman with the tattoo. He shrugged, and worked his way to a raised walkway on the narrowest side of the crowd, that green coat silently finding him a place where he could see the spectacle over the heads of those nearer the action. He had been standing there a few minutes when he heard his name called from somewhere back in the crowd; he turned awkwardly in the crush and saw Jodis. He reached towards her, grabbing her reaching fingers, and pulled her through resisting bodies to stand crushed beside him; too close for comfort. They elbowed more room, Jodis laughing, Eachan with a foolish grin on his face. The edge of the stone paving crumbled under Jodis' foot and she slipped. Eachan steadied her. Jodis craned her neck to see whether her footing was safe, and crouched awkwardly, her back against the roof support, to pick up the loose stones.

'Here,' she said to Eachan handing him a small flint, 'a souvenir.' She pocketed a couple more flints and turned to face him, trying to stop their bodies actually touching.

'So,' Eachan said, 'what brings you out in this crush?'

'Not any desire to see the Queen,' Jodis murmured mockingly, 'my master is here, decked out in his finest, hoping to attract attention.' She pointed out Doran, in the second rank of military leaders about the offering circle. Eachan focused on the dark russet cloak, the same colour as Jodis was wearing. He watched Doran, wondering why it was not possible to tell by looking at the man what manner of torturer he was.

'I'm glad to have met you,' Jodis said happily. 'I've news.'

'For me?'

'For Ahern's daughter. Couldn't she be let out from the horses even today?'

Eachan focused carefully on Jodis' face, trying to divine any sense of irony.

'Brede does not look after the horses.'

Jodis frowned, puzzled, and then dismissed the thought.

'The daughter, Neala —'

'Yes?' Eachan asked urgently.

'I'm not definite, but there is a girl at West Gate Inn who could be her.'

Eachan took in a breath, and his concentration on Jodis' face became so intense that she couldn't ignore it. She shifted awkwardly in the crush, turning her face away to break his gaze.

'This really matters to you?'

Eachan sighed and rubbed the scar beneath his blind eye. He did not attempt to explain.

'Tell Doran, if he's a mind to sell, I'll buy any horse of your breeding. I'll buy all of them.'

Jodis stared at him, silently calculating.

'Would it be enough?' he asked.

Jodis sighed.

'It would help.'

Eachan nodded, and turned his eye away from her, giving her time to recover her composure. She pulled the concealing scarf from her neck, blotting tears, and laughed a little shakily.

'This wasn't the news I was expecting when I left the garth this morning.' Eachan glanced at the glistening metal about her neck, and away. The metal was smooth from constant wear, and the thick links were some kind of alloy of which the main component was gold. Jodis' hand covered the bond collar, then pushing the scarf into a pocket, she stood defiantly, the collar glinting slightly in the sun. She kept her eyes away from Eachan's face, staring determinedly at the square and the cluster of officials still hiding the Queen from the waiting crowd. Eachan followed her gaze, his eyes drawn to the horse she had chosen for the Queen.

'Brede approved your choice,' he said quietly. Jodis ducked her head slightly, hiding a smile. 'She also thought you should have offered one of your own.' Jodis lifted her dark eyes to regard him thoughtfully. 'I agree with her,' Eachan said, keeping his eye on Jodis' darting uncomfortable gaze, wanting suddenly to be somewhere quiet with her. Jodis ducked her head again and said nothing, awkward under his regard. Eachan smiled wryly and turned back to the square. Jodis reached and squeezed his hand, and the smile broadened.

At last Grainne stepped forward, flanked by her bodyguards. The trumpets sounded, but there was hardly any need, the crowd were ready to listen, ready to accept almost anything Grainne, their Queen, who was not after all dying, had to say.

Only Jodis, with new thoughts of freedom to distract her, had eyes for anything but the strong, straight body of the Queen. She gazed distractedly at the whole group beside the offering circle, her eyes dwelling particularly on Doran. He glanced around, as though aware of her gaze and their eyes met. Jodis looked away quickly, focusing nearer, and saw Brede. At first she was pleased, then where Brede stood hit her. She checked the rest of the group, sure she was mistaken, but no, there was no question; Brede stood at the side of the Queen, green-clad, her bodyguard.

The crowd was in uproar, but Jodis was oblivious. She stared in dismay at the woman beside the Queen, rapidly reviewing every word that she had said to Brede. Her fingers strayed to the tattoo on her temple, then the bare collar about her neck. She fumbled for the scarf in her pocket, and her hand closed over two pieces of flint.

Brede scanned the crowd, anxious to distinguish the tones of the response to Grainne's announcement. She couldn't honestly call the sound enthusiastic. She glanced at Sorcha, who smiled, a slow, warm, promising smile, distracting her for a moment. Grainne saw the look pass between them and frowned.

The missile struck the edge of the offering circle, sending splinters flying. Instinctively Brede threw herself flat and Grainne with her. There was blood in her eyes. She was aware of screaming somewhere, a tangle of limbs about her, Maeve's voice urgent but in control, issuing orders. The second missile hit her shoulder, numbing her arm. Brede rolled with the blow, frantic to get the blood out of her eyes and make sure Sorcha was safe. Her eyes clear momentarily, Brede stared down into Grainne's face, splattered with her blood, but alive, and then swiftly across to Sorcha, crouching over them, both arms spread protectively above Grainne's head. Sorcha's eyes grazed hers, and there was no smile this time. Brede glanced around; a wall of green coats blocked her view. She scrambled to her feet and pushed through the dense grouping of Maeve's mercenaries, knowing what was happening somewhere out in that crowd, something she must stop. She looked across the rapidly clearing square, knowing the direction that the second stone had come from. A tight knot of people among the dissipating crowd told her where to go. She dropped from the edge of the offering circle, and walked towards them as fast as her unsteadiness would allow.

The raised walkway was almost at waist height. Brede saw a limp arm in a torn russet sleeve trailing over the crumbling flint-faced edge. She pushed an onlooker out of the way, and caught a glimpse of dark hair, a glint of bond collar, no more than that. Eachan caught at her injured arm, and the pain forced her to turn away.

'I couldn't stop her,' Eachan said faintly. Brede cradled her arm against her chest and turned to look again.

'I couldn't stop them.' Eachan said harshly. Brede shrugged him off.

'Let me see,' she demanded. She was ignored. 'In the name of the Queen,' she said loudly, grateful for her green coat. A reluctant shifting. Brede leant her injured arm on the walkway and turned the face of the dead woman towards her. She could barely make out the tattoo in what was left of Jodis' features. She looked at the people about her.

'Did any of you see what happened?' she demanded.

A man stepped forward: well dressed, his gold-edged cloak the same colour as that torn sleeve. He was vaguely familiar. Brede frowned.

'This is my bondswoman. As soon as I realised she was responsible I dealt with her.' Brede blinked, trying to work out how much time had passed; it seemed only seconds.

'And you are?' she asked, choosing not to admit that she knew his name.

'Doran.'

'The archer.' Brede said. Doran inclined his head. 'And this was your – *storm*-mare.'

Brede pushed away from the support of the walkway, shaking her head. She saw a length of cloth at the foot of the walkway, she scooped it up, and saw the simple outline of a running horse painted onto it, barely more than waving lines unless you knew how to look. Brede knew how to look. She wrapped the cloth about her hand, pulling the fine fabric between and about her fingers.

'Eachan will take care of the body,' she said. She glanced about her, recognising more faces now. Killan, and Ula – furtively wiping blood from her hand. She turned to find Corla at her side. She glanced at Corla's hands: finding them unsullied, she gestured at Jodis' body.

'Will you help Eachan?' she asked. Corla nodded and began to force people out of her way.

Brede turned back to the offering circle, absently dabbing blood from her forehead. She knelt at Grainne's feet.

Grainne looked at her silently then took a tight breath.

'I suppose it is too much to hope that the culprit has survived.' She turned to Sorcha: 'Get me away from here.'

By the time Brede had gained her feet the Queen was gone. She stared at the questioning faces of Maeve, Tegan, and even Phelan, expecting some sense from her.

'A Plains woman,' she said at last, aware that Tegan and Maeve at least would make something of that. 'A makeshift sling and a couple of flints from the walkway. Doran's bondswoman.'

Phelan nodded, satisfied. He turned his horse and headed back to the tower. Brede looked furtively at Maeve, then Tegan.

'What now?' she asked.

Tegan sighed.

'Back to the barracks. Grainne will want some explanations.'

'She won't get many.' Brede said shortly. The feeling was beginning to come back into her arm, and with it, a certainty that Grainne was not the target of those chips of flint. Tegan had to help her onto Guida's back.

Grainne pulled away from Sorcha's protective touch the second she was within the chamber.

'That shouldn't have happened,' she said fiercely as she struggled with the fastenings of her ceremonial robes. Sorcha caught the falling cloak, and flung it over the back of Grainne's chair. Grainne strode to the window, flinging the shutters wide, anger and fright keeping her moving, restless, impatient.

'Where's Brede?' she asked irritably, but as she spoke there were steps on the stair and voices at the outer door. Sorcha opened the inner door, but it wasn't Brede, it was Phelan.

'Are you hurt?' he asked immediately, his eyes scanning Grainne's white, drawn face.

'No,' she reassured him immediately.

'There's blood on your face.'

Grainne nodded.

'It isn't mine.'

Phelan relaxed.

'Sit down cousin, before you fall down.' He took up the bottle of wine and poured two glasses.

Grainne's hand shook as she clutched the glass. She raised the glass to Phelan, allowing him to see that weakness.

'I will confess that I did not expect this. I did not think my citizens enjoyed war so well that they would react brutally to the suggestion that it end.'

'Not one of your citizens. A slave. One of Doran's.'

'Are you suggesting he was the target?'

Phelan laughed, pleased that Grainne could make light of the incident.

'I've asked him to join us, perhaps we'll find out. It is possible that he thought so, as he was amongst those to see to it she threw no more stones.'

'Was he?' Grainne said angrily.

More voices at the door. Doran and Brede arrived together. Brede allowed him precedence through the door, glad to let him mask her entrance a little. She slipped into her accustomed position and kept silent.

'Your bondservant, Doran?' Grainne asked.

'My lady, I have no idea what could cause her to commit such an act.'

'But you killed her all the same.'

'It was my duty as your loyal subject.'

'Quite.' Grainne's angry eyes strayed to Brede.

'Did anyone see what actually happened?'

Doran stayed silent. Brede made an effort.

'Eachan was beside her.'

Grainne considered Brede's bloody face and clothing.

'Sit down before you fall down,' she said echoing Phelan's words to her, but not his tone. Brede lowered herself carefully onto a low-backed chair, trying to hide the lack of strength in her left arm.

'Her name was Jodis. Daughter of Ute of Storm Clan,' Brede said dully.

'That explains the choice of weapon,' Phelan commented. Doran said nothing, but began to take more notice of Brede, divining her accent, and her knowledge of his bondswoman's bloodline.

'It seems an impetuous action,' Brede continued. 'The sling was her scarf, the stone from the facing of the walkway.'

'Even so, we can't assume she was working alone,' Phelan said firmly. 'Had she family or friends in the city?'

Brede had a sudden vision of Jodis' children being tracked down and killed to satisfy Phelan's lust for punishment.

'She was there at the instruction of her master,' Brede said swiftly and with a touch of malice. Doran met her eyes.

'Your stable-hand knows more of this woman than I do after six years in my service. Is that not strange?'

Phelan snorted.

'She knows what Eachan knows. Eachan bought a horse from you only yesterday. Jodis handled the sale. Unless you go out of your way to get to know your bondservants, Doran, I would place no reliance on that kind of comparison.'

Grainne gestured impatiently at Doran.

'You can go.'

He looked startled and relieved. He made a bow and left.

Grainne observed Brede.

'You'd best talk to Eachan more, but go and soak your bruises first. Let Tegan's healer have a look at that cut, I don't want any more of your blood on me.'

Brede struggled to her feet and bowed, unable to disguise the limpness of her arm this time. Grainne frowned, catching Sorcha's anxious gaze on Brede. She turned back to Phelan.

'I think this will turn out to be nothing,' she said firmly.

'You still want me to go to Lorcan?'

'Definitely.'

'Very well. I will leave as soon as I can be ready. Two hours perhaps?'

'Good. Thank you, Phelan.'

Phelan shook his head.

'A strange birthday. Shall we announce that you are persuaded the woman was alone and crazy? The midsummer festival will be out of sorts, else.'

Grainne laughed.

'You think of that now?'

'Popular support is fickle, my dear. If the traders suffer from the uncertainty of an unresolved attack on the Queen, much of today's good work will be undone.'

Grainne nodded.

'Would you arrange that before you go?' she asked contritely.

Phelan bowed.

'Your command is my heart's wish. I'd better get on with it – unless you have reconsidered your answer of this morning?'

'My answer?'

'Your hand?'

Grainne frowned.

'Go away, Phelan, I am weary of your jests.'

He swept another bow, deeper than the last and went.

'He didn't kiss me,' Grainne observed.

'You do have blood all over your face.'

Grainne nodded, accepting this explanation. Suddenly she seemed to collapse in on herself.

'Goddess, I've had enough. I can do no more today.'

Sorcha glanced into the bedchamber, with an anxious frown on her face.

'There are hardly any herbs left, how much have you been taking?'

'I have taken more, when I didn't want to wake you.'

'You should have told me. There aren't enough there to get you through the night. I can't leave you to get more until Brede is back. I shall have to stay with you, unless you can manage?'

Grainne shook her head. She reached up and removed the crown, placing it gently beside her.

'I can't, my mind is too full of other things. I'm sorry to burden you.'

'It is not a burden,' Sorcha said quickly.

Grainne caught her eye and said nothing. She rubbed at the dried blood on her face.

'Help me up, Sorcha, I can't stand.'

Brede went first to find Corla, but found Tegan.

Brede cleared her throat, warily.

'I was looking for Corla. I need her to look at this cut.'

'The witch too busy to bother with you?' Tegan asked, then cursed and interrupted Brede's reply. 'No. I'm sorry. Corla is laying out the Plains woman.'

'Where?' Brede asked.

'Leave that for later.' Tegan inspected Brede thoughtfully. Brede tried to straighten her shoulders and sighed.

'Can you help me?' she asked. 'I can't get out of the mail.'

Tegan stepped close enough for Brede to feel her breath.

'I am sorry about your sister,' she said at last, taking the weight of the mail while Brede snaked out of it.

'Thank you.' Brede shook her hair loose, caught up the mail in her good hand and went out into the yard, heading for the bathhouse. Tegan was relieved that she did not walk into Maeve, who, happily oblivious to Brede's progress, was caught up in deep conversation with Killan by the gate.

And what is he doing here? Tegan wondered, heading over to join and break up the huddle of gossip at the sentry post.

Brede did not have to struggle with the tubs, several willing hands found hot water, and helped her out of her clothes. Eager for rumour, Brede's audience listened to anything she was willing to say about the morning's events. They were disappointed with her terse comments, and eventually Brede sank below the surface of the water to escape their questions, but the water started the scalp wound bleeding again, and Riordan went to find Corla, declaring that she would bleed to death else.

Corla inspected the cut without touching it, calling Riordan to get fresh hot water. She washed her hands while Brede waited docile, blood pouring down her face and curling into the cooling bath.

Corla probed the wound gently.

'It's a flesh wound, there isn't even much bruising. If you'd only let it clot you'll be fine. Hot water wasn't the most sensible thing to do.'

'That was for my shoulder.'

Corla glanced down, observing the bruise seeping up through the skin.

'Can you move it at all?'

'Now, yes.'

'You'll live,' Corla said. 'I'll find some salve to speed up the healing.' She slid off the side of the tub and crouched down so that she was level with Brede's ear.

'Eachan would be glad of your company,' she said softly, then she was gone.

Brede eased out of the tub, and dried herself quickly, rejecting Riordan's joking offer of help. She dragged her clothes on somehow and trailed her mail shirt after her round to the stables.

She found Eachan sitting beside Jodis' body in an unused stall. He did not stir as she entered. She flinched at Jodis' ruined face.

'What happened to the collar?' she asked at last.

'Doran – removed it. It amused him to have his servants wear collars that reflected their worth to him. Jodis was worth quite a bit.'

Brede nodded, and gently tied Jodis' scarf about her neck, hiding the gouge where the careless smith had struck the collar from her lifeless neck.

'The stones were meant for me,' Brede said, sitting beside Eachan.

'Yes, I think you could be right.'

'Why?'

'She didn't realise what you were until you were standing there, being bodyguard. I suppose, to her that was shocking.'

Eachan turned his head slightly, but Brede was on his blind side, he couldn't see her expression.

'I can't be sure,' Eachan said. 'She said something to me that makes me think that's so – she said something else too –'

'What?'

'No. I must check first. If I'm right, I will tell you.'

Brede reached out to trace the tattoo on Jodis' temple.

'The children?' she asked suddenly.

'I don't know. I don't know how many, I don't know how old. I don't know where. Did she say anything more to you?'

Brede shook her head, regretted it as her vision swam.

'Doran said he'd had her six years. They must all be infants. Where –'

Eachan raised a hand in caution.

'It would not be wise to draw attention to them just now. You couldn't afford them, Brede, nor could I.'

Brede withdrew a little; surprised at the rough anger of Eachan's voice, and the way he anticipated and answered her unspoken questions.

'Why should you?' she asked.

'I've known Jodis for under three days, but I think I owe that woman something. I'm not sure yet. You know, when she called to me this morning, I thought – only this morning? I thought –' Eachan covered his face suddenly. 'Foolishness I expect. I'm turning into a foolish old man.'

'Not old.'

'Not foolish?'

'No, not foolish either.'

'What if it was all planned? What if she was fooling us both? What if she came here trying to find a way in?'

'What she told us was the truth – wasn't it?' Brede was suddenly assailed by doubts.

'Yes, she told you the truth, I'm sure of that. What I'm not sure of is why.'

Brede stayed silent for a long time. Eachan at last turned his head fully to look at her.

She would not meet his gaze.

'This could have been my sister,' she said quietly, gesturing at Jodis' broken body. 'It could have been me; it could have been any one of Wing Clan. But it was Jodis, and it was Jodis because she tried to help me, and because I didn't trust her. I didn't tell her everything, even when she asked.'

Chapter Twenty-Three

Brede returned to Grainne's chambers to find Riordan on guard, and silence and darkness within. She slipped quietly through the main room to the door of Grainne's bedchamber. It stood open, and she saw two recumbent forms on the bed, Grainne held close within Sorcha's naked arms. Brede stood motionless for several minutes, and then moved an experimental hand across the threshold. She met gentle resistance. Wards. She turned away, seeking her own bed, desperate to put the distance of sleep between herself and the morning's events.

Sleep, and dreams of Falda's hand-fasting, a quiet affair: their mother's Marshland birth had meant that Falda and Carolan must ask permission of the Clan.

Brede smarted at her sister's humiliation, bristling at her side during the protracted deliberations, but Falda put her arms about her, laughing,

'No one is going to say no, it's just a game.'

And no one had said no, because Falda, for all her mixed blood, was Wing Clan to her core. Brede dreamt the dancing, Falda and Carolan skipping joyfully about ,yelling promises to each other, and then Brede dreamt Falda, eight months pregnant, staggering as a horse barrelled into her in the darkness and confusion of the last gather, and then Falda surrounded by dozens of children, Falda lying in the straw of a horse stall, her face ruined and a bloody gash in her neck.

Brede woke to the soft touch of Sorcha's lips against her eyelids. She stirred, confused, as Sorcha's lips caressed upward to the wound in her scalp. She heard the faint hum of Sorcha's song purring into her throat, and the wound tingled under Sorcha's mouth, shaping words against her skin, healing the torn flesh. The stirring spread through her body, waking, warming, exciting. Brede lifted her head slightly, lips against Sorcha's throat, feeling the vibration there. Sorcha sighed and the humming faltered. Sorcha lowered her head slowly, so that she could see Brede's face.

'I'm running low on herbs,' she whispered. Brede stopped her with a kiss. Sorcha twisted away laughing and reached for Brede's injured shoulder. The humming resumed, a little louder, the words a shade more distinct. A sudden surge of feeling in the torn nerves, and Brede's newly mobile hand caught at Sorcha's shirt front, winding fingers into cloth, pulling Sorcha close once more. Sorcha's hand slipped from shoulder to breast, and Brede's found places to kiss that had Sorcha giggling.

'I have to get more herbs,' she whispered. Brede let the cloth between her fingers slip a little.

'I thought you didn't need them anymore?'

Sorcha sighed.

'I can't be awake all day and night. It takes drugs to keep her out of pain when I'm not there and – she's been lying to me about how much she's using.'

Brede reached to stroke Sorcha's face, aware that she was close to tears.

'I'll take care of her, go and get whatever it is you need.'

'I won't be long,' Sorcha promised, and before Brede could acknowledge her words she vanished, as abruptly as a snuffed candle. Brede's reaching fingers refused to acknowledge the absence of her warm skin. She scrambled for her sword, and held the hilt tight between both hands, trying for something of which she was certain. She sat staring at the space where Sorcha had been, and then she shook herself, pulled on clothes, and walked swiftly into the main chamber, checking the doors, the windows, even the fireplace, with a thoroughness she knew to be unwarranted.

Grainne stirred from sleep, and moaned.

Brede started at the sound and went to the bedchamber door. Grainne's eyes opened, and Brede straightened to attention.

'Is that you, Ahern's daughter? Come talk to me.'

Brede pulled a stool through from the outer room and perched beside Grainne with the sword across her knees.

Grainne forced herself into a half-sitting position so that she could see Brede's face. Her eyes grazed the sword, and a half smile twisted her lip.

'You don't trust me, do you?'

'Madam?'

'It is hard to be close to Sorcha and not be with her.'

Brede sighed, and dropped her eyes to the blade across her knees. The silence dragged and she realised that Grainne expected her to speak.

'Sometimes I wish she wasn't here at all.'

Grainne nodded.

'Sorcha has a tendency to flirtation; I've seen her making eyes at you across the back of my visitors.' Brede kept her eyes down, hot to the roots of her hair. 'It is not kind,' Grainne observed, 'to you, to Sorcha or to me.'

'What do you want of me?' Brede asked, goaded into risking a glance at Grainne's face.

'You're deaf and blind to everything but Sorcha. You watch her every move; you contrive to touch her at any opportunity.' Brede sat stiffly silent.

'I trust you with my life, Brede.' Brede turned the sword over, restless under Grainne's scrutiny.

'You are still alive,' she said at last.

'But the Plains woman is not. I told you that I want anyone who raises their hand against me alive.'

'Is this because I am a Plains woman? Do you think I am implicated?'

'No. I think perhaps Doran – she was his servant, and he was amongst those who brought her down.'

Brede hesitated, wondering whether to tell Grainne the little she knew of Jodis.

'I could not protect you and her.'

Grainne laughed.

'You were not protecting me, Brede, your first thought was for Sorcha, I saw you. It was only chance you brought me down. Where would you have been if you'd been forced to choose between us?'

'That isn't so,' Brede protested softly, ignoring the accusation, her mind full of the broken body on the walkway. 'If I could have reached her, I'd have protected Jodis.'

'You knew her?'

'We'd met.'

'And did she know what your duties here were?'

'No.'

'And did she ever come within these walls?'

'Not for me, but she sold Eachan the horse you rode this morning, she may have come in then.'

Grainne stared thoughtfully at Brede's down-turned face.

A footstep in the outer room. Brede was at the door in a moment.

Sorcha stepped back from the sword, a song half sung. Brede lowered the sword, and stepped back. Sorcha watched the blade-tip touch the floor. She gathered up the herbs she had dropped, without speaking. Brede's hand tangled with hers, silent reassurance. Sorcha returned the quiet embrace of fingers, almost furtive. She was suddenly aware of Grainne's eyes upon her. She turned to face her; one hand still caught in Brede's.

'This is not for you,' Sorcha said sharply.

Grainne's eyes widened in surprise and she jerked her head at Brede, dismissing her.

Grainne waited for Sorcha to come close enough and caught at her shaking hand.

'That was careless.'

Sorcha shook her head.

'Brede was closer to death than I; doubly careless. I didn't expect her to be in here with you. How did she come through the wards?'

'I invited her.'

'What were you talking about?'

'The Plains woman. Trust. You.'

Sorcha shook her head again, the tremor in her hands gone. She mixed the new herbs in the proper proportions. She handed Grainne the drugged wine.

'Drink,' she said gently. Grainne took a steady swallow, watching Sorcha over the rim of the cup. Sorcha kissed Grainne on the brow, so close that no more than breath was required, certain that Brede would not overhear.

'Stop interfering, Grainne, it is hard enough already.'

Grainne grabbed at Sorcha's hand, preventing her from moving away with an unexpected strength.

'For my sake, Sorcha, bed her and have done. You are putting my life at risk with this. You can't concentrate.'

Sorcha forced her wrist out of Grainne's grip.

'You have no right,' she said sharply. 'You have no claim on me that gives you the right to speak to me like this.' Rage took her across the room without even thinking where she was going.

Sorcha shut the door from Grainne's chamber firmly, and leant against the solidity of the wood. Brede glanced up to see her setting wards.

'What are you doing that for?' she asked.

Sorcha shook her head.

'Giving in to my temper,' she said, pulling the binding from her hair and shaking it loose.

'Grainne has made you angry?'

Sorcha nodded. Brede breathed deeply, filling her lungs with the scent of herbs. 'How is it possible?' Brede asked softly. 'Is this friendship of thirty years at risk?'

Sorcha laughed.

'I wouldn't go that far. It is only that I am –'

'Tired, hungry, lonely, burdened, frightened..?'

Sorcha raised an eyebrow; half tempted to argue with Brede too.

'Yes; but more than all of those. I am failing Grainne, and failing you.'

'Grainne said that, but it was me she was blaming. I don't know how to be the person she thinks I should be. She set me to guard, but she expects more; she thinks I'll discover her enemy, but I've no idea how.'

'She can't expect –'

'If I were to solve this riddle for Grainne – I think – perhaps – I hope – you will stop looking haunted, perhaps you'll stop look at the world askance –

maybe you will look straight at me; maybe Grainne will release us.'

'Do I not look straight at you?'

'No. Everything you do is warped by worrying about Grainne – but Grainne sees you look askance because you are thinking about me. And she is right, Sorcha – I think the same – I *do* the same. I can hardly think of anything but the glorious smell of your hair.'

'Brede –'

'My preferred suspect is Madoc, but he wasn't here and I can see no cause although Jodis was bonded to Doran, who is Madoc's man – I think Jodis' stones were meant for me, but Grainne's paranoia is catching. I'm suspicious of everyone, even you. Bewitched, so I am. Tegan tried to tell me, and I didn't believe her, but how can I ignore Grainne, who has known you thirty years, and knows why you do not look that age, who *knows* you can disappear into thin air?' Brede let go of Sorcha's hand and stepped away. 'You scare me,' she said abruptly.'What do you want of me? You can't need me; I'm useless to Grainne, and to you. You have isolated me,' Brede took a shaky breath, incapable of finishing that thought, burdened as it was with so much. 'But for what purpose?'

Faint voices on the stairs prevented Sorcha from any answer. She turned swiftly and went in to Grainne. Brede bit down on her uneasiness and went out to the stairs, and found Tegan.

'How is Grainne?' Tegan asked.

'Looking for someone to blame.'

Tegan frowned. 'I'll need to see her later, there's something I must check first – but I've a message for you, from Eachan. He says you might find something of interest at West Gate Inn. Does that make sense to you?'

'Not necessarily.' Brede frowned, trying to fathom Eachan.

'Why did Grainne choose you?' Tegan asked. 'Why didn't she ask me?'

'She did ask you, Tegan. She said that she wanted the use of your eyes, remember? She wanted you out there looking.'

'That's true, but she's not listening to what I see.' Tegan held Brede's gaze for a while. 'You've been avoiding us these last months. We are of the same household; we have the same employer. We need to talk more.' She hesitated. 'We are still friends?'

Brede clasped Tegan to her, in an easy, light grip. 'Don't be such an idiot,' she said softly. 'I'm long past doubting you.'

Tegan gazed into her eyes, and rested a hand against Brede's face.

'And Eachan says you have issue to take with Madoc.'

'I have.'

'Have a care. That one was always trouble.'

'I'll remember that.' Brede said dryly. The door opened softly behind her and Tegan glanced across catching sight of Sorcha.

'I must go,' Tegan said, and kissed Brede lightly on the mouth, then pulled away, and took the stairs two at a time.

'What was that?' Sorcha asked.

'I'm not sure,' Brede admitted. She reached for Sorcha, pulling her into her arms, seeking reassurance, holding her far closer and with greater urgency than she had held Tegan.

'Well,' said Sorcha, 'you lose no time, one lover kissed and another embraced, in the time it takes to spit.'

'But are you my lover?'

'I hope so,' Sorcha answered. 'Is Tegan?'

'No,' Brede said, dismissing that almost closeness from her mind. 'Whereas,' she said, holding Sorcha even tighter, 'I have reason to make plans, where you're concerned.'

'As do I. Grainne has – suggested – we take some leave.'

'Now?' Brede asked, perturbed.

'Immediately. She wants to be undisturbed by us.'

'Are you happy with that?'

'How can I be? It is insanity. But she is the Queen.'

'And what shall we do with this unwanted freedom?' Brede asked.

Sorcha blinked. 'There is a festival on. We could dance? We could – we could sing, get drunk – spend some of our wages –'

'Can you think of nothing better than that?'

'I'd be glad to take Macsen out.'

Brede frowned, not sure that she was being teased.

'I'll go see about his gear, then, shall I?' she asked, starting for the stairs.

Sorcha allowed her a few steps before calling after her, 'I'll meet you in the stables.'

Brede stopped, and looked back at her.

'I must make sure Grainne is as well as she can be. I shouldn't leave her, whatever she says, but if she insists, I can't enjoy myself if I'm worrying about her.' Ask Eachan if he knows any inns with comfortable beds.'

'Why should I do that?' Brede asked, irritably.

'I thought you'd want a comfortable bed, if we're to be in it for as long as I plan,' Sorcha whispered.

Brede watched her go, her words settling into her mind, blanketing, smoothing, and disguising the uncertain ground beneath.

Chapter Twenty-Four

Brede had both horses saddled by the time Sorcha appeared at her shoulder. She smiled, unnerved by the promise of uninterrupted time together. Sorcha's answering smile smouldered, and Brede found a sudden urgent interest in a buckle on Guida's bridle.

Sorcha grabbed a handful of Macsen's mane, and hauled herself onto his back.

'Are you coming with me, or are you going to admire the grease on the tack all day?' she asked. Brede pulled Guida about and led her into the yard where she could mount without hitting her head.

'Where to?' she asked.

'Away,' Sorcha said abruptly.

Brede persuaded Guida close to Macsen and touched Sorcha's forearm, intending comfort. Sorcha glanced down and frowned.

'What?' Brede asked indignantly.

'Gloves,' Sorcha said accusingly, and then her eyes travelling along Brede's arm and upward, 'sword, knives, mail.'

Brede removed her hand from Sorcha's arm, pulling the leather glove from her hand with her teeth. She tapped Sorcha's arm with her fingernail, producing a faint ringing.

'Not exactly silk-clad yourself,' she observed, throwing the glove across the courtyard, 'Come on, I thought you wanted to exercise your horse.'

It was strange for the streets to be so full of people, laughing and spending such money as they had. This kind of celebration was all too rare. And now it was as though the very thought of war and of the attempt on Grainne's life had been excised from the minds of the revellers. Out beyond the stone walls of the tower, the rest of the city had forgotten fear, and was full of light-heartedness. It felt dangerous.

There were children in the streets, a beggar playing pipes by the fountain. So normal, so carefree – no one paid attention to the mail-clad riders. Brede wondered if they remembered the army out beyond the walls; whether they knew they weren't safe and cherished this unexpected happiness, as she cherished it. She wanted to lose herself in the colourful noisy throng, to be with Sorcha in an easy companionship, but the thought of Jodis kept her unwelcome company.

Forcing her hand away from the hilt of her knife, Brede tried to glance about her in a casual fashion. If everyone else could be at ease, wrapped in their own concerns, so could she.

They reached the market place, where the crowds made it harder to be together, impossible to force a way through, even on horseback, for this was a place for brisk sallies between one stall and another, not a head-down dash across the square.

On her way out to the walls, with half a mind to go beyond, Tegan walked into Eachan and had to put out a hand to steady him. It wasn't until he thanked her that she realised how out of character it was for him to be unsteady, and more so for him to be grateful for assistance.

'What's wrong?' she asked.

'Have you seen Brede?' he asked.

'Yes,' Tegan said, 'she's up with Grainne as usual.'

'No, no she isn't.' Eachan swore, tucking a glove into his belt in an absent-minded fashion.

'What is it?' Tegan asked.

'Trouble,' Eachan responded. 'Madoc is back. I want her to stay away from him. And if you gave her my message she's off in search of the daughter.'

'West Gate?' Tegan asked. Eachan nodded.

'But she's taken her horse,' he observed. 'She wouldn't do that, would she, if she was only going there?'

Tegan was motionless, doubt assailing her.

'Well if Madoc is here, and she's gone, there's no danger of Brede crossing swords with him,' Tegan said carefully, wondering why Madoc was back, and beginning to make connections.

'That is something to be grateful for,' Eachan agreed, with more of his usual assertiveness, 'Madoc would cut her to ribbons.' Tegan walked on, but stopped again, not catching what he said next.

'What?' she asked, sensing its importance.

'If it is the girl –'

Tegan nodded, finishing his sentence for him.

'She'll go looking for him.'

Out of the crowds at last, Brede put Grainne from her mind, and got her foot into the stirrup. Hauling herself into the saddle, she glanced at Sorcha.

'You're frowning,' she said.

Sorcha raised her chin, and continued to frown. Brede turned Guida awkwardly, and bringing her round close to Macsen's side, she reached over, pulling Sorcha's plait. Sorcha turned her head, so that her cheek lay against Brede's ungloved hand.

'Where are we going?' she asked.

'We can't go outside the walls, but I've found the river a good place to exercise the horses.' Sorcha nodded. She wasn't likely to forget that. Brede lifted her chin slightly, part defiance, part mischief. 'Then we're going to an inn, remember?'

'Which inn?'

'West Gate.'

Sorcha gave Brede a considering look.

'Comfortable beds?'

'I didn't ask,' Brede said archly, and gave Guida a sharp kick, which set her off at a reasonable pace towards the river.

Brede was grateful for the wind in her face, and the certain strength of Guida's muscles, putting more and more space between herself and the claustrophobia of Grainne's chambers. She allowed Guida to choose the pace, and thought of nothing.

Sorcha watched Brede riding ahead of her with wistful jealousy. No matter how much she sang to Macsen, he would never be half the horse Guida was, nor would she ever have a tenth of Brede's skill. However, she was prepared to try. She kicked Macsen lightly, encouraging him to greater speed. He surged after Guida, and, briefly, Sorcha understood Brede's insistence that horses shaped her life, and that she could never be complete without them.

With that thought in her mind, Sorcha came level with Brede, and called out to her. As the horses slowed to a walk, Brede reached out, snatching at Macsen's rein, pulling him close, so that he walked shoulder to shoulder with Guida for a few steps, then idled to a halt, content to nuzzle thoughtfully at Guida's head strap. Brede twisted about, gathering Sorcha into her arms, awkward, passionate.

Guida stepped away from Macsen; unhappy at being close to a beast she knew to be vicious, and forced them apart.

'What is it you are so afraid of?' Sorcha asked, nudging Macsen close again.

'Being wrong.'

'Wrong?'

'You don't say much. You keep secrets, perhaps one of those secrets is that you don't really want to be here.'

'Dear Goddess, what gave you that idea?'

'Silence, mostly.'

'Were you not listening up on the roof, Brede? I was listening to you. I want to be here. No, that isn't quite true – I want to be with you, I want to be out of this mail, in a bed, with you.' Sorcha glanced at Brede's face and laughed. 'Right now,' she said firmly, and walked Macsen close again so that she could reach out and touch Brede's arm. 'Right now.'

Brede ducked her head as she passed under the lintel of the stable. Guida protested softly at being brought back inside so soon, objecting to being brought through the crowds to no better purpose than this, a strange stable.

A child scrambled to her feet, reaching out an impatient hand for the reins, and Guida chose to complain at this too. Brede scolded her impatiently. The horse flicked an irritable ear, but restrained her awkward movements. The child's hand dropped and she stared at Brede, taking in the sword and mail, the lack of saddlebags, the apparent lack of bond-collar. She could see the horse hadn't come far, and was suspicious. She also recognised the words the warrior had used to her steed. Brede's eyes met hers, as she dismounted and handed over the reins, almost questioning, but as swiftly dismissing.

'You'll be careful of the other,' Brede said,. 'He's difficult.'

The child nodded, recognising the accent, not listening to the words. As soon as she got a good look at Macsen, she grinned; the meaning behind the voice becoming clear. She nodded again.

'I'll mind,' she answered, accepting the coppers Brede held out.

Sorcha gripped Brede's hand. She was so used to the weight of keeping Grainne free of pain that she had almost forgotten what it was to not be holding her up. She hadn't been as free as this since the horse market – since she first heard Brede's voice. She considered her companion: what was it about her voice?

The Innkeeper was not unduly interested in them. Festivals often brought strangers in search of a room for an hour or two, to sleep off a hangover, to strike a deal in private, more often a meeting of bodies than minds. He scarcely glanced at them.

And at last there was a barred door between them and the world, and the whole city between them and anyone who might need them. A moment to be treasured then, a moment to linger over.

They stood a little apart, listening to the noise outside the shuttered window, tasting the rather foetid air of the closed room. Sorcha could not speak; any word of hers might appear to be witchery and, indeed, might be so.

Brede glanced about the room checking the security, and stopped; there was no danger here, but still. 'This doesn't feel right.'

'How can it not be right?' Sorcha protested. 'Isn't this what you and I have been wanting for weeks?'

'*Yes.*' Brede's word exploded in the quiet. 'Goddess, yes; with every bone in my body, but I wanted to – *find* our time, not be given permission.'

She pulled the sword belt roughly over her head, and rested the blade against the door – unconsciously barring it.

'What then?' Sorcha asked. 'Would you rather –'

'*No.*' Again, explosive near-anger. Sorcha withdrew a step, listening with every hair, every pore of her body, trying to get past Brede's words, trying to hear what it was she wanted.

Splashes of sunlight lit the darkness where the shutters had rotted. Sorcha watched Brede unlace her mail shirt and stepped forward to help her out of it. The weight of the metal on her hands felt strange, every muscle in Brede's body screamed with restrained violence, but yes, as Brede said, every bone whispered desire. The splash of sunlight moved across Brede's face as she turned. Brede's hands guided Sorcha's metal coat over her head, taking care not to catch her hair in any of the rings; tender. So close then, almost touching. Sorcha worked her hands free of the metal, acutely aware of the dull slithering thud as the mail hit the floor.

And still there was that reserve in Brede; that caution. Sorcha stood back.

'Would you rather it was Tegan here with you?' she asked. Brede's startled glance met hers and turned back to a frown.

'No,' she said shortly, then, catching Sorcha's expression, she hesitated. 'No,' she said again. 'If Tegan and I had truly wanted –' She couldn't finish, suddenly unsure if what she had been about to say was true. 'Tegan and I would always have been fighting each other. But you – I would fight *for* you.'

Sorcha laughed, puzzled. She let her eyes fall, away from Brede's anxious expression, to the taut line of her neck. Almost without thinking, she raised her hand, laying her fingers against the pulse in Brede's throat. Muscles jumped at her touch, and the rough sound of Brede's breathing filled her.

'Forget why we are able to be here,' Sorcha said quietly, running her fingers up the ridge of tendon to Brede's jaw, then on to her ear. Her lips followed the same journey, kissing from base of throat to lobe of ear. She could feel the heat of her own breath plume back off Brede's skin. Brede bent her head and sighed, and the tension in her body was abruptly changed.

'It seems I don't need to fight for you,' Brede said reaching to enclose Sorcha in her arms. Sorcha's arms folded about Brede, pulling her closer, protective. She buried her face in Brede's hair, breathing in the warmth of her.

'Now,' Sorcha said quietly.

Brede stroked her hair thoughtfully.

'Now what?' she asked.

'Just *now*. Not *soon*, not *later*, not *when we can*; but *now*.'

Desire quickened, and Brede smiled uncertainly, not sure what to do with that infinite spread of *now*. Sorcha had no such doubts; she buried her fingers in Brede's hair, revelling in the warmth of her scalp. She clasped her hands about Brede's head, holding her possessively, shaken by a molten rage of longing.

Slowly, she told herself, placing her lips very gently on Brede's brow. Brede blinked, surprised at the lightness of that touch, so at odds with the pent energy in the hands against her head. She shifted, and the grip relaxed. Encouraged, she snaked her arms about Sorcha, reaching under her shirt for warm flesh. As her fingers touched Sorcha's ribs, Brede felt her flinch suddenly, and she laughed, pulling her towards the bed.

'I never thought we'd get this far,' Sorcha admitted.

'No?' Brede asked, exploring the warmth beneath Sorcha's shirt.

'No, I thought –' Sorcha's thoughts trailed into incoherence as she listened to the new messages flowing through Brede's bone, sinew, flesh – and her own.

Coherence returned with her immediate needs satisfied, and a more leisurely exploration of Brede's body. Under her seeking hands and lips Brede relaxed into happy anticipation, then that relaxation melted into a waiting stillness of such intensity that Sorcha was disconcerted, feeling that Brede was no longer with her, that somewhere in her mind, Brede was far away. She drew away slightly, and Brede's heavy-limbed immobility stirred and she opened her eyes, and remembered to breathe. Her breath was ragged, and her puzzled, seeking eyes were half-blind, as she turned to Sorcha, a protest half-voiced. The protest died, and Brede turned her face away.

'Don't hide from me,' Sorcha whispered.

Brede shook her head, and laughed, but the laugh caught, and became a sigh, and then a deep shaky breath. And then, another gasping breath, and another. The waiting stillness dissolved into shuddering, and the gasps into sobs. Brede wound shaking limbs tightly about Sorcha, hiding tears, muffling confused laughter.

Sorcha held her; waiting for the shaking to still, for the leaping pulse beneath her lips to steady.

At last Brede pulled loose of their tangled limbs, her lips seeking Sorcha's, still too caught up in emotion for words. There was still an urgency to those kisses that overwhelmed Sorcha.

She pulled away once more, and gazed at Brede's face.

Brede's expression was filled with fear and hope and laughter. Such openness, such vulnerability, that Sorcha ached for her, wanting to assuage all that need. Here, at last, was the face that matched the gentle richness of Brede's voice.

'How long –' she asked divining part of Brede's response.

Brede blinked and said without the slightest hesitation, 'Nine years, three hundred and sixty-two days, and about seventeen hours.'

Sorcha laughed, not believing her.

'As precise as that?' Then the calculation bit. 'Midsummer Gather, year five, on the banks of the Muirghael River?'

Brede flinched, beginning to build her defences once more.

'No,' Sorcha said quickly. 'Stop hiding from me.' Brede turned back, but her expression was guarded. 'Please?' Sorcha softened her anguished command. Brede shifted silently then sighed.

'Her name was Devnet, and I do not want to talk about her.' She untangled her arms from Sorcha and worked her fingers into her hair, pulling gently, raising the hair away from her scalp, letting the sweat cool and dry.

'So Tegan –'

Brede laughed in protest. 'I've told you twice already. Why do you find it so hard to believe?'

'You look at her as though she had been your lover, as though there was something unfinished between you. She looks at you as if she regrets you.'

'Does she?' Brede asked, concerned more at the tone of Sorcha's voice than whether what she said might be true. 'I'm not going to trawl through my entire life story to reassure you that you are the most significant –' Sorcha stopped her words with a long, deep kiss. Brede pulled away, '– significant lover in my life so far,' she continued. 'Because you must know that you are, and I do not want to prompt comparisons from you as to where I am on a scale of the doubtless hundred lives you have graced.'

'You don't really think that do you?' Sorcha asked.

'I don't know what I think.'

'Brede –'

'Not now. This is our – our *now*. I don't want to think about any before, nor what follows. I want to think about how to make sure you never forget *this* now. I want you to be able to say in ten years, should anyone ask you, *Midsummer festival, year fourteen, Westgate Inn.*'

'And who do you think would be asking?' Sorcha asked, but Brede did not reply, caught up in making sure of the *now*.

Chapter Twenty-Five

Sorcha strayed from sleep, woken by hunger, thirst, and a need to relieve herself. She lay, revelling in the ordinariness of the urgency of her body, finding great pleasure in being woken by her own needs, rather than by Grainne's. She looked down at Brede's motionless sleeping huddle, so deeply lost in her dreams that she could scarcely hear her breathing.

She scrambled into clothes and pulled a knife from the muddled pile beside the bed, and went in search of the privy, and then the kitchen. The inn was busy with the festival, there were sleeping bodies laid about the floors as ready tripping hazards to the unwary, but Sorcha was careful.

The kitchen was a low, dark room; and at this hour of the early morning, was unattended, save by a sleeping bondservant, a restless cat, and rows of unbaked loaves, left to rise overnight. Soon, someone would be up to place the first consignment into the waiting oven, but that wasn't Sorcha's concern. She hoped for some bread already baked.

The bondservant stirred, woken by the slight change in temperature as the kitchen door opened. She sat up, and saw what appeared to be an armed warrior standing in the doorway. The cat, observing movement, made an enquiring noise.

'I suppose you'd know where they keep leftovers?' Sorcha asked the cat.

'She does,' the bondservant answered, 'but she can't open the cupboard.'

'Well then,' Sorcha suggested, 'perhaps you'll oblige me?'

'You'll have to pay,' the girl warned.

Sorcha merely nodded, and waited. The girl opened a heavy door, and hauled out half a loaf and a corner of cheese.

'Is that all there is?'

'All there is that I can get at without keys.'

'Any water? Anything sweet?'

The girl nodded, waved a hand in the direction of the water pail, and climbed up to the high shelf where the stone jar of honey was kept. As she handed the heavy jar down, the bondservant got a better look at her visitor.

'You're with the Plains woman?'

Sorcha nodded cautiously, dipping the mug for a second time.

'Ask where she got her horse. It's stolen. So's yours, but you wouldn't know; she does. I've seen the mark. Tell her that.'

Brede pulled the blanket about her shoulders and leant against the wall, as she settled beside her.

'Food,' Sorcha said, 'how long have you been awake?'

'A while. What did you manage to find?'

'Not a great deal, there's no one but the stable-hand in the kitchen at this time of night. Enough.'

'What time is it?' Brede asked uncertainly.

'A couple of hours 'til dawn.'

Sorcha edged onto the bed, careful not to spill the water. Brede sighed in appreciation as Sorcha handed her the mug. The water was warm, slightly bitter – but exactly what she needed. Her thirst slaked, Brede brought her attention to the slightly dry bread, rich cheese, and the small portion of honeycomb. Sorcha licked honey off her fingers with great concentration.

'You'd best not leave any crumbs, you'll attract the rats into bed with us,' Brede said.

Sorcha gave her a considering look. 'What crumbs?

Brede picked a morsel of bread from the lacing of Sorcha's shirt, collecting crumbs with the tip of a honey-coated finger. Sorcha loosened the shirt and threw it into a far corner, crumbs and all.

Brede glanced from Sorcha to her own honey-covered fingers. Sorcha followed the glance, and made a grab for Brede's hand.

Brede evaded her.

'This is my share of the honey, and I'm having every last taste of it, thank you.' She set to licking her hands clean.

Sorcha soon discovered that Brede had not been successful in removing all the honey from her fingers, setting her body alight with a feeling so intolerably precious that she feared to let Brede out of her arms. The reality of the world outside the room became uncertain, and all that mattered was the *now*, Brede, warm and lithe beneath her hands, and the sensations that Brede coaxed from her body.

Brede dozed in Sorcha's arms, not sure whether it was still the same day, not much caring; almost content to lie in the warmth and ease of slaked desire, to relish the nearness of her lover, and forget the world, but it was not so simple. She rubbed her face, trying to banish the unease.

Sorcha's lips against her shoulder traced the lines of her scars, and idled against her neck in gentle anticipation of rekindling passion. The quiet space about them no longer seemed infinite, and Brede was no longer listening to that comforting silence.

The roar of the market had subsided somewhat, settling into individual noises: an argument between two drunks, grumbling against the wall of the inn, the grate and thump of a stall being dismantled, horses stamping in the stables immediately below the shuttered window.

Those lips on her shoulder, the scar beneath Sorcha's questing mouth told her what it was that disturbed her peace.

Sorcha felt restlessness of the wrong kind quiver through Brede and ended the journey her mouth had been taking along the contours of Brede's body.

'What is it?' she protested.

The sun had moved round to once more force its ragged way into the inn's smallest bedroom. The patches of light from the rotted shutter lay across them, lighting Brede's shoulder, Sorcha's breast. Brede raised herself on one elbow, casting about the room, looking for her sword, her clothes.

'We should not be here,' she said impatiently.

'What is there for us to do?' Sorcha moved to prevent Brede from rising, wanting to recreate the sense of timelessness and ease that had held them safe for so brief a while.

A sudden, sharp cry from the stable below stilled her motion.

Brede froze, trying to identify the sound. Stamping and shouting, cursing, a young voice raised in protest. Were it not for their quiet, perhaps she would not have heard; no one else seemed to have remarked the disturbance. A voice cried out in pain and fury. Brede couldn't ignore it. She leapt up, groping for her abandoned sword.

Sorcha scrambled after, throwing clothes on, but wary of interfering.

Brede tried to place what it was that cut through the threads of her desire.

Again the voice cried out, and she knew it. The child in the stable called her, screaming for help in a language she was no longer glad to hear in this city.

Brede forced the shutters free and flung them wide. Sorcha blinked in the unexpectedly bright sun and wordlessly handed Brede clothes.

They could hear, now, the stamping and snorting of horses, a general cacophony of distress in the stables.

Brede couldn't see the stables for the roof under the window, which covered the outermost stalls. She thrust her arms into sleeves, scrambled into her breeches. She glanced at Sorcha, and almost laughed, so rumpled and dishevelled a pair they made.

'I may need you,' she said as she climbed awkwardly from the window to the sloping roof, hoping it would take her weight.

Sorcha grabbed her own sword and climbed out, sliding down the roof to land in an undignified heap in the yard. She looked around, and cursed.

Brede crouched over a still figure, one outstretched hand touching the man, her expression hidden by her loose hair. Sorcha reached her in two strides, and turned the body over.

'What did you do to him?' she asked, disquieted at the bloody mess.

Brede shook her head.

'Not me.' She looked about, seeking the cause of the man's brutal death. 'Your horse, I think.'

Sorcha stared up at the great bulk of Macsen, standing apparently docile but for the set of his ears, and the blood and brains spattered up his legs.

'Be easy,' Sorcha suggested.

He stamped his blood-splashed hooves: a threat. Sorcha backed away, disturbed by this challenge from a beast she thought she controlled.

'Macsen,' she sang, and his head drooped toward her. 'Am I the enemy, great one?'

The horse shuddered, acknowledging her. She stepped forward, raising her hand to his neck, waiting for permission before she touched.

'So, what is it then?' she asked, gentling his twitching. She stepped closer, running her hand along his side, feeling the sweat on his skin. He backed, flinging up his head once more, and she slapped him impatiently and spelled him to stillness, no longer prepared to be polite. She glanced around the stable.

'Is this the one who called you?' she called to Brede, indicating the huddled child, crushed into the corner of the stall.

Brede pushed past her and knelt beside the child.

'What is your need?' she asked, in the soft syllables of her father's language.

The child uncurling from her fear, stared up at Brede.

'I called you,' she said, barely more than a whisper, 'and the horse answered, he trampled that man.'

'Yes,' Brede agreed, pulling the child to her feet. 'Are you hurt, by the man or the horse?'

'No. The horse protected me.'

Brede twisted to look at the horse.

'Well, Macsen, there's a sudden change of character. He doesn't usually care for children.'

'I'm not a child.'

'Well, Macsen doesn't recognise any child in you. You know he has killed the man?'

The child wilted, abruptly heavy in Brede's encircling arms.

'Come on. You don't need to hide behind Macsen now. I have you safe.'

Brede pulled, and the child followed, still dazed. Sorcha took the child from her, singing gentle encouragement. The girl wrenched herself out of Sorcha's arms, gazing suspiciously. Sorcha folded her arms and met her gaze.

'Interesting,' she said, 'Which Clan are you?'

The child remained silent. She would never reveal her kin to anyone she didn't trust, and she didn't trust witches.

'Tell her how you came by your horse, Brede,' Sorcha suggested, suddenly making connections. Brede ignored her suggestion, and rested a hand on the child's shoulder.

'Wing Clan, my blood,' she said, still speaking the Clan language.

The child turned to her, a look of painful hope on her face.

'Kin I call you, then. Wing Clan, my birth.'

Brede stared at the child, trying to see who she might be, under the dirt and hard use. Not a child, but young for all that, not more than ten years, surely. Brede's hand tightened on her shoulder, and she shook her gently.

'Are you telling me the truth? I don't know you.'

'I've never ridden with the Clan.'

Brede's mind skipped again to a conclusion that she couldn't bring herself to believe. *Running before the wind,* she told herself.

'Your mother and father?'

'My mother is dead. I've never met my father, although I know his name.'

'And? This is important, girl.' Brede could hardly contain her impatience.

'I can see that, you are not the first to come asking these questions. My name is Neala, daughter to Carolan of Wing Clan.'

So – then she must be – she must be.

'Your father was alive last I knew,' Brede said, dismissing Carolan – it was the girl's mother who mattered. Her mother, who was dead.

'Your mother?'

'Falda, daughter to Ahern of Wing Clan.'

Brede made a strangled sound, half laugh, half sob. She crushed the child to her, not quite believing her still.

'Blood kin I name you then, Neala, Falda's daughter. I am Brede, daughter of Ahern of Wing Clan.'

Neala struggled out of Brede's embrace, staring into her face.

'Yes, you are. Riding one of my mother's horses, too.'

Brede's eyes fell for the first time on the links of the chain about Neala's neck. She hooked her hand beneath the collar, and pulled it gently free of the scarf that obscured it. Neala's hand joined hers about the warm metal, loosening Brede's grip, and tying the scarf once more over the symbol of her enslavement. Suddenly, her hand snaked up, pulling the jerkin away from Brede's neck: no chain She let the leather loose, finding nothing to say in the face of the unexpected hope that writhed in her mind.

Brede forced herself out of contemplating the child. There was a dead man lying at their feet; something must be done.

'Do you know this man?' she asked her niece.

'No. I think he was after stealing your horses. He went for me when I tried to stop him.'

'You did well,' Brede said, seeing the child's face pinch with fear.

'Not so well as the horse,' Neala replied, trying to throw off her distress.

Brede smiled. A strong child, this.

Sorcha touched her shoulder. 'I know this man,' she said.

Brede's waited for an explanation. Her restless eyes discovered the two long knives at the man's hip: an assassin.

'Phelan's man.'

Brede swore, painfully aware of the child at her side, wondering what the implications of this death would be.

'Sorcha,' she said, casually, 'we can't go barefoot and half dressed – can you get the rest of our gear? I'll saddle the horses. We need to be gone from here.'

Neala's face crumpled, hope snuffed out. She turned to go back to the kitchen. Brede's hand closed on her upper arm.

'You too, next-kin.'

'I can't leave,' Neala protested. 'I'm a bondservant.'

Brede swore again, and flung the child towards the horse. 'Bonded to whom?' she asked. 'On what authority? You are a child; as your next-kin I say any bond is dissolved. Now help saddle that horse, and let's be gone from here.'

Sorcha still stood unmoving.

'Grainne isn't going to like this, not assassins, nor your next-kin.'

'Grainne will survive it – besides, she promised me.'

Sorcha shook her head doubtfully, and glanced up.

'I can't climb back up that roof without help,' she said patiently, remembering the barred door.

Brede glanced at the roof, which was sagging already from their swift, careless descent. She laughed, and kissed Sorcha, at first lightly, and then reluctant to stop.

'And you a witch,' she protested.

'Not one that can levitate,' Sorcha said.

She could get back into the room, but the child had already shown enough distrust, no need to frighten her more.

Brede gave her a little shake.

'No need for that, you have yourself a tall horse that will stand as still as stone if you but ask it of him.'

Chapter Twenty-Six

Sorcha made no attempt to disguise her urgency as she dismounted and threw the reins in Corla's direction. Corla bit down on the protest that came to mind, shouting after Sorcha, 'Messages – for you, I'm thinking. You'd best hear them.'

Sorcha slowed minimally, turning her head in Corla's direction, but continued walking. Corla raised an eyebrow at her impatience, and took a few steps after her, still not absolutely sure this was the woman Tegan had meant.

'Tegan said to tell you Phelan is back, and expected within the hour.' She caught at Brede's sleeve, 'Eachan said to tell you Madoc has returned, and gone again. He also said there's more than old times between those two. He said he has things to tell you.'

'I must see Grainne at once,' Sorcha said. 'Is Tegan with her?'

'No. She's out in the city somewhere. She said she had things to attend to.'

'Did she say what?' Brede asked.

'The usual. Trying to find out what's going on with the rest of the world. She's worried.'

'I'd noticed,' Brede said.

Corla's eyebrow crooked itself once more. 'What's afoot?'

Brede shook her head. 'You'll find out when the dust settles,' she said, and Corla frowned at being shut out.

Brede turned away, and was brought up short by the sight of Neala.

Sorcha anticipated the hesitation.

'Take Neala to Eachan,' she suggested. 'She can help stable the horses. I'll meet you in Grainne's quarters.'

Before Brede had a chance to answer, she was gone.

Corla glanced at the child. 'And you are?' she asked.

Neala glared in silence at Corla. Brede answered for her.

'This is my sister's daughter, Neala.'

Corla raised an eyebrow.

'Tegan will be pleased.'

Brede nodded. That scarcely mattered now, she felt too crowded about with other concerns to think about the value of Tegan's friendship.

Neala looked at her expectantly.

'Come meet Eachan,' Brede said, wearily.

Eachan scarcely glanced up as the two horses were led into the stable.

'You're back then,' he said, giving a final sweep to the coat of the horse he had been grooming, before he turned.

'Ah,' his eye met Neala. 'We've met before, haven't we?'

Neala nodded; a child of few words. Eachan put his brush aside, and stretched his back, giving the horses a considering look.

'Managed to give these beasts a run? And the bay? Did she get any exercise?'

Brede stared at him blankly, and then blushed furiously.

'I thought that was Tegan's private joke.'

'Nothing is private here.' Eachan said. 'Have you not learnt that yet? Jokes, passions, loyalties... Everyone knows everything. You don't know what you give away – You don't need to answer me, I can tell merely by looking at you.' Eachan's mocking slipped at Brede's enraged expression. 'I'm happy for you. I'd be grateful for your friends if I were you.'

Brede held up a hand in protest, trying to stop the flow of words. She pulled Neala slightly forward.

'This is Neala, daughter of my sister, and my next-kin.'

'Ah. I thought she might be. So, is she going to take over your sadly neglected duties in the stables?'

Brede shrugged.

'I think Grainne has other things on her mind now, but I want a formal breaking of the bond that innkeeper claims, and quickly. Then I should take Neala back to her kin – this is no place for a child. If she'd like to help with the horses, I'd be glad for you to keep her occupied, until I can speak to Grainne.'

Eachan turned his eye on Neala once more, and caught the glimmer of metal about her neck.

'There's something more immediate we should be doing with you, girl.'

Brede followed his gaze and nodded sharply.

'It's a heavy chain, that,' she said to Eachan. 'Have you tools for it?'

Eachan shook his head.

'I leave that sort of thing to the smith.'

Brede pulled the links free of Neala's hair once more, peering closely at each in turn.

'How fortunate that we have a smith to hand then,' she said, as her fingers found a link that was poorly made. She glanced at Neala's narrowed eyes. 'Will you hold still and trust me?'

Neala nodded her assent, but her eyes widened as Brede pulled a short broad-bladed knife from the top of her boot. Brede worked the knife tip into the link and twisted it, then forced it further, eyes fixed, not on the chain, but on Neala's vulnerable neck. For a fraction of a second she thought of the gouge in Jodis' neck and hesitated. She turned the knife a little further and the link gave. She threw the knife down.

'Hold the chain away from your throat,' she said, and gave a swift yank at the chain, which parted easily. Neala gave a startled yelp, and held the limp sway of metal up to her next-kin.

Brede took the chain and wrapped it twice around her knuckles and closed her hand over the shattered link.

'Well, girl?' Eachan asked Neala, 'What's it to be? Help me with the horses, or trail at Brede's heels, where you can trip up the Queen with a bit of luck?'

Neala bared her teeth, an approximation of a smile.

'The horses, so please you. Especially this one,' she slapped Macsen as high up his shoulder as she could reach. The horse lowered his head and breathed into her hair in an unusually amiable fashion.

'You are welcome to him,' Eachan said, pleased at the beast's unexpected docility. He nodded to Brede. 'I've things to say to you, concerning a certain general.'

Neala's expression became guardedly curious. Eachan gave her an uncomfortable look.

'Have you had a chance to talk?' he asked.

'No,' Brede said. Neala shook her head.

'Well, if the young lady will forgive. Madoc has been back.'

Brede glanced at Neala, who was white-faced and scowling.

'And gone again, Tegan says. He has powerful protectors that one, I wouldn't tangle with him were I you.'

'No, not yet.' Brede narrowed her eyes and the metal about her knuckles bit into her flesh as she clenched her fist. Eachan frowned in response.

'Have a care, girl.'

Brede held out the chain to Eachan.

'First in your collection. Any news –'

'No.' Eachan cut across her question. 'None.'

Brede reached a hand to Neala. 'You'll be all right here for a while?' she asked, uncomfortable with her new responsibility as next-kin, itching to ask the girl more, but with other matters more immediately pressing.

'Go talk to the Queen,' Neala said calmly.

'Change first,' Eachan said. 'You look a sight.'

Brede shrugged, gathered her discarded knife and made her way toward the barracks. She ignored the thought of hot water and clean clothes and pulled her jerkin straight. As she turned towards the tower, she spotted Tegan and raised her hand in greeting. Tegan joined her at the base of the stair.

'I need to see the Queen,' Tegan said at once. 'And I need your support, if you can give it.' They hurried up the steps.

'What –' Brede began.

'Not here.' Tegan reached the top of the stairs first, dismissing Ula with a tilt of her head. She waited until Ula was out of earshot. 'I don't know who I can trust with this apart from you.'

She opened the door and walked into the Queen's outer chamber, Brede at her shoulder. Sorcha came to the inner door, a sword in her hand. Tegan swore under her breath.

'Urgent business with the Queen,' she said and swept past her. Brede and Sorcha followed, and caught her unceremonious greeting to Grainne.

'You asked me to use my eyes, and I've done that. If I'm wrong –' Tegan's worried glance flickered from Grainne to Sorcha, to Brede, and back to Grainne. 'Tell me, of all your trusted friends, whom do you trust the most?'

'I do not have 'trusted' friends any longer; I have only friends who have proved themselves. Sorcha, Phelan, you.'

Tegan flinched, then discarded caution, too urgent for cowardice.

'Who has been at your shoulder? Who has stood beside you in all things? Who leads your armies out to fight?'

Grainne did not want to hear this, not from Tegan, not from anyone.

'What is it you know to Phelan's discredit?'

'I don't know, I *suspect*. So I ask you: who would know that the Dowry blade was missing? Who would know where it ought to be?'

'And?'

'Who controls your armies; who speaks for you to them?'

'We are winning,' Grainne protested.

'Who tells you so?' Tegan asked quietly. 'I see no victorious troops, I see only deserters slinking home, an unexpectedly early start to this year's campaign, and with Ailbhe's death – scouting parties, Lorcan's, under the very walls of your city. And no one can tell me why that is. My first campaign was with Phelan; we trained together. I know him; he isn't how he used to be. Grainne, you must stop thinking with your heart.'

'You go too far.'

'You asked me to use my eyes and this is what I have seen. If you do not want me to report what I see, what must I do?'

Grainne stared wildly at Tegan's impassive face, at the trembling in her shoulders, and her anger waned suddenly. 'No, Tegan.'

Grainne buried her face in her hands. Tegan stood, thinking she was dismissed.

'Sit down,' Grainne said. 'Sorcha, what do you think?'

Sorcha took a wary breath, her mind spinning, watching pieces of the puzzle fall into place, wincing away from the pattern they formed.

'She's right about deserters. But the Dowry blade? Phelan? If it is true – Phelan can't be working alone.'

Grainne nodded, turning her weary gaze back to Tegan.

'Maeve and I are the only captains to report directly to you. All other reports come to you through Phelan. He is the only person who could mislead you. You are not winning this war, Grainne. If he were guiltless, he would have discovered the treachery and told you of it. You've lost control of the army, and you no longer know who controls your troops, which divisions are conscripts, which mercenaries. Do you know who is in charge of the defence of this city?'

'Doran.'

'No; Doran sits at home breeding horses, and slaves. There is no one in charge, there is next to no defence. The mercenaries have not been paid, and they distrust you. Half the conscripts have run away, the rest are on the point of mutiny. They have homes and families they have not seen in too long. They could be harvesting; instead they are killing people. If Lorcan were to attack this city, you could not defend it.'

Tegan stopped, wondering if Grainne was listening, her face had lost all expression. The silence dragged, until at last Grainne whispered,

'But Phelan? What could he gain by this?'

'He is Aeron's half-brother, your closest kin after Lorcan,' Sorcha said hesitantly. 'If he took that sword to Lorcan, intending Ailbhe's death, might he not intend to use Lorcan's strength to take your place, then kill Lorcan? The boy is scarcely into manhood, after all.'

Grainne shook her head. '*If* he took the sword. This is Phelan we are talking about. My next-kin – my – Phelan is not a religious fanatic, there are other ways to kill a king, why choose that way? And he would never consider the throne for himself, it is sacrilege.'

'All the more reason to use the sword, surely?' Sorcha asked. 'If he could imply some righteousness? Treating Ailbhe as a traitor?'

'Not a traitor, no,' Tegan shook her head. 'Treating him as a consort who has provided an heir for his queen.'

Grainne closed her eyes. They sat silent for a while, watching her reject the argument. Sorcha tried again.

'Would Phelan know the sword was gone? Would he know where to find it if he needed to take it?'

'Yes, of course he knew. He is Aeron's brother, Muirghael's son, my nephew. Of course he knew. But that doesn't mean he took it, or used it.'

Sorcha watched the spinning of her puzzle. 'The sword makes sense for Lorcan, but not for Phelan. There is still no gain for him. And he loves you, for pity's sake, he is hardly going to be conspiring with Lorcan.'

Tegan sighed. Neither of them were listening, neither of them understood.

'You sent him to Lorcan to talk peace,' she said at last. 'And he is on his way back.'

Grainne's eyes opened.

'What can I possibly do that is anything but a betrayal of the loyalty Phelan has shown me all his life?'

Brede felt warily for something safe to say.

'Has Sorcha warned you that we were followed by one of Phelan's men?'

'Yes, but that doesn't mean – '

'He sent an assassin,' Sorcha said faintly, as another piece dropped into place.

Grainne shook her head dismissively. Brede leaned forward. 'You have forgotten something, Phelan doesn't have the sword, nor does Lorcan. We do,' she said gently. 'Does Phelan know you have the sword safe?' Brede asked.

'No.'

'Then confront him with it.'

Tegan exploded. 'Are you from your wits? Would you present him with the opportunity to use it?'

Brede smiled; a slow smile of remembrance.

'There are no holy slayers any more, Tegan. If he so much as makes a move towards it, he will have betrayed himself.'

'Yes,' Sorcha agreed. 'He might have supplied the sword, but it is Lorcan who took a blade to his sovereign, not Phelan. Besides it need not be Grainne who confronts him, although she should be a witness.'

Grainne nodded, accepting Sorcha's assessment of the danger because she was sure of Phelan.

'If it will satisfy you. It will prove you wrong and then you can concentrate you energies on finding my real enemies. I've no cause to doubt Phelan.'

Sorcha watched the weariness in Grainne's strained face, and touched Tegan's arm. Tegan jerked from her touch as though burnt, and walked stiffly from the room. Brede followed Tegan, closing the door behind her.

Tegan turned from the empty fireplace.

'What *is* this witch doing here? Is she really just tending to Grainne's ills?'

'She is keeping her alive.'

'But is that all? What is in it for her?'

Brede frowned.

'She loves Grainne,' she said, patiently, and her words bruised her heart.

'So does Phelan,' Tegan said despairing.

Sorcha came out from the Queen to join them beside the unlit hearth.

'If it is Phelan, what will Grainne do?' Brede asked.

'What would you do if someone you trusted, as much as Grainne trusts him, turned against you?' Sorcha asked, and shuddered. 'I know Phelan, although he has forgotten me. There's more than trust between those two. Grainne loves him. Phelan is – was a brother to us both. It can't be true – you've seen them together – how he is with her – how can it be possible?' Sorcha asked. She shook herself. 'Phelan will be back to report in a few hours. Tegan, you must watch for him, we cannot afford to be surprised. Brede, do you have that sword safe?'

'You know I do. It's under my bed.'

'Under your bed? Dear Goddess. You are more used to handling swords than I am; you'd best have with you – and keep a close grip. We can't risk Phelan getting even one hand to it.'

Chapter Twenty-Seven

'Is everything as you want it?' Brede asked.

Grainne gazed uncertainly around the room. Sorcha had moved a table, partially obstructing the space between the door and Grainne's seat.

'Pull the shutters closed.'

Brede went to the window, and stared down at the river. She pulled the shutters across, the sun blinding her briefly as the gap between them narrowed. She was reminded of the sun through the shutters in the inn, and smiled to herself, although these shutters were unrotted, and covered with fine blue paint.

The shutters cut out some light, disguising the intention of the moved furniture.

'The sword,' Grainne said urgently.

Brede crossed to the side chamber, brushing close to Sorcha as she went. She seemed scarcely aware of Brede's existence, drawing slow, steadying breaths into her lungs, preparing herself.

Brede discarded the red cloak, giving a critical glance to the blade. She wondered if Phelan would actually recognise it in the dimness of the Queen's chamber. Passing near the door, she heard Riordan's voice, faintly, from the foot of the stair. Sorcha's head jerked up, and they scrambled to their places.

Brede had barely straightened into her position when Phelan walked in. He didn't look in her direction, used to her presence. He did not see the sword.

Grainne shot Brede an agonised look over his bent back as he leant to kiss her cheek.

'Well cousin, young Lorcan's face was indeed a picture.'

'Never mind his face, Phelan. What did he say?'

Phelan pulled his gloves slowly from his hands, inspecting Grainne.

'You are unwell?'

'What did he say?'

Phelan sighed.

Doubting Phelan, Brede listened more carefully than usual, listening not for the words but the tone. And she heard.

'He said no.'

'No? Why?' Grainne's voice was husky, barely a whisper.

'He said that if you were weak enough to offer, he wanted capitulation not accommodation. He said that he will be at your gate within the week, and expects to find that gate open. I told you he wouldn't wait.'

Phelan walked as he spoke, restlessly turning in the awkward space, which he had yet to notice, and which he should have observed at once.

Brede gripped the hilt between her hands the more securely. She was certain now, and angry, but she wasn't sure that Grainne understood.

Sorcha closed the door quietly.

Grainne could not bear the tension. She couldn't hear what Phelan was saying. She smiled thinly, and did not try to hide the shaking of her hands.

'I am not myself today, old friend,' she said faintly, interrupting him. 'You'll have to save the rest of what you have to tell me for tomorrow.'

A look of concern passed over his face.

'I will leave you then, cousin,' he responded quickly, stooping to kiss her frozen face. 'A swift recovery, my dear.'

He turned, coming face to face with Brede in the confined space. Brede hefted the sword slightly, cradling the hilt in the crook of her arm. It was a perfectly normal movement, the sort any guard might make, in preparation for moving aside. Conveniently, it drew attention to the sword, to the fact that it was too long and heavy for her, and consequently, to what manner of sword it was.

And Phelan saw what manner of sword it was. He schooled his reaction quickly, but not sufficiently.

Grainne nodded, and Sorcha sang a short phrase of song. If there were words, Brede did not decipher them, they were not meant for her.

Phelan's eyes moved, a frantic darting from the sword to Sorcha. Recognition lit his eyes and his breathing quickened. No other muscle in his body would respond to his bidding. Brede swallowed uneasily. She had seen Sorcha use this spell before, on the enraged horse. The same nervous twitching that set sweat on Macsen's hide, now tortured Phelan. Brede stepped around his motionless body, avoiding any contact and passed the sword to Grainne.

The Queen used the Dowry blade to balance herself as she slowly rose to her feet. Grainne nodded to Sorcha once more, her teeth gritted against the pain in her body, the pain and disbelief and anger in her mind.

Sorcha's song forced Phelan to turn and face Grainne. His face was bathed in sweat as he fought Sorcha's bindings. Brede took the sword from his belt and found two more blades in his clothing.

'Well, *old friend*,' Grainne said, her voice hoarse with rage. 'I am well served: A horse breeder and a witch for guards, and an old mercenary for my eyes. Would that I had friends also. It seems I must search amongst my enemies for people to trust. Where would I have to look to find your friends, or your conscience?' she sighed, and lowered herself back into the chair, unable to stand longer. 'Do you like your handiwork, does it please you to see the life sucked out of me?' She flicked a finger in Sorcha's direction. 'Let him answer.'

Sorcha's voice shivered over a few notes. Phelan coughed violently. Sorcha had abandoned her disguising softness, all her concentration for the spell. If she chose, she could stop his breathing, or still his heart.

Phelan sucked air into his lungs unsteadily, aware of that possibility.

'Is this how you treat your loyal friend – your kin?'

'Are you loyal? Are you?'

'You know I am. What cause have you to doubt?'

'What motive have you to betray? You recognise that sword, Phelan.'

'Of course I recognise it.'

'Why? You've never had reason to see it, I haven't had need of it since I came to be ruler, and Aeron never so much as glanced at it once her marriage ceremony was over. It has been kept hidden all that time. How did you come to know where it was?'

'I've always known.'

'And who stole this blade and gave it to Lorcan? Who gave *my* sword into the hands of a patricide? And who spread the rumour that it was missing? No one knew it was gone but you. I told no one else. Whom did you tell?'

'It was not I.'

Grainne closed her eyes against the calm denial. 'Can you make him tell the truth?' she asked Sorcha.

Sorcha had been expecting this. She took her time before she answered.

'It is possible.' She frowned at Grainne's eager movement. 'But it is difficult. If he tries to lie, you will know. But Grainne, I can't keep him to it for long, do not ask too many questions.'

Grainne nodded. She almost believed that Phelan was lying to her, almost; but she needed certainty before all those years of love could be put aside.

Sorcha's melody was as fierce as walking on knives. Grainne winced at the sharp clarity of the sound, capable of whittling the most heart-deep secret from an unwilling mind.

'Phelan. What did Lorcan say?'

'He said what I t…' Phelan's eyes widened in horror. He gagged on the remainder of the sentence, and his entire body shuddered.

'What did he say?'

Phelan's mouth worked, trying to find a way around the knife-edge insistence of Sorcha's song.

'He laughed,' he said at last.

'Who are you working for?'

'No one.'

That came so easily that Grainne looked at Sorcha questioningly. Sorcha spread one hand in a shrug and changed the tone of the song a shade.

'Does Lorcan believe you further his cause?'

'Yes.'

'And do you?'

'Yes.'

Grainne pushed the sword slightly.

'You took this?'

'Yes.'

'And Lorcan struck off Ailbhe's head?'

'Yes, but I wish I might have done it.' Those words came easily, in a rush.

'Why?'

'I loved Aeron.'

'We all loved Aeron. Why work against me for Lorcan?'

'He is her child.'

That tremor again.

'What else?'

Silence, as Phelan struggled against the spell. At last he spat out the words. 'He is *not* ...Ailbhe's.'

Grainne stared in disbelief at the tears coursing down Phelan's face.

'Yours?' she asked at last. '*Yours?*'

'Yes.'

'Does Lorcan know?'

'No.'

Grainne's hand tightened around the blade of the sword across her knee, drawing blood. She glanced at the cut then raised her eyes to him.

'So the poison was you,' she said at last.

Phelan fought once more, but at last the word hissed from him.

'*Yes.*'

Grainne couldn't believe it. 'You?' she asked weakly, and again, 'You?'

'Yes,' Phelan whispered. 'Yes it was me.'

Grainne shook her head. Even with his confirmation she couldn't bring herself to credit the idea. She watched the tears still streaming down his face. Pain? Remorse? It was beyond her understanding, and she still needed to know who had been party to Phelan's schemes, who could have had sufficient influence to warp the mind of someone she still thought her dearest friend and ally.

She asked her many questions in the teeth of Phelan's sobbing, and Sorcha's white face and clenched fists. Grainne buried his answers in her mind, hearing names she dreaded to hear, more people she once trusted, condemned unwillingly by Phelan's tortured voice.

Brede couldn't watch Phelan writhe in the grip of the spell; she hated to listen, but couldn't shut out the horror of it, a horror made worse by the cold beauty of Sorcha's voice. Beautiful: not the words, not the tune, but the voice...

Brede watched Sorcha, and recognised her for what she was at last; not a witch, but a power wielder, a terrifying and dangerous being. This woman she had lain with – this woman – Brede tried to peel away her horror, struggling to feel anything for Sorcha in the face of this nightmare, and saw the strain in her wide unblinking eyes. There was a lack of personality in that look, as though Sorcha had lost herself in her song.

Brede dragged her eyes away, looking at Grainne, almost as tormented as Phelan; relying on her anger for strength. Sorcha did not have that support. Brede watched her mouth shaping words that destroyed, watched the shaking of the hand that rested against Phelan's shoulder, watched the tears streaming down Sorcha's face unchecked; and saw that the spell was failing.

'That's enough,' Brede said, desperate to make herself heard against the confusion of sound already battering at Grainne.

Grainne couldn't hear her. She had reached the all-important question; her voice was fierce, clear against the frightening whirl of noise, the strange unearthly voice of Sorcha's spell.

'*Why?*'

'I would have been satisfied to have been your consort,' Phelan said, easy now with the truth, willing to tell her this, glad even. 'I knew you were too old to have a daughter, I knew I would be safe. I would have been proud to have been at your side, I would have been glad to destroy that upstart Ailbhe for you, and we could have raised Lorcan together – *but you scorned me.*'

Sorcha stopped singing. Her hand fell away from Phelan's shoulder; she staggered as she stepped back, and collapsed.

Grainne glanced swiftly at Phelan's unmoving body and, reassured that he was still in Sorcha's thrall, she closed her mind on the last of her questions.

'How long will this spell hold him?' she asked.

Sorcha had to make an effort to answer, her voice scarcely more than a whisper. 'Until I end it – but you had best bind him,'

Grainne was satisfied. She beckoned Brede to her, holding out the sword.

'Put this away,' she said, 'then find Tegan and Maeve, and set them to find those this traitor has named; bring someone back to take my – cousin – to the dungeon.'

Brede took the sword, wondering if leaving it under her bed, as she had done for the last months would suffice, and decided that it would not. She hurried down the stair and out into the practice yard in search of Tegan, with the Dowry blade still in her arms.

Chapter Twenty-Eight

Brede left the Dowry blade safe with her riding gear in the stables, hidden under a pair of saddle cloths. Then she went about Grainne's business with a heavy heart. There was no sign of Tegan, but she found Maeve quickly enough.

'Maeve, I have orders from the Queen.'

'What orders?' Maeve asked, puzzled by her abruptness.

'You are to place Phelan in confinement, and there are others, including some under your command.'

'Phelan?' Maeve paled, wiping her hand across her mouth. 'And who else?'

'Madoc, Doran, Chad, Oran, Murdo and Ula and their crew,' Brede glanced quickly down, 'and Killan.'

Maeve hesitated between disbelief and horror, stunned at the names; surely there must be a mistake? She pulled herself together quickly, as Brede reeled off thirty more names.

'Households as well where relevant?' she asked, and when Brede nodded, turning her eyes away, 'I'll make the arrangements, then I'll come for Phelan myself, if he can be left that long. Word of his – confinement – would send a warning to the others.'

'He's not going anywhere.'

Maeve shot Brede a look, taking in her grim expression.

'Is Tegan...?'

'How could you think it?' Brede's eyes widened. 'Tegan warned us – although – where is she?'

Maeve shook her head, she had no idea. Her mouth twisted in fear and frustration, missing Tegan: she couldn't delegate some of those arrests to junior officers. She nodded to Brede, and calling to Corla, grabbed up her smarter cloak as she strode away to collect her troop together.

'I'll be with you presently,' she said to Brede, calm and in control of the situation for now, despite the sickening doubt in her mind.

As soon as Brede had gone, Maeve shuddered, not knowing how she could bring herself to give those orders. She caught Corla's anxious glance and straightened her shoulders.

'We're to take certain people into custody,' she said, 'but it must be done with the utmost courtesy, no dungeons, just well-guarded guest rooms. And find someone who knows where Tegan is. I need her here.' Corla went at a run.

Maeve watched her go, for something to focus on while her mind shuddered with uncertainty once more. When Grainne came to her senses, Maeve did not want the embarrassment of having ill-treated her prisoners – and if Grainne did not recover good sense, how long before someone remembered that many of those alleged traitors were friends of Maeve's – intimate companions – how long before Maeve herself was under arrest?

Grainne stared at Phelan. The immobility, the silence, dragged at her memory, forcing her to consider every nuance of every word he had ever spoken, every action, every touch, every kiss, every gift. She caught her breath.

'Your midsummer wine.'

Phelan would have liked to turn his eyes away from her, but he couldn't.

'You drank the same poison you gave me?' Grainne thought about that midsummer wine, thought about Brede handing her the glass. If Phelan had drunk the same, he must have an antidote. Then she thought about him taking her hands, both her hands in his, in his mockery of fealty, asking his yearly question, and when she gave her annual refusal, he had handed the glass back – *no* – there was no antidote, and there was no poison until she refused, and each time she refused – Grainne shuddered.

'I trusted you. I trusted Aeron – why would she – she would have told me – Lorcan is truly yours?'

'Yes.'

'Why?'

'You would not have me.'

'No, Phelan. Do not try to blame me.' Grainne's mind painted pictures for her, casual laughter at Phelan's teasing protestations of love; that absurd leap from the roof to escape his more amorous advances. And he had still hoped? She couldn't believe it. And he had asked her to hand-fast every year for fourteen years, and he had not, could not have started poisoning her that long ago.

'What changed?' she asked. 'What made my refusal worth poison?'

'You were always so self-sufficient.' Even though Sorcha no longer held him to truth, Phelan told it, exhausted and past caring. 'I thought if you were weaker you would rely on me, need me, want me. But you stayed strong, despite everything. The more I hurt you, the stronger you got, and the more I loved you, and wanted you more.' He laughed, and would have shaken his head, if only he could, and he would have wept, but Grainne might then think he was lying still, and he would not have her misunderstand him now.

Maeve nodded to Inir, and Cei. Inir because he, like her, loved Killan; Cei because he did not. She could barely wait to saddle her horse. Inir pulled the tangle of reins from her hands.

'Roof?' he asked. She blinked, looking across the river at the mill and nodded. They set off running towards the fastest possible route for their goal.

Brede stayed away as long as she dared. At the door to Grainne's quarters she stopped. She didn't want to go back in.

Would she have done this if she were Grainne? Would she? She could smell Phelan's fear, his humiliation, his distress; it disgusted her. And worse, there was Sorcha. She took a steadying breath and pushed through the door.

A constant tremor shook Phelan's limbs. Sorcha was sitting at Grainne's feet, her face buried in the Queen's skirts. She lifted her head as Brede entered, and turned a tear-stained anguished face towards her.

'Maeve will come,' Brede said, feeling nothing for Sorcha, wanting an end.

Grainne inclined her head stiffly, refusing to lower her guard now. The smell of fear was so tangible and rancid that Brede gagged. She went to the balcony shutters and threw them open. She filled her lungs with the clean warm air, and stared wistfully down at the riverbank below. Brede sensed angry movement behind her, and turned, her heart pounding. Phelan hadn't moved. The Queen looked straight into Brede's furious fearful eyes, and let her objection die.

Wing Clan, she reminded herself, pulling her gown closer about her neck, against the faint breeze that stirred the foetid air. She felt cold to her marrow, but she couldn't expect a nomad, used to the Plains wind, to understand that.

Phelan felt the breeze against his back, and was grateful. The tremors faded.

Inir checked that his sword was loose in its scabbard for the fourth time. He glanced at Maeve, her face pale as the moon, and as impassive.

'We'll take this as gently as we can,' she said softly.

'We need someone up on the wall,' Inir suggested. Maeve glanced up.

'We do? You think he'll run?'

'You know he will.'

Maeve fought a constriction in her throat. *Did she?*

'Is there something I should know?' she asked.

Inir loosened his sword again.

'If we're right to be arresting Killan, he has been fostering our confidences, he has been betraying us, you and me, not just whoever it is he thinks is his enemy.'

'*If.*'

'Maeve, you know it, I know it. It makes sense doesn't it? As soon as you rejected him, he turned to me. He wanted a conduit for information about what we were doing, what the duty rota was, how many guards. He had no reason to be here, he had no real work. We were duped, used.'

'He'll try to run.' Maeve moved into shadow.

'We may have to kill him.'

Maeve nodded slowly, considering whom she could trust to do that, if it came to it.

'Could you?' she asked, her voice unrecognisable.

Inir wiped sweat off his palms and shook his head.

'You?'

Maeve raised her head again, sighting along the edge of Killan's roof. She considered what she might have told Killan that he could use, and her heart twisted with grief, and anger, and doubt. She weighed him in the balance of her heart.

'If he makes me.' She gripped the hilt of her sword, thinking about Killan's hands twining into hers, thinking about her blade in his flesh. She shuddered. 'I'll take the wall. Wait for me.'

Inir stood motionless in the alley, his eyes flickering from the lighted window in the attic, to the wall above, until he saw Maeve silhouetted against the evening light. He turned to Cei, pointing down the street.

'If he goes for the roof, he can get down at the corner. Stay here. If he gets by me, stop him, if he gets to the roof, go there and meet him.'

Cei nodded curtly. Inir cleared his throat, and leant on the door, pushing his way into the poorly lit stairway. He made his way up the familiar narrow treads which seemed even more precarious now. At the doorway he hesitated, listening. Killan was not alone. Nothing for it, he rapped briefly on the doorpost and pushed through the curtain.

There was a swift giggling scuffle from the bed. Inir caught sight of a woman who he was relieved to not recognise, and Killan untangled himself from his bedding laughing.

'Inir! I thought you were on duty tonight.' Killan sounded warm, welcoming, slightly drunk.

'That I am,' Inir replied, pleasantly, sauntering to the middle of the room, putting himself between Killan and the sword belt draped over the only chair. The woman pushed hair out of her eyes, and reached for the clothing strewn beside the bed.

'So, this is business?' Killan asked, his voice levelling into caution. The woman glanced up sharply, thrust her unclothed feet into her boots, grabbed her breeches, and sidled to the doorway. Inir held the curtain aside for her.

'I'm here to arrest you, Killan,' Inir said softly, his hand resting on the hilt of his sword. 'Please don't make this difficult.'

'Difficult?' Killan threw back the bed covers, revealing his utter nakedness. Inir let his eyes wander over his body, his hand groping for the back of the chair and the shirt tangled with the sword belt. He threw it at Killan. Killan nodded slowly and drew the shirt over his head. 'I owe you that.'

'This is deadly earnest, Killan. I hope it's a mistake and will be sorted out by morning, but I must assume it isn't.'

'Breeches, boy,' Killan said tersely, searching under the bed for his boots. Inir caught the breeches up for the floor, and for a second his eyes were not on Killan. There was a knife in Killan's boot top, and there was a knife in the air, and Inir was flinging himself sideways, and Killan was out the window. He didn't get far, Maeve's blow struck him to one side of his neck and he crumpled at her feet. She crouched beside him, turning his unconscious face toward the light. She stroked the side of his face absently, then peered in through the damaged shutter, at Inir lying in a tangle of clothes.

'Are you all right?'

'Yes.' Inir fought to his feet. 'Just feeling stupid. I hadn't drawn my sword.'

Maeve shrugged.

'We both wanted not to have to. Come and help get him in.'

Inir came to the window.

'Are we going to get him dressed?' Maeve considered the bared thigh by her foot, and curled her toes against the urge to kick Killan really hard.

'I don't think so, no. Let's get him bound up and out of here. He'll be awake by the time we're in the street, I expect. What's the humiliation of walking Broad Street in nothing but a shirt compared to what he's dealt out to us?' Inir shook his head unhappily. 'I really thought he cared for me.'

Maeve sighed.

'I think perhaps he really did – and for me, but it didn't make a difference, beyond making it easier to get us to talk to him.'

'Do you think you ever said anything really damaging?'

Maeve closed her eyes and nodded.

'Probably. Perhaps even enough to get me hanged.' She gazed at Inir, 'You?'

Inir nodded. They looked at each other. Maeve uncurled her toes. 'If you're thinking what I am, about the drop from this roof, and the silence of the dead, I hope you realise that as a sworn officer of the Queen's bodyguard our first duty is to bring justice to this – piece of shit, whatever the consequences.'

Inir nodded, 'Duty,' he said firmly.

'That's right.' Maeve leant and yanked Killan away from the drop, towards the window. Inir reached to help her haul him in over the sill.

'Bastard,' he said coldly.

Maeve leant once more through the window and whistled for Cei. She saw his shadow detach from the corner.

'I have to get back,' she said quietly and stepped back out onto the roof. She measured the leap required at the end of the alley, glanced quickly at Inir to make sure he was coping, then ran, and leapt.

At last, footsteps echoed on the stone stair outside. Brede went to the door, sword at the ready.

Maeve stepped back slightly, seeing the drawn blade.

'Steady,' she said, making a half question of the word, recognising how on edge they all were, her own heart pounding and her breath uneven gasps which were not solely the result of her break-neck rush across the roofs of the city.

She glanced furtively at Phelan's immobile form, then expectantly at Grainne, as she bent her knee into an approximation to a bow.

Grainne gestured her upright, then rested her hand on Sorcha's shoulder. 'It is time,' she said.

Maeve couldn't understand Phelan's unresisting silence, but recognised that Sorcha had something to do with it. So it was to Sorcha that she looked now.

The warriors drew their swords, ready to escort their prisoner. Sorcha forced herself to her feet. She looked Phelan in the face, searching for something – remorse, or perhaps forgiveness. She saw only loathing. She mustered her resources, sang a few notes, and set him free.

Phelan felt the sudden jumping of muscles at last his to control, but not controlled. He forced the trembling into a dull shudder, fighting the urge to let his knees bend under him. He looked around slowly, relishing the movement. It was as he thought; the room as he remembered, the escort as he anticipated. He stepped toward them, warriors he once commanded, now ready to kill him, unarmed and bound though he was, should Grainne give the word. He was certain that she would not give that order; she wanted him alive for now. Phelan took another step forward, testing the strength of his legs; sufficient for what he planned. His eyes swept over Sorcha, and he shook his head slightly.

'I would not have thought this of you,' he said, his voice rasping on the last word. Sorcha flinched away.

He bowed his head to Grainne.

'Cousin,' he said, unrepentant still, undaunted. She half raised her hand, a fluttering in the corner of his eye, no time to think what it might mean: Phelan moved swiftly. He made no attempt to harm Grainne, no bid for freedom. He dived for the balcony, the open shutter, and the freedom of the air.

Maeve's fingers grazed his shoulder as she lunged after him but no more than that, and Phelan flung himself from the parapet, out and down, falling three storeys.

Maeve stared down in horror, her warning to Inir stark in her mind.

Far below her, Phelan stirred. His arms still pinioned, he began to crawl, with agonising slowness, forcing himself toward the river through sheer will. Maeve scarcely heard the commotion behind her, too shocked to take in what else was happening.

Brede reached Phelan first. She made no attempt to touch him; she simply stood between him and his goal, understanding what he was trying to do. If he died, he could not be forced to bear witness at any trial, there would be only her word and Sorcha's that he had confessed, and that he implicated those others who should stand trial with him. Grainne might be accused of his murder, which would further discredit their evidence. Phelan must not be allowed to die.

So, Brede stood between the man and his drowning, and hated herself. He was bleeding and broken, and he cursed her with steady loathing. If ever cursing might be effective, this cursing should be.

Corla arrived, out of breath, and tried to assess his injuries. He screamed at her touch, and Brede pulled her swiftly away. Corla gagged quietly, heart-sickened at Phelan's broken struggling and at Brede's grim refusal to allow him to die.

Brede tried not to think of what she was doing. She wanted nothing more than to allow Phelan to welcome the embrace of the Scavenger – nothing.

Sorcha now, collapsing to her knees beside Phelan, setting about his healing; grim faced, icy voiced, visibly shaking. She sang, and willed his body to mend, but Phelan's will was stronger. To heal, the body must wish to be healed. Sorcha was so tired already, and he wished to die. And still Phelan cursed.

Sorcha sat back on her heels, taking her blooded hands away from the tensed, unmoving body.

'I can't hold you,' she said quietly, and the tension left Phelan in a rush, and with it, his last breath.

Brede closed her eyes, relief weakening her.

Sorcha reached out once more to Phelan, smoothing his hair. Now that he was gone, she could afford to remember him as he had been, the amusing young friend of her youth, the reckless laughing boy, the vulnerable one, always in love with someone – always in love.

'I would not have thought this of you,' she whispered.

Somehow she must find the strength to stand. Somehow she must get to her feet, and somehow she must tell Grainne that Phelan had beaten her. She stared without thought at Phelan's bruised, distorted face, slackening in death. At last she held out her hand to Brede, asking for help to rise, and looked up into Brede's face for the first time. She met an expression that she could find no words to encompass – the blindness in Brede's eyes, the bleached-bone pallor of her skin. Brede eyes dropped to that outstretched hand and she stepped away. Sorcha made to wipe her eyes, and understood Brede's involuntary wincing away. She wiped her hands against the thin grass, but it was not enough to clean the blood from them. Slipping on the sloping ground she forced herself to the water's edge, plunging her hands in to the ice-cold water.

Brede helped Sorcha back to her feet, offering no apology nor explanation.

Sorcha went, trembling, to explain to Grainne.

Brede watched her go, and a sudden need to see nothing but a horizon engulfed her – no walls, no monarchs, and no witches. She closed her mind to the exhaustion in Sorcha's walk, and allowed her to get to the gate before she started after her. She didn't plan to go back into Grainne's tower, or anywhere else, with Sorcha. She turned sharply towards the stables, her mind icy.

Maeve was still in Grainne's chamber, stiffly at attention. Sorcha met her eyes, and shook her head. Maeve, to her surprise, found new depths for her despair. She had not thought to fail so completely, and she had liked Phelan – She didn't understand why she was still standing there, why Grainne had not ordered her execution. Grainne saw the shake of Sorcha's head and sighed.

'I need to sleep, Sorcha. How can I sleep?' she tried not to sound like a petulant child, but she was too distraught to be dignified.

'I am here,' Sorcha replied wearily.

'No, you've done too much already. I've asked too much of you; you and Brede. Now I have tasks I do not think I can ask of either of you. Maeve shall be my guard for the next watch, and after her, Tegan, if she has returned. Find me drugs – that's all I ask. You need rest; take as long as you need.'

Sorcha considered Grainne levelly. She translated her words – *Get away from me. I can't bear to have you here now.*

Well enough, Sorcha preferred not to be close to Grainne now either. She bent her knee, formal, contained. She put the herbs where Grainne could reach them, gathered up a cloak, and left the Queen's quarters.

Sorcha ran down the stairs, almost blind with anger and exhaustion. The halls seem strangely unpeopled. She forced herself to stop her headlong flight, and fought for calm. This was an unnatural quiet, as though the whole city held its breath in fear. Even though several feet of stone closed off the courtyard, Sorcha could hear the flurry of pigeons on the walls. She closed her eyes. She thought of Brede, and the terrible, closed expression that had passed over her face inflicted itself upon her memory. Sorcha shivered, and pulled the cloak close about her. Walking slowly now, she stepped out of the grey light of the tower into the brightness of the courtyard that separated the tower from the barracks. She glanced up at the pigeons, lead-grey wings spread, as she passed under the arch into the practice yard. Here too there was a feeling of desertion. Across the yard then, and round to the stables. If Brede could not be found, there would at least be the horses. Macsen would be a poor substitute, but she could pretend he understood.

Grainne looked at Maeve's immobile face.

'You have failed me, Maeve,' she said, 'and now I must deal differently with those you arrested for me this day. Do you understand me?'

Maeve nodded, unwillingly.

'You will deal with them personally. I have no choice but to believe I can still trust you. You will not fail me again.'

Grainne couldn't bear to look at Maeve. She longed for Tegan to return, Tegan who had told her nothing but the truth, even when she hadn't wanted to hear it. The silence stretched and she turned back to Maeve, waiting for her answer.

Maeve paled, but at last she inclined her head in response. She was a soldier, she must follow orders. She must deal with the prisoners, as soon as Tegan could be found to relieve her of her present duty. She wished abruptly that she had thrown Killan from his roof; it would have been easier – she recoiled, seeing again Phelan's broken determination to die. Maeve took an unsteady breath, trying to imagine what must come.

I can't, she thought, *I can't do it – I can't, I can't –*

Chapter Twenty-Nine

In the familiar darkness of the stables, Brede headed straight for the corner where Guida's tack was stored. She wrenched the bridle from the hook and slung it over her shoulder, then hauled the Plains saddle from its rest, cradling it against her chest as she moved the few steps that took her to Guida's side. She settled the saddle hastily in place and pulled the bridle over Guida's head. She swore bitterly as Guida pulled sharply away from her fumbling.

'Leave the poor beast be,' Eachan said, taking the leather from her shaking hands.

Brede tried to get her breathing under control, willing her eyes to stop smarting. Neala pulled at her elbow.

'Which way is the wind blowing?' she asked, her voice husky and her accent shaky. Brede looked down at her next-kin.

Towards death she thought.

'Kinward.' Her voice sounded tight, even to her own ears. She ushered Neala away from Guida, who was beginning to stamp at too many people too close.

'My kin?' Neala asked uncertainly.

'Yes,' Brede said fiercely, 'I will claim Clan Right for you. You're blood of Wing Clan on both sides, they'll not refuse you.'

'Even though I sound like a city dweller? Even though I've no horse?'

'Even so. Carolan will be grateful to have something of Falda again.'

'Are you sure?'

'Certain. And if by some lunacy he does not, you have kin in the Marshes too. My mother would welcome you with open heart.' Brede put a reassuring hand on Neala's shoulder, and briefly the child looked so like Falda that it stopped her breath.

'I need to know,' Brede said abruptly. 'I need to know how and when and –'

Neala laid a hand over Brede's, and nodded quickly.

'My mother died at midwinter four years ago, of a fever. She'd been ill for a long time. Nothing particular, only that she got thin and tired and had nothing left to fight with when the fever came.'

Neala looked up at Brede's shadowed face trying to gauge how much she should say, wanting to move away from that memory. Brede winced at that calm, adult explanation. Neala caught the look, but didn't know what to do with it.

'She spoke of you often. She thought you were dead. She said she saw you struck down;' Neala made a slicing movement with the side of her hand. 'She grieved for you, more than for any of her kin, save Carolan.'

'She was so close? I couldn't find her. I couldn't see her.'

'She had no chance to go to your aid, she was captured almost at once.'

'By Madoc?'

'The same.'

Brede waited for Neala to continue, but the silence dragged.

'He sold you when Falda died?' Brede prompted. Neala nodded, a slight movement that kept her eyes hidden. She tied knot after knot into the cloth of her belt, pulling each one tight, then wrapping the loose end around her fingers.

'I was no use, once she was dead; a burden. He used to allow her to teach me Clan ways, provided he was there. I hardly saw her but he was there too. He wanted to know everything there was to know about the Clans.'

Brede shuddered, remembering Madoc's offer to Grainne. Neala glanced up suddenly, a fierce grin on her face, the belt unravelled from her fingers.

'We taught him a thing or two, before he got good enough with the language. It was days before he realised that what we'd told him was the correct greeting to another Clan was actually *I am your enemy.*' The smile slipped. 'He thought it amusing,' she said, her voice utterly bleak. Brede reached out, intending comfort, but Neala shrugged her away and slipped past, to take Guida's reins from Eachan.

Brede heard steps behind her, and turned. Sorcha's eyes flickered from her face to the horse.

'Leaving?' she asked.

Brede looked away, taking the reins from Neala and twisting them.

'I've fulfilled my contract.'

Sorcha rubbed her hand across her eyes. No comfort then. She gazed about the stables, grasping after some way of expressing the depth of her distress.

Eachan saw, and beckoned Neala to him.

'Come and help me wax some saddles,' he suggested.

Neala trailed reluctantly after Eachan.

'I must take my next-kin back to our Clan,' Brede said, her voice husky, angry with herself for making excuses. 'I needed time to talk to Neala.'

'Has it helped?' Sorcha asked, aware of how short that time had been.

'Yes.'

Sorcha didn't need the saddled horse to know that Brede was on the point of walking out of her life.

'Phelan was my friend once,' she said at last, feeling her way through the litter of possible causes for Brede's rejection.

Brede sighed restlessly. 'Have mercy on your enemies.'

'It was a long time ago. He was young, charming, ambitious, wild. The sort of man who gets his way. I suppose we all indulged him, Aeron, Grainne and I.'

Sorcha rubbed patterns into Guida's hide, frowning.

Brede checked Guida's girth, pretending that what Sorcha was saying was idle chatter, but when Sorcha's voice trailed into silence, she looked up, straight into Sorcha's eyes, too close for comfort. Brede went to collect her saddle roll.

'Aeron indulged him more than either you or Grainne realised.'

Sorcha hunched a shoulder, bemused.

'I think that hurts Grainne more than anything else, that she had no idea.'

'Or because she is jealous?'

'No, she could've had Phelan for the asking, but Aeron always came first with Phelan, and with Grainne. Losing her hit them both hard.' Sorcha sighed deeply. 'Grainne can't cope with this.'

Brede placed the saddle roll across Guida's back, gently shifting it to lie level. Sorcha reached a hesitant hand to stroke Brede's fingers. Brede jerked away momentarily, then took Sorcha's hand and turned it palm up, sniffing at it.

'Between us – Grainne, Maeve, you and I – we killed this man who was your friend.'

Sorcha shook her head.

'It was his choice.'

'We drove him to that choice, and you allowed him to die.'

'I couldn't stop him.'

'He cursed me, Sorcha, he cursed me with such – hatred – I could feel the words sticking to me, just as his blood stuck to your hands.'

'Just words.'

'No, Sorcha, no more than your songs are just words. I feel stained – marked.'

Brede rubbed her forehead gently with the side of her thumb.

'Is that why you're running away?' Sorcha asked.

'I don't imagine I can outrun a curse, but I can't stay here any longer.'

'Why not?'

'I can't. There is no why.' Brede lapsed into her own language suddenly. 'The wind is blowing,' she said softly.

Sorcha wrapped her arms about herself, seeking comfort.

'I feel it,' she said.

'Feel it?'

'The wind. I never have before, but you are right. It is no longer safe here.'

'What about Grainne?'

'Grainne.' Sorcha's voice had a sombre tone to it. 'Grainne is an old friend. Well, I allowed one old friend to die today. Grainne has asked more of me than she has a right to, and I've done it, in the name of friendship, without thinking. I have allowed her needs to become my own.'

'So, now?'

'I can't. I promised her.'

Brede frowned. 'Loyalty?' she asked.

Sorcha's mouth twisted. 'She still needs to try for peace; she still needs the strength I can give her. Not for long now, one way or another, and then I will be free of what Grainne needs. It must be loyalty, mustn't it, for it feels like a burden now.'

'What was it before?'

'Love.'

Brede tested that word against the terrible doubt in her heart and found it still held her, there was still some spark of value there.

'Talk to me,' she said. 'Tell me who you are, or what you are. Tell me why you can keep Grainne alive, why the whole course of the war depends on you – and don't tell me it doesn't, I won't believe you. I am staying, but only while you talk. The wind is at my back, I will listen; but not for long.'

A slow smile spread across Sorcha's face.

'I love you,' she said softly. Brede's fingers clenched about the leather.

'That isn't what I meant.'

'It is what I mean, with every bone in my body. It isn't who or what I am, but it could be.'

'You don't mean that. Your sense of duty is far too strong.'

'Is that what you think? I came here because I was running away from duty. I crept away to be with an old friend who needed me, and I left behind duty. I thought of this as an adventure, as freedom.'

'This was freedom?'

'Yes, but – so irresponsible; a mistake. I should have sent someone else, someone who would have kept Grainne strong, and no more. I'm too close to Grainne, I couldn't see where I should stop, only that I could meet her needs.'

'What are we talking about?' Brede asked, confused. Sorcha reached suddenly, gripping Brede's wrist.

'Power. That is what you're asking me, isn't it? Who I am, what I am. You know that I am a witch. You know how strong I am.'

Brede nodded impatiently. 'A Songspinner.' She pulled against Sorcha's hand; reassured that she had chosen physical force, to keep her still.

'More,' Sorcha continued, abandoning caution. 'I'm *the* Songspinner.' She shook her head suddenly. 'I've been deceiving myself, in blaming Grainne. I chose every step I took. But it's too late now. I have to finish what I've begun.'

'And if you had not begun?'

'Then I would be free to come with you – but you will not have me.'

Brede pulled free of Sorcha's grip and took a sudden interest in Guida's mane, finding snarls that were invisible to Sorcha.

'Tell me what you are afraid of,' Sorcha said. 'Tell me what I have to do to convince you.'

Brede shook her head.

'What does the – Songspinner? – want with me?'

'Love.' Sorcha said, barely a whisper. 'Desire, need.'

'Need?' Brede asked doubtfully.

'Need,' Sorcha said firmly. 'Like water, like air, like the movement of wind on tall grass.'

'You don't expect me to believe that,' Brede asked, shaken.

'Expect? No, but hope – for pity's sake Brede, stop doubting me. Stop building walls and expecting me to knock them down for you. If you can trust *Grainne*, if you can *love* Tegan; you can show *me* a reason for my meagre hope.'

Brede slapped Guida's shoulder, edging her out of the way. Very slowly she stepped forward so that she was within touching distance of Sorcha. Sorcha risked a glance at Brede's eyes. She could see no softening of Brede's resolve, no understanding. She tried to swallow the tight knot of distress that choked her.

Brede's fingers traced the spasm in Sorcha's throat, barely touching, a flicker of flesh against flesh.

'It isn't the same,' Brede said. 'I hope for nothing from Grainne, so it costs very little to trust her. I resisted Tegan; I put my life in her hands, but never my heart.' She lifted her hand, caressing the side of Sorcha's face. Even to think of the trust she had offered Sorcha was to be reminded of desire, which seemed like a betrayal now. 'So much power,' she said, and her voice was no more than breath. 'You frighten me.'

Sorcha reached a hesitant hand to Brede's hair, which was coming loose from its bindings.

'Stay.'

Brede laughed – a strange sound, like anger – like despair.

'I can't.'

'Stay,' Sorcha said, again, more assertively.

Brede pulled free, alarmed at the quickening in her blood at Sorcha's touch.

'I can't,' she said, very gently. 'I have to get Neala away.'

'Will you come back?' Sorcha asked, watching for a shift in Brede's granite resistance.

'No,' Brede said at last. 'Once I'm back with Wing Clan, I'll not return.'

'If you didn't have to go, would you stay with me?' Sorcha asked, echoing Brede's question.

Brede thought, and thought, and finally reached out to hold Sorcha.

'How can I say what I think, or what I hope? I can't speak my heart. There are no words.'

'So?' Sorcha asked, hoping that the tremor in Brede's arms spoke of passion.

'So,' Brede said. 'This is where we stand.'

'So,' Sorcha echoed, 'you will go to Wing Clan.'

'Yes.'

Sorcha reached to pull Brede closer.

'But not until morning?'

'First light,' Brede said firmly.

'Sunrise,' Sorcha compromised, winding her arms about Brede tenderly; feeling the tremors still, resistance ending.

'Sunrise,' Brede agreed.

Chapter Thirty

Maeve waited until Grainne drifted into sleep before she slipped away. She couldn't wait any longer for Tegan. Right now, she did not know how to control the feeling of betrayal and contamination and hopelessness that smothered her. She was afraid she might hurt Tegan if she saw her; if Tegan didn't strike her down first. Closing the door softly behind her, she breathed more deeply, and leant against the cold wall.

What now? Her mind slithered away from that other betrayal, those friends whose treachery led her here, to these choices. She half knew that she was about to make a bad choice, but still her mind screamed at her, *I can't, I can't,* and at end, there was only this one, last, dreadful, thing left for her to do. Maeve rubbed at her face, and pushed through the outer door. She stumbled down to where Riordan guarded the stairs. She glanced from her brother to Cei, and could find no words. Riordan's eyes flickered across her face, and he drew his sword, slowly – not wanting to precipitate anything. Maeve glanced at the blade, and found the strength to straighten her back, to smile in reassurance.

'A guard is needed above,' she said, her voice husky.

Riordan nodded, and gestured Cei away up the stair.

'Maeve?' he asked, his voice barely a whisper, the sword still in his hand.

'What you do not know, you can't be blamed for,' Maeve said, gripping his shoulder. 'I have orders from the Queen, and I…' She shook her head sharply, it wasn't safe. 'I'm sorry,' she whispered and walked briskly towards the barracks.

Riordan didn't sheathe his sword. His mind raced, telling over the prisoners and his sister's expression. He had to do something, but he could at least give her some small moment of grace, As soon as Maeve was safely out of sight, he called Cei back, and sent him for reinforcements.

Maeve slipped through the stable, loosening the tether of her horse, gathering saddle and bridle. Aware of the increased amount of activity between the barracks and the tower, she scarcely stopped to ensure the buckles of the saddle were secure before she mounted, and was away.

Stealing out of the city, Maeve was forcibly reminded of Tegan's anger at the lax security, and for the first time allowed that she was right – although she no longer cared. As soon as she could safely do so, she allowed her horse free rein, riding along the river as fast as the horse could go in the darkness, wanting only to put a good distance between herself and any hunt that might follow.

It was only when she was challenged by the sentry that Maeve realised that she had forgotten the first rule of a warrior's life. *Enemy territory.*

She stared down at the spear point levelled at her heart, at the red marking on the shaft, and made a swift decision.

'I have news for Lorcan,' she said calmly, 'from Phelan.'

Disturbed by the distant clatter of hooves on cobbles, Brede stirred, and began to dream, and woke suddenly from that dream, afraid. A rider burst into the courtyard, almost falling as she dismounted a horse that hadn't quite come to a stand. Brede dragged her clothes into a semblance of order and went to investigate. Sorcha wasn't far behind her.

Tegan grabbed a torch from its sconce, calling out for Maeve. She scarcely glanced at Brede, save to nod to her.

'Is Maeve still with Grainne?' Brede murmured to Corla, as the crowd in the yard increased in size. Corla shook her head.

'Horse has gone,' Eachan muttered, a sense of unease gripping him.

'Who's Maeve?' Neala asked, her clear voice piercing above the uneasy muttering. Brede gave her a brief description. Neala nodded in understanding.

'She rode out of here shortly after the hour,' she said.

'She did what?' Tegan asked. 'Where was she going?'

'How could I know?'

Brede sensed a ripple of anxiety pass through the small crowd of Maeve's warriors; each and every one of them knew what had occurred this day, each of them save Tegan. Quickly she drew Tegan by the arm, pulling her into a corner of the yard.

'Phelan's dead,' she said bluntly. Tegan gasped.

'Hush,' Brede said. 'I've not done. He threw himself from the balcony of Grainne's chamber. Maeve let him fall. There are prisoners, Killan and Ula among them. Grainne will have given Maeve orders.'

Tegan's face became drawn, her distress apparent even in the uncertain light of the torches.

'Has she carried out those orders?'

Brede glanced at the knot of warriors, noting who was absent.

'Those set to guard are not here, but their horses are, so you can hope they're still at their places,' she said. Tegan closed her eyes, understanding what would push Maeve into flight. Those traitors were Maeve's drinking companions, friends, and closer even than that.

'Then she has gone.'

Tegan pulled away from Brede's grasp, unable to contain her anger at

Maeve, nor her grief for her. She strode once more to the centre of the yard, calling for attention.

Tegan put aside grief.

'There is an army out beyond our walls,' she said, her voice suddenly soft, but carrying for all that. 'Lorcan's army, brought here by Phelan, and now it seems that Maeve may have gone to tell the enemy what has befallen him and his spies. I'm going to find out what our liege lady wants us to do.' Her words fell into a silence, broken only by the hiss of Eachan's breath, drawn through his teeth. Tegan beckoned to Sorcha. 'I think Grainne may need you.'

Eachan grabbed at Tegan's arm, furious with her.

'You don't know what you're saying. How could Maeve *know* Lorcan would be out there? If she has found him she's probably dead.'

'I hope she is,' someone in the group of warriors muttered.

Tegan pulled her arm free of Eachan's grip, unheeding.

'Grainne needs me,' she said coldly.

Eachan turned to Brede, hoping she would talk sense to Tegan, and perhaps even to Grainne, but he saw the drawn, disquieted look on her face and asked a quite different question from the one he had planned.

'What ails you?'

'Is Grainne going to have them all killed? Without trial?' Brede asked faintly.

'They are traitors,' Eachan said, hushing her firmly, turning her by the arm, back into the seclusion of the stables.

'Are they? I hope you're right, Eachan, because if they are not, none of us are safe, and I have been ...' She couldn't finish. 'Whatever the outcome of this battle, I'm leaving as soon as it is safe to do so. If it isn't too late already. I have to take Neala back to Wing Clan.'

'More frightened of staying with the witch than of going home finally?' Eachan asked gently. Brede pulled sharply away from him.

'Neala needs to be with her kin.'

'And you don't? Why are you so afraid to go back? You could have gone back any time in the last ten years if you'd wanted to, but only now, when there's something that might be worth staying away for, you go back. It makes no sense.' Eachan reached to clasp her shoulder. 'Rumour has it that Maeve let the General fall, but it was you provided him with the chance, opening the shutters as you did.'

Brede had been trying to dodge that memory.

'You're finally in danger of making enemies, girl. Keep your head down for a while, if Grainne will let you. See if she still loves you. We might as well all be on trial for our lives just now, thanks to Maeve.'

'Don't blame Maeve.'

'I don't, but Grainne will. I'll keep an eye on your next-kin. Go build bridges while you've the chance.' Eachan gave her a shove between the shoulder blades that set her off balance. 'Go on, Grainne listens to you, see if you can dig us out of this, before you go.'

Uncertainly, Brede made her way to the foot of Grainne's stair.

Riordan let her pass, but Brede went no further than the outer chamber. Sorcha caught sight of her and stilled her impatient walking, holding her arms out in welcome. Brede kissed her briefly, and drew away.

'Why are you still out here?' she asked.

'Tegan is with her.'

'I don't hear anything.'

Sorcha shrugged helplessly.

'She won't be shouting, with Maeve's brother at her door.'

'Does this change your plans?'

'It must. Lorcan is at the gate. Any peace talks must happen at once.'

'But after that?'

Sorcha shook her head and set her mind to their more immediate preparations, and started by searching under the bed for the discarded greatsword. It gave her a moment to recover.

'We don't need that, do we?' Brede protested, at the thought of the blade. She had come to hate that weapon.

'Grainne will need it,' Sorcha said, suddenly wanting to smash the sword and Grainne with it.

'For what?'

'As a symbol of her sole rule – to remind Lorcan that his bid to use Phelan failed.' Sorcha straightened from her search. 'Perhaps to behead her traitors, I don't know – where is it?'

'In the stable.'

Sorcha sighed.

'Why did she choose Maeve?' Brede asked.

'Revenge. She wanted Phelan alive, Maeve failed her. Be grateful she didn't choose you.'

'Has she some other revenge planned for me?'

Sorcha gazed at Brede. So soon after her rage at Grainne that question chilled her. She couldn't shrug the uneasiness away.

Brede walked to the inner door, shamelessly pressing her ear against it.

'I still can't hear anything. Nothing at all.' She caught Sorcha's look, lifted the latch and pushed hard on the door.

'How is it with the Queen?' Sorcha asked, trying to steady her voice.

'She sleeps,' Tegan said quietly.

Sorcha could think of only one way Grainne could sleep now.

'What are you thinking, Tegan? Would you let her slip into death so quietly? Why did you say nothing sooner?'

Tegan's impassivity slipped from her face, and pain and exhaustion and grief were there, like bruising.

'I'd willingly let her sleep, and yes, let her die, if that's what she wants,' she said defiantly, but she could not meet Sorcha's enraged, wide-eyed anguish. Sorcha pushed her aside, flinging herself down at the bedside.

Sorcha took her friend's hand in hers, lacing her fingers between Grainne's. *Not dead yet.*

'Go guard the door, Tegan,' she said, as kindly as she could bear to be. 'This is my work to do now.'

Tegan withdrew reluctantly.

For a moment Brede thought she might follow Sorcha into Grainne's room, might in some way assist. She caught the intense concentration on Sorcha's half-turned face, and found no place for her.

'So –' she turned away without finishing the thought.

Sorcha gazed at Grainne's face, seeing that her spirit was far withdrawn from reality. It would be so easy to let her slip away now, peacefully, as Grainne must wish to go. Sorcha let the Queen's limp hand fall, and checked the herbs that she had left, so conveniently within reach. If Grainne truly wished to die, the dose she had taken would free her, but if she did not wish it, she could fight the numbing of her thoughts, the slowing of her heart – perhaps it was even an accident. Sorcha hesitated to discover Grainne's choice, but, despite Tegan's challenge, to leave without trying to revive her was beyond her.

Sorcha considered, weighing her resources against her friendship. She decided, despite her own mind-numbing exhaustion, to be gentle – to use her own strength rather than Grainne's. Sorcha lay beside the Queen, her hands entwined with Grainne's. What she planned was dangerous; she didn't want to slip out of consciousness and fall. She chose her song with care, winding gently into Grainne's mind, smoke from a dying fire.

Grainne had slipped a long way out of herself, needing a great distance to find her peace. Sorcha stirred her gently, igniting the embers of her consciousness. She found a taint of death there, Grainne's long illness, and now this flirtation with the Scavenger. Sorcha felt Grainne's awareness of her, the half protest and then – clawed despair – pulling them together into the abyss.

Sorcha tried to draw back to the surface of her wakeful mind, but she couldn't bring Grainne with her. Grainne clung to Sorcha within their shared consciousness, holding her back, pulling her deeper into the darkness. Sorcha stared down into the dark, trying to assess the depth. The darkness was velvet soft, uncertain – nothing to hold onto, nothing to take a bearing from. Sorcha tried to work out how far Grainne had sunk, how far Grainne had dragged her – and suddenly she was struggling against the gentle silence, not to save Grainne, but to save herself – aware that her body couldn't support that effort for long. She fought to free herself of Grainne, panicked into a silent screaming, lashing out with all of her power to free herself of the suffocating nightmare that was Grainne's death. And still Grainne clung to her.

The song died on Sorcha's lips, as she stared into the face of the Scavenger. No nightmare this, but cold reality – Sorcha hadn't expected the harbinger of death to be beautiful, it was a heart-stopping shock. Just for a moment she stopped struggling. The Scavenger untangled Grainne's limbs from Sorcha's with slow patience, determined to make her give Grainne up. Sorcha forgot to fight, forgot to think, forgot to breathe. Grainne's limp arms draped about the Scavenger in a travesty of an embrace, as it collected her to its breast, gently, lover-like – and still the Scavenger's eyes held Sorcha's.

Tegan sat with her back against the door to Grainne's chamber, with her drawn sword across her knees, and hoped for the song that pulled against Grainne to end; yet when the song finally drifted into silence, she waited, unwilling to discover the result of Sorcha's efforts. When she still heard nothing, no movement from beyond the closed door, she knew she could wait no longer.

Grainne lay motionless and blank-eyed, one hand trailing over the edge of the bed, almost touching the floor. Sorcha sat beside the Queen, her hands clenched into Grainne's hair, rocking in silent grief. Tegan looked at the Queen, who lay, so clearly dead, in the room she should have been guarding. Were it not for Sorcha, and the almost silent gasps of despair that racked her, Tegan could feel relief at the sight. Quietly she pulled the door shut, and walked the few yards to the outer door where Riordan stood guard.

'Find Brede,' she ordered.

Riordan saw Tegan's haggard expression and drawn sword, and stilled his urge to question. He vanished down the stairs as though the Scavenger were after him.

Tegan leant back into the door frame, seeking the support of stone, and finding it inadequate to her need. Slowly she allowed her body to sink to the floor, the sword still in her hand. She laid it carefully down, across the threshold, and waited for Brede to come.

Chapter Thirty-One

Brede climbed the stairs to Grainne's chamber, head tilted upward, as though expecting ambush. At the sight of Tegan's foot lying against the top stair, she leapt up the last few steps, to find Tegan slumped in the doorway.

Tegan stirred, and held out a hand for Brede to help her up. Tegan pulled her into the chamber. Brede stumbled, almost catching her foot on the hilt of Tegan's sword, laid across the threshold.

Tegan pushed the door shut and leant against it.

'Grainne is dead.'

Brede stepped back, an involuntary movement, quickly checked. It wasn't as though she hadn't been half expecting this. She went to the inner door.

Sorcha sat on the bed, cradling Grainne, stroking her hair. She didn't look up as the door opened. She smoothed Grainne's brow, then lifted her burden slightly and kissed her closed eyes.

Brede shuddered. She had often felt Sorcha's lips placed against her own eyelids in that caress.

'Sorcha,' Brede whispered.

Sorcha raised her head.

'You shall not have her.'

'I don't want her,' Brede said. 'I want you.'

Sorcha was silent, unmoved, unmoving. Brede stepped towards her, one slow cautious step.

'Grainne should have her crown, she should have her guard –' Brede tried.

'She hated the crown.' Sorcha's eyes followed Brede's slow approach suspiciously. She glanced down at Grainne, a sudden frown on her face.

'I never thought it would be beautiful.'

'What?'

'It. The Scavenger. So beautiful.' Sorcha's gaze rose once more, but it wasn't Brede she saw. 'I will recognise it next time,' she said. 'I will be ready for it. I shall guard against it.'

'Sorcha –' Brede edged onto the bed, one hand reaching out to Sorcha, but not touching. 'You can't guard against death itself. No one can do that.'

'I can.' Sorcha said angrily, slapping away Brede's hand. '*I* can. It won't steal anyone from me again.'

Brede bit her lip. At least somewhere in her grief Sorcha did seem to know that Grainne was dead, but Brede didn't know how to separate the Queen from her over vigilant guard.

'Sorcha.' The eyes drifted back to Brede's face. 'Tell me who I am.'

'You are Brede,' Sorcha said, content to answer without wondering why.

'What am I?'

'Trouble.' Brede recoiled, despite the softness of Sorcha's tone. 'Trouble,' Sorcha said again, rubbing at her eyes as though they pained her. 'Glorious, wonderful, troublesome Brede.'

'Why trouble?' Brede asked.

'You get in the way.'

'Do I?' Brede asked.

'Wherever I turn, there you are, in my mind, blocking out everything else.' She loosened her hold on Grainne, reaching her hand towards Brede, touching her face, brooding. 'This face,' she said. 'Always there.'

Brede closed her own hand over Sorcha's, bringing it to her lips, kissing her knuckles, her palm.

Slowly Sorcha's other hand untangled from Grainne's hair, and wavered towards Brede's unkempt plait.

'I never stop thinking about you,' Sorcha said, frowning deeply.

'Nor I you,' Brede said, beyond surprise. Sorcha stayed silent for a long time, unmoving, her eyes almost closed. Then her eyes opened once more and she focussed on Brede as though seeing her for the first time.

'Hold me,' Sorcha said, staring out of nightmare at a beacon of hope.

Brede held her close, pulling her away from Grainne's limp outstretched hand, off the bed, onto the floor, holding her tight, so tight.

'I will never let you go, never,' Brede whispered into Sorcha's hair, feeling the shudders storm through her body. Sorcha sobbed incoherently, turning her face away, trying to fight her way out of the dread that still held her.

'Never,' Brede said again, desperately, not knowing what else to do.

Sorcha took a long shuddering breath, and then another, half choking. She leant her head back against the side of the bed, eyes tight shut. A gentler breath and she turned slightly so that she could see Brede.

'That's enough,' she said abruptly. 'You can let go now.'

Brede loosened her hold a fraction, startled at the normality of her tone.

'I'll never let you go,' Brede said furiously.

'Enough to let me breathe?'

Brede loosened her hold a little more.

'Are you safe?'

'No, no I'm not – but I'm not dangerous.'

Brede nodded and pulled away, putting sufficient distance between them that she could see Sorcha's face properly.

'Am I really troublesome?' she asked.

'Exceedingly. It's one of your most irritating virtues.'

'Virtues?'

Sorcha nodded, wiping tears from her face with her sleeve.

'Never stop being troublesome. It is a rare and wonderful gift, and I love you for it.'

She smiled, an attempt at reassurance, and struggled to her feet.

Brede blinked. Sorcha moved away, and stood over Grainne's body.

'Is this peace?' she asked, folding first one limp arm and then the other across Grainne's wasted body. 'Is this what you wanted?' Sorcha pulled Grainne's robe into a semblance of order, then smoothed her hair. She sighed. 'I failed her, with everything I had to give her, I failed her completely.'

Brede scrambled to her feet. 'She's gone,' she said swiftly.

'Yes,' Sorcha covered her eyes, trying to blot out the sight. Brede laid a hesitant hand on her forearm.

'I thought I'd lost you.'

Sorcha stared at Brede for a long time, before she answered. 'Never.'

Brede could think of no answer to that. She allowed the silence to last, almost content. At last, Sorcha broke the silence.

'What do we do now?'

Brede took her hand before turning to Tegan. Tegan shrugged miserably.

'There's no hope of defending the city. The defences have been undermined with great efficiency. There's nothing to be gained from trying.'

'What do you suggest?' Sorcha asked.

'You want my honest opinion?'

'Of course.'

'I'm a mercenary, not a politician,' Tegan warned, 'I think we should let free the prisoners, be exceedingly polite to them, and open the gates to Lorcan. Let him walk in. There's nothing to be lost. Phelan planned to betray Lorcan, after all; I doubt Lorcan will rue his passing. He could only have been a threat now that Grainne is dead.'

Sorcha moved slowly across the room to the shuttered window. Dawn was beginning to filter into the dullness of the sky. She squinted through the slats.

'You can see them now,' she said softly, rapping her fingers against the shutter. 'It is the sensible thing to do, there is no question. But why should he get what he wants?' she turned abruptly from the window.

Tegan stiffened in frustration, beginning to doubt the calm reason of Sorcha's voice.

'What are you planning?'

Sorcha glanced at her, struggling to remember what Tegan knew, and what she did not.

'Be careful of Lorcan. He is Phelan's.'

'Phelan's?'

'His son. According to Phelan. And according to Phelan he does not know it, but he might have guessed. Lorcan's killed one father; he may not grieve over the other, but all the same, be careful what you say to him of Phelan.'

'You'll not be here?'

'It is not safe. Lorcan is not Grainne. He – distrusts – power in others. I must leave at once.'

'Where will you go?' Brede asked softly, feeling the world begin to slip away from her, hardly daring to grab after it, for fear of setting a landslide in motion. Sorcha was already half way to the door.

'With you,' she said, puzzled.

The world righted itself again, and Brede laughed, dizzy with relief.

'We should leave at once,' Sorcha said.

She flung open the door, and glanced down at the sword, lying so neatly across the threshold. She had a sudden desire to kick it away.

'There is some significance to this?' she asked Tegan.

'Tradition,' Tegan said. 'It keeps out evil spirits.'

Sorcha sighed. 'Pick it up.'

Brede glanced from Sorcha to Tegan, doubting, but she stepped forward, and lifted the sword from the stone floor.

'Grainne's dead, Tegan, you can't guard her any more, from spirits or mortals,' Sorcha said sadly. 'So let us see what we can do for the living?'

Tegan nodded, and took the sword from Brede's outstretched hand.

'I'll get you out of here if I can,' she agreed.

Reaching the bottom of the stair, Tegan considered the guards. Under her eyes Riordan stood straighter, wondering at their silent approach after the commotion of voices at the top of the stair. Tegan took a deep breath.

'The Queen is dead,' she said. 'The next person to climb those stairs will be the new king, who is even now approaching the city. No one apart from Lorcan is to go up without my presence. If I am not with them, kill them.'

Her eyes raked Riordan's face, then she nodded her satisfaction, and rejoined Sorcha and Brede.

'A little excessive?' Sorcha asked.

'The crown is up there and I don't know who we can trust any more.'

Sorcha raised an eyebrow. It all seemed so petty now, nothing to do with her. She clutched at Brede's hand, hardly daring to think about the future.

Neala was asleep in the hayloft, one of the many stable cats draped about her shoulders. Eachan sat beside her, listening to the deep rumble of contentment from the cat, and feeling the transient nature of the quietness. As he waited for the peace to be broken he cleaned a sword. Hearing footsteps below, Eachan slid forward to the edge of the loft and peered down.

'You won't need that,' Tegan said, as her eyes caught the glint of metal.

'Ah,' Eachan climbed down to face her; 'she's gone?'

Tegan nodded, and stretched trying to get the tensions out of her back.

'Poor lass,' Eachan said. He eyed Sorcha. 'You'll be taking off away from here then? Surprised you've not gone already. Not got one of those disappearing tricks tucked away handy?'

Sorcha shrugged.

'Can't carry three that way,' she said cautiously, not sure how much Eachan really knew.

'You'll be wanting your horse then, and a Plains saddle perhaps?' Eachan glanced the length of the stable to where Macsen was tethered. Brede hauled her own Plains saddle from its resting place and carried it to Guida, talking to the horse in a soft murmur as she did so. Tegan thought hard.

'Use the north gate,' she said, handing Sorcha a pass, 'and wait until you've heard the trumpets sound. I plan to give Lorcan plenty to think about, get away while he's busy.'

'I will,' Sorcha said.

Tegan nodded, considering. She slapped her gloves against the wall with nervous energy.

'Were I you, I'd not come back,' she said, 'and don't let anyone who knows you see you leave.'

Sorcha scarcely nodded, silent and withdrawn, now that there was the semblance of a plan.

Tegan smiled wanly, wanting to be gone. She glanced at Brede, involved in bridling her horse. She flicked her gloves against the wall again thoughtfully, then walked out of the stables at a brisk speed, before she said something she would regret.

Sorcha climbed to the hayloft and shook Neala awake.

'Come, we're leaving.'

Neala struggled out of her nest dislodging the reluctant cat and followed Sorcha down the ladder.

'Ready?' Brede asked as Eachan led Macsen into the yard.

Neala nodded and mounted Guida in a fluid movement that brought a smile to Brede's lips. Sorcha was on Macsen's back almost as swiftly. Brede looked for Tegan.

'She's gone off in a sulk,' Eachan said.

Brede frowned, and pulled at the straps that held the saddle pack in place. She glared closely at the pack and discovered a lack in it. She glanced about, trying to think what it was that was missing. Eachan offered her the sword. Brede raised an eyebrow.

'She can't use it now,' Eachan said softly, anxious not to draw Sorcha's attention to their transaction. He wasn't quite sure what prompted him to put the Dowry blade back into the hands of the Plains woman and in so doing, place it out of Lorcan's grasp.

Brede thrust the sword beneath the straps of her pack, making it secure.

'Tell Tegan –' she said, then stopped, struggling with the weight of all the words that would be necessary.

'Don't worry, Tegan knows,' Eachan said gently. He cleared his throat suddenly and scowled at her. 'Get the horizon behind you, girl. Rumour has it that Lorcan doesn't care for Plains folk, nor witches.'

Brede pulled herself up behind Neala. She glanced down at Eachan.

'Be strong,' she said, finding nothing more original to encompass what she wanted to say.

'Stay safe,' Eachan responded, suddenly anxious for the danger he had put in her way. He turned away swiftly.

Brede set her heels to Guida's flanks, and followed Sorcha's impatient lead out of the stable yard, and across the barracks forecourt, at speed, hoping that Tegan was keeping her warriors busy, and they wouldn't be seen.

Maeve's heart sank at the sound of trumpets. She wrapped her reins another turn about her hand, in readiness. But the trumpets continued to sound, not in defiance as she first imagined, but in valediction. The white stallion next to her stirred uneasily. The boy on its back pulled on his reins, unnecessarily brutal. Maeve glanced at him, recognising that fierce control for fear.

'What are the trumpets for?' Lorcan asked.

'Grainne,' Maeve said softly. Lorcan's breath caught into a surprised laugh.

'Dead?' he asked incredulously. 'Fate smiles.' His eyes rose to the walls of the city, eager for some sign. The trumpets continued their grieving, and the gates remain closed.

'What's keeping them?' The King asked, as the tone of the trumpet changed, becoming a welcoming fanfare and the gates swung open.

Maeve kept her head down passing under the gateway. She had thrown away her honour for nothing.

Lorcan had not been within these walls since his early childhood, and for a second his confidence failed him and he wasn't sure which direction to take. He glanced at Maeve's grim expression, and found himself amused. With greater assurance, he turned his horse to follow the broad street to the tower.

Maeve followed, sending a silent word of gratitude to the Goddess for Tegan's good sense. She could not meet the eyes of the silent guards at the tower gateway, but she heard the soft hiss of anger as she passed. They dismounted in the courtyard, and Eachan came, grey-faced, to take Lorcan's horse. Maeve allowed Lorcan a few paces away before she turned urgently to Eachan.

Eachan turned his blind eye toward her. Maeve scowled, wondering if she would have to live with the scorn of her old friends forever. She hurried after Lorcan, catching him at the foot of the stair, where Tegan waited.

Tegan's eyes locked with Maeve's. She could think of nothing to say. She led Lorcan up the stairs. Maeve followed, a careful few yards distant, disassociating herself from Lorcan, and from Tegan.

Lorcan could scarce hide his impatience, pushing past Tegan as soon as they reached the door to Grainne's chamber. He barely glanced at Grainne's body, as he turned to search the presses and chests. His hand closed on the crown almost at once, and he flung it onto a chair, then continued searching. Tegan stood stiffly to attention, her eyes following him.

'Where is it?' he asked her at last.

Tegan thought how to answer that. Lorcan was not Grainne; he would not encourage the easy familiarity Grainne had allowed.

'Sir?'

'The sword.' Lorcan's eyes narrowed, as he stood before her, close enough for her to see a fine glimmer of sweat on his face. Too close.

'I don't know,' Tegan said, wondering how he knew the sword had ever been there; but even as she spoke, her thoughts twisted and she realised that she did know, precisely, where the Dowry blade was. She unfocussed her eyes so that she need not look at Lorcan's face.

'I do not think that is the truth,' the new king said, very softly.

She saw Maeve's blurred presence move forward, and recognised that movement for protest, Maeve pleading with her to be sensible.

Tegan forced Lorcan's face back into focus, and saw the determination that sat so uneasily on his still childish features. She knew with sickening certainty that she would, eventually, tell Lorcan everything that she knew. But for now, Tegan drew her body up straight and returned his gaze as levelly as she could.

Chapter Thirty-Two

Approaching the gates, it was evident to Madoc that many things had changed while he had been out on the Plains. The red banners on the city walls told him so. He had considered removing his green coat, but decided not – a wise decision.

The guards were civil enough, his rank, and the fact that at least one had seen him about Lorcan's camp, gave him sufficient leeway to gauge his position while their captain accompanied him to the tower. He kept his eyes sharp on that short journey, taking comfort from the mixture of green and red coats in the streets. This had not been a bloody change of government. The captain left him, to walk nervously in an anteroom until the door opened.

'Madoc.' The general turned to see who had called him by name, and was relieved to see a face he recognised, a green coat with a red sash hastily tied about the sleeve.

'Doran, I see things are not as I left them.' Doran nodded, lifting a cautioning hand. He came fully into the room, closing the door and laying his outstretched hand on Madoc's sleeve, guiding him away from the door.

'I'd have sent word, had I a way of knowing where to find you. Grainne and Phelan are dead. Lorcan is in charge.'

'In that order?'

Doran looked at the general blankly, then saw the implication of it.

'No. Phelan first, two days ago, at Grainne's hand; Grainne within hours of him, accident probably. Lorcan chanced upon the aftermath and took advantage.'

'So that's why everyone is being so polite.'

Doran's face twisted.

'Not everyone.'

'How has Lorcan taken Phelan's death?'

'Indifferent in public, angry in private.'

'Did he suspect?'

'Yes, but the situation was muddied, thanks to Maeve.'

'Maeve?'

'She didn't take to being ordered to slit Killan's throat. Took matters into her own hands. She's provided an excellent confusion, without realising what it was she was hiding. She thinks Phelan's treachery was solely towards Grainne, and it is so evident she believes what she says that even Lorcan struggles to push his search for traitors.'

Madoc smiled his relief, and started to plan once more.

'So, why does Lorcan still doubt?'

'The Dowry blade is missing.'

'Of course it is.'

'Yes but it's not so simple. Phelan did not have it.'

'How is that?' Madoc asked, alarmed.

Doran shrugged. 'I know where the blade was. It is not there now.'

'So where is it?'

'I don't know, but someone does.'

'Who?'

'I think, perhaps, Tegan.'

Madoc removed his gloves, and leant against the wall, squinting at Doran's closed expression.

'Lorcan is in a difficult position without that sword, and with Phelan gone, who do we think his heir could be?' Madoc asked softly.

'Heir? I think the only candidate is the girl – Grainne's third cousin – what is her name?'

'Armorel,' Madoc said impatiently. He had made a study of the possible claimants; he knew perfectly well how the situation stood.

'Yes,' Doran agreed, misinterpreting Madoc's frown. 'But Lorcan does not take her seriously.'

'So, without the sword – and without Phelan –'

Doran laughed, a short fox bark. Madoc and his lieutenant shared a smile.

'You're not considering seeking the sword yourself?' Doran asked.

'Not yet. This is a time for consolidation. If I were to turn on my heel so swiftly, how might Lorcan react? No, the situation is more – interesting than I anticipated. I don't want to raise suspicions. I shall stay here until Lorcan gets his answers for himself.'

The night air was ice cold; the muggy, midsummer warmth had vanished as swiftly as the light. The travellers shivered over their meagre fire. The flames provided only a semblance of heat, but enough smoke to discourage the ever-present insects.

Neala licked the last fat from her fingers and glanced furtively at the remains of her next-kin's meal. Brede caught the wistful expression and passed the bone to her.

Sorcha pulled her cloak tighter and allowed her eyes to stray about their meagre encampment searching out dangers she had no idea how to face – listening for the soundless step of death. Her eyes lit and caught upon Brede's saddle, and beneath that, a length of metal; nothing but a faint glint in the feeble light of the fire. At last she forced herself to move. She pulled the sword out.

'What is this doing here?' she asked.

Brede glanced up, and slid away from Neala. She took the Dowry blade and pushed it back beneath the saddle straps.

'I brought it away with me. The Goddess never intended Lorcan to have it.'

'What have you done, Brede? You've brought away the *one* thing that matters to Lorcan now that Grainne is dead. Without this, his claim to be King is almost sure to fail. He'll be after us as soon as he finds out who has it.'

'How would he find out?'

'How long do you imagine it will take Tegan to work out where this has gone? Or Eachan? How will they protect you in the face of Lorcan's capacity to harm them? You've put them in danger, and Goddess knows what you've brought down on us. I must take it back.'

Sorcha took up the sword once more, shivering with disgust.

Words would not come: as soon as she shut her eyes she fell, drowning in the silent depths of the Scavenger's eyes, drowned in Grainne's death. She pulled the air to pieces with her song, but could find no words. She stilled her voice, shuddering, and forced her eyes open. She was still by the smouldering fire, out on the plain. She flung the sword from her, and scattered the remaining embers of the fire, fearful now of pursuit.

'Where can we go? What must we do?' she asked.

'Put the horizon behind us,' Brede said gathering up her saddle, and the Dowry blade.

Sorcha forced the pace all night and all the next day. Dusk was long gone, and full darkness had closed about them before she at last permitted a camp to be made for the night, and even then she scanned the darkness, certain that she could hear the soft rustle of a familiar tattered brown robe, sure that any moment that strangely beautiful face would be lit by their fire, the dark wells of those eyes drowning her once more.

'What is it?' Brede asked, watching her restless pacing.

'We must set wards.'

Brede caught an unfamiliar emotion in her voice.

'You can't do it?' Sorcha shook her head sharply, and Brede reached to take her hand. 'What is it?'

'The Scavenger,' Sorcha said at last, and Brede felt a tremor of released tension flow through her arm. 'It touched me,' she whispered. 'It fought me for Grainne, and it won. I gave everything I am, and the Scavenger won. It took something from me; it *knows* me – it – it has my *scent*.' Sorcha met Brede's gaze. 'I'm not imagining this, Brede, I swear to you. I can no more sing a spell than

I can – than I can raise Grainne from the dead. I can't spin the simplest spell to keep us safe. Even you could make a better stab at it.'

Brede stepped back, waiting for Sorcha to realise what she'd said. Sorcha raised her eyes to meet Brede's gaze, and frowned.

'I'll set wards,' Brede said. 'What do I do?'

'Pick a tune you are easy with,' Sorcha said, grateful for the distraction. 'Something short, with words that you can adapt to tell the song what you want it to do – something purposeful.'

Brede couldn't remember a single tune, not a single song, as though she had never sung at a fireside, never got roaring drunk at a Gather – Plains songs weren't particularly purposeful.

'*Roll, turn, spin?*' A sleepy voice suggested from behind her.

Brede threw her next-kin a glance of gratitude. A simple melody, with childish words that could easily be turned to her use. She managed to stutter out a warped version of the song's chorus. Sorcha eyed her critically, building a fragile humour from her fear.

'The song won't do it for you,' she said. 'You need to persuade it.'

Brede nodded.

'Purposeful?' she suggested.

Sorcha agreed.

'Well?' Brede asked, flinging herself back to the ground and gathering up her blankets.

Sorcha said nothing, startled to find that what had begun as a distraction had become protection after all. Something she had always known filtered into her mind, the subtle strength of Brede's voice.

'They'll serve their purpose,' Sorcha said, weakly. 'Can you not see them?'

Brede shook her head. 'I've never been able to.' She turned her gaze to Neala. 'You: go to sleep or Sorcha will sing you a sleep skein.'

Neala laughed, and settled back into her blankets.

'Except that I can't,' Sorcha murmured, seeking the comfort of Brede's arms. Brede instinctively stroked Sorcha's hair away from her face, as though the darkness in her mind could be brushed away with the same ease.

Sorcha shuddered at that touch: death could be gentle; there could be no comfort in tenderness.

Chapter Thirty-Three

So many days now, with no sign of danger – Brede had begun to relax. They were far into the plains, with no hope of cover, when the clouds at last spilt their burden of rain. And then, at last, there was a smudge of motion on the horizon, far to the east. Brede watched, uncertain. She did not believe it was the feared pursuit. Not even Lorcan would send so many at such speed as a hunting party, not even for the sake of the Dowry blade; but it might still be an army. She wasn't used to identifying horses in rain – most of her herding experience was gained during the drought, when a cloud of dust would have been the first sign, visible from much further away. So she waited to bring the blur to her companions' attention until it finally solidified, and was indeed a herd of horses.

Brede encouraged Guida into motion. She felt Neala tense against her.

'It may not be Wing Clan,' Brede warned.

Neala shrugged. 'It's a Horse Clan.'

Brede laughed at Neala's pretended calm. The first time she joined a herding on these plains she had almost choked on her excitement.

Closer now, the horses were clearly visible. The herders had seen them; their pace had increased noticeably, and three of the outriders were diverging, making towards the strangers.

Brede's breath came short, waiting for hailing distance, but the riders wheeled into a defensive stand, waiting for the strangers to come to them.

Sorcha pulled Macsen in, slowing his pace. The herders each carried a spear, where once the only weapon on the plain had been a sling and a handful of stones. Brede rode further and stopped within range of those spears, and waited for the herders to speak. She searched for a face she recognised.

'What do you want?' asked the older of the two women.

Brede baulked at the use of a trade language but replied in her native tongue.

'I look for kin. I am blood of Wing Clan.'

The woman relaxed slightly, but her eyes stayed wary.

'Who are you?'

'Brede, daughter of Ahern. And you?'

'Muirne, daughter of Toole and Brenna.'

'You are Wing Clan then?' Brede asked eagerly. 'I didn't recognise you. Does Toole still keep that vicious stallion he bought from Cein?'

'Toole is dead. The horse is a good stud beast, but still unmanageable. He runs in my string now.'

'I am sorry for it. Will you tell me, is Carolan still riding with Wing Clan?'

'Your sister's hand-mate is with this herd –' Muirne shook her head slightly. Brede felt Neala's grip tighten, and shook her arm free of her niece's clasp. 'I have Carolan's daughter with me.'

'His daughter?' Muirne was frowning now, and unease fluttered under Brede's ribs.

'Falda was carrying a child,' Brede said cautiously, 'when we lost her at the last Gather. She was taken into captivity and bore her child safely, but she died four years ago.'

Muirne's frown vanished once more. She urged her horse forward; until she could look Neala straight in the eye, could search for signs of her parentage. She reached out a hand and smiled.

'Well, and what did she name her daughter?' she asked, as though this were a chance meeting beside a horse ring.

Neala stretched awkwardly across Guida's neck, and took the hand she was offered. With quiet dignity, she introduced herself. Muirne laughed aloud.

'Your sisters will be glad.'

'Sisters?' Neala asked, wondering how swiftly her unknown father had forgotten her mother.

'My daughters. I hand-fasted with Carolan six years ago.'

Brede swallowed the muddle of emotion at Carolan's hand-fasting, at least Neala had been offered some form of acceptance. The last time she had seen these riders they must too have been children. In that dreadful searching, they had shivered and wailed as Wing Clan gathered them safely together, like herding foals away from their mothers. How many had been lost – she did not recognise any of these three riders from that last memory, nor from earlier memories of the child-herd running in amongst the horses and their elders at the Gathers, shrieking and whooping and laughing.

Muirne reached again and absentmindedly rubbed her hand along Guida's neck; she found the tattoo.

'Falda's,' she said softly. 'We have a few of her mares still and many of their offspring,' she smiled at Neala. 'You will have a good string to start your herd.'

'Me?' Neala asked confused.

Muirne nodded, and raised her eyes to Brede. 'You too, we found a few of yours running loose after you'd gone. Carolan and Devnet kept them for you, in case you came back.'

Brede gazed at her in silent astonishment.

'I have horses?'

Muirne laughed. 'We buy or steal any horse we come across with an uncancelled mark.'

Neala twisted to glare in triumph at Brede and mouthed *You see?* Brede clasped her shoulder and gave her a gentle shake.

Muirne glanced at Sorcha.

'So,' Muirne said, recovering her poise. 'You and Neala are kin. Who's this?'

Brede twisted slightly to beckon Sorcha forward. Macsen behaved, stepping delicately and docile, holding his head so that any horse breeder would know he had more mettle than he chose to show. Sorcha murmured him to absolute stillness, and spoke.

'My name is Sorcha.' She faltered, what was she, now? 'I am Brede's – hand-mate.' Sorcha chose that word with care, regardless of its limited truth. She caught Brede's startled, pleased glance, and smiled slightly.

There was a hostile stirring and the young man murmured 'City dweller,' at the sound of Sorcha's accent.

'So are you riding one of Brede's or Falda's horses? He's clearly Plains bred.'

Sorcha glanced helplessly at Brede.

'No,' Brede said. 'He's another stolen at the Gather. One of Cloud's, but I don't recognise the mark.'

The man started forward at that, and Muirne nodded to him, saying 'Murtagh will know.' He rode across to Sorcha and searched Macsen's neck.

'Macsen,' he said. Sorcha started. He glared at her suspiciously, and Macsen sidled, feeling the tension between them.

'Macsen is what I named him,' Sorcha said quietly. Murtagh considered.

'Well his breeder is long dead, it serves well enough for the horse to bear his name as well as his mark; though by rights this horse should come back to Cloud.' Murtagh shrugged, relinquishing Cloud's claim.

Muirne stared anxiously after the disappearing herd.

'Murtagh, ride after them, tell them to wait.'

Murtagh dipped his spear point slightly, kicked his horse into an easy canter, and chased after the receding herd.

Muirne spoke swiftly. 'Murtagh is one of the few of Cloud left. They ride with us now; they were no longer viable as a Clan.' Brede nodded, mind reeling at the thought of a Clan so depleted. Muirne bit her lip. 'A lot has changed since the last Gather; I hardly know where to begin telling you – it really isn't the same.' Muirne shook her head, and turned her horse abruptly to follow the herd.

Brede caught her breath at the size of the herd. Muirne frowned at the glance she swept across the herd.

'It is enough,' she said curtly. 'We don't have so many Clan members to feed these days. You were not the only one to give up the plains.' Brede was about to protest, but Muirne hadn't finished her explanation. 'We can move more swiftly with this number, and they are the finest beasts I've ever raised. They fetch a good price when we choose to sell.'

Murtagh came forward from the waiting herd. Brede recognised the man with him at once. Carolan glanced apologetically at Muirne, who did no more than raise a shoulder. Brede grinned at him; close kin, someone who had been a friend, a counsellor to her youthful, half-forgotten self.

Carolan considered the woman before him, searching her face for the child-woman he remembered – wincing away from the metal-clad warrior that girl had become. At last he allowed his eyes to drop to Neala, another child-woman, he realised at once, another warrior. He measured the serious, eager, frightened, demanding countenance Neala offered him and opened his arms in welcome, beyond speech for the moment.

Neala ran to her father's horse, placing her hands against rein and saddle. She looked up at him, a little solemn, but ready to forgive him for being a stranger with a new hand-mate and daughters. Carolan leant to her, offering a hand and Neala sprang up to sit before him on the saddle, managing the leap neatly.

Carolan gathered up his reins, encircling his newfound daughter, holding her gently, wonderingly. He inclined his head to Brede.

'We're almost at a watering place. We'll camp there, and you can tell us,' he hesitated. 'You can tell us.'

With the horses corralled and fires lit, Carolan gathered his people to him. They huddled beside the main fire, waiting for the strangers to speak.

Carolan hugged Neala close to him, remembering, with fleeting clarity, the moment when his hand slipped from Falda's as they ran from arrows in the darkness of the last Gather. He was not about to make the same mistake now.

Brede scanned the faces about the fire, uneasy with the role of news-bringer. She would rather sit quiet by a fireside, and drink, and later explore her new-found herd. She would rather talk privately with Carolan about Falda, although Neala would have more to say than she could – no: it was the private mourning she craved, surrounded by people who had known, had loved her sister. She found she could remember some faces from that terrible morning after all. This woman, she remembered as an older girl, drawn and trembling, cradling her lifeless young brother against her – she would not be parted from him, crazed with grief. Well they had all been crazed then, Brede as much as any other. Brede's heart lurched with sudden realisation – all crazed – yes. All this time she had been blaming Devnet for something not of Devnet's doing, nor within Devnet's power to mend. *Not Devnet's fault:* she had felt the same pain and fear as any of Wing Clan that dreadful morning. If Tegan could be forgiven, how not Devnet?

Brede found her suddenly. She met Devnet's gaze, and tried to make that dagger-intensity soften.

Devnet – Brede forgot to breathe. *Devnet* – her first lover, her first real friend; but now –

Devnet watched Brede with curiosity. She observed how strong she was in the shoulders, how her face had thinned and her eyes deepened. She moved like – like a warrior, surprising, impressive. There was just a hint of the young Brede, in the way her hair refused to stay bound, in the way her hands wouldn't stay still. Devnet let her glance encompass those hands, stirring uneasily, pushing the mailed sleeves up her arms, exposing scars that hadn't been there before. Strong, capable hands. Devnet remembered, and smiled.

Sorcha watched for the Scavenger. She examined each face, each stance, and couldn't recognise anything that Brede had claimed for her kin. No strength of mind or spirit presented itself, in the ninety or more Plains folk before her. Pride, suspicion, even fear. And something else, something even less welcoming. Sorcha searched for it, and caught the gaze of a woman sitting the far side of the fire, one leg bent under her, and her chin resting on the knee of the other, hands clasped about her shin. The tension, the curiosity, the intensity of her gaze alarmed Sorcha. The haze from the fire between them made her face seem to waver, but her eyes did not. It was not Sorcha she watched, but Brede. The woman smiled a slow, feral, threatening smile. She closed her eyes slightly, and turned her head. Brede started at the break in the contact.

The shuffling and murmuring died to a waiting silence. Brede rose to her feet, feeling that her welcome was not as certain as she would like.

'Greetings to Wing Clan,' she began formally, 'from your kinswoman, Brede, daughter to Ahern of Wing Clan.' She smiled suddenly, warmed by a sudden recognition of what those words meant. *Kin.* 'There are some here who remember me, across the ten years we've been apart. I had a sister, hand-fast to Carolan of this Clan. We all thought her dead at the last Gather, but it wasn't so – Falda was taken into slavery. She bore a child away from the plains, away from her kin, in bondage,' her voice failed her for a moment, 'to a man named Madoc.'

She felt rather than heard the stir in the crowd, and hesitated, looking about for who had reacted, trying to divine why. She caught up the thread of her tale again.

'My sister died in bondage, her child was sold. But I have found her, and brought her home to her father. She is called Neala. I claim her rights for her.'

Brede waited for Carolan to acknowledge her claim.

'I recognise this child as my daughter; I offer her a share of my fire, a share of my herd, a share of the sky. Would any gainsay her?'

A soft murmur of acceptance spread about the fire. The rain was easing, making it easier to distinguish individual voices. Carolan squeezed her hand gently, and Neala, in her turn, stepped forward.

'Greetings to Wing Clan, from your kinswoman, Neala: daughter to Carolan and Falda of Wing Clan. I accept my share of the fire, the herd and the sky,' Neala grinned round at her kin, 'joyfully, after much hope and long waiting.'

She was welcomed with laughter and whistles. She looked anxiously at Carolan, and he nodded, beckoning her to sit beside him. Carolan inclined his head to Brede. She smiled, more confident now. Riding the wave of good humour, she gazed at the Clan, and picked Devnet from the crowd again. Devnet's face was a mask of fury. Brede glanced quickly at the people on either side of Devnet, they were edging away, and there was furtive wariness in the glances that shot from other groups, at Devnet, but also at Brede.

'You speak ill of a friend of this Clan,' Devnet said. 'You speak ill of kin.'

Brede glanced at Carolan, confused.

'Madoc is hand-fasted to Wing Clan,' Carolan muttered.

'What?' Brede asked in shock, her tongue running ahead of her mind.

'Devnet,' Carolan responded, still keeping his voice low.

'Devnet?' Brede took an uneasy breath. 'Well, there is more I would say concerning Madoc.' *How to say it?* 'Some more things that you won't wish to hear, Devnet.' Brede took a steadying breath. 'He is a general in Grainne's army. Did he tell you that much, at least?'

Devnet heart raced suddenly, but she didn't let that show on her face. 'That is what was said, kinswoman. But I also heard there was a Plains woman acting bodyguard for the Queen. I didn't believe it until I saw you, with your mail shirt, and your green cloak. So now I believe the general, with this evidence before me. So why should I disbelieve what else he said?'

Brede nodded slowly, trying to control the fury that made her limbs shake dully with the need for movement. 'Madoc told you about me, did he? Have you forgotten how we escaped the carnage of that massacre together? Have you forgotten the scar I bear across my shoulder, and how you pulled me out from under that blow, to safety? Devnet, you can't tell me you've forgotten.'

'I've not forgotten,' Devnet agreed, thinking of Brede, raving with wound-fever, blaming her for Falda's death, blaming *her*.

'You don't know who it was commanded those troops,' Brede continued. 'And you couldn't know until now who carried off my sister to die slowly in captivity.'

Brede glanced at Carolan, and was certain that his hands were shaking, where they grasped his newfound daughter.

'It was Madoc who kept Carolan's hand-mate and daughter in slavery.' Brede wiped tears from her face, scarcely aware she was weeping, she reached out, half believing she was still talking to the Devnet she remembered from her youth, trying to say something to reach her. 'But worse, Devnet, it was Madoc who commanded that raid, Madoc who scattered Wing Clan and destroyed Cloud.'

Brede caught Murtagh's incredulous look, and the way his body shifted, away from Devnet.

Devnet was on her feet in an instant, hearing only that Brede was somehow blaming her again.

'What kind of – jealousy – revenge – is this, Brede?'

Brede tried to keep her voice level, but she couldn't keep the tremor of grief and anger from her words.

'Not jealousy, Devnet, not revenge; *truth*. Madoc's raiders, Devnet, and his sword, in defiance of the orders he was given. No one else is to blame for the loss of our kin, no one but him.'

'I don't believe you,' Devnet said, her voice harsh, rage twisting her face. 'You've spent too much time in the city, you've been – corrupted, you – you are not my kin.'

Not her kin? There was nothing worse than that. Brede shook off Sorcha's restraining hand.

'Madoc is no kin of mine,' Brede said, her voice jagged with shaking. 'Any who claim kin with him are kin to a murderer – and a slaver. Those actions are his; and they are the actions of any who claim kin with him.'

'This is madness,' Devnet said, desperately, half believing it as she said it.

Brede fought a pain in her chest, drawing her breath in tight gasps; 'You haven't seen the slave markets, Devnet,' she said, and her voice died. She swallowed and tried again. 'You haven't seen women tattooed by your hand-mate's friends, you haven't seen slave collars, or watched children sold away from their mothers. If you take Madoc to your fire, that is where you are taking this Clan. That is madness.'

Devnet sprang to her feet, a knife in her hand. Brede turned swiftly to Guida, scrabbling for a knife, but her hand closed on the hilt of the greatsword and she had to struggle to disentangle the long blade from her pack. Devnet was faster, leaping across the space between them, slashing through Brede's outstretched hand, her knife connecting with flesh and bone, and sticking there. Brede cried out, and grasped the knife with her other hand. Forcing it out of her flesh, she flung the knife at Devnet, but missed. Carolan was on his feet, shouting for order; eager hands dragged Brede and Devnet apart.

Sorcha clasped Brede to her. Brede's harsh sobbing breaths filled her ears and gave her the beginning of the notes she needed to mend that wound, but not the words. She stared in silence at that blood, and then with great deliberation, Sorcha laid her hand over the ragged tear in Brede hand and wrist, which might lose her the use of her fingers. Her own fingers were slippery with Brede's blood and she could almost feel the throb of pain in the spurting heat. Sorcha filled her mind with that blood, refusing to see the Scavenger, waiting just beyond the heat of the fire. She mined deep in blood for words, dragging them out of herself. It took time for her to be certain, but once she was, she sang the tendons and muscles back into line, the skin to wholeness.

Sorcha let Brede's hand drop, trembling with relief that she had not, after all, lost her skill. The Plains people stepped away from her.

'You see?' Devnet said, scornfully.

Carolan turned his head slowly away from her, away from Sorcha, looking out at the slow waving of the grasses.

'It is time we moved on,' he said quietly.

Sorcha crouched beside Brede, suddenly fearful for their safety.'I think we should leave –'

Brede shook her head. 'Devnet can challenge me if she wants, no one else will interfere – but she won't challenge me now, she has already cast me out of the Clan. She can do nothing worse.'

Brede got to her feet with difficulty; her bones felt heavy. She folded her arms across her chest, to hide their shaking, and that new-healed scar.

'If Wing Clan will not listen to what I have to say, will you ask Neala who it was sold her to an innkeeper?' she asked.

She was met by silence. Carolan shook his head.

'For my part, I've heard, and seen, enough. I give credit to your words, and your intention – but I've seen how swiftly dissention grows here. A lesson well taught, Brede. Arms are not for the Clan, nor is a revenge that turns us against each other.'

Devnet started to protest, but he waved her to silence.

'Devnet is right about the corruption of too close a link with outsiders. You are your father's daughter in truth, Brede, so easily to turn away from your people to suit an out-clan hand-mate. But Devnet, you've made the same choice. Where one is condemned, so too the other. Devnet – and Brede – neither of you are welcome among the horses of Wing Clan. You are not our kin.'

'Carolan –'

Carolan shook his head. He raised the greatsword and used its weight to force the blade into the ground at his feet. He turned his back.

Brede looked around wildly for some support. Only Neala met her gaze, used as she was to the casual violence of the city and only beginning to understand that she had gained a father and lost an aunt in the space of a few minutes. She turned her puzzled angry gaze from one to the other, wanting an explanation, to apportion blame.

Devnet did not wait; she didn't need Wing Clan. She had other kin, other friends, and a hand-mate to turn to. And now, too, she had information to barter with. Madoc had told her about a certain sword, and it seemed to her that where there was a witch and a blade of the quality Brede carried, there were conclusions to be drawn.

Devnet chose the one horse an outcast was permitted. She collected her weapons, her tent and blankets. She made no comment, did not try to argue with Carolan, or any of her silent, stunned not-kin. She took a last look at the Dowry blade, determined that she would be able to describe it accurately.

Brede gritted her teeth, and began a studious untangling of Guida's mane, trying to find something safe to give her mind to.

Devnet was mounted and gone by the time Brede looked up, the other Clan members were astride their horses, the temporary corral dismantled. Wing Clan moved quietly, collecting and herding horses, the only sounds were the whistles that moved the herd on, the occasional complaint from the horses themselves, and a confusion of hooves.

Brede turned her back on Wing Clan, and didn't take her eyes from the ground until the sound of hooves had faded.

Sorcha watched the great herd of horses vanish. There had been as many as three thousand beasts here and perhaps ninety people – and now there was no one and nothing save the smoking fires to show where they had been, vanished ghosts – Grainne drifted through her mind.

Brede fought with Guida's hobble, so that she wouldn't have to meet Sorcha's gaze, dreading that she might lose her too. It was too easy to lose people. Brede felt the fierce rawness of the new skin on her wrist and hand and thought fleetingly of her mother, and how she had walked away, leaving Leal to her slow sinking into apathy in the Marshes.

'I should have taken Neala to my mother,' she said. 'She would be glad to know she had a granddaughter. She might stop grieving for Falda if she knew.'

Sorcha was startled at this abrupt change of direction.

'To the Marshes? I thought you hated it there.'

'I owe Leal that much don't I, to give her something to rejoice in? She never cast me out. She loved me, in her way.' Brede slapped Guida's neck, perhaps harder than she meant to, the horse shifted reproachfully. Brede soothed her quickly and mounted. 'I never knew my father was condemned for his choice of hand-mate. I thought he stayed away from Wing Clan all those years because that was what Leal wanted. I blamed her. I wanted what they had, the Plains, the sky, *kin* –' her voice dried and she ran her hand through her hair. 'What now? Do I come with you to your kin?'

She need hardly say that she had nowhere else to go. Sorcha thumped Brede on the knee.

'Of course you come,' she said. 'I want you with me. If that is where you want to be?'

'It is,' Brede said with sudden certainty. '*Hand-mate.*'

Sorcha glanced at her uneasily.

'Did you mind?'

Brede shook her head.

'No, I liked it; but now,' her voice became unsteady once more, 'now I have no more kin for you to tell.'

'I still have kin,' Sorcha said.

Brede's eyes followed the faint movement on the horizon, which was all that was left to be seen of Wing Clan.

'Can you still say Phelan's curses can't hurt me?' she asked.

Chapter Thirty-Four

Lorcan found his answers, eventually. He chose his hunting party with scrupulous care. He would not trust any of Grainne's people, not even the uncertain Maeve. Not for this hunting. A small band, no more than ten: Madoc, of course, for his knowledge of the Horse Clans. And to lead? Lorcan would trust no one for that. The Dowry blade was too valuable to entrust to anyone else.

Madoc thanked the Goddess for his time out on the Plains, which had given him an opportunity to distance himself from Phelan's treachery, and had provided him with an invaluable knowledge on which Lorcan must now rely. He had a fair idea of where to find his hand-mate and her kin, but he found her sooner than he expected. Devnet rode into their camp on the second night, ignoring the shouted challenge of the guard. She stayed on her horse, waiting for him to come to her, refusing to say more than his name.

Madoc looked up into Devnet's face, and felt uneasy.

'Hunting?' Devnet asked, at last.

'Yes.'

'For a witch? For a sword?' Madoc couldn't prevent the look of surprise that flickered across his face.

'What is she saying?' Lorcan asked, impatiently.

Madoc had almost forgotten how young Lorcan was. Spending time with him, his youth was the last thing to strike the mind, despite his appearance. This thin, overgrown youth, barely sporting a beard, controlled a nightmare mismatch of an army, somehow keeping all the disparate factions under his hand. A hand capable of the murder of his own father.

Madoc considered the boy-king standing before him, uncertain of his reaction to the knowledge that the witch was within reach, with Grainne's ritual sword at her side.

'My liege,' he said, waiting for permission to speak. Lorcan nodded impatiently. 'She asks if we are hunting a sword.'

'Tell your little princeling that I know where the witch is.'

'She knows where the witch is.'

'Where?'

Devnet turned her eyes on Lorcan, correctly interpreting his question.

'I can lead you,' she said, and waited for Madoc to translate.

Lorcan saw the concern that flitted across the faces of these seasoned warriors at the thought of that sword. he remembered the feel of the hilt in his hand, the weight of it as he swung it – and wished he did not. He could feel the uneasy bristling of the warriors, gathered about him. He had only a weak grasp on them and although the sword was essential to his claim, the use he had already made of it was damaging.

'When are we leaving?' Lorcan asked, pulling his warriors back into the reality of the moment.

'As soon as horses can be saddled,' Madoc said stiffly.

'Good,' Lorcan said softly, still dreading the reappearance of that blade. 'I want that sword.'

Only now did Devnet dismount, turning her back on Lorcan, who was not her leader. Madoc tried to cover her deliberate rudeness, but Devnet scorned to dissemble.

'I have no kin but you, now, hand-mate. Be sure I do not regret my choice; revenge is a lesson I have learnt well.'

'And why this revenge? What is the witch to you?'

Devnet considered telling him, but the wound of lost kin was too raw to be eased by mere talking.

'I have chosen,' she said. 'I chose you.'

Madoc did not understand the darting look Devnet shot him: he didn't recognise the seed of doubt that struggled in the infertile soil of her choices.

The river spread before the warriors, so broad the bank was scarcely visible, but relatively shallow. The water was fast, gathering its strength for a fall of half a mile when it reached the edge of the plateau.

Devnet held up a hand, warning the warriors to stillness and silence. Madoc scanned the riverbank trying to see what had attracted her attention. It was beginning to get dark, the thick cloud hiding the setting of the sun. Devnet led her horse away, stepping delicately over the pebbled bank. Madoc did not question her methods; he was content to let Devnet hunt in her own way, in her own time. She reminded him of a falcon, and like a falcon she would return at his call.

Brede waded a short way into the river, prodding ahead of her with the greatsword, searching the fast running water for invisible dangers. It seemed safe enough to ford and soon the moon would set; for that short while it would be too dark to continue searching for a safer crossing. Brede did not want to wait for dawn, she had a bad feeling about this river, and she wanted to be across it speedily.

Sorcha let the horses drink, leaving their reins to trail in the water, her mind far from the glistening pebbles and the unseen far shore, oblivious to the water tugging at her ankles.

Brede laid the sword down and adjusted Guida's saddle slightly – the horse had lost weight, and the girth needed constant attention. Guida complained, and Brede smiled, but the smile faded at an answering call from behind her. The breath stilled in her chest, and she had to force herself to turn.

The rush of the river masked her approach, Now Devnet gathered a swift handful of pebbles from the riverbank and pulled her scarf from her neck, dropping one of the pebbles into the cloth sling. Brede took a step towards her. She swung the sling to and fro, idly threatening.

Brede backed up, towards the sword, and Sorcha.

'Sorcha, Devnet's here.'

Sorcha dragged her thoughts together, searching for words, a tune – Brede pushed her towards Macsen, forcing urgency into her movements and Sorcha scrambled for the saddle. Devnet flung her missile.

Sorcha cried out, falling; and Brede lunged to stop the fall of her unconscious body, so that she slumped across Macsen's shoulders. Barely secure: Brede wrenched her shoulder making another shift to get Sorcha safely across Macsen's back. Breathlessly she glared at him, daring him to move, and snatched the sword from where it lay at the water's edge.

Devnet smiled, swinging her sling, the next stone ready.

Brede cursed. Those pebbles had glistened so innocently at the water's edge: her only resources were the horses, and the greatsword, and like the fool she was, she had chosen the sword.

Another stone spat out of the growing darkness, and Macsen shrieked, his short temper frayed. Another stone and another, striking sparks from Brede's armour and screams from the horses. Brede fought Macsen for a second, forcing him back to a stand. She heard Devnet's voice, but couldn't make out the words, then a man's voice; again the words were unclear against the river's rushing – and the sound of many feet on the grinding pebbles. Brede turned to her one certain weapon. She whistled to Guida, setting her dancing and screaming towards the unmounted warriors, hooves flailing dangerously. It would not take long for Devnet to control her, but it would be long enough. Brede took that half-second of Devnet's distraction, found the binding at the back of the saddle and was on Macsen's back. Brede whistled to him, and kicked harder than she had ever kicked a horse in her life. Macsen stretched and exploded into speed.

Devnet hauled the loose horse round, pulling viciously on the reins, and made terrible threats. Guida quietened. Devnet glanced after her prey; it was not too late to use the sling. She gathered another handful of pebbles.

Lorcan cursed. Why was there no archer when one was needed? He waved Devnet away, contemptuous of her skill with stone and sling; he wanted certain death, not broken bones.

'Doran?' he roared, and those about him flinched, Lorcan's unspoken scorn was molten lead poured over them. Doran stepped uneasily forward.

'You can use a bow?'

'I can; my liege.'

'Then find one.'

Lorcan glanced at the Plains woman, with her sling and pebbles, and the horse wild of eye and jumpy at her shoulder. He looked around for Madoc.

'Tell your savage to keep that horse under control,' he snarled, giving the beast a cuff as he passed.

Madoc met Devnet's eyes, and saw a dangerous spark there. He chose not to translate Lorcan's words.

Chapter Thirty-Five

Brede raced Macsen along the edge of the river, splashing into the uncertain water. Grateful for the remaining dark, oblivious to everything but her need to have Sorcha safe away. Seeing, at last, the ford she had been looking for, and distantly beyond it, a stand of trees that would provide cover, she set Macsen to plunge across the river.

The footing was difficult, and the water deeper than she expected, splashing into her face as Macsen ploughed into the current. He slowed, struggling against the weight of the water, but Brede would not let up. Only when they were safely out of the water and well into the woodland on the far side, did she allow him to catch his breath. Macsen picked his way through the thick undergrowth, obedient to Brede's calming hand on his neck, urging quiet. Brede twisted in the saddle, trying to gauge the pursuit, trying to hear above the rush of the river. She couldn't tell, and Sorcha still slumped barely conscious before her.

'Sorcha,' she whispered, leaning forward to breathe into Sorcha's ear, dreading to make sound, but desperate to have her stir back into consciousness. She reached for the water and trickled it over the side of Sorcha's face. Sorcha started, shifted, felt how insecure she was, felt Brede's protective hand at her shoulder, Macsen's loud breathing far too close, and slid to the ground, desperate for solidity. She staggered, and stepped clear of Macsen's restless hooves, then staggered again, falling to her knees. Brede's hands were there again, her arms enclosing, supporting, protecting.

Sorcha leant into Brede's body with relief. There was water – she wet her lips cautiously, then swallowed a small mouthful.

'How badly are you hurt?' Brede asked softly, hardly daring to ask. Sorcha reached a reassuring hand, not yet trusting her voice. 'We're not safe.'

'Safe enough,' Sorcha croaked, wiping away Brede's tears. 'Nothing to cry for,' she said gently, almost laughing, and instead finding her voice trembling into tears of her own. Brede struggled to speak, to say something, anything, which would make Sorcha understand.

'I know,' Sorcha said painfully. 'I know.'

'We are not safe here. Is there anything – ?'

Sorcha shook her head, and regretted it at once.

'I can't.' There were no words. 'Is it only Devnet?'

'No.' Brede paused; surprised at how much she had taken in of their pursuers in the split second she had seen them. 'We have warriors at our backs, mounted. At least eight.'

Not just warriors, Sorcha thought, *the Scavenger is hunting us*, but she could not say that aloud.

'They'll not go away. Wards won't be strong enough to hide us from warriors who know we're here.' *Nor from the Scavenger.*

Brede prepared to argue, but Macsen shuddered and screamed, twisting away from a sudden pain.

She whistled to him, and half heard Sorcha singing a similar few notes. She fought Macsen's fore hooves back to the ground. Brede's groping hand found a bloody score across Macsen's shoulder. Her mind registered relief, and then fear, in one heartbeat, *arrows*, and she leapt to his back, a safer place to control him, dreading losing him. Grabbing Sorcha about the forearm, she pulled hard, feeling Sorcha's other hand scrabbling at the saddle behind her. Brede leant away from her weight and strained, willing Macsen to stay still a fraction longer. Sorcha found the purchase she needed and scrambled onto Macsen's back. She clung to Brede, acutely aware of the smell of her hair, of her body heat, barely discernible through the mail shirt. Macsen's muscles bunched beneath her, and the air moved against her face, touching every pore of her skin.

I know what this is, Sorcha thought, aware of each breath she took, the jarring of her teeth as Macsen's hooves collided with the ground. *Stolen time.* Her heart jolted violently, her mouth became dry, and she had to close her eyes, overcome by nausea.

She heard their pursuers, heard them in the tremor of hooves echoing through the earth. She had no thought for the songs that might stop the hunters, or hide their own passage through the woods. She concentrated on the immediate, the physical – the rub of the stirrup straps against her leg, the flicker of half-light between the trees, the leather between her hands where she gripped Brede's belt; the jolt of Brede's ribs against her arm as she forced Macsen sharply through the thick undergrowth. She could not think beyond those sensations, because there was nothing beyond them but death, and fear of death.

The trees ended and Brede forced yet more speed from Macsen. It was better to be moving at speed, but they were exposed out in the open and Sorcha felt her back muscles flinching involuntarily. She hoped the horse could keep up that speed, wounded as he was; it was their only hope of evading the hunt. *Hope.* She smothered that; she could not afford to hope.

The hunters reached the edge of the woodland, and Lorcan called a halt, watching the horse speeding away from them, a darker blur in the darkness. His eyes narrowed against the rain that fell once more.

Lorcan looked to Doran, pointing his desire, meaning too potent for words. Doran notched the arrow to his bowstring, and pulled smoothly until the fletching lay against his cheekbone. He listened for the distance and direction, not trusting his eyes in the darkness. He let loose the arrow.

For a split second there was no pain, only shock, but then Sorcha tried to take a breath. The Scavenger had her scent. Time had run out.

Doran lowered the bow. Lorcan nodded in satisfaction. He turned, searching his band of breathless followers. He gestured to Madoc, the least trusted, Doran's friend, Phelan's man.

'Go with Doran, make sure of them.'

Madoc was an excellent tracker, a better killer, the obvious choice; but Lorcan thought him an ambitious man, willing to strike out on his own. He offered Madoc sufficient rope to hang himself, and Madoc grasped it with both hands. If he didn't do what was required of him, out here with only Lorcan's men about him, he was a bigger fool than Lorcan gave him credit for.

Madoc pulled his cloak closer about him against the rain, and followed the archer across the heath. They knew the lie of the land; their quarry did not. There was no hurry now that the fugitives had chosen this route.

Macsen's hooves went from under him. Brede instinctively hauled on the reins, struggled to keep him upright but the footing was not there, the brush that went by so fast was not going to stop their falling, the slipping and sliding and scattering of stones could end only one way. She lost hold of the reins, lost contact with the horse, lost her sense of which way she was falling. The earth rose up to block her path, flinging her from one brutal battering to another.

At last it stopped. Brede lay, grateful for stillness, and fought for breath. Pain dulled her sight, her hearing. She gazed up at the cliff above her. Logic told her that the pain would only get worse, that she was not safe where she lay, that she must move. She raised a hand off the ground, then let it fall again. *Impossible.* She turned her head, reached about her with the other hand. Her fingers brushed hair. She twisted further, glimpsing a dark hump of bloodiness. *Macsen.* Her fingers trailed away from the warmth of his body, falling back to rain soaked soil. She concentrated on breathing a while longer, trying to get her brain to untangle the horizon, but pain ate at the edges of her understanding and darkness encroached.

Sorcha clung to consciousness; she would not allow it to slide from her. She turned her head with difficulty, and found Brede lying close. She reached out but couldn't touch her – couldn't move further. She pulled her energy together, forcing the spark of life to reach her tongue, to call Brede. With agonising slowness Brede raised her head. There was blood mingled in her hair, but she was aware. Now that she knew Brede was still alive Sorcha could hear her whimpering, as she had not before, deafened by her own pain. She couldn't make out all Brede's hurts; she did not have the strength. She willed Brede to move closer to her; she needed to touch her, needed to have her close.

Brede inched across the sodden ground, stopping often, overcome. Sorcha felt the burning in her lungs, the torturing of her body that ordered her to cough, but she did not dare, afraid of what more it would do. She stifled the need, breathing shallow, as far as the pain and no further, but the pain was there sooner, and sooner. Brede's fingers found hers, and Sorcha dragged her hands to her, careless, ruthless in her need.

Sorcha steadied herself against Brede, allowing her body to feel its pain and weakness for a second, aware of the bitter choice before her. There was nothing to cling to, save Brede's cold, trembling hands. All she could do was protect Brede, and call help.

Sorcha coughed, unable to prevent it any longer, and choked for so long that she was too weak for anything more. Brede scarcely stirred, but for the sobs that shook her. Sorcha felt Brede's strength ebbing from her, felt the grip on her hands slackening. Somehow she found breath, found words, found a tune. She must, she *must* sing. She spun her tune from love, from her joy in Brede, strengthened it with responsibility, with need. The words were simple, a calling, of anything that might help.

Sorcha slipped in and out of consciousness. She felt the weight of unspoken grief and loneliness in her heart, the weight of the song on her tongue, and imagined she was singing when she was not. As awareness returned, she struggled back into the song, layering it, adding her own harmonies, discords, anything that might bring help. She started again, then drifted once more, searching for more words, anything to bind Brede to life.

The call was so violent, so urgent, that it caused Kendra acute pain. She woke with her mind screaming, as the one who called was screaming. Her lungs were filling with blood, closing her breath, burning her veins. Kendra hit her head as she scrambled from sleep into wakefulness, gasping in horror. She lay back, struggling with blindness, her heart pounding. It was not the dark that confined her movements, but the pain and fear. Kendra answered the screaming as well as she could: *I am coming.*

She could scarcely breathe for the calling. She would not be in time. The earth beneath her fingers was damp and the air smelt of rain. Kendra crawled from her cave, running before she knew which direction to go, pulled against her will into the dawn.

Dawn is no time for dying.

She could sense the voice weakening, a human voice it must be, for as she weakened, her insistence grew stronger.

The rain was heavy, sheets and sheets of water, the world was drowning. It made the new day silent in its birth, creeping quietly from dark to half-light, without the usual rush and burst of noise. Night was reluctant to leave.

Kendra wiped the water from her eyes; she could smell blood. It couldn't be far, the very strength of the call told her so. No, there was more than closeness to the strength of that call, she could taste a difference. This was not the thoughtless scream of the injured creature, human or otherwise. She did not merely cry out, she called Kendra deliberately. Kendra listened to the screaming in her bones more carefully, and recognised the resonance. It was more than a calling, it was a spinning of song. Kendra told her again, *I am here.*

Wandering from confusion back into her waking nightmare, Sorcha saw a figure approaching across the rain-drenched ground, and relief stilled her tongue. She closed her eyes, to conserve the shreds of her strength, and the figure was still there behind her eyelids, She searched the face that hovered above her, and recognised it for what it was.

Dread turned her joints molten. She struggled to find her voice, but there was no song left. She could not feel Brede's weight against her; could not feel the pain in her chest. She took in a breath: *no pain.*

You may not wait here, the figure said. *Come, you have no need to stay now.*

Sorcha shook her head, clinging to Brede – she could not feel the hands she held.

This is no longer your place. There is a Gate to pass.

The Scavenger of Souls reached down a hand and pulled Sorcha gently to her feet.

I will guide you.

Sorcha took a hesitant step away from her body, letting out her breath in one last defiant word of love, drifting slowly to settle like a cloak over Brede's shoulders.

Sorcha straightened her back, took another, firmer step away – and her heart stopped beating.

Chapter Thirty-Six

Kendra stumbled over the body, too confused by the call to see it. As she got to her feet, she saw the horse – past calling, that one. She was near then; she stepped over the cruelly angled neck, searching. *Yes.*

The calling ebbed; she knew Kendra was here. Kendra limped away from the horse to the huddled body – two bodies.

She could feel the calling here: not in the limp mortality at her feet, but tangible in the rain and trees. Kendra trembled. This should not be possible. She was already dead, and yet she still called.

Kendra knelt cautiously beside the tangled bodies. The rain was already dispersing the blood. She pulled gently at the nearer body. It rolled easily, unconsciously, away from the other; but the hands were tangled together with those of her companion, tightly caught.

Kendra felt for the flicker of life as she prised the fingers away. It was there, just, but there was something more pressing in her mind. Kendra needed to know who called her.

She stared down at the face gazing sightlessly up at her, as she had known she would. This one would not meet death with her eyes closed; but a Songspinner need not pass that gate at all. She could easily save herself, she need not lie in the mud and choke out her last breath calling for help.

Kendra considered the living one. Her hold on life was tenuous. She needed to be moved, out of the bone-chilling rain. She gathered the unconscious body to her. So slight, these mortals.

The presence that had hovered about her was gone. This was what the dead one wanted; she did not call for herself, but for her companion.

Kendra gazed down again, at the pale, determined, frightened face, still taut with her fight for existence.

Well then, Songspinner, she told the fallen one. *I have your precious one, I will do what I can.* But the grief she would feel for any creature that had fought so hard for life and lost, was tainted with anger. She didn't care to be compelled where she would have given aid willingly.

She tried to shrug off the anger. The light was here now, and the rain was easing. Night had lost her hold; perhaps death would acknowledge defeat also.

Kendra carried the limp, crushed creature to her cave, laying her as gently as she could upon the ground. She didn't stir. It did not bode well, although it made the setting of broken bones and binding of wounds easier.

The flicker of life was still there. Kendra didn't understand it. The injuries alone should have carried her past the gate; the blood loss and the shock and the chilling rain might easily have taken her, but still she hung on, by so faint a thread – she didn't seem to fight for her life, and yet... It was wrong; an echo of that calling brushed Kendra's mind. She didn't like what she believed the Songspinner had done.

The mortal was as safe and as comfortable as she could make her. The time had come for Kendra to return to the carnage in her woods, to the place at the foot of the precipice, where the Songspinner lay.

The rain still fell, less torrential, more of a grieving; water on leaves, the taste of death was in the air.

Witches burn their dead. Kendra sighed, so she must sacrifice her wood to their beliefs. Well, she would do it. If the Songspinner's companion survived, it would help her to know that the right rituals were followed, even if the songs were beyond Kendra.

She knelt once more on the blood-drenched soil. The rain had kept away the crows, but she could feel their presence up in the rain-rocked trees. She would disappoint them.

Kendra had felt the Songspinner drowning in her own blood. Now she saw the arrow that was the cause. Slow, that way, slow and hard.

Well, Kendra told her, *it is over. It is ended.*

She stroked the woman's hair, as she might straighten the feathers of a dead sparrow. All endings were alike. Her fingers caught on something bound into her hair. She teased it out: a row of small blue stones. Kendra knew the meaning of that: The woman was, as she had thought, an extraordinarily skilled Songspinner. She had never seen these stones before, but she had heard of them.

Why? Kendra asked her, as she cut the stones from her hair. she wrapped the stones carefully in the edge of her shirt and tied a knot to hold them safe. She gathered up the dead witch, as she gathered up the dead badgers, the fledglings fallen from their nests.

As she turned to go, she heard a voice in the distance, no, not so distant. The rain had hidden their approach, now it muffled their voices, but they were close. Kendra leant up against a tree, shifting her grip on her burden.

The shadows under the branches, the constant movement of the rain, her own stillness, would not be enough. They were searching, and therefore they would see.

Kendra thought *tree. Branch and root,* her breath slowed: *Leaf and bark,* and *stillness and age.*

I have grown here more than three hundred seasons; she told the air about her, *I am nothing strange. I am part of the wood: I am the wood.*

Two men stepped into the clearing. The taller halted, abruptly holding the other back. He pointed cautiously with his sword. The other nodded, impatient. He wasn't interested in the horse. He pushed away the restraining hand, stepped forward. He glanced up at the cliff face above him. The marks of the fall were there, the skidding in the wet mud, the bent and broken plants. It was a long way to fall. The horse had broken its neck. He glanced at his companion.

The swordsman was kneeling, pressing his hand to the sodden earth. It came away stained faintly with blood. He sniffed his palm lightly, and stared about the clearing, a slow and careful sweep. The other, who carried a bow, crouched beside him, inspecting the ground, looking for footprints. He would not find any. Kendra made no mark upon the earth.

The swordsman tasted the air, as a fox would do. His head swivelled, until he faced her. His eyes narrowed, sensing something not quite right in the shadows. But he didn't see what he searched for, and therefore did not see that she was not the tree she wanted him to see. He was made uneasy by her all the same; half knowing she was there, half understanding why. He stood. He wanted to go, but did not know how to make his companion leave. The archer did not find the footprints. It worried him. A dead horse, enough blood to have stopped anyone in their tracks, but no body, no footprints.

'They are dead?' he asked, more for reassurance than anything else.

Madoc shrugged, the urgency of fear making him careless of their search. The length of metal, which still lay somewhere in the mud and ruin before him, the cause of this hunting, was forgotten. He no longer wanted to know what had happened to the witch and her companion. He didn't believe anyone would survive the fall down that escarpment, therefore, despite the lack of bodies, he believed they were dead.

'You saw her take your arrow. You know they're dead. If we tell the others so, they'll believe us.'

Still the archer hesitated, doubting. He scanned the ground again. *Who knew what happened to a witch when she died?* He accepted what he wished to believe. He nodded; decisive, relieved.

Kendra unthought her branches, withdrew her roots. She breathed. She made a promise to the trees that sheltered her, that they would have her special attention in future.

Chapter Thirty-Seven

Lorcan leapt up at the sight of Madoc; eagerly he reached out his hands. Madoc stared blankly at the mailed gloves.

'The sword,' Lorcan said impatiently. 'The Dowry blade.'

Madoc's eyes widened, horrified. Instantly he knew his forgetfulness to have been caused by witchcraft. Equally he knew he couldn't admit it.

'They no longer had the sword. They must've thrown it down,' he said desperately, hoping he could rely on Doran to back him up. Doran nodded.

'We found them both, and the horse – broken neck, no sword –' he asserted, trembling in the face of Lorcan's mounting fury.

Lorcan considered his still outstretched hands. Madoc had tangled himself firmly in that proffered length of rope, but perhaps not firmly enough. He curled one hand into a mailed fist and struck Madoc a backhanded blow across the face.

Madoc reeled under the blow, but managed to stay upright. He turned back to face Lorcan. For a moment he bitterly regretted Phelan's death.

'My liege,' he said, very quietly.

'You will find me that sword,' Lorcan said coldly, 'if it takes the rest of your life.' He turned his back, calling his horse to him. 'I'm going back to the city,' he said unnecessarily. 'Bring me the sword there, swiftly.'

The grey horse disappeared into the uncertain light. The men about Madoc mounted their own steeds, and moved away speedily, all save Doran.

'They are dead?' Doran asked again. Madoc shrugged, unready to admit his doubts. Doran grimaced, and collecting Guida by the lead rein, rode away through the trees, glancing nervously about him. Madoc turned to Devnet.

'What are you still doing here?' he asked.

'You are my hand-mate,' Devnet replied. Madoc quelled the temptation to hit her.

'I need to find that sword.'

'For the princeling?' she asked scornfully.

Madoc rubbed the bloody weal across his face thoughtfully. 'Not necessarily,' he answered.

Kendra carried the dead Songspinner slowly, reflecting on which trees to sacrifice to the human need to dispose of mortal remains. Depression settled over her shoulders as she silently marked out the infirm and the dying among her flock. Kendra rarely used wood herself. She grieved, and tried not to think. She returned to her cave. There could be no funeral pyre until the rain finished, until she was sure the pursuers were gone.

Kendra laid her burden in the outer chamber. She stepped into the further cave, bending her head low to pass under the arch of tree roots. As she straightened, she saw that she had a visitor.

She came, as she usually did, as the Scavenger. Dressed in her tattered brown robes, her face ever hungry, she waited to tidy away the loosened ends of this human tragedy. She had come before, to wait for one she considered hers, to snatch away from Kendra the failing breath of her charges.

She sat with her face close to that of the unconscious woman, intense concentration keeping her features immobile. Kendra moved silently to stand over her ward, placing herself between the fallen one and death. The Scavenger raised her head, and her voice whispered into Kendra's mind.

Mine.

She did not waste words. Kendra shook her head and spread her gnarled hands in a protective barrier between them. A frown flickered over the usually impassive face of the Scavenger.

Kendra had stood between death and its intended many a time. This one came in many guises, to guide the fallen, the falling, to the gate of the world. She could be the reaper of the young, the gatherer of the lost – she could be the saviour of the ancient. She was the Battle Maiden and she came often as sharp knife or burning fever. Kendra had seen her once, rolling an avalanche of smouldering rocks before her, as a child might roll a discarded wheel rim. Some said that she came as a lover to the suicide, but Kendra had not seen it, for she was death's enemy, and Kendra could never love that one's messenger.

This time, she was the Scavenger, hungry for any left-over, half-used soul, such as the tattered exhausted being with the ruined body that lay now beneath the protective spread of Kendra's fingers.

The Scavenger of Souls raised her hands to Kendra's, but didn't touch. Kendra's time would come, but her soul would never be for the Scavenger to hold. There was an opportunist look to the Scavenger, hoping to take advantage of the weakness of this one's defences. Kendra risked moving her hands.

The time is not yet, she told her visitor, and beckoned her away.

The Scavenger came readily. She could afford to wait, to play games. All things fell to her hand eventually. She seated herself beside Kendra, as though they were a pair of longtime companions, a couple of gossips waiting out a deathbed. Although they had sat like this before, with Kendra's will pitted against the impassive certainty of the Scavenger, Kendra could feel a difference this time, and a dull dread, for it was not Kendra fighting this battle. The Scavenger did not recognise this yet; Kendra provided a distraction. She saw only the nearness to death, waiting to claim her prize for her mistress. Kendra did not think that she could.

Will you play the stones for it? the Scavenger asked, casually, as though wagering for some petty trifle.

She had asked this often over the years. Kendra had always refused. It was a game, a trick. The Scavenger only offered this when not certain of her catch. And this time, when the Scavenger should be sure, she was not. Kendra stared into the cold of her fathomless eyes.

Yes, I will play, Kendra smiled. *But I will only play with these stones.*

Kendra untied the knot in the hem of her shirt. The four blue stones rolled onto the ground at the Scavenger's feet. She stretched out her thin brown hand, but her fingers could not touch.

What have you done, Kendra?

She reached her hand towards Brede, as though she would rip the living heart from her, an expression on her withered features that Kendra had never thought to see there. *Grief.* Why would the Scavenger grieve?

This is wrong, Kendra, you must undo it.

It is not my doing.

It is not what this one wants, she wants to die.

Kendra would not believe her, were it not for that startling grief and pity on the face of the Scavenger of Souls. The Scavenger shook her head. She placed her papery hand on Kendra's shoulder. Cold seeped in.

You will have to work hard with this one, Kendra. I think that perhaps this will be the last time we argue over the fate of one of your scavengings.

Kendra rubbed her shoulder. The cold ache would not leave.

I look forward to our next meeting.

The Scavenger turned on her heel, giving Kendra a careless wave, an old friend, a neighbour; not an enemy. The harbinger of death walked out of the cave, alone.

Kendra sank gracelessly to the floor and rested her face in her hands. The stones pressed against her, moulding her flesh, making her uneasy. She rethreaded them for safety, and laid them beside Brede.

She was depleted, irrationally grief-stricken. She wanted to return to her sleep, her dreams, her silence, but she had a responsibility now. She believed that her charge would survive, although the recovery must be painfully slow. She would not sleep as she wished to sleep for many turns of the moon.

Kendra breathed deep of the damp earth, its promise of growth, trying to rid her mind of the smell of death, and the anger that battered at her heart. She sighed restlessly and went out among her flock to collect the wood for the pyre.

Kendra made her sacrifices, gave the dead one her rites and puzzled over the Songspinner's web, woven from the threads of her song, of her ebbing life; stronger than any Kendra had yet met: even the Scavenger could not break it.

She did not stay to watch the flames.

Returning to the cave, Kendra settled once more on the cold earth. She closed her eyes wearily. For the first time in her conscious existence, she didn't know what she should do for her foundling. She drifted into herself, she wasn't needed yet, and there was time to seek rest and nourishment from the earth and silence that sustained her.

Brede woke in darkness. Pain roared through her and she couldn't understand how she had shut out the raging for so long. She stilled the whimpering fear, her training overcoming her desire to scream aloud.

Enemy territory? She forced herself beyond the pain, listening.

Silence? Not quite – there was a soft dripping of water onto earth, a constant soughing of distant steady rain, unless it was a river? An irrational dread followed that thought. She stretched her perceptions, but couldn't persuade herself that she knew what she could hear. She tested the air, heavy, dark, earth-laden, but she could sense that there was space about her, and that gave her hope.

She concentrated, forcing the drugging confusion of pain away: There was light, or at least, a lack of total darkness. She was in some kind of cave, alone.

Brede allowed some of the tense alertness to leech away, and the pain flooded back. She fought it, identified each hurt, told herself this hurt is only so much, and this, even less – forcing her body to believe her.

She could tell that her wounds had been tended, but she was so weak. She did not try to move. She allowed her mind to range, seeking out an explanation for how she came to be here, searching her memory for a time and place of which she could be sure, and found Sorcha. Involuntarily, she moved, trying to reach out to her memory. Pain lanced her, but it was nothing compared to the fear.

She had been falling.

Sorcha isn't here.

Someone had bound her injuries, that someone must be Sorcha.

Sorcha would not need bandages, would not leave her in such pain; Sorcha would not leave her.

Sorcha is not here.

The need to find Sorcha welled up in her, trying to voice itself in a gasp of impotent fear.

Brede felt a disturbance of air close by and her heart quailed. Something detached itself from the wall of the cave and came to her side. In the darkness she could see only that it was unthinkable. So tall, so roughly made, so almost human, so outside her understanding. It reached out a hand and Brede shrank away. It did not attempt to touch her. It picked up something from the edge of the makeshift bed where Brede lay.

She focused her eyes with difficulty. Hanging from the creature's immense hand, swinging slightly, there was a thread of beads. Despite the darkness, she identified them. Not beads: *stones*. Four of them.

Brede struggled to find her voice, to deny what her heart told her. There was only one way that those stones would have left Sorcha's possession.

All that disturbed the thick silence was an incoherent, ragged gasp. Brede heard the sound and could make no connection between it and what her mind held – such a shallow meaningless gasp for the ravaging of grief and terror that was ripping her apart. She could not bear the sight of those swinging stones. Behind her closed lids the movement continued. She closed her mind against it, the winding pain in her bones a welcome distraction now.

'No,' she whispered to herself, her heart shrinking within her, recoiling.

Kendra sensed the withdrawal, the hopelessness. She closed her hand about the blue stones, angry with herself. She had just undone all the healing of the last days. The scent of despair rankled in her. She strode out of the cave. There were others in need, who would not fight her with despair. She stayed away for days, and when she returned she expected to find a corpse.

Brede stirred uneasily in her determined sleep, pain and grief forcing themselves to the surface of her mind. She cried out, and in her turn, Kendra drifted back into consciousness, out in the forest of her own sleep. She pulled herself back into the world and walked reluctantly back to the cave, and the stirring that might mean life, or might mean death. There was a sense of crowding in the cave, of waiting, of many lives twisting in an uncertain knot, a smell of damage. Perhaps this was the time. She glanced about, filled with unease.

I'm looking for the Gate, Brede said to a being that she could barely see.
Death nodded.

Kendra listened to Brede's breath wane, smelling the despair that leeched from her pores, begging for release.

I am the Gate, Death said, puzzling over the mortal and her shadow. *I am the Gate of the world, all things pass through me. No one comes who is not welcome. No one leaves. There is no Gate.*

But Brede couldn't hear. The thread that bound her to life pulled her back, winding itself tight about her. She didn't struggle; the spell that bound her was too strong for her to break.

Brede stirred once more, and her breathing changed, gasping, fighting, choking. Kendra reached protectively and found another's hands there before her. She felt flesh she couldn't see, she heard a soft murmur of comfort, a skein of words, from a mouth closed by death. Kendra shuddered, and stepped well clear.

Death thought about the shadow. It kept Brede away from her and it understood the Gate. There would be another time. All things passed through her, for she was the Gate.

The presence had gone. The silence of the cave was the deeper for that absence. Kendra waited beside her foundling. Consciousness rose; she felt the reluctance with which it came. The eyelids flickered and closed tighter in protest.

Kendra smiled, tasting acceptance. She had given up on dying; now she would start to mend.

Brede's eyes opened. It was still dark, but not as dark as the last time. She was ready for the pain, ready for the gaping loss that surrounded the island of her self. She was not ready for Kendra.

She gazed silently for a while, accommodating the fact of Kendra's existence to her knowledge of the world. She had to stretch her mind to do it.

'How long have I been here?' she whispered.

Kendra shrugged. She didn't measure time the way Brede measured it. There were dawnings, but she didn't see them all, there were turns of the moon, but she could never be sure it was the same turn each time she greeted that silver light. She judged time by the fall of leaves, the growth of bark. There was the growing season and the waiting season. She couldn't answer Brede's question; insufficient time had passed to register on her reckoning of such things.

Brede did not mind the lack of answer. She wasn't really expecting the creature to speak. She tested her injuries: they were starting to mend. She tried to judge how long it must be.

'I ought to thank you,' she said, feeling beholden, and ungrateful.

Kendra shook her head, understanding her reservations, smelling them in the tone of her voice. Brede recognised that Kendra had answered her, that they could communicate. Curiosity overcame her grogginess.

'I am Brede,' she offered.

Kendra inclined her head, and made a sign with her hands. It was the sign for her name, which was the same as the sign for wisdom. Brede blinked, taking in the sign, divining that it was a name, but she could only guess at its sound. Kendra made the sign for *strength*, and inclined her hands towards Brede. Brede accepted her interpretation of her name, without understanding what it was.

Chapter Thirty-Eight

Try as he might, Madoc couldn't remember seeing the sword in that clearing with the dead horse, and he had come to believe that perhaps Brede had thrown it down after all. So his search was slow and methodical, covering ground he had walked twice already. The persistent rain, almost blinding in its determination to fill his eyes, his ears, and his mouth made the search more difficult. Away from Kendra's confusing influence, Madoc no longer believed Sorcha was dead. He saw the smoke from Kendra's fire, but said nothing to Devnet.

She barely acknowledged Madoc's existence, and took no part in his search. Unimpressed by the significance of the sword, Devnet followed Madoc at a leisurely pace, apparently oblivious to his anxiously bent back, his searching eyes. Having made her choice to stay with Madoc, Devnet was uncomfortable in his presence. She brooded on Brede's words, wondering why she was so adamant in her accusations. She watched Madoc's search as though she could divine the truth from the way he moved. It took two days to reach the edge of the gorge, by which time Madoc's thoroughness had driven Devnet from scorn to rage.

She stood at the brink of that drop and peered cautiously over the edge.

'You think they survived this?' she asked incredulously.

Madoc shrugged.

'They weren't there. Plenty of blood. Perhaps, perhaps not.'

'And that smoke?'

Madoc sighed. 'I don't know,' he admitted, irritably.

'I'm not taking my horse down there,' Devnet said, developing a deep unwillingness to discover what lay at the bottom of the gorge.

'I wasn't planning it,' Madoc agreed. 'It's hard enough on foot with the rain.'

He looped his horse's reins into a bush that clung to the edge of the precipice, and started cautiously down the slope with scarcely a glance at Devnet. She followed unwillingly, slipping in the mud, clinging to thorny bushes to slow her descent. She reached the floor of the gorge covered in mud, bloody of hand and in a raging temper.

'It had better be here,' she muttered, as she waited for Madoc to complete his slow descent. He hung from the bushes and gazed carefully about hoping for a glint of metal among the bushes and boulders. Reaching the foot at last, he rested against a rock, and inspected his cut palms. Devnet hauled him to his feet.

'You came here for a purpose, look for your blasted sword, and then let's get away from this place.'

Madoc glowered at her, trying to remember why it had seemed such a good idea to hand-fast with this bitch. He rubbed the blood from his hands onto his jerkin and strode away to where the remains of the horse lay.

Devnet recoiled from the crow pecked corpse; she was fond of her horses. Madoc quartered the ground around the beast, but found nothing, not even his own footprints. Devnet wandered away, and he thought nothing more about her, until he heard her sharp exclamation.

Madoc raised his head at Devnet's call, and leapt up to follow her, almost colliding with her as she backed away from her find. Madoc found himself automatically providing a comforting and protecting arm, and to his surprise, Devnet accepted his support. Madoc gave her a reassuring hug, and went past to see what had caused such unexpected weakness.

Ashy remains of a large fire. The torrential rain had prevented the fire from completely destroying the bones at its centre. Madoc's stomach turned in response. He retreated swiftly, and resumed his embrace of Devnet, as much for his own benefit as for hers.

'We don't burn our dead,' Devnet said softly. 'Brede wouldn't do that.'

But the witch would, Madoc thought, assessing the situation. If the witch was alive, and she took time for funeral rites, she might still be somewhere in this wood. And what kind of grudge would she hold now? He shuddered, the recovery of the sword fading in importance.

Devnet pulled out of his arms. She had to remind herself that she had wanted to kill Brede herself only a few days ago, but this was different, and she wept: not for the woman who forced her to question her certainties, but for the woman of ten years past, who had laughed with her, who had sung with her, who had shared her blankets. Devnet looked up into Madoc's grim face, her hands flat against his chest, thinking about his single-minded pursuit of that sword. She had seen the blade, it was nothing special, but she understood the struggle for power that the blade had engendered. Devnet thought about Madoc's eager searching after power, and her heart went cold within her.

Walk away, she told herself. *Walk, while you still can.*

'Brede spoke of you,' Devnet said quietly, knowing the risk she was taking, but unable to keep silent.

Madoc saw the way Devnet's eyes narrowed, the way her trembling stilled.

'She said that you led the raid against the Horse Clans. She said you held her sister in captivity until she died and that you sold her next-kin to an inn-keeper.'

Madoc said nothing. Devnet waited for him to answer her accusation, and the moment stretched. She listened to the water dripping from the leaves about her and she stared at her hands, where they pressed against Madoc's rib-cage.

Walk away, she told herself again.

Devnet did not look him in the eyes again. She took a careful step backwards, and withdrew her hands from Madoc's body. A bloody palm print remained on the fabric of his coat.

'You are not my kin.' She turned away, feeling that sudden loss as a freedom. She walked between the trees, towards the faint noise of a river, listening, listening; waiting for Madoc to come after her. She held her head high, expecting a blow to her unprotected back. It did not come, and the sense of freedom grew and the trembling tension loosened her limbs, until Devnet felt she might fly. She did not look back.

When next she woke, Brede was alone. The pain was slightly less. She moved cautiously, testing her limbs, trying to work out what was injured, and how badly. One arm seemed usable. Brede ran her unimpeded hand across her body, telling over broken bones and bruising and worse, and wondered at her waking. She longed for enough light to see by. Her seeking fingers found the string of stones. She clutched them compulsively.

There was a greater pain then, a wave of desolation, threatening to drown her. The hollowness inside her, the aching silence that should contain Sorcha. In the darkness Brede could find nothing to cling to except those stones and she held them tightly; feeling them bite into her flesh, and in spite of herself remembered the touch of Sorcha's skin against hers.

Well then, she told herself.

She stared into the pressing darkness, building a picture in her mind with slow deliberation. She put together impression after impression, the tangle of Sorcha's hair in the mornings, the way the light fell across her shoulders on one particular evening, the touch of her hand, the touch of her lips on Brede's closed eyelids – Brede cursed. Nothing could make her believe it. *She would not believe it.*

She peered at the stones in her hand. She tried to remember their colour. Blue, she decided, concentrating on the texture of the surface. Not all quite the same colour, shading into almost grey, dusty looking. She rubbed her thumb across them, feeling the slight variation in size. They were in the wrong order. They had been taken from their string, and rethreaded without care. She tried to tease the knot loose, using her teeth. The leather thong came loose only gradually. She was tired. The knot untied, there was no way of keeping the stones safe whilst she sorted them. She could get them off the thread, but would not be able to put them back, nor retie the knot. Brede leant her head back, wrapping the end of the thong around her finger, and let tears roll down the side of her face.

Kendra felt threatened now, and protected the boundaries of her domain.

Only someone who knew for a certainty that her woodland existed would find a way into the green dusk of her land. None of the many search parties that Lorcan sent after the Dowry blade could find a way in, and only Madoc remained to disturb Kendra's uneasy quiet.

In time, Madoc believed he understood this place. Devnet's theft of his horse helped determine his continued search. The gorge was full of sounds, but no voices. It was not Madoc's natural habitat and he was made uneasy by it. He liked voices, preferably loud ones. Trees and rivers and small animals and birds made him feel isolated, and when Madoc was isolated he feared, and what he feared, he wanted to destroy; but there was still the sword. Madoc's certainty that the sword lay somewhere in that gorge kept him there, searching.

Brede believed she had allowed herself enough time to heal. She had unbound her ribs; she had stretched and strengthened her damaged arm. She strengthened the muscles in her back and arms much as a fledgling bird prepared its wings for flight, with furious bouts of determined exercise. She had been patient, but time was an uncertain thing in the darkness. She balanced her craving for light and certainty against the pain – diminished, but still there, gnawing at her.

She removed the splints from her mangled leg; she tested her joints, flexed and stretched her injured limbs. The pain made her dizzy; she sweated with the effort it cost her to make those small movements. She shook helplessly with fatigue, but gradually, as days stretched into weeks, it took less and less effort, to bring her knee to her chest, or any of the other tasks she set herself. She was afraid of the uncertainty of time here. She didn't know how long she had lain in the darkness. She knew only that she had neither hungered nor eaten. She wondered if this was what lay beyond the Gate, if this was, in fact, death. Only the pain persuaded her otherwise.

Brede used her voice less and less, in deference to Kendra's silence. The silence gave her too much space to think, and she filled her time with her desperate exercise, and with learning the signs she needed to speak to Kendra.

The shapes and signs that Kendra made on her hands, slowly impinged on Brede's brain, and she repeated and elaborated on those signs, until she could ask questions and understand the answers. In the darkness, those signs were read by touch, and Brede was astonished at the roughness of Kendra's skin, which was as creviced as the bark of an ancient tree, and made the gentleness of her touch all the more remarkable.

In her mind, Brede called Kendra *Tree*, despite having found that the sign for Kendra's name wasn't the same. Discovering that her own name sign meant *Strength* made her wonder whether Kendra chose that sign for her as encouragement.

Once Brede had achieved her ambition, and threaded the Singer stones back onto their thread in the correct order, she tied them into the hem of her shirt, and put them, and Sorcha, from her mind.

Kendra's hold on her territory was firm, and Madoc had no hope of finding the cave, any more than he had a hope of seeing Kendra when he looked straight at her. He only sensed a strangeness, a disjointedness, as though shadows fell where there should be no shadow. He was drawn to watch those uncertain places where the trees weren't quite as they should be, where there was a silence in the constant roar of wind through the branches, but there was nothing to see.

Kendra was aware of the watcher, aware of every bough he broke, every twig he burnt, every fish he stole from the waters of her river. She watched as he searched, and recognised him. She remembered him sniffing the air like a questing dog. Kendra saw how he recognised the confusions she set him, not for what they were, but for their existence. She wondered if she drew him towards her with those disguises, and so she set arbitrary confusions all about her domain, finding spots where the light fell strangely, where silence gathered, encouraging Madoc to spread his search, to spend hours staring at an uncertainty in the air that hid – nothing.

Kendra wasn't immediately aware of Brede's first faltering attempts to stand. It wasn't until Brede fell and Kendra felt her cry of pain and rage and despair that she broke her communion with the earth to seek out her foundling.

Brede was hardly aware of the arms that gathered her up and laid her gently back on to the makeshift bed, as though she were no more than a child.

She turned her head away from Kendra, feeling betrayed by her body, and angry at her own weakness.

Kendra forced Brede's fist loose, and spoke on her fingers, *Too soon*, and closed Brede's hand back into its fist.

She watched the tears running back from Brede's eyes into her hair. Brede coughed, and wiped her nose angrily on her sleeve.

I know, she signed, then let her hand drop limply onto her chest, too worn to even pretend she was not crying.

Kendra stepped away into the darkness, unwillingly reminded of something that might help. She returned, carrying an object that she held awkwardly. She placed it beside Brede, wiping her hands against her legs.

Brede turned her head, not understanding what it was that lay beside her.

She reached her hand to touch, and recoiled from the coldness of metal.

The Dowry blade.

Of all the things she had hoped never to see again. The cold of metal clung to her fingers, and she closed her hand, trying to warm her fingertips, but the icy sensation crawled through her arm, across her chest and clutched at her heart, a caress of darkness, a hand catching her lower ribs and tugging sharply. Brede gasped in shock and flung herself away from the sword. She sat up, twisting round to get her legs over the side of the bed.

Kendra watched, puzzled. She reached for the sword, meaning to offer it once more. As her hand closed over it she felt the calling in it. Kendra dropped the blade at once. Her eyes met Brede's. She raised her hands to try to warn, to explain what the sword was, and could find no words. Brede ignored those hesitantly raised hands. Slowly she pulled the blade to her once more, feeling the cold as a comfort, a right-ness. She hefted the sword, and placed its point against the earth by her feet. If Lorcan could only see his precious sword being used as a crutch.

Kendra stepped away from the unsheathed blade.

Brede hooked the belt over her shoulder, so that she couldn't lose the sword, then, centring her weight on her stronger leg and the hilt of the sword, she stood.

Her balance had changed. She wobbled dangerously, accommodating that unexpected imbalance, and put her foot to the ground. Even with the support of the sword, she could put no weight on the leg. The slightest pressure, even the fact of being upright, set pain clamouring through her, in a way that she hadn't imagined possible. It was worse than the initial pain of the injury.

Brede collapsed back onto the bed.

Too soon, she signed, reluctantly.

For all that, she would not give up, and gradually, the leg healed enough for her to walk, after a fashion. It took weeks before she could walk far enough to leave the cave, but there was a need in her now, a craving to move, to be gone.

Madoc had forgotten his purpose; he watched now, for the sake of watching, half mesmerised by the ways of this place. He had no understanding of how long he had waited, there was only a certainty that there was something here that he wanted, and that if he waited long enough, he would discover it.

When Doran at last found him, he scarcely recognised his general. The metal of his armoured coat was rusted, the leather cracked and mouldering. Madoc's hair had been allowed to grow unchecked by comb or braid, into a tangled mass full of twigs and dead leaves. Were Doran not appalled at the change, he would have laughed.

'General?' he asked cautiously.

Madoc had not seen his approach, had not heard his horse's hooves on the mossy rocks beside the river. He had become so used to listening for silences, that he did not recognise the sounds for what they were.

Madoc blinked at the sight of bright mail. He stared at Doran without recognition.

'General.' Doran tried again. 'Have you found the sword?'

Madoc tipped his head back. The sword? He began to laugh, softly at first, but soon the noise bounced back from the great rock wall above the river.

'The sword?' he asked.

Doran lowered his head, and pretended an interest in his gloves, waiting for the laughter to die.

'No.' Madoc said, the splash of a stone into water.

Doran raised his head and smiled.

'Good,' he said. 'Let Lorcan wait, let him hire all the witches he can find to search for his precious blade. There are friends searching for you, General: friends who no longer look to Lorcan for leadership. You have many friends.'

'Witches?' Madoc's eyes seemed to focus on Doran for the first time. Under that steady regard, Doran wondered if they had made a mistake. Madoc's hand rubbed against his face, thoughtful; and Doran remembered Lorcan's mailed fist striking Madoc. No, they hadn't made a mistake. Madoc nodded.

'Lorcan, without the Dowry blade – yes,' he agreed. 'If he is asking witches for help he must be desperate.'

Doran reached down a hand to help Madoc to the back of his horse, and tried not to flinch as the smell of decay invaded his nostrils. Madoc caught the look on his face.

'Don't wince at me, Doran,' he said.

Doran did not reply. He turned the horse and retraced his route beside the river. He looked at the glittering sun-splashed water and wondered why it had taken five days for him to find a way into the woodland. Madoc glanced back, seeing one more shimmering doubt in the air. The witch was still here, somewhere, and so was the sword. Well, it could wait. When he had Lorcan, he would come back for the sword. He would burn down every tree if necessary, but he would find the blade.

Chapter Thirty-Nine

Brede chose night for her first foray, fearing the brightness of day after so long underground. Even so, the moonlight seemed harsh, making her feel exposed. She shivered at the stirring wind, after the still closeness of the cave. Strange to feel the cave as safety, after years of longing for the wide sky of the Plains. She gripped the hilt of the sword, adjusting her awkward hold, so that she could put more weight on it and ease her leg slightly.

From the mouth of the cave, Brede surveyed the immediate territory, setting herself tasks. If she could walk to here, there was a boulder to rest against: to here, a convenient tree. She sat on a massive tree root, and planned her small battles, her fragile victories.

Brede laid the sword beside her and rubbed abstractedly at the scar across the back of her hand, the slight ridge, the momentary smoothness of scar tissue, pale even against the pallor of her sun-starved skin. Rhythmically she traced the length of that mark, trying to remember a time without pain, flinching from the memory buried in that scar and its sudden painless healing. She blanked her mind to the remembered touch of Sorcha's hand on hers, holding that torn flesh together. Brede clasped her hand against her chest and sighed, a soft uncertain noise in the shadows.

The air stirred and Brede glanced back into the cave.

Kendra stood in the entrance, her head almost touching the rock that arched above Brede. She glanced about, watching for the searching man, the watcher who had invaded her world.

Brede at last saw her silent companion in light. What she saw didn't surprise her, as it might once have done. Kendra was at least two feet taller than Brede. Her body must once had been lithe and strong, but she was old now. Her joints were gnarled, awkwardly twisted, but she still walked with grace, still stood with her back straight. Her skin was a silvery brown, and seemed so old, so used up and dried, that Brede winced, and rubbed her hand against her own forearm. Kendra's hair was as grey as willow leaves. The slight breeze rustled about her. Looking at her, Brede no longer wondered at the choice of the sword as a crutch.

Kendra closed her eyes, not wishing to meet the mortal's gaze, feeling herself reflected there, as she did not wish to be. When she opened her eyes, she gestured to Brede, the latest of her foundlings, her strong one.

Walk for me, she suggested.

Brede picked up the sword, and hauled herself to her feet. Slowly, laboriously, she walked the few steps to the boulder that was her next landmark.

Kendra couldn't bear to watch that painful journey. It took too long, this healing. She covered the same ground in two strides, and gathered Brede up into her arms. Brede moved to protest, but Kendra ignored her.

After the initial shock of Kendra's arms lifting her, once the fear of falling had subsided, Brede enjoyed the feel of the bark-rough skin against her, it was a safe feeling. Kendra felt Brede relaxing into her clasp, and smiled. She carried Brede to the river that ran through her domain, and set her gently down.

There was a small still pool where the current had forgotten its urgent shifting, where Brede might strengthen her leg more swiftly, less painfully.

Brede stared at the water. It was so still, so quiet; but it was a river. Brede hesitated. Rivers had never held much luck for her, even in times of drought. Her mind flickered to another river, its waters tugging at her as she waded the shallows, the current trying to pull her further into its depths. She pushed that thought away, only to have another catch her, the noise of a horse racing through that same river, the bite of the spray thrown up to spatter her – and the warm body leaning against her; an incoherent jumble of thoughts dripped into her brain. Brede shuddered.

Precious, they whispered in astonishment and gratitude, at the waters-edge of her memory.

Lost, Brede screamed back across the distance of time, and closed her mind.

The stones were slippery; Brede gazed miserably at the expanse of rock for a while. Realising that she should not have taken Brede by surprise before; Kendra waited to be asked before she carried Brede to the pool's edge.

The coldness of the water closed around Brede with a suddenness that made her wince and she clung to Kendra's arm, suddenly afraid. Kendra stood patiently, awkwardly bent, until Brede understood that the water was shallow, that she was safe, and loosened her hold.

Kendra sat with her feet in the river, whilst Brede cautiously tested her muscles against the drag of water, breaking the stillness of the surface.

Kendra stayed motionless, save for her eyes, questing about in the darkness. There was no sign of Madoc, no scent of him. Kendra listened, tuning out the noise of the river, of the birds and animals, even their breathing, even their heartbeats – nothing. The man had gone. There was no need to fear for Brede's safety.

Brede watched the moonlight break off the dark ripples of water with a quiet pleasure, unexpected contentment taking some of the knots from her muscles. She stayed for as long as she could bear the numbing cold.

Resting her hand on Kendra's knee, Brede indicated her readiness to leave. Kendra stared down at her thoughtfully, before reaching down to pull her very slowly from the pool. The drag of the water was dreadful, and Brede struggled with a moan at the sudden reassertion of her own weight. Kendra cradled her gently as she pushed to her feet and stepped across the slippery stones in one stride. Brede was asleep in her arms before they were back at the cave.

Kendra was aware that Brede's only thought was of leaving the safety of her woodland domain. For every improvement in Brede's twisted, damaged leg, there was another sign of Brede's determination to leave. Kendra was tempted to keep Brede with her, and nurture their fragile communication, but she had been tempted this way before and it was foolish, there could be no long-term bond between mortals and beings such as Kendra. So Kendra was careful of herself, pulling gently away.

Brede was aware that Kendra was withdrawing from her, and feared it. She had been spending more time away from the cave, relearning the skill of walking. She rediscovered hunger, thirst; and drank greedily from the river. She used her unsteady progress through the woods to gather mushrooms and berries, edible mosses, the occasional bird's egg.

Brede put her weakness down to hunger, which was a constant now. Kendra encouraged Brede's sorties, not for the exercise alone, but for the sustenance she discovered on her forays. As Brede spent more time away from the cave, as she found her own food, her reliance on the essence that fed Kendra lessened, and gave Kendra hope that Brede would survive without her. She would not allow Brede to fall to the Scavenger through any lack of effort on her part. Brede was her last charge, her last responsibility, and she would see her safe. But to do that she must find a horse. Horses weren't commonplace in her land, stumbling in by accident, and that rarely. And so she must go outside her domain, to the nearest farm, and take a horse.

Kendra had not left the narrow strip of woodland that was her world for so long, that she had only a few broken images to supply her memory of what the rest of the world looked like.

She hadn't always been tied to the wood. There was a time in her green and eager youth, when she had been tempted out of her safety, to follow a smiling lad, who had forgotten her as soon as he reached the next town; never realising he owed his life to her care, never realising what she was, or what she might had been to him, had he let her into his heart.

Time had warped for him, and when he at last left Kendra's arms, his wife was long gone, hand-fasted to some new man down the valley, believing him dead. So Kendra had got her revenge for his leaving, his forgetfulness.

She wondered whether she wasn't falling into precisely the same trap with Brede; pouring out her days on someone who would not remember her, who would dismiss her sacrifices as nothing. But no, Brede was not another smiling careless one. Kendra had seen the worried frown play across Brede's face, when she had allowed her foundling to see her own doubts, her weariness: Brede wouldn't forget her. They had communicated in their rough and ready silence, in a way the smiling one never attempted. For him, Kendra's silence had implied devotion and agreement, which had rapidly ceased to exist. Kendra couldn't remember, now, why she had followed him; but she was glad that she had, for it was to Smiling Conal's farm she went, to steal a horse for Brede.

Conal had substantial fences about his field. Kendra stood in the shadow of the nearest trees, measuring the distances, trying to smell if Conal was about, and whether he kept dogs. She moved so slowly across the clearing that between the forest edge and his fence, that her movement would only be seen if someone were to look straight at her. The horses didn't notice.

Kendra laid her hand gently on the dead wood of Conal's fence. Her skin looked almost as dead as the bleached and dry paling. She gave a tug, and the post pulled from the earth as though it were water. One of the horses raised its head, startled by the unexpected movement.

She pushed the crossbar gently, and the fence folded in on itself. The horse looked at her curiously, puzzled at the sudden appearance of what appeared to be a tree. He walked towards her, stretching his neck out so as to investigate from as safe a distance as he could. Kendra offered a hand, and he scratched against her bark-like skin.

The other horse started out of its reverie, and whinnied shrilly. A dog started barking, and there was an abrupt jerky movement from the porch of the shack-like building on the far side of the field. The horse shied from Kendra, stepping away uncertainly. Kendra stared across the field at the bent old man woken from his afternoon nap. She didn't recognise him, for this wasn't Conal after all, the smiler had gone with the Scavenger many years past. This one might be his son's son, or even further down the generational ladder. This one was not so tall, and not so ready to smile as his handsome ancestor.

Kendra sighed to herself, and resolved to banish any remaining tenderness for Conal's memory. She beckoned the horse closer and took hold of its halter. She led the horse carefully over the broken fence. She ignored the cry of protest from the other side of the field. She might not move swiftly, but she was faster than the old man and the horse came willingly.

There was no sign of Brede at the cave. Kendra tethered the horse, and ducked under the entrance.

No Brede, but there was another.

What are you doing here? Kendra asked, angry and taken aback.

Kendra, the Scavenger said, in soft reproach.

The word span across the space between them and uncoiled into Kendra's being. She stepped back, trying to escape the strange feeling of disintegrating.

What are you doing? she asked, frightened now.

I've come for your soul, the Scavenger replied.

It is not time, Kendra protested, her certainty of that fact failing her briefly.

No? I thought I felt something – the Scavenger turned her head thoughtfully from one side to another. *I thought I heard something dying? But here you still are.*

I have no soul, Kendra offered.

Yes you do. You've had a soul ever since you picked up that bleeding boy, and kept him from me. You have picked up a veneer of mortality. I can smell it.

Conal? Kendra asked, startled into it, with her memories of him so recently woken.

Was that his name? the Scavenger asked. *You've kept me from my work too many times for me to remember them all. I remember the first, and I will remember this last one. I look forward to taking them most, when you go wherever it is you go.*

Have them now, and welcome, Kendra signed, confident that the Scavenger could harm neither her, nor her charge. She did not hold Brede's soul, nor did she need any soul she might have.

The Scavenger was startled at so easy a capitulation.

How will you manage without them? she asked, not understanding even now, that Kendra was not mortal in the way the Scavenger understood.

She got no answer; Kendra had moved to the cave mouth. She had heard something, felt something, and was drawn by the cry, as she was always drawn.

But the Scavenger had told her that there would be no more souls for her to rescue, that Brede would be her last charge, and so, that cry must go unanswered. Kendra had a momentary fear that the cry might, after all, be Brede. She feared that she had been tricked into giving away her protection of Brede. She turned back to the Scavenger, her hands raised to ask, and saw the disappointed frown on the face of death's messenger.

Kendra smiled. She had won.

Brede's grip on the sword altered as she entered the cave, alerted to potential danger by the horse outside.

'Greeting,' she said politely, although there was a chill in her heart that made her tremble. Brede had never known Kendra be so still, so tense. Her voice was scarcely a whisper it had been used so little of late, but it hit the stillness and something of the tension broke.

Yes, Brede thought, that immobility had been fear. Anger for Kendra's dread reminded her tongue of how it once made words. She punctured the silence again.

'Is that your horse outside?'

That other, the uncertain being that she couldn't quite see, answered casually, 'No, I believe it is yours.'

But there was nothing casual about this meeting. Brede sensed the purpose tightening at her throat. Although that other had spoken, Brede was aware of no voice. Mostly she was conscious of an absence, an emptiness about the figure, which seemed intent on drawing her in.

Brede glanced at Kendra, hoping for an explanation of the terror. Kendra smiled uneasily, still half listening to the crying out in the woods.

'Who are you?' Brede asked.

'You don't need to know that,' the Scavenger said. 'Not yet. But I shall not forget that you asked. I'll even give you the advice that Kendra can't bring herself to give. Leave here at once. The horse is for you, a gift from Kendra. Be grateful. You've made better progress than I would have thought possible.'

Brede stepped towards the stranger, sensing that she was about to leave, trying to restrain her. The Scavenger raised a warning hand.

'I would not advise you to touch me, not this time. We will meet again.' The Scavenger turned to Kendra. 'I am disappointed, and puzzled. I don't understand how you have kept this one from me.' And she walked through the Gate, and vanished.

Brede turned to Kendra, sensing a tremor of delight in her companion.

It is over, Kendra signed, *and now you must leave. Take the horse, get away from here, go and find your own kind.*

I don't know if that is what I want, Brede offered, trying to fathom the urgency of Kendra's fingers.

You must. It is time.

Brede nodded reluctantly.

'Kendra,' she said aloud, trying out the name, recognising why the sign for the name was as it was.

Kendra gazed at her for a while, measuring the life in her, feeling that the balance had been reached. There was nothing more to be done. She felt Brede's voice slide into her heart, felt her name spoken with love for the only time in her life. She smiled, grateful for the Scavenger's carelessness, in allowing Brede that knowledge, and herself this unexpected luxury, to hear her name from Brede's lips.

Take your horse, take that blade, make a life.

Brede glanced at the weapon. The sword was blunt and dull now.

'It's not my sword,' she said aloud. Nor ever had been, yet here it still was, a curse, clinging to her. Well, there was an answer to that.

I will take it back to Lorcan. Let him have the monstrous thing if he wants it, and my curses with it.

It is only a sword, Kendra signed. *There is no curse on it, no special secrets. It is only metal, wrought by an intelligent smith into something that has been used for evil. It is a tool, nothing more.* Even as she built the words Kendra was rejecting them, knowing they were not her words, not her persuasion. She couldn't stop her fingers building the half-truths.

Brede shook her head. At every turn, since she found it, the blade had marred her life. The only solution now, was to be rid of it.

It is time, Kendra signed again, feeling the pain of losing this, her last foundling, and wanting it over swiftly.

Brede stretched her arms to embrace the rough solidity of Kendra's body. Kendra placed careful hands on Brede's shoulders, remembering with painful clarity, the last time anyone embraced her. It must be two hundred seasons or more. She sighed.

Brede stepped away from her, gathering up the sword. She glanced about the cave, and gathered up the mushrooms, tying them into a corner of her ragged shirt. Then, with one last look, she turned, and limped from the cave.

Kendra watched her go, and then thought herself into the earth, roots delving deep, seeking solace for the silence of her being; a comfort that seemed, for once, elusive.

Chapter Forty

Brede stumbled from the cave, her mind full of the journey ahead, Kendra already half forgotten. She ran a cautious hand over the horse's shoulder. Certainly not Plains bred. Not even an animal trained to be ridden, more of a plough beast. Brede glanced back at the entrance to the cave, feeling guilty at her silent criticism of the beast. Kendra had done what she could. But with no saddle, riding an untrained horse would be difficult.

She led the horse to the boulder that had been one of the milestones in her recovery. She steadied herself, scrambling painfully onto the stone, and whispered a terrible threat to the horse, should it dare move whilst she tried to get across its broad back. The animal flicked a deprecating ear, and stood still.

Brede settled cautiously into the familiar position on the horse's back. Her bare feet reached uncertainly, and she wondered how she would manage to get back to the ground. The horse raised an inquiring head, not, as she had feared, unused to being ridden. She collected the rough rope rein in her hands. She was a child again: too far off the ground, on a horse too broad in the shoulder for her. Frightened, but exhilarated. It was hard to get the horse to respond to her weakened kicking, and she was grateful for the horse's ploughing, for it responded to spoken commands.

To ride, after so long scarce able to walk, was at once a luxury, and a torment. New muscles were pulled and twisted into a fire of pain. Brede wasn't sure she could stand it for long. She walked the beast in a slow circle about the clearing. Possible, perhaps even wonderful. Brede grinned – a certain fearful delight. She glanced once more at the cave, wanting to say goodbye, but uneasy with the thought of dismounting from the horse. There was no sign of Kendra. Hesitating only a second longer, Brede sketched a farewell into the air, and encouraged the horse into a more purposeful walk.

As she rode out from the trees Brede was overcome by a haze of memories that she did not wish to examine, full as they were of terror, and of Sorcha. She blanked those thoughts with scrupulous care, and mapped out the lie of the land in her mind, tracing the distances she must cover, the direction to follow. She scarcely noticed the certainty she had for the route. There was a road, and the sun weak in a cloudy sky to give her a hope of finding her way.

She wasn't as cautious as she should have been. She rode carelessly along the road, without a thought as to the progress of the war, or who held these lands. It was hard to turn her mind to those concerns again, to scan the horizon for signs of habitation, or for riders; her mind was too full of pain and how to endure it.

The first farm Brede came to she entered, careless of danger, hoping only to confirm her tentative mental map. The gate was smashed, the hearth cold. Brede sifted the jumble of rotting furniture quickly, hoping for anything that might be of use. She found a belt, but not, as she had hoped, any food or any boots. She couldn't continue barefoot indefinitely. Sure sign of a stolen horse, riding barefoot, bareback. She couldn't afford those suspicions falling on her.

On then, harder to get to the horse's back this time, her muscles refusing to translate her wishes into motion. She had to lead the horse to a wall, and scramble up. Her muscles leapt in protest, and she was grateful for the patient indifference of the horse, which allowed her to spend many moments gripping his mane, waiting for her body to accept the shock of the climb up the wall, before permitting her the risk of the horse's back.

Brede started to look about her, at the empty fields, rock strewn, dusty. There had been no drought, so the crops must have either never been sown, or have been destroyed by some passing army. She tried to reckon the time of year. There was a cold bite to the air, and the leaves had turned, some trees already reaching bare branches towards the unpromising sun. Time had been passing, and she hadn't seen it. She tried to reckon it up. It must be at least two years since she had fallen into that gorge, into Kendra's land, perhaps a little more. Her reckoning faltered, it could as easily be three years, four – it was not so late in the year. Brede's mind avoided the thought, trying not to remember the falling, the pain, Sorcha. And another thought lodged, limpet-like. An army, set on starving the villages here, but who, and why, seemed irrelevancies; there was only danger.

And so, darkness. The cold deepened, and her threadbare clothing didn't keep out the wind. Cold and pain and hunger kept her awake; kept her moving.

Only when dawn greyness lit the sky did Brede stop, brought up short by the sight of a river, and the charred remains of a bridge. On the other bank there was a building, an inn perhaps, with smoke rising in a lazy trail from its smouldering ruins. Brede walked the horse a few paces into the water, determined to cross, but the bank shelved steeply, and the footing was difficult, many-coloured pebbles shifted noisily under the horse's hooves.

Pebbles.

She stopped. So bright they seemed, those small rounded stones, water-splashed and shining in the wan sunlight. She gazed across the river again, trying to pull her memory into order. This was the same river: she was a few miles further upstream, but it was the same river. Brede forced the horse around, unwelcome memory dragging at her mind as the water dragged against the movement. Out of the water once more, Brede scanned the bank, and the stony path that led alongside it, overgrown with straggling late brambles. The horse, distracted, pulled a meagre mouthful of leaves from the nearest bush. Brede glanced at the plant, and approved the animal's choice. She pulled an eager handful of not yet rotten berries from the stem, stuffing them into her mouth. The almost bitter juice and the coating of dirt caught her throat, but she swallowed hard, stripping more berries from the bush with concentrated urgency until she had eaten all that she could reach. The acid sat uneasily in her stomach, burning, curdling.

Brede urged the horse along the track, aware that the path had been used recently, despite its overgrown state – the brambles were trampled in places, there were skid marks in the stony earth. Someone had come this way recently, and in a hurry. It was then that she saw the body, lying half in the water. The horse shied away, and Brede allowed him his head, a few steps only, and the beast calmed, but refused to go nearer.

Brede slid from the horse's back. Her leg collapsed under her, suddenly useless. The horse stepped away, startled, and Brede had to grab the rope rein, to prevent him bolting. She was dragged a few steps, before the horse would settle. She bit her lip against the new pain of the grazes on her unprotected shins, reminded of her first meeting with Sorcha, and Macsen's ill-tempered stamping. At least this horse hadn't tried to kill her. Brede folded that memory away, in the part of her mind where she refused to dwell, and tried to work out how to get her legs to move.

The horse had wandered a short distance, its head sunk almost to the ground. Brede whistled to it and it walked back to her, hoping for a handful of oats. Brede pulled herself up, using the horse to rest against. The horse still refused to go any closer to the body, so Brede took the long sword as a crutch once more.

She leant heavily on her sword, bending reluctant knees to get down to the level of the body. She hugged the cold metal to her, desperate for something to hold on to, as a spasm of pain shot up into her back, leaving her gasping. Brede put the sword to one side with slow determination. All she could do was wait. Slowly the worst of the pain ebbed, and Brede turned once more to the body beside her.

The head and one arm trailed in the water, and it took some effort for Brede to drag him clear of the river and turn him over. An oldish man, his throat cut. Brede wiped her hands uneasily. She glanced about her, but there was no sign of anyone nearby. The body was quite cold, losing the first stiffness of death. He had lain here long enough for his murderer to be far away. Brede shifted awkwardly away, wanting no more to do with this ending. She glanced almost furtively at the body. Her eyes strayed to his feet.

Boots.

Her feet were freezing. Brede shuddered, thinking of Maeve going through the pockets of the woman she had killed. She eyed the boots again. Too big, but not much too big. She stretched a cautious hand to the man's foot, gave an experimental tug. The boot shifted easily; too big for him too. Thanking the Goddess for the waning stiffness in the body, Brede worked first one boot, and then the other off the corpse's feet. Another wave of disgust hit her. She placed her bare foot beside the boot, measuring. She would need to wrap her feet to stop them slipping and rubbing.

She tore lengths of cloth from the remains of her cloak, trying to keep the cloth smooth as she forced her feet into the boots. Scrambling to her feet, the boot dragged her damaged foot straight for the first time, forcing it into alignment with her shin. Brede hadn't been aware of her limping tendency to turn her toes inward. The boot acted as a splint, but too late for mending the defect. She gasped, gritting her teeth against this new pain, wanting to rip the tormenting leather from her and throw the boots into the river. The dead man's bare feet accused her, the toes pointing vainly at the sky. Brede struggled to the horse, every step setting fire in her bones. She stared up at the horse, wondering whether she had the strength in her arms to pull herself up onto its back, with no saddle to give her purchase. She decided that she had not, and headed back to the ruined bridge, and the damaged footing that would give her the height she needed to remount.

Secure on the horse's back once more, Brede re-examined the riverbank; there was no question of fording the river here. There was no obvious track away from the bridge in the other direction, Reluctantly she turned her back on the water, and took the horse slowly back along the road, looking for a turning. She found one almost immediately, disguised by the gorse and hawthorn growth, but visible now in the early dawn light. This track was more regularly used, and swiftly curved back to follow the river downstream. Barely out of sight of the road, she came upon more bodies. Irrationally, she was grateful that the man had not died isolated from his family. She was shocked at being comforted by carnage. The small farm by the river was deserted now, the raiders long gone, whoever they were. Brede searched through the few remaining possessions scattered across the yard. She took a blanket, and a half loaf of bread, not too spoiled for eating. She thought of her parents, victims of just such a raid, and remembered picking through her own scattered belongings, delirious and in pain, hoping for anything that might still be serviceable. Nothing here could be of use to the slaughtered owners. She forced her thoughts away from the sprawled bodies, determined to prevent herself from trying to work out the relationships between each cold, motionless form. Taking what she needed, she remounted the horse, using the mounting block in the silent yard.

Sunlight spilt across the river, lighting those silvery pebbles, stained dark with blood. Brede encouraged the horse back onto the riverside track. There might be a bridge further on, but there might also be the raiders. Brede wanted only to cross that river and ride as fast as the horse would permit her. She didn't plan to stop again. It was not so far: if she rode fast, she could be at the city in a matter of days.

Chapter Forty-One

Exhausted by days of riding without sleep, Brede was surprised that she could find the way to the city. It seemed centuries since she had first come here. There was still a sense of danger in the country immediately around the city; she flinched fearfully from any sound, watching for any sign of warriors.

So, the northern gate, and an area not overly familiar to her. She was not challenged at the gate, although the women on guard gave her a sharp look, before letting her through. Brede was glad she had made no attempt to hide the greatsword. Although most people were not armed, each knot of refugees had at least one blade amongst the bundles, goats and hens, and children; she would have been out of place, suspicious, without a blade readily to hand. Some soldiers still wore green, but with red badges on their sleeves, an attempt to create a link between the old enemies, but the tension and the heavy guard at the gate didn't speak of reconciliation, and the red-coated warriors did not all wear corresponding green badges. She walked the horse towards the warriors' quarter, and the barracks; disconcerted to find several of the bridges dismantled or barricaded. At last she crossed the main bridge, the only stone bridge, hoping for someone with answers for the questions that crowded her mind.

Brede sat her horse and, trying not to let her glance stray to the shuttered windows of the tower above her, watched the traffic through the gate; watching for someone she knew. She didn't wait long. Several people she recognised, but who did not recognise her, came through the gate, and then Corla.

Corla was preoccupied, but she was well trained; she noticed the stillness amid the bustle. She pulled her horse to a stand; turning her head to stare curiously at the stranger waiting just far enough from the gate to be unobtrusive, just close enough to be noticed, if she wished to be noticed.

Corla walked the horse towards the stranger, drawn by her watching, her stillness. Closer now, she saw the face, and recognised it, but could give it no name.

'Corla,' the stranger said quietly, by way of greeting.

Corla recognised the voice, despite the effort it cost Brede to make her vocal cords work after nearly two years of silence, and realised that above all, it was that stillness that had confused her. She had never thought of Brede as still; and the horse was such poor quality –

'You should not be here,' Corla said, keeping her voice low.

She reached out and touched Brede's shoulder, for the benefit of anyone watching, indicating that this was a welcomed chance meeting, although that was not the truth; and the touch was as much for her own benefit, to convince herself that she was not hallucinating.

'How so?' Brede asked, her voice rasping painfully.

'Lorcan's not forgotten you. He thinks you're dead, but he hasn't forgotten. If you're seen here, you will be in danger.'

'I have something of Lorcan's that I wish to return.'

'What?'

'A sword. It has brought me nothing but trouble. I'd be glad for him to have it back.'

'Are you out of your mind? Look, come with me; get away from here. If Maeve sees you —'

Brede turned her horse, allowing him to fall in step with Corla's youthful roan.

'Maeve is here then?'

'Yes.'

'And Tegan?'

Corla shook her head.

'I'll take you to Tegan. I was going in that direction in any case. She'll know what to do with you.'

Corla surveyed Brede thoughtfully.

'Is it only two years?' she asked wonderingly. 'I'd not have recognised you — but cover your head, shade those eyes, you still look like a Plains rider. That isn't wise.'

Corla fished awkwardly in her saddlebag, and handed a battered broad-brimmed hat to Brede.

Brede pulled the hat well down, shading her eyes from view. She felt ridiculous; she had never worn a hat in her life.

'So,' Brede said. 'Where is Tegan?'

'Keeping an inn.'

Brede laughed.

'She said she would, when she got sick of soldiering. Where?'

'West Gate.'

Brede didn't respond, a fleeting image of a splash of sunlight in darkness; lighting Sorcha's shoulder and neck, her own hand, not quite touching Sorcha's face —

'Maeve wouldn't let her go further, wanted to be able to keep an eye on her. I think Lorcan would like Tegan well away, out of his lands; or dead, of course, that would suit him well enough – but Maeve is valuable to him.'

'Maeve is close with him?' Brede asked.

'Not so much close, more useful. He won't argue with her over Tegan.'

'I didn't know Maeve was so ambitious,' Brede said quietly.

'Nor did any of us – although it kept her alive, and us too I don't doubt. She is tolerated, and plays the consummate mercenary,' Corla said. 'Brede – you should not have come here.'

They rode the rest of the way to West Gate in an uncomfortable silence, Corla restless to be out of Brede's company, Brede unsettled and uncertain.

Tegan greeted Corla with pleased surprise, and was puzzled when her old comrade merely lifted a shoulder and grimaced.

'What is it?' she asked sharply.

'Not what, but who,' Corla responded, beckoning Brede from the shadows.

Tegan saw a woman who would have been tall, if she could have stood straight. Her dragging limp was painful to watch, and disguised a walk Tegan might otherwise have recognised.

Brede pulled the hat from her head, and ran a hand through her hair, as far as the tangled braid would allow. That gesture Tegan recognised, but couldn't believe she had seen.

'What is this?' she asked, abruptly feeling unsafe. 'What is this?'

Brede waited in silence, as Tegan stepped closer, peering at her face. She didn't believe she had changed so much that Tegan would not recognise her.

Tegan did not doubt the identity of her visitor. It was the how and why that concerned her.

'What are you doing here?' she asked, keeping her voice low, pulling Brede back into the shadows, keeping her body between Brede and anyone who might glance in her direction. Tegan wasn't pleased to see Brede, and yet for all that, she wanted to keep a hold on her, perhaps even embrace her. A strange feeling, after so long.

Tegan drew away, glancing at Corla. The warrior caught the look, shrugged.

'I've places to be,' Corla said. 'Stay safe.' She left swiftly. Tegan hoped she would keep silent about this meeting.

'I've brought Lorcan his sword,' Brede said at last, feeling as she spoke that this was not, after all, why she had come.

'And how were you planing to deliver it? Between his ribs?'

'I don't much care. I don't want it. If Maeve has access to him, perhaps she –'

'No,' Tegan said swiftly. 'No, you aren't going to deliver that sword, through Maeve, or any other way. Sell it, if you can, or lose it. It has been nothing but trouble, and there is enough of that already. Can you imagine what kind of furore there'd be if it turned up now?'

Tegan stared once more into Brede's face, hardly able to trace anything she recognised there, save the dark watchful eyes.

'I thought you were dead,' she whispered, and hugged Brede fiercely, her arms loosening from Brede's shoulders reluctantly, registering the uneven shoulder blade, the thinness –

'So did I,' Brede said, but her voice cracked, failing to make a joke of the pain in Tegan's words. She shook her head abruptly, refusing to dwell on it. 'I was told it isn't safe for me here?' she asked, afraid of the response.

'We've things to say to one another,' Tegan said. 'Come and sit down.'

She led Brede through to her private quarters, issuing terse instructions to the boy in charge of the barrels. She tried not to watch Brede's painful progress, resisting the temptation to take her arm, to assist her.

Brede lowered herself slowly into a chair, and glanced about, imagining she would recognise something; she did not. Tegan frowned, and took a bottle from a shelf, and a couple of mugs. She poured, and handed one mug to Brede.

'You look as though this might help,' she said.

Brede took the mug without comment, and took a small mouthful. The liquor was harsh, shocking to her mouth after so long, but welcome.

'So,' Tegan said. 'Tell me where you've been, and why you look as though the Scavenger spat you back.'

'I don't know where I've been, exactly. I know I'm alive, and for now, that's more than enough. I need something to do with my life, and none of the skills I've trained for are the least use to me. I thought I'd deliver the blade to its owner, then take my bearings from there. That sword has been an unreasonable burden, ever since I found it.'

'You should've left it there.'

Brede didn't answer. She couldn't imagine what her world might have held, had she not taken the sword from its resting place.

'Perhaps you should take it back?' Tegan asked.

'No. *She* didn't want it. I doubt I'd find the place now. Tegan, there are things I would ask you. I don't know – how the land lies, I don't know who my friends are. Tell me what has been happening.'

'Where have you been that you don't know?' Brede shook her head, having no answer. Tegan frowned at the continued silence, then said: 'Well. Lorcan has taken the crown, you must know that at least?'

Brede nodded, and took another swallow of Tegan's brew.

'Lorcan made promises, far too many to be able to keep. Many who were loyal to him throughout the war are no longer so, feeling that they have been sold short. Others – not so loyal – have been found out, and are on the run, making common cause with anyone with a grievance – Madoc for one. They're in revolt.'

Brede made a face. Madoc *again* – she couldn't pretend she was surprised.

'The Horse Clans are in turmoil,' Tegan said, trying to sort through the chaos to find the issues that would matter to Brede. 'There are factions within factions, and confusion on all sides. The war isn't over; perhaps it will never be, now. There are still those loyal to Grainne's memory, or at least to the principle of female rule, who don't accept Lorcan's claim to the throne – the loss of that sword hasn't helped him there – although who else has the right?'

'That's where you stand is it? No other choices, so accept the inevitable?'

'Why not?' Tegan asked, surprised that Brede hadn't reacted to mention of the Dowry blade.

Brede shrugged. It didn't seem to matter as it once did.

'I've hung up my sword,' Tegan said softly. 'My concern now is to make a living here.'

'And Maeve?'

'We're no longer close. I do not ask.'

'Corla told me.'

Tegan shrugged, determined to turn the conversation away from Maeve.

'Well, and have you been in contact with your Clan kin?'

'No.'

'No?'

'I have no kin in Wing Clan, save Neala. They cast me out.'

Brede cast her eyes down. Tegan turned away, on the pretext of refilling her mug.

'You and Sorcha have been blamed for Grainne's death. You had, to all intents, stolen the sword, and run for your lives. Lorcan needed someone to blame. You were conveniently expendable. No one much cared what happened to you, it wouldn't have jeopardised any future treaty to put the blame on you.'

Brede handed Tegan her mug to be filled once more. The alcohol was beginning to deaden the pain in her leg, but more was needed to deal with the ugly images her mind insisted on conjuring.

'And rumour takes hold so swiftly, doesn't it, when no one says it's false. You knew, Tegan, yet you said nothing?'

'Who would want to hear that Grainne died by her own hand?'

Brede shook her head.

'Corla said that you and Lorcan don't see eye to eye?'

'How could we? But Lorcan knows me for a mercenary, so for him, that is the role I play. *What do I care who pays me?* I told him. And when that viper Doran came back with your horse on a lead, and said you were dead; what point was there in saying the rumours were untrue? It would only have drawn Lorcan's attention. Besides, it was the sword he was concerned about, not Grainne, and you did have the sword.'

Tegan shook her head, shifted her gaze elsewhere. Brede tried not to think about that silence, but she had to know.

'And who told Lorcan that?'

Tegan continued to look away.

'So,' Brede asked. 'Was it you? Or Maeve?'

Tegan drew in an unsteady breath. 'I was asked. Lorcan can be – persuasive. Riordan knew I'd been in Grainne's quarters, perhaps he even saw you take the sword. There was nothing to be gained from silence, once you were safe away.'

Brede drained her mug again.

'Safe?' she asked softly.

'How could I know?' Tegan asked.

'Sorcha –' Brede couldn't find the words.

Tegan winced. She hadn't even begun to think about Sorcha, but now a vivid memory of Doran, and the horse, and exactly what he had said on his return burnt with acid clarity.

'Lorcan hunted us –' Brede's voice faded in the face of saying that aloud.

'She's dead.' Tegan said for her.

'Did you imagine I'd be here if she were not?'

Tegan shook her head.

'They said she was dead but – there was no word from the witches, no complaint – I thought she would have found a way to get herself out of trouble .'

'Not at my expense,' Brede said sharply.

Tegan winced. 'I bought you time, girl. What did you do with it? I kept silent for days in the face of Lorcan's ways with persuasion. If you want someone to blame, look elsewhere.'

Brede forced her legs to work, and stepped close to Tegan, too close. Tegan put a hand up, fending her off.

'I no longer owe you a life, Brede,' Tegan said fiercely. Brede caught something in her tone that puzzled her. Fear. More fear than she had ever heard in Tegan's voice before.

'No.' Brede struggled with memories and emotions that she had long forgotten. One sharp image fixed itself behind her eyes, snow on the ground, Tegan asking – *What are you willing to die for?* She laid a hand against Tegan's face and listened to the intense silence. At last Tegan's hand met hers, acknowledging all that remained unsaid between them.

'I owe you nothing,' Tegan said softly, pulling Brede's hand away from her face.

'You can't help me,' Brede said, subsiding back into the chair and reaching for the empty mug, twirling it between her hands, first one way, then the other.

'You can't stay here, it wouldn't be safe, for you, nor for me.'

'I can see that.'

'Lorcan's a dangerous enemy. Whatever you have or haven't done, you're a threat to him, and you don't have Sorcha to protect you now, not that Lorcan has much respect for Songspinners.'

'Mightn't that be because he has killed the greatest of them?' Brede asked, feeling burdened with her knowledge. How could the Songspinners not know?

'I don't know, Brede,' Tegan said anxiously. 'You must not speak of it.'

'I must.'

'Not here,' Tegan said tersely, spurred to anger by the guilty fear that anything she once said might have caused Sorcha's death, and fear of Lorcan, should Brede be traced here.

'That's how it is, then?' Brede asked, her anger easing through her misery, and Tegan an easy target. 'Would you rather I had stayed conveniently dead?'

'Brede,' Tegan protested.

Brede shook her head abruptly.

'No, I think not. I'll not bring risk to you, Tegan. I'll not stay where I can't trust my welcome. Be strong.'

Brede struggled to her feet, her will to be away overcoming the numbing stiffness and pain.

'Brede,' Tegan said again, regretting her fear. 'Stay.'

'No.'

Tegan hesitated. The Brede she remembered would know she was being ridiculous and unbend, given a silence to do it in. Brede fumbled with the hat she had been wearing. Corla's hat, Tegan noticed for the first time. The hands that tried to untangle the band about the crown were shaking. Brede wasn't going to laugh at herself this time, wasn't going to forgive.

'Well if you won't, let me tell you something at least.'

'I'm listening.'

'If you hope to leave the city, do so at once. Corla says there is an army massing to the west, and that Lorcan rides out in the next few days to confront them. The gates will be barred behind the army, and you'll be trapped here.'

'And where would I go?' Brede asked angrily.

Tegan ignored her words, intent on passing on her information.

'Another thing, Brede; listen to me, for pity's sake. You must understand that it isn't safe for you with me. Lorcan has always had an eye for my movements.

I'm barely tolerated, for the sake of Maeve's protection, and only if I keep my head low. And he's not forgotten you, nor that sword. I've had people here asking questions recently, even after all this time – asking about you, about the sword; and here you are, back with the – *blasted* Dowry blade in your hand. I've heard rumour that there has been a witch in the city for a while now, up in the tower somewhere. Goddess knows why, but it might be something to do with that blade, there are too many coincidences to be ignored. Get rid of it, if you value your life.'

'The Songspinners don't care about the Dowry blade, Tegan. They aren't interested in what the rest of the world does, unless it affects them – or people they love.' Brede laughed. 'Can Lorcan inspire that kind of love?'

'He'd try, for something he wants as badly as he wants that sword, yes, he'd try. You've always underestimated the significance of that thing.'

'I wouldn't expect any Songspinner to indulge him.'

'So why did Sorcha help Grainne?'

'Sorcha loved Grainne. She knew how to love.' Brede said defiantly.

Tegan met Brede's eyes, and then she turned away.

'I grieve for your loss,' Tegan said, belatedly.

Brede took a breath, testing herself, seeing if she could respond with civility.

'Goodbye, Tegan,' she said quietly; it was as much as she could manage.

Brede stumbled out to the stables to collect her horse. No rotting thatch here now, no bondservants. Tegan had a firm grip on her new trade. Brede glanced upward – new shutters at that low window, firmly latched, painted soft ochre. Well, she was right at the gate; she might as well make use of it. She scrambled onto the horse's back, and rode out onto the narrow street.

To her surprise, she was challenged at once. Brede peered up at the woman who stood on the wall, her bow at the ready.

'Is there something wrong?' she asked mildly.

'We've orders to confiscate all horses leaving the city.'

Brede continued to twist her neck awkwardly, trying to meet the woman's eyes, hindered by the concealing hat. She considered the horse. If it had been Plains bred, she could have made a run for it.

'Why?' she asked.

'You don't need to know.'

'But I do, this horse is the only valuable belonging I have. If you're going to beggar me, you might at least explain your reasons.'

The woman smiled thinly.

'My reasons are that I have orders. You're free to leave the city, if that is your intention, but the horse stays. You'll be recompensed for the value.'

'I can't leave the city without my horse,' Brede said softly, fondling the animal's ear.

There was no use in arguing. She was in no position to win her point. Brede glared at the boy who sidled up to take the rein from her. She shrugged helplessly, and took her time getting down from the horse, making sure her weight was mostly on her sound leg as her feet hit the cobbles. Even so, light-headed from alcohol and anger and lack of sleep, she couldn't control the landing and staggered. The boy's hand was under her elbow before she had a chance to adjust her balance. She turned and found his face too close to hers for comfort.

'Leave me be,' Brede said, snatching the sword from the makeshift carrying sling and leaning heavily on it. The boy backed away.

'Are you taking this animal or not?' she called after him.

The woman above dropped from the wall and took the reins.

'I'm sorry,' she said. 'But I have to follow my orders.'

Brede nodded, wanting to cry for the loss of the horse, but knowing the horse had nothing to do with the feeling of utter powerlessness that swamped her. She couldn't leave the city on foot; she couldn't walk far enough to make it even worth considering the effort.

The guard offered Brede a slip of paper.

'What is that?' Brede asked.

'If you take it to the barracks they'll give you money for your horse.'

'How much?'

'What it's worth.'

Brede sighed. She couldn't risk another visit to the barracks, and the horse was worth very little in money terms, but she took the piece of paper and tucked it away. She reviewed the half thought out plans she had made, before Tegan told her of the imminent closure of the city. Once she had thought to find work here in the horse market, but if horses were so scarce her ploughing beast was confiscated, the market would be merely another windswept meaningless open space by the river.

'Do you have any suggestions as to what I might do now?' she asked the woman. Her question was met by awkward silence. 'No,' Brede answered herself. 'Go and join the other beggars in one of the squares.'

For a moment she considered going back into the inn, asking Tegan for shelter; but she couldn't bring herself to do it, Tegan was terrified to have her under her roof. Her heart sank – how could Tegan, of all people, be afraid? West Gate Inn was no place to find help.

Brede turned her back on the open, beckoning gate. Most of the traffic at the gate was inward, refugees fleeing the uncertainty of open ground for the safety of those walls. Soon the city would be closed, preparing for siege, and the hunger would begin. Brede refused to look up at the stone, and limped away into the city, one rootless, dispossessed stranger among thousands, caught up in Lorcan's battles.

Brede chose her spot with care: she could remember the first time she saw beggars and what a shock it had been. Now she saw them again as though for the first time, considered herself as one among them, thought about the techniques that had rung coins from her in the past. She chose a sheltered spot near a food stall at the foot of a bridge, where people were likely to notice her, as they were putting their money away, as they were about to satisfy their own hunger.

There were many more beggars than there had been – refugees from outlying settlements, ex-soldiers incapacitated by wounds. A great many beggars, and far too few people with money in their pockets. Brede sat for days, her face covered, unable to think of looking at passers-by, and not wanting to risk being recognised. A few coins came her way, and she learnt to fight her fellow beggars for scraps from the food stall. It was miserably cold, even in the sheltered spot she had chosen, and she dared not leave her post for long, lest she lose it to some other desperate vagrant. But, she gradually found, she recognised faces among the crowd of increasingly ragged and hungry beggars. And recognition led to something more. A group of children stoning pigeons drew her away from her bridge, to show them how to use a strip of cloth as a sling, and the gangly nine year old who first brought one down, smiled at her. That smile kept her warm a whole hour, and later, as she struggled with sleeplessness, in the ancient abandoned stables where many of them spent the night in careful, rigidly maintained but imaginary privacy, the boy's mother brought her a sliver of the pigeon, cooked, and half a loaf, stale, but still. The woman smiled at her, and whispered 'You have a sword. Can you use it?'

Brede nodded.

'The respectable folk who live near have been making complaints, the town guard –'

Brede shook her head impatiently.

'Why would the town guard care about us?'

'We're trespassing.'

Brede shook her head again. She didn't want to draw the attention of the town guard. She thought briefly of that lesson in stone and sling – skills that could draw attention her way also. Reluctantly she rejected a source of food. Too dangerous.

The woman frowned, shrugged, and went back to her little knot of family. Brede watched them, then fell to gnawing the bread. She slept more easily with food in her stomach.

From her vantage point by the bridge, Brede saw the army leave, early next morning. She watched the barricade drawn back, saw them march past, the few horses reserved for officers. She recognised a few warriors, but none that she could put a name to. Watching the slow shuffling of the foot soldiers, the grim-faced riders, Brede wondered, for the first time, why there were so few horses that her plough horse was of use to the army. These horses were well trained, fit; they didn't look like the beast that was taken from her. Slowly her mind ground the information and she remembered that Muirne had told her that the Clans were not selling horses to Grainne, or Lorcan. That situation must still hold. Perhaps those stolen horses were held in reserve, against a time when there were no trained beasts left. Perhaps, Brede reflected grimly, they were being held against the siege lasting to the extent that the horses were needed as food for the starving.

Chapter Forty-Two

The army returned from battle well before sundown, too soon for the outcome to have been successful. There was disarray among the troops crowding the streets, much shouting from the officers; a lack of control. Brede shrank against the bridge footings to avoid being trampled. The numbers were noticeably depleted and she had a fleeting impression of a face she recognised among those crowding across the bridge. Maeve, looking as angry and wild of eye as Brede had ever seen her. Brede followed her difficult progress, furtively, not wanting to draw attention to herself. Keeping Maeve in view, she managed to recognise Corla also, slightly behind her, tears pouring freely down her face, her green tunic dark with blood. Brede made an involuntary movement that drew Corla's eye. Scarcely more than a glance, and no way to push through to where she was, but Corla had marked her out.

Brede guessed at defeat, but the gossip by the bridge was swift to correct that impression, replacing it with far worse. Given the opportunity to be beyond the gates of the city, many of the warriors had slunk away, some few to join the rebels, but many more had run for home – thinking on land abandoned in drought, which was now recovered, thinking on planting crops, on survival. With the choice between that, and a long starvation in a besieged city, or death on the battlefield, Lorcan's charismatic control of his army had unravelled.

So said the gossips by the bridge, as they chewed their sweet pancakes, oblivious to the beggars. Another rumour was slower in its circulation, but that very laggardliness burdened it with a smell of truth: the rebels had captured Lorcan. Desperate to instil his warriors with some pride in themselves, some sense of commitment to his cause, he had led a raid deep into the enemy lines. And lost his gamble.

A rumour it remained, no official confirmation was given, but before it was dark, Corla was back, standing over Brede pretending an interest in the murky depths of the river. Brede glanced sideways and upward at the blood spattered green cloak.

'Alms for an old soldier?' she whispered.

Corla pretended to notice her for the first time.

'You should've got rid of the hat, that's what I recognised.'

'Have you said anything to Maeve?'

Corla shook her head, and narrowed her eyes at Brede.

'Should've got rid of the sword too. No one's going to give money to someone with something of value they've not sold yet.'

Brede shifted the blade against her shoulder, protective.

'I might need it.'

'Can you still use it?'

'If I have to.'

Brede flicked the edge of Corla's cloak,

'Whose blood?' she asked.

'Riordan.'

'Bad?'

'Dead.'

Brede winced and wound her hand into the cloak, forcing Corla closer. Corla shook her head, yanking the cloth free.

'Don't waste your breath. This is anger, and it will do fine to keep me from grieving for now. Maeve, though, she's fit to kill.'

Brede nodded, remembering Maeve's protectiveness of her young brother, and the temper with which she disguised her feelings.

'How?'

'Trying to protect that – bastard fool, Lorcan.'

'Ah, it's true then?'

'Thought he could throw himself into the lion pit and get out again, and happy to take his own with him through the Gate.'

'Is Lorcan dead then?'

'No, more's the pity. But the rebels have him prettily trussed.' Corla smiled at that, but her heart wasn't in it. 'I'd kill him myself given half a chance,' she whispered.

Brede nodded. 'Grainne called Lorcan a viper.'

'That he is; poisonous and slippery. It's revenge I want now. Join me?'

Brede laughed weakly, remembering her one brief glance at that brash young man, so eager to prove his right to command. She thought of his awkwardly jutting jaw, his angry voice.

Revenge? she wondered, and had no answer for Corla.

She had tried so hard not to think of Sorcha, but now she couldn't shed the feeling of Sorcha's hands against her skin, and that sensation of falling: she stood at the edge of a precipice, the howling wind trying to drag her down into the abyss. She leant her head into the wall, pressing her forehead against the rough stone of the bridge footing and cursed and sobbed, and wished that she were safely out of her mind, where she could not torment herself.

Corla listened in bewilderment. She gripped Brede's shoulder briefly, and hurried away.

Brede didn't notice she had gone; she stayed huddled against the wall until it was dark, then crept away to sleep in the rotting musty hay of the old stable.

Corla hesitated at the foot of the bridge, trembling with rage and loss, and recognising the slender difference between how she felt and Brede's anguish. It frightened her. She headed west, in need of friends, and balm for her heart.

As Corla stepped into the fire-lit smoke-filled warmth of the inn she glanced about for Tegan. The boy at the barrels spotted her and raised a hand in greeting.

'Tegan not about?' Corla asked lightly. The boy nodded.

'Out the back, but she has a visitor.' Corla crooked an eyebrow. 'Maeve,' the boy said. Corla crooked the other eyebrow, and shrugged.

'I'll have me some ale then, and wait.'

'Food?'

Corla considered, and then shook her head. The boy's eyes fell to the blood splattered across her cloak and nodded again. He handed her a filled tankard, and fished on a high shelf for a small leather bottle.

'What's this?' Corla asked, pulling the stopper and sniffing.

'Strong.' He grinned. 'On the house.'

'I can't decide whether you are a demon or blessing. Goddess knows where Tegan found you.'

'The slave market.' Corla froze, and gave a swift glance to the boy's neck. He pulled his shirt loose. There was no bond-collar. Corla considered the boy's features and sighed.

'Jodis' boy?'

He nodded. Corla shook her head slightly, and handed over the payment for the ale. She glanced about the inn. Quiet still. She felt a great disinclination to talk to Maeve. That could wait for midnight and the full weight of whatever was in that leather bottle to take effect. She chose a dark corner where she could watch the door to Tegan's private quarters and took a slow sip of the ale. It wasn't what her body wanted. She tried the bottle. Fire ran down her throat and spread tentacles through her stomach, unravelling the knot of silence and tension. She gasped. She sensed eyes on her and glanced at the boy. He nodded. Corla closed her eyes against his knowing look. A child that age ought not to understand how she was feeling, ought not to know how to deal with her hurts.

Corla had finished her ale and was a third of the way through the bottle by the time Maeve emerged. She leant further into the dark corner, and kept still, but Maeve had no eyes for what was going on about her. Tegan on the other hand, noticed her at once. She waited until Maeve had walked out into the darkness, then raised her hand towards Corla and waited.

Corla smiled weakly, gathered the bottle to her and followed Tegan through to her private rooms.

As soon as they were in the better light Tegan looked long and hard at Corla.

'What have you to say that you couldn't share with Maeve?'

Corla looked at Tegan. Her eyes were red and puffy, and the frown line between her brows was more pronounced than usual.

'I didn't think Maeve would come to you for comfort.' Corla said, dropping into a seat.

'I don't know that she did.' Tegan stirred the fire, and joined Corla at the table. 'She came to tell me. I've known Riordan since he was a child. He was almost-kin.'

'Yes.'

'And Maeve never knows how to share anything, even grief.'

'Yes. She'll want it all for herself.'

Tegan sighed and smoothed the frown line with her thumb.

'And you and I?'

Corla shrugged, and held out the leather bottle. Tegan smiled.

'Juhel's a clever lad, but be careful how much of that you drink, it could kill you.'

'I should care?'

'Corla, you might not, but I would.'

Corla nodded.

'I know when to stop.' She hesitated, not wanting to talk about Riordan yet. 'I didn't know you had taken on Eachan's reclamation plans.'

'Juhel, you mean? It's not something I'm going to shout about.'

'Have you found any more?'

Tegan shook her head.

'He's probably the only one old enough to know for himself who his mother was. Without that, there's no certainty, and we have to be careful who and how we ask.'

'It's not Eachan you're doing this for, is it?'

Tegan held Corla's glance.

'You know better than to ask.'

Corla took a slow swig from the bottle, watching Tegan over the top.

'She's still here.'

'What?'

'Brede. I saw her on the lower bridge.'

'What in hell is she doing here still?'

'Begging.'

Tegan made an incoherent noise of anger and despair, and put her head in her hands. She shook her head, her eyes still buried in her palms.

'I don't believe this. What is going on? Has everyone gone stark mad?'

Corla sat back, considering that question.

'I think Brede may have. She's not making sense.'

'I told her to go. I warned her about the witch.'

'The witch?'

'She still has that sword.'

Corla sat up and put the bottle on the table. Her hands were shaking.

'What sword?' Corla asked carefully.

Tegan's head jerked up. She said nothing. Corla pulled her hands sharply away from the surface of the table, to tie them in an uneasy knot out of sight of Tegan's stricken expression.

'Oh,' she said lightly. 'That sword.' She dropped her eyes, gazing intently at the bottle. She pushed it jerkily towards Tegan, still not meeting her gaze. Corla felt burdened and panicky. Tegan took a large swallow from the bottle.

'What will you do?'

Corla shook her head.

'Corla, I have to know.'

'Or what?'

Tegan frowned, her hand tightening on the bottle. Corla watched the hand metaphorically wringing her neck and sighed.

'I wish you hadn't told me.'

'So do I. I thought she was gone, I thought she was safe.'

'The witch hasn't found her yet, and she does have a sword with her, I suppose it's that one.'

Tegan shrugged. *What other?* Corla shook her head. The thought of Riordan stabbed through her fear; fierce, impossible to ignore.

Will it be like this forever? she wondered, winding imaginary bandages about her hurt. *Will I be beating my head on walls and screaming in two years' time?* She pulled the bandages tight; feeling the throb of pain stifled, but not cured, and doubted it.

'I don't care,' she said calmly. 'Brede can go to hell, and all the rest of them. I don't care.' She sighed. 'But you do, don't you, Tegan – so I will help.'

Tegan shunted the leather bottle from hand to hand, thinking. Corla waited impatiently, then snatched the bottle away. She moved it to the far side of the table.

'Bring her here, protect her, take the risk?' She moved the bottle to the other side. 'Get her away from here, somehow?'

Tegan sat still, her hands flat on the table, staring at her fingers.

'Well?'

'Whichever I can persuade her to.'

Corla stood.

'Fine, come on then.'

She led the way, the leather bottle cradled against her. Tegan grabbed up a coat and followed.

They walked the short distance to the bridge in silence. Corla strode slightly ahead, impatient, angry, wanting to be getting on with her grieving, not dealing with this. Tegan kept up, just; equally angry, but afraid, trembling with uncertainty. Corla reached the bridge; loped down the slope and reached for the shoulder of the huddled form in the turn of the stonework, and looked down into the startled, sleep confused eyes of a complete stranger. She swore sharply and stood back.

The beggar swore at her, and pulled his blanket more tightly about his shoulders, waiting for whatever abuse was about to come his way.

'Where's the woman who is usually here?' Corla asked. He shook his head. Corla got a grip on the blanket and yanked at it. 'The woman with the sword and the leather hat, where is she?'

Tegan loosened Corla's grip and held out a coin. The beggar took it.

'Don't know. You're not the first to ask, though.'

'Who else?' Another coin.

'Pretty woman, lovely voice. She smelt good. Had an escort of soldiers.'

'What did she say?' Another coin.

'"It's been here recently, I can hear it."'

'Did they ask about the woman?'

'Not exactly.' Yet another coin.

'What then?'

'Something about a sword. Course, I knew who they meant. Isn't anyone but she with a blade.'

'What did you tell them?'

'Didn't tell them anything. They smelt of death.'

'That's quite a nose.' Corla said hoarsely.

'Can smell what you've been drinking. Can smell what you think, too.' The beggar's eyes gleamed palely. 'Grief and fear and blood and anger.'

Corla backed away.

'Come on,' she said sharply.

Tegan followed reluctantly, back towards the West Gate.

'If they haven't found her already,' Corla said softly, slowing her walk enough for Tegan to keep pace. 'Our looking will draw them to us, and perhaps to Brede too.'

Tegan nodded, and held out her hand for the bottle of spirits. Corla handed it over and let her drink deep before demanding it back.

'I'm going back now. Go see to your business, Tegan.'

'What will you do?'

'What I ought to be doing. Helping Maeve get through tonight, let Maeve help me get through it.'

Tegan looked thoughtfully at the bottle, then nodded.

'There's not enough left there to kill both of you, but don't have too much more yourself. What about tomorrow?'

'Whatever tomorrow offers, I won't be out looking for beggars with swords. You shouldn't either.'

Tegan nodded, then hugged Corla to her, her arms fierce with pent up anger.

Corla worked her way free and walked swiftly towards the barracks. Tegan walked as quickly back to the inn, flinging the door wide as she entered. She glanced about the drinkers crowding the room, then strode over to Juhel. He considered his employer, and reached down another leather bottle. He thrust it into her hand. Tegan looked from the bottle to the boy and frowned. Then she pushed her way through the door to her private rooms, turned, and bolted the door.

Chapter Forty-Three

Brede woke to voices, faint, but angry. She glanced around quickly but none of the refugees and beggars she shared the stable with stirred in the pale dawn light. As sleep receded, she realised that the thin wooden wall beside her formed part of the next building. Listening to snatches of conversation had become a habit, providing a welcome, if unsuccessful, diversion from hunger. She closed her eyes, the better to concentrate. The argument concerned Lorcan's capture, and the possibility of persuading a witch to take up the government's cause and win him back.

Brede lay in the musty straw, staring with great concentration at the grain of the wood beside her, and the patterns that woodworm had made. She wondered what could possibly persuade a witch to rescue Lorcan, and where they would find one with enough power to do it. She wondered why the rebels hadn't simply killed Lorcan.

The louder voice thought the plan unworkable. Brede approved his scepticism, and then remembered Tegan saying that there was a witch in the city. Probably there were hundreds, but if there was one who was known like this, then she must be a Songspinner.

The quieter voice, the more reasoned, and perhaps more desperate, said something about mutiny. Brede's mind latched onto that word. She wondered who those voices belonged to, and whether they meant what they said or were speculating. The meagre remnants of Lorcan's army would not hold together without his hand on the leash. It was only a matter of time before the restless and undisciplined ones decided to open the gates to the rebels, or to loot the city themselves. The few who continued to hold fast in the face of that destruction had no hope of controlling the situation. It was a time for drastic action. What alternative could there be? The argument the other side of the wall continued – a mustering of the townsfolk untrained and frightened – could they really consider arming them and sending them out to fight? Why not try to persuade a witch?

Curiosity made Brede struggle out from her nest in the hay, scramble carefully over the sleeping bodies about her, and limp around the stables to look at the building adjoining her shelter. It had an abandoned air to it – just an old house, although a fine one, and well secured. Brede was about to turn away when the door opened. She slid to the ground, and sat with her back to the wall of the building opposite, hand out in the familiar beggar's posture. Peering out from under the brim of her hat, Brede watched two men leave the building. They wore no identifying badge nor uniform, but there was no doubt in her that they were Lorcan's generals. Brede kept her head down, not wanting her interest in them to be recognised.

As they passed, Brede caught a murmured comment; the soft-voiced one, still almost angry.

'She owes us. The sword is not returned for all her promises.'

Brede had to force herself to keep her head down. She had no doubt as to the meaning of that. The witch, or Songspinner, or whatever she was, had promised Lorcan his sword back.

Brede ran a finger down the hilt, and out along the guard, remembering the sour ache of the sword when she'd touched it, lying on her makeshift bed in Kendra's cave. She hadn't thought, until now, why she had returned to the city. Now she wondered: had she been called back? If Tegan was right in her guess, she should get rid of the sword, before it could drag her into a trap. But she had been in the city long enough, why had the witch not found her?

Brede's thoughts strayed back to the generals and the possibility of mutiny. Abruptly she worked her body upright and limped down the alleyway that led back to the bridge, where she could listen to the gossip, and hope for some food. At least she could be prepared for what would come.

Her usual place was taken. Brede considered whether she was prepared to fight for it. The man who sat in her preferred corner raised his head sharply at her approach and rose. He scuttled towards her, arms raised, his tattered blanket wings flapping as he lurched. Brede stepped back into a doorway, startled. He pressed up against her, staring beyond her shoulder, at the hilt of the sword.

'People asking for you, swordswoman; asking for sword. Not wanting to buy, I'm thinking.'

Brede shuddered, put a hand in his chest, and pushed. He fell back, grabbing hold of the remains of her cloak as he did so, ripping it from ragged hem to neck. Brede swore, helpless with rage.

'Soldier gave me money,' he said righting himself, and smoothing the torn strip of cloak over her shoulder. 'Smelt of blood. Didn't want the sword, wanted you. Mentioned the hat.'

'So?' Brede asked, guessing at Corla.

'So I'm telling you. Stay here, they all find you, leave, they all not find you. Good pitch, –'

'– Find your own pitch, you've got money, I haven't.' Brede pushed him roughly away and made for her corner.

'They'll find you,' he called again.

Brede glared at him, and laid the sword carefully beneath the crook of her knee.

'Let them come,' she muttered, trying to make either half of her cloak function as a garment. But once her heart had stopped hammering rage, an uncertain rhythm took over, and she watched every passer-by, jumping if someone came too close, wincing away if an eye stayed too long upon her. No way to get alms, no way to be inconspicuous, but she stayed, rigid with cold and fear, beyond finding the will to do anything but wait for whatever came to find her.

For days nothing happened. The gates remained closed, the gossip became fanciful, and the food scarce.

Dozing fitfully in her corner by the bridge, Brede was joined once more by Corla. She slid down beside Brede, and shifted her back uncomfortably against the roughness of the wall.

'Still here?'

'You sound surprised.'

'Still alive, which is more of a surprise. You know you're watched for?'

Brede raised her chin a fraction. Corla watched the motion out of the corner of her eye, and tried to fathom it – *Indifference? Bravado? Stupidity?*

'What would you say if I told you that there are a great many people who'd gladly let the rebels in?' Corla asked.

'Mutiny? I'd say it was common knowledge.'

'And if I say that Lorcan with no Dowry blade is just a man in enemy hands?'

'I'd say that he has never been anything else.'

'And if I said that rumour had it they've already executed him?'

'Not without the Dowry blade,' Brede said, alert to how close her rival beggar had come, drawn by the sight of a green cloak.

'Not without the blade, no. Do you still have it?' Corla glanced furtively about, not seeing the tell-tale length of metal. Brede didn't answer, didn't move.

'You know it's the blade they're looking for? Given a straight choice between handing over the sword and starving to death, why do you hesitate?'

'I've grown attached to it, and I've no mind to help Lorcan.'

'It's only a matter of time before the witch ferrets you out.'

Brede shrugged.

'It's taken her long enough so far.'

Corla smiled wryly, and eyed the blade that Brede's protective hand had drawn to her attention.

'She's probably walked passed you twice, seen that thing and decided her instinct was wrong.'

'As might yours be.'

'Brede, Tegan told me.'

'She knows I'm here?'

'That you're still in the city at any rate.'

'She's not come looking.'

'Yes she has. You weren't to be found. If you want refuge it's on offer; if you want help to get out, she'll try to help with that too, although it'll be a lot harder now.'

Brede shook her head impatiently.

'Why are you still here?' Corla asked. 'Why are you sitting there with the most sought-after weapon in the country under your knee waiting for disaster to creep up on you?'

'Do you think Lorcan can do worse to me than he has already?'

'Frankly? Yes, I think he, or his kind, can do far worse.'

'I was called here. I can't leave.'

Corla turned her head slowly to see Brede's face clearly. She let the idea that Brede might be completely mad flow through her.

'Why are you wasting your time on this, Corla?' Brede asked wearily.

Corla shrugged.

'I like you. I'd rather you gained from that thing than I walk up here one day and find your corpse in the river, and the sword gone to glory. And no, that isn't a threat. It's honest concern. But you're right, I'm wasting my time.' Corla pushed herself upright. 'One of the details to slip the general's mind is the paying of the troops, but if you ever admit to desperation, you know where to find me.'

'There is something you can do for me,' Brede said, suddenly reminded. She searched her clothing until she unearthed a scrap of paper. Corla took it, glanced at the writing, and sighed.

'This is worthless,' she said. 'We ran out of money to pay those whose horses we took about eight days ago.' She glanced at Brede's rigid expression. 'It's only for a few coppers anyway. You can't trust anyone to give you the true worth of anything these days.'

Corla fished in her scrip, and glanced dubiously at the coins that remained.

'I'll help you if I can,' she said.

'I'll remember,' Brede agreed, pocketing the coppers Corla offered. Corla nodded, looking long and hard at Brede.

'Tegan would help, too.'

'No.' Brede's expression turned wintry. 'I'll take no help from Tegan.'

'If you stay here, you'll have no choice. She'll come looking again.'

'Then I shan't stay here.'

'All right. Stay strong,' Corla said softly, and sauntered away. Brede glared at the sharp-eyed beggar who had worked his way round into a nearby doorway. He turned his back, pretending a fascination in the paintwork of a shutter. Brede wondered whether he was planning to seek out one of those searching for her, and let them know she was back. She wondered if she cared. She worked her way to her feet, and hobbled off intending to search for fruit from the market spoil heap, and somewhere less conspicuous to fail to wring alms from passers-by, somewhere quiet, where Tegan could not find her, somewhere the witch could kill her without raising attention if she was so minded.

As she walked, she cradled the sword, wrapped in her ruined cloak, a precious burden, loved child. Her steps took her down the bridge-side onto the river-walk, along the bank away from the markets, toward the castle. She half-noticed when she slipped on wet cobbles that she was in unfamiliar territory, but still she walked, away from light and hope of food, away from the relative safety of crowds. She shuddered as she walked, feeling pushed and pulled and buffeted, as though trying to force her way through a throng of people, but there was no one there, as she made her way beside the high walls of the river-garths. Her leg hurt, and her shoulder ached with the weight of the sword, and still she walked, recognising the gate to Doran's garth, locked and lit. She heard voices from the far side of the wall as she passed, indistinct, a child crying. She did not slow. There, on the far side of the water, girded by the bend of the river, stood Grainne's tower.

Finally Brede stopped. She felt nothing but animosity, gazing at the deep slow running water, at the stone rising from the banks, at the lighted windows above. The sword slipped from her arms, and she let herself down on her hands and knees beside it, staring into the water at blistered warped reflections of lights – Grainne's chamber, the shutters wide open, the room above, a mere splinter of light, and above that, torches on the roof walk. It seemed half a lifetime since she had stepped out on to that roof. Brede closed her eyes, dazzled by flickering yellow in the winter darkness. It didn't seem as though that half lifetime was in any way to do with her. Her hand closed on the hilt of the sword, and she felt a tugging at her rib cage. She tightened her grip, raising the sword and plunged it into the earth.

'I know you're there,' she said, watching that sliver of light in the uppermost chamber. 'And you know that I – *we* are here. Call all you will, I cannot swim. All you have to do is look out, I'm not hiding from you.' She hauled herself upright and dragged the sword from the soil.

'I'm not hiding.' She walked a few steps along the river's edge, her eyes on the high window. Just for a second a shadow blocked the light and her heart jolted – *all you have to do is look out* – without question, someone stood at the window for a long moment, then turned away. Sorcha would have known. Brede smiled, not such a clever little witch after all. She turned away, snatching windfalls from below the immaculately plastered wall of the garden that backed onto the river here. Brede found a dark corner out of the wind, and recited her nightly ritual of warding song, without the slightest faith in its efficacy.

The town guard were up at dawn calling the news: telling the populace that the rebels were advancing on the city; that every able-bodied citizen should report to the barracks to be issued with a weapon. As she made her way back towards the market, Brede listened to the rising noise of concerned voices, and assumed that the Songspinner had chosen to leave the city, refusing whatever enticement was offered her to rescue Lorcan. Relief flooded her. For all her insane challenge of the night before, she feared the witch.

But now there was a new threat, or perhaps a new opportunity. She started the long walk along the riverbank to the barracks. Not that she needed a weapon; she had the longsword, blunt though it was, firmly strapped to her back. What she needed was the food that would be handed out to every willing volunteer. She would gladly take the army on single-handed if it would get a proper meal into her, even if it did meant saving Lorcan.

Brede wasn't the only beggar with the thought of real food in their minds. The first citizens to reach the barracks were the poorest: the destitute, the refugees; the ones who could not avoid hearing the criers, as they crawled from their holes beneath bridges, down alleys, under carts.

As Brede walked the cobbled streets, she pulled her clothes straight, brushing off as much of the filth as would came. Her hands were shaking. She tried to steady them, she didn't want to be sent away.

There was already quite a crowd. Brede settled onto the side of a horse trough to wait her turn. She could see the green and red-cloaked captains moving through the assembly, taking names, issuing slips of paper, giving directions. She watched the gradual shifting of bodies, and pulled her hat down over her eyes. She could smell horse bran. It seemed that would do very well under the circumstances.

A green coat blocked her line of vision.

'No,' the captain said immediately, recognising her, and starting to turn away. Brede made a swift grab at the tail of her coat.

'Maeve. Don't turn your back on me.'

Brede was very glad that her leg would not allow her to go on her knees, because the temptation was there, and she would sooner die than give in to it. She had every intention of taking the food, joining the march out of the city, and then melting into the nearest trees, and making her way somewhere, anywhere else, no matter how slow her progress. With the witch gone, there was nothing forcing her to stay, she had choices again, and the city was too dangerous now.

Brede kept a firm hold on the green cloth. The back remained turned. Brede shaped her lips around *please* but couldn't force the word out. She would beg on the streets, but she would not beg a friend for help, nor would she beg Maeve, who had never been a friend.

Maeve pulled the coat from her grasp. She surveyed Brede, her hands planted on her hips.

'You must be out of your mind. We're after volunteers, not mercenaries.'

'So I'm volunteering.'

'Why?'

Brede shrugged, then decided to tell the truth. She stood up.

'Look at me. Do you honestly think anyone would hire me? I can't remember the last time I ate something I hadn't stolen. You want anyone who can hold a sword. Well I can do that. So I'm volunteering.'

'I am looking, Brede. What I see is a wreck. Can you swing a sword as well as hold it?'

Brede reached for the longsword. Maeve held up a steadying hand.

'Not here. I don't want a demonstration. I'm not going to send you onto a battlefield you aren't fit for, Brede. I don't want you dead.'

Brede subsided onto the edge of the trough.

'And what will you say to Tegan, when she comes?'

'Tegan knows what she is about. You don't,' Maeve said distractedly. She sighed, doubting Tegan would come and pulled a slip of paper out of the scrip at her belt. She gave it to Brede. She was prepared to bend the rules and get some food inside her, but she would not take her into battle. Maeve didn't need Brede's brand of trouble; she had enough of her own, and Brede had always been trouble. Brede waited for an explanation.

'Food.' Maeve reviewed the condition of Brede's clothing and she pulled another piece of paper loose and held it out. 'A cloak. Take it to the quartermaster. For Goddess' sake, Brede, you know the drill. Then get out of my sight, so I can forget I ever saw you here.'

Brede was not given a chance to thank her. Maeve was away and about her business. Brede looked at the pieces of paper. At least she knew where the quartermaster was.

There were queues forming. She joined the one for food: her most pressing priority. She recognised some of her fellow refugees from the stable. The young lad, and his mother – they exchanged the slight nod of recognition allowed amongst their caste. A beggar had no friends, at least, not amongst other beggars. Brede smiled. *Maeve, of all people.*

Brede reached the top of the queue, and carried away the bowl of thin broth and slice of bread. She found a corner to crawl into and gave her mind to the problem of getting her stomach to recognise warm food. It seemed determined to spit her offerings back. Chewing the bread made her jaw ache. The broth burned her. She had to take it slowly, and rest afterwards, allowing the solid lump in her belly to settle. She took her precious piece of paper and joined the next queue. The true citizens were beginning to filter through now; youngsters, eager for blood, older folk, grim, silent; turning their new weapons over, doubtful and alarmed.

Brede collected her new cloak and wandered slowly out into the practice yard, still careful to disguise her limp as far as she could. The more eager recruits were being given some last minute training in the use of their short stabbing swords. Brede watched, wincing at their ineptitude – she didn't expect that any of these untried volunteers would return from the battle. Brede saw them only as vulnerable skin, with blood pulsing too near the surface, and she wondered at the gibbering intensity of fear that drove them. Brede turned her thoughts away from the feast there would be for the Battlemaiden, and leant on the fence rail, surreptitiously taking the weight off her leg. She had been there some time when she heard another familiar voice, giving full vent to fury.

Brede turned. A small burly man was fighting with a horse that towered over him. It was an ugly brute, hopping on its back legs, attempting to concuss him with its front hooves. Brede considered the shape of its head, the set of its ears. *Plains bred.* She whistled sharply, two short bursts. The horse stopped hopping, grounded its front feet, and stood stock-still. Eachan wrapped the reins swiftly about the rail next to Brede.

'And you're no better, you arrogant mare,' he said to her, his face still thunderous. 'Make yourself useful and bring out the other beasts, instead of standing there daydreaming.'

Brede laughed.

'It's good to see you again, Eachan.'

The master of horse stared through her.

'I'm glad to see they've had the sense to hire me someone who knows horses. I'm grateful for your help, *Stranger*. The last time I had proper help with the beasts was when we had a lass from Wing Clan. Now they know their horses. She's been dead more than two years now.'

Brede's heart sank, recognising the same response she'd had from Maeve and from Tegan. Like having a ghost rise up at your feet.

'Not a safe place this city now, too many people asking questions. If I had any sense I'd hie me off almost anywhere else. Now are you getting those horses or not?' Eachan risked a real look at her. 'You look terrible,' he said bluntly.

Terrible didn't cover it. The woman he remembered, even when she had been pining for the Plains, had a spark to her, an inner vibrancy that was gone. She was too bony to look fragile, but she looked ill, much as Grainne had done towards the end, exhausted and lacklustre. He watched as Brede draped her new cloak over the rail and headed into the stables. He shook his head, guessing at what had lost her that spark and left her so shadowed.

The smell of the stables was so welcoming it brought tears to Brede's eyes. It was not the familiarity of the horses alone that affected her; she had been so lost in her loneliness for Sorcha that she hadn't realised that she was lonely for her friends. She was grateful for Eachan's kind word, so grateful for his warning, useless though it was, that she couldn't control a new rush of grief. She wiped her nose on her sleeve, and slapped the nearest horse on the rump to make it move over.

She worked as steadily as she could, saddling, bridling, leading out. She recognised some of the horses, and deduced that she had better stay out of the way when their riders came to collect them. Reluctantly she accepted the lack of strength in her body and rested regularly to still the tremors in her arms and legs. It was an unexpected pleasure to be among horses, talking to them, touching them, their hot breath fluttering about her neck. She was almost content.

When the last of the horses was ready and many were already being walked about the yard, she hovered in the stable, mucking out, refilling the mangers, exhausting herself; waiting for Eachan to come back.

By the time he arrived she was fast asleep in the hayloft.

Eachan stared down at his onetime assistant, sprawled in the hay with the Dowry blade beneath her hand. Eachan kept his eye away from the blade after the first startled glance. He felt a yawning guilt at his impulsive action so long ago, putting that blade into her hand; and a yearning to make everything right for her, if only he knew how. She looked younger asleep, even more vulnerable. He was alarmed at how thin she had become, at the lines etched into her face. He tried to remember how old she was. She had always seemed so young, but now – Eachan didn't want to wake her. He went quietly away, down to the paddock.

Leaning on the rails, he watched the few spare horses, the ones no one trusted to ride into battle, despite the lack of mounts; among them, a speckled grey, with a distinctive white streak on its back. Brede's own horse. She should have been to the knackers long since, but Eachan was getting sentimental about animals in his old age. He whistled her up.

Guida's ears pricked in surprise. She came willingly, looking for treats, but the old man opened the gate and let her through. He walked her, without touching, up to the yard. She was happy to walk beside Eachan, as he talked to her companionably about nothing. Into the stable she went, and stood still for him to saddle her. Placid, content.

Eachan wasn't sure that he was doing the right thing. Guida was distinctive, but he couldn't let Brede have any other horse. What use she made of his rashness was for Brede to decide. Eachan filled the saddlebags with grain. He brought in Brede's cloak from the practice yard, and went to his own strong box, and took out the two long knives that had lain there ever since Guida was led back, saddled but riderless. They were well polished and sharp, he had taken good care of Brede's belongings. He strapped them onto the saddle. He remembered the long length of the Dowry blade lying under that very saddle strap. *A mistake.* And this?

Eachan inspected his handiwork. He thought Brede would understand. He didn't go back up to the hayloft. He didn't want to have to say goodbye again.

Chapter Forty-Four

A clear, sharp light fell across the field of battle. The generals were satisfied. The ragged army – a handful of warriors leading a mismatch of butchers, smiths, midwives and children – was massed at the foot of the cliff. They had made sure they had no room to retreat – they must fight or die. On the ridge above, the generals stood; the marshals, the messengers, the herald – and the witch.

An oddity here, unmailed, bareheaded in the freezing wind, her blue robe fluttering as she lifted her arm to shield her eyes; she took a long slow look at the enemy.

'Can you do it?' the general asked. She nodded slightly, bringing her breath under control, measuring distance and the direction of the wind. Oh yes, she could most certainly achieve the task they had set her.

The marshal strode past her, invading her quiet space. The witch glanced contemptuously, and he jerked to a halt, and backed away slightly. She searched the blur of motion on the far side of the heath, a much larger army than the frightened chaos below her. And somewhere among them; the king, held captive. And that was, in some way, her fault. She had failed these people once, although she could sense the nearness of that sword, an irritation in her skin. So close, but too late now. So she must make amends, she must win this battle for them. It would not be easy, but she could do this. The witch smiled to herself, and raised her hands, pulling in the wind, moulding it to carry the ultimate weapon against that massing army. The generals stepped away, frightened at the sudden roaring of the wind, and at first, they didn't hear the sweet, clear notes that were borne away on the air, to settle on the enemy. They watched as the witch tied the rebel army in chords of deathly music, as pure as the ring of hammer on anvil...

Killan was not the sort to be at the forefront in a battle. He sought out the generals and the marshals, people who would need messages taken, who would remember the good-looking, helpful, available, efficient – people who would remember him.

But this was no ordinary battle, and it seemed he was expected to get in there and fight. He was, after all trained, unlike so many. Away in the distance was a drift of banners, red, green – people he knew were there, people he – no, it would be too much to say people he loved. People he hated. Maeve. Inir. Perhaps even Tegan would have dragged herself away from her inn for this? And what would he do, forced to fight, if he found any one of them at arm's length? Killan raised his arm to rehearse a killing blow, and found that he could not. A disconcerted murmur ran through the people around him. No one could raise their weapons. Killan let his sword fall from his hand, tried a step, and then another, away worked, towards did not. Well enough. The green and red banners were on the move, Killan turned and ran. It was not long before he heard screaming, and a handful of his fellow rebels caught up with him as he raced for the tree line and what he hoped would be safety.

News of the victory had reached the city, bells rang out, and the singing had started. Ashe flinched away from the noise, smiling nervously at the joyous faces about her, hiding the fact that she didn't rejoice with them.

She found a market stall that was as oblivious to the merrymaking as she and managed to stock her satchel with food by pointing at what she wanted and counting on her fingers. Annet was patient in a bored fashion, and stared through her when Ashe discovered that she had been short-changed. Annet knew that a mute was hardly about to call the town guard. Ashe scowled and left. She needed to be gone from here before the army returned, and with it people who would recognise her, what did a few coppers matter? Despite the angry indifference her mind was holding, her heart was leaping with anxiety.

Annet's eyes followed her, noting the route she took. She couldn't quite credit what she had seen, but she knew there would be gold for the information she had, if it was believed. She glanced round quickly, and caught the eye of a beggar-child watching her stall with bright focus. She beckoned it over – she couldn't tell the sex, too young to be significant.

'Do you know your way about here?'

The child nodded cautiously.

'If you take a message to the miller at the tower mill, I'll give you enough food for a whole day. He'll give you a token to show you delivered the message, bring it back and I'll feed you.'

The child nodded again.

'Can you speak?' Annet asked sharply.

'Yes.'

'Well then you say to the miller: the songster is walking home.'

'The songster is walking home.'

'Off you go.'

She watched the child scuttle across the market in the right direction and went back to her wares.

Brede started awake, confused by the sudden clamour of bells. She peered out at the yard below her. The battle was over so quickly. She climbed stiffly down the ladder to the stable, and there she discovered Guida, saddled and ready. She understood. She would hie herself off somewhere, anywhere, else – but Brede wasn't ready to go, not quite yet. She stilled her excitement and impatience. She petted her horse, who didn't admit to recognising her, until she spoke to her in the tongue of the Horse Clans. Then Guida blew hot air onto her face, and laughed, in the way of horses. Brede slapped her, impatient, but pleased. Guida was too old to be ridden hard. So where to go, other than away?

Brede had no intention of returning Lorcan's sword to him, determined now to escape the witch's calling spell, but she didn't want to wander aimlessly. She thought briefly of the Marshes. The mere idea of being tied down in the cold dank atmosphere of her mother's home made her desperate.

The child clutched the little bag of flour the miller had given her and caught her breath for the long walk back to the market. She glanced up at the sky to judge the time and saw a man silhouetted against the light, on the roof of the mill. As she watched, he leaped down on to the roof of the house next to the mill, and set off at a run.

Killan caught the whistle as he was closing his street door. He glanced up and moved swiftly back into the house. As he reached the top of his ladder, Haran from the mill pushed the shutters in.

'Message,' he said quietly. 'The songster is walking home.'

'Doesn't seem very likely. Says who?'

'Annet, on the market. No imagination that one – if she says that's what she saw, then it is.'

'That's so. Thank you, I will pass this on.'

Killan waited for Haran to go, then went thoughtfully down to the lower floor, crowded with wounded rebels, those who had run for their lives, understanding the limitations of the witch's spell, those far enough back in the ranks not to have met the first onslaught of Lorcan's rabble.

'Revenge, anyone?' he asked, as the general pulled himself through the trap door from the cellar. Madoc regained his dignity.

'Always revenge,' he said softly. 'What do you know?'

Brede was still sitting in the stable, undecided, when the first of the soldiers came back. She started up guiltily, hissing at the pain the too swift movement caused her, but it was Maeve. She looked sickened and angry, and scarcely gave Brede a glance.

Still here? her gaze swept the saddled horse, and a smile flickered into the corner of Maeve's mouth. She gestured to Guida, and spoke to her companion, a woman Brede didn't know.

'Warriors have become butchers, and dog meat gets dressed up as riding material. Why not? And a ghost to ride it.'

Brede waited, uncertainly. There was a strained quality to Maeve's voice that she had heard before, a dangerous sign. The stranger took Maeve into her arms, and Brede felt the brush of armoured glove against mail as if she were between them. It hurt, that gesture. She tried not to think of Sorcha's hands, not wanting to see warmth between these two, not wanting to think about the possibility of caring for anyone.

'It is not your fault, you didn't know,' the stranger said, her voice soft and protective. Maeve didn't concede to the tone, remaining harsh.

'But I should have. They should have told me.'

'Told you what?' Brede asked, unable to contain herself. The stranger released her metallic grip on Brede's ex-captain.

'Told us they'd hired a witch. Told us we weren't fighting a battle, but committing a massacre. We had a right to know, a right to make a choice.'

Brede frowned. Why had the volunteer army been sent out to fight, if the generals had persuaded the witch to help? Why a massacre?

Maeve crossed her arms, protective, defensive.

'I'm a soldier,' Maeve continued, sounding as though she needed to convince herself. 'It's a profession. There are rules, things to respect, but this? It's no use expecting volunteers to behave like an army. They don't understand the rules. We could have won the war without spilling a single drop of blood with the witch, but now? The worst thing is, our glorious leaders liked it. They have no respect for us. If they want to do this sort of thing, they can do it without my assistance.' Maeve's voice cracked on that last word. And she trembled. Brede laid a hesitant hand on her arm. Maeve shook her off impatiently.

'What will you do now, Brede? This city isn't a safe place for you. I can't think what possessed you to come back.'

Brede shrugged. A new notion was taking root in her mind. She hugged Maeve to her, for the first time, for the last time.

'Stay safe,' she said. 'Be strong'; meaning it more than she ever had before.

Brede pulled the brim of her hat down to shade her eyes, and headed for the eastern gate. The time had come to visit the witches, to hand over to them what little she had left of Sorcha; it was time to start her life again.

An hour on the east road, and only a few others had decided to leave the safety of the city yet, unsure of the thoroughness of the destruction of the rebels. Brede rode briskly, but not at a speed that might indicate fear – purpose was the impression she needed to give, that and her new green cloak should protect her for a while. Ahead of her she could see someone from whom fear radiated – a beacon of terror, limping already from unaccustomed haste.

As Guida's shadow fell over the woman she flinched to the edge of the road to let her pass. Brede slowed to a walk beside her.

'Walking doesn't seem to suit you, lass,' she said gently.

The woman kept walking, glancing back nervously. Brede considered what she must see, the bony shaggy horse, none too clean; her own patched and dirty clothes and battered riding boots, the long, dull-edged sword banging gently against her shin. And the incongruously new green cloak, draped across the hilt of the sword and caught on the saddle. She would be frightened herself.

'I was going to offer you a ride, but –'

The woman waved her on, still not risking eye contact.

'I was thinking to myself, here's a foolish rich woman in clothes that are totally unsuitable, going for a stroll in the forest, thinking her money's safe because she's hung it between her breasts.' Brede paused and the silence was broken only by the persist clatter of metal and creak of leather. 'Don't worry; I've no designs on your money. I'm thinking: has she run away from her hand-mate who beats her?' It was not what she was thinking at all, but Brede kept up her gentle, non-threatening, one-sided conversation.

The woman shook her head, raised a protective shoulder, annoyed perhaps, now, as well as frightened.

'No? I was thinking, I should do the sisterly thing and help you out.' Brede eyed the young woman with curiosity, taking in the short silky hair, the absurdly fine clothing. She was feeling generous, secure in her sudden wealth of friends. 'But you're not running away, are you?' Brede continued, testing out the new persona she had found for herself, this new, friend-rich person, who it seemed, could talk forever.

Ashe shook her head. She stared up at Brede, trying to judge what to think of her, how far to trust her. She was not unlike her horse: bony, grubby, and older than was comfortable for what was expected of her. A battered, broad brimmed leather hat disguised much, but Ashe could see greying hair, tightly bound, and a face that was scarcely more than an impression of sharpness harshly lined, the cheekbones prominent from long hunger. A hawk-like nose, the shadow from the brim of that disreputable hat disguised her watchful eyes. Ashe wondered, in a distracted fashion, what colour they were.

Brede bowed with exaggerated courtesy.

'Will you accept my offer?'

Ashe, ashamed, shook her head.

Brede sighed, and gathered up her reins.

'No need to thank me.'

Ashe looked up, stung by the reproach. She grabbed the reins and hesitantly placed her fingers against her mouth and shook her head. Brede frowned, thinking suddenly about silence, thinking about Kendra. Had she imagined that?

'But you can hear?' she asked at last.

Ashe nodded.

'Do you sign?'

Brede let go of her reins again, stripping off her gloves. Hardly believing that she had found a use for her laboriously learnt skill, she made one sign after another. Ashe shook her head, and absently admired the strength in Brede's long fingers.

'That means we are two women alone.'

Ashe saw that she was offered communication, and hope gave a small, uncomfortable lurch. She repeated the gestures awkwardly. Brede gazed at her consideringly, wondering whether she really wanted a companion, whether this involuntary urge to assist was misguided.

'My name is Brede.' She shaped the sign, smiling to herself at its other message, *strong*; well, perhaps. She moved her hands again. Ashe watched closely, trying to make sense of it.

'Will you ride with me?' Brede repeated aloud.

The witch stared at that hand, it was not the hand of an old woman, worn, certainly, but strong and strangely beautiful. She glanced back up at the ravaged face, puzzled. Their fingers made contact and Ashe marvelled at the feel of it. She couldn't remember the last time she'd touched another person's skin.

Brede could feel the lack of experience with which Ashe scrambled up behind her grabbing the scuffed and ragged leather of her belt, forcing the sword into movement as she balanced its weight.

Ashe glanced at the sword, and her breath stilled. She had to drag her attention away from that plain hilt – she would like to laugh. She would like to tell her companion that it was no accident that they had met. She ought to touch that hilt, and close off her last spell, but that felt more of an ending than silencing herself had done. Let it stay, for now, a whisper of power, a reminder of what Ashe could no longer do.

Accustomed though she had become to silence, Brede was consumed with curiosity about her companion.

'Where are you going?' she asked, then almost immediately, 'Are you continuing east?'

Ashe cautiously unhooked one hand from the belt and held it up where Brede could see it, in the sign of agreement used in the market. 'How many days?' Brede asked.

Ashe spread her hand then held up four fingers.

'Four days, maybe?' Brede interpreted. 'Walking? You're going to the witches' city then?' Brede's voice was husky with unease.

'Do you think they can cure you?' Brede asked, tentatively.

Ashe signed *no*.

Brede shrugged; her uneasy curiosity unsatisfied.

'It's your business. Me, I'm going there. I'm aiming to get cured, even if you're not.' An unexpected kind of truth: a kind of healing. 'Besides, it's not safe for you to wander about on your own without even a weapon, not that you could use one I suppose? I can cut a day or two off your journey. You can pay me with the food that's doubtless in that bag of yours. I've nothing, but I'm not drawn to brigandry.'

Unused to the sound of her own voice, Brede felt over jovial, and false; *enough talking*. She wished the woman could sign, she could find a comfortable familiarity with that. And had she been able to sign, what chance she would have used the same system as Brede had learnt? Brede half laughed. Even Kendra's *yes* had been subtly different.

Hours later, far into the forest and with dark falling, Brede found a reasonable camping ground, prudently far from the road, and Ashe struggled to the ground. Her feet were agony; the muscles of her legs would scarcely hold her.

Brede made an effort. Helped by the stirrups, she swung easily from Guida's back, but on the ground she was once more awkward and slow.

Ashe watched her and realised that no one could heal that damage, or that pain. She began to understand that look of having lived through more unpleasant experience than should be crushed into any one lifetime.

War, Ashe reminded herself.

They prepared a meal together and huddled over the meagre fire. Brede attacked her share half-raw and scalding; unaware of Ashe picking at the food she could scarcely stomach. Brede stretched, and limped a slow circle about the camp singing quietly. Ashe touched Brede's arm, making the only sign she knew for what Brede had done. It wasn't a flattering one. Brede laughed abruptly.

'No, not me. I learnt that from a witch I travelled with for a while.' Brede hesitated, wondering what had brought her to speak of Sorcha to a stranger. She shrugged, 'I don't really know if it works, just – superstition.' Brede looked curiously at the woman beside her, at the dark smudges beneath her eyes. 'You don't miss much do you?'

Brede settled into her cloak to sleep. She glanced at Ashe, still rigid and uneasy.

'You rest. I can hear in my sleep. Anything that disturbs us, I will deal with.'

Ashe discounted this assurance, but knew they were safe within the wards.

Brede rested on her elbows, too full of curiosity to quite relax.

'I don't understand why you can't sign. You look rich enough to afford the best teachers. Are you only recently mute?'

Ashe nodded. Far more recently than Brede could imagine.

'But surely you've connections at court, couldn't you have gone to the witch they hired for the battle instead of traipsing out here?'

Ashe let her hair swing forward so that her companion would not see the hot flush of shame on her face, terrified that Brede would follow her thought to involuntarily discover the truth. If she had travelled with a witch she might yet guess.

'Squeamish about blood are you?' Brede asked, trying not to show scorn in the face of this woman's delicacy. 'Don't worry, I wasn't there, so I can't upset you with details. They wouldn't hire an old warwound like me even for the child's play they were at this morning.'

Child's play?

Bitterly Ashe condemned all warriors, and this one in particular.

She huddled her knees closer to her chest, making a protective barrier between herself and the casual cruelty of the warrior's words.

Brede saw that movement as a flinch.

'Oh,' she whispered, shocked at the thought that bubbled into her mind.

Ashe saw her eyes gleam in the fading firelight.

'You're one of the rebels aren't you? That's why you were leaving – running away. No wonder you couldn't go to the witch to be healed.'

Ashe gazed at her in astonishment. Brede had woven her two theories into such a glorious mess that Ashe could only admire her imagination, yet she was horrified at where it might lead.

Ashe shook her head slowly and emphatically. Brede was sure she was right, it was the only logical explanation for this naïve young woman to be on the road without an escort; but she shrugged and lay down.

Ashe stayed upright, sleep far from her mind; nursing her aches to her as some false consolation for the pain she had caused others. At last she lay down to sleep, but every time she closed her eyes she saw that bloody field and all the lives wiped out. Ashe peered at her hands, obscured by darkness, and imagined them dripping gore. She wiped her palms against her legs, and despaired.

Chapter Forty-Five

Ashe started awake from fitful, nightmare-filled dozing to a slow and feeble dawn and mist hanging from the trees.

The wards flickered faintly and her companion slept. Ashe struggled to her feet and the horse snorted in shock, having forgotten her.

Brede did not stir. Ashe smiled to herself; so much for her great hearing. Ashe shook Brede's shoulder gently and she rolled suddenly away, clutching at the great sword but completely unable to get to her feet.

Brede woke fully and swore, incapable of being civil.

Enemy territory, she reminded herself, thinking of Maeve, and suddenly missing her scorn. She could use someone to keep her up to the mark. Away from the constant threat of the city, secure with a horse, *her* horse, once more, she was already getting careless. Using the sword as a crutch Brede hauled herself up. The damp earth had aggravated her pain. Ashe saw all of this. It would take only a few notes of a simple song to ease, and she couldn't do it. Brede staggered bad-temperedly away to relieve her bladder and Ashe set about seeing to some food and a warming drink to drive the cold and damp from their limbs.

Now that they were some distance from the city, the urgency had left Ashe, and there was only a nagging ache in her mind that told her to get home. She had an odd dryness in her throat that caused her anxiety, for she had no way of healing it.

Brede returned, her temper under control, and devoured food with no less ferocity than the night before, ignoring the pain in her stomach, desperate to end her weakness and get strength back into her muscles. She scrambled from a fallen tree to Guida's back, closing her mind on the lack of dignity, the shame of a Plains woman struggling to mount, somehow more acute now she had her own, Plains-bred horse again; as though Guida was noticing and sneering at her rider.

She tied Ashe's belongings to the saddle and helped her up. Ashe watched the wards fade as they passed them and wondered what her sisters would make of her devastating choice of silence.

Brede whistled to Guida, a string of subtle communication that had Guida's ear forward and alert, good spirits surfacing easily. Ashe half listened, and hope rushed over her.

Whistling: surely she could whistle? She could still use tune, it wasn't the same as song, but there were some small things that didn't need words, some small things that could be hers again. She would not be able to set wards, but she could bring sleep and, perhaps, take some of the pain from Brede's leg – if she could find the right tune. No words – damage came only from words.

Ashe hadn't whistled in years. She wasn't sure she remembered how.

The forest stretched before them. Brede kept a wary watch for the suggestion of other paths, and or trouble.

With nothing else to occupy her, Ashe inspected the trees, noting which had lost their leaves; distracted by the way the earth smelt and the way the light fell, green and strange, peaceful. Her throat ached, and she coughed fitfully – leaning against Brede's back to draw breath.

'If you will travel half-dressed you can expect to catch cold,' Brede observed. 'Sorcha used to dress so, but then, she could keep the cold away.'

Sorcha.

Ashe knew that name. It shook her. Goddess, yes, she knew that name. Surely there couldn't be another?

Sorcha of the voice like molten sunlight, of ice turned water? Sorcha who had enough skill for twenty: Sorcha *the* Songspinner? Could she be the witch this woman once travelled with? Was it possible? Ashe shook Brede's shoulder.

Brede turned, but Ashe couldn't explain. She reached round Brede and pulled at the reins, forcing Guida to stop.

'What are you doing?' Brede asked, exasperated.

Ashe fell from the horse, replacing pain for pain, and scrabbled in the leaf mould. Brede stared at the writing, then at Ashe. She understood that what she had written was important, but they were doomed to silence between them.

'I can't read,' Brede said.

Ashe glared at her in disbelief, and still crouched in the dirt she buried her face in her hands, giving way to the frustration and anger and grief that had been brewing for a day and night, weeping until she had exhausted herself.

Ashe wiped her face on her sleeves and straightened. Brede was settling the edge of Guida's saddlecloth with great concentration. She looked up at last with an expression Ashe didn't recognise and offered a hand to help her up, and brushed the worst of the dirt from her clothes. Ashe tried to explain. She made the sign she knew for witch and pointed at Brede, then again wrote *Sorcha* in the earth. She hissed an 'S'. It was the best she could do.

'Sorcha?'

Ashe nodded, relieved that Brede understood. Brede wished she did not.

'Sorcha?' her voice shook, but she must know. 'You knew her?'

Yes, *no*: how could Ashe explain without telling Brede who she was? Could she afford to risk that? Could she make herself understood? Hesitantly Ashe shook her head. A drained look passed over Brede's face, and Ashe decided to trust her. She made the ugly shape for witch again, then pointed at herself. This time Brede was sure she had misunderstood.

'You? You can't be a witch. You're too young, besides, you've got no voice.'

Brede's own voice faded and she covered her mouth, understanding at last, and that terrifying precipice was at her feet once more.

'Who did that to you? Who took your voice?'

Ashe shook her head and pointed again at herself – when Brede shook her head in confusion she touched her throat and closed her fist against her chest.

'You did it?' Brede asked at last.

Ashe nodded. Brede took off her hat, and drove her fingers into her hair. '*Why?*'

Ashe shrugged hopelessly. How could she explain even if she had speech? Brede thrust the hat back on her head, and helped Ashe back onto Guida. Ashe settled on yesterday's bruises and wondered what Brede's silence meant.

Brede's anger melted at last, but she had no compassion. She twisted her head, unwilling to respect Ashe's self-imposed silence.

'So you're – you're a witch. And you took your own voice. Why didn't you just kill yourself?'

Ashe recoiled from the bitterness, recognising a quality in Brede's voice, an undertow of power. Ashe tried to avoid her question, but it persisted.

Why didn't I? Because that wasn't the point – even as she thought, Ashe doubted. There was no way to encompass how she felt about herself, no way to atone, and no way to explain.

'Sorcha lived for her voice. She couldn't have lived without it,' Brede said, trying to understand. She continued her one-sided discussion, castigating Ashe for being everything that Sorcha was not; for being *alive*; building a wall of dislike for Ashe, as protection from the rawness of the loss of Sorcha. 'She'd never have given away everything that she was. What could you possibly have wanted that was worth the loss of your voice?'

Ashe winced away from Brede's scorn. She couldn't undo what had been done; but she had at least made sure she could never do it again.

'Sorcha's dead, did you know?' Brede said.

Ashe heard the careful control of that tone and recognised the effort it cost Brede, and the jagged anguish it attempted to disguise.

No, Ashe didn't know. She bit hard on her knuckle, trying to drive away the pain by a physical hurt. Her eyes stung.

Dead?

Brede wondered at the shocked intake of breath, but made no attempt at further communication; blanking her mind to any thought of Sorcha, refusing to look any further into the dark uncertainty that Ashe had so unexpectedly illuminated.

Hunger prompted Brede to halt at last. Ashe refused to eat at all. Brede shrugged, and ate Ashe's share. Ashe watched the food vanishing without regret. She crouched against a tree, unconsciously rocking forward and back, chewing the skin beside her thumbnail.

Brede wandered through the trees, to walk some of the stiffness out of her legs, and to put some distance between them. Ashe stood abruptly, staring at her hands, thinking of Sorcha. There were too few Songspinners left. She should never have discarded her heritage with such haste – she saw again that field covered in blooded bodies.

Sorcha, dead? Ashe remembered her voice, so full of life. Her voice had cut the air, lifting words into power, lifting Ashe out of herself. Her throat ached to pour out a tribute to Sorcha and tears threatened again. She forced them down, forced the ache from her throat, breathed. Then she tried, hesitantly, to whistle.

It was ugly at first, then she caught a note that told her something. She followed where it led and there was a tune she didn't recognise. A fine tune and there must be words for it if she but knew them. She faltered. It made no difference if she knew the words. She tried again. Phrase followed phrase and she knew that there was something in the making here. A strong sense of spinning. She had stumbled on a song of rare power– it was a song of pain and grief, and of hope and defiance and love and – abruptly, she lost the sense of where the melody led and fell silent. She wanted desperately to know whose song it was; there was a scent of belonging to it.

She listened to the horse snorting and stamping one foot impatiently, and to the hurried, scrambling, uneven, footsteps of the horsewoman. Brede crashed through the undergrowth. She came to a halt staring wide-eyed at Ashe, her hat crushed in one hand –

'That tune,' Brede said carefully, controlling the urge to strike out at Ashe and twisting her hands into the leather to hide their trembling. 'Sorcha sang that when she was dying.' Brede reshaped her hat and thrust it back onto her head, glaring at Ashe. 'You really are a witch,' she said sourly. She caught up the trailing reins. She half turned, an unthought-out word on her lips, but she rejected the momentary urge to confide and mounted, holding out her hand to help Ashe onto the horse.

Chapter Forty-Six

As Ashe took Brede's hand a strange sensation took hold with it. Dizziness held her still, so that Brede pulled against resistance. Ashe shook her head to clear the confusion and scrambled up.

She held on to Brede's belt, but part of her wanted to put her arms around Brede's waist. She sat more upright on the horse, and instinctively used her knees for balance and control; as though she had taught herself to ride.

She opened her mouth to say something to Brede, her silence forgotten in her excitement – *Silence* – Ashe listened to the deadened sound of the horse's hooves on leaf mould and mud, and the occasional break of a twig – there was no birdsong, no movement from the small animals that had scurried away from them before. The horse's ears swivelled and Brede slowed her, turning to one side then the other, listening, waiting; recognising the signs, trying to judge in which direction to run.

Ashe shuddered, feeling that there was another presence waiting with them, that if she were to turn her head she would see someone at her shoulder.

A flurry of motion and a ring of blades surrounded them. The horse shied and Ashe clutched Brede's arm. She stared wildly – there were only seven swords, but that was more than enough.

For the first time Ashe looked death in the face, and wondered if this was the presence that had waited at her shoulder.

It was too late to run now; there was only a faint hope of talking their way out of trouble.

'What do you want of us?' Brede asked, looking for a weakness in that barrier of swords.

A woman near Guida's head caught the reins and replied, 'We want the witch.'

'I know of no witch.' Brede said firmly.

'She rides at your shoulder, woman. We recognise her.'

Ice-cold heat ran through Ashe – a kind of terror she had never felt before in her life. The lurking presence at her shoulder reached out, and entered. *Death*, her heart whispered to her; and somewhere in the dark void of fear that engulfed her, she was glad.

'This woman is mute, you must be mistaken.'

'She wasn't mute yesterday morning.'

The woman gestured with the knife, and one of the men grabbed Ashe, pulling her down from the horse. Her head spun and she staggered, backing away. Was this it? Was this her answer? She straightened quickly. *Atonement* – perhaps she had been fooling herself, perhaps this was what she deserved, perhaps she had no right to choose her own punishment. She shook her head, seeing double.

Brede drew her long knife.

The finest feather touch of hope brushed Ashe, painful in its slightness. She had not been forsaken. But it was pointless against so many and Brede knew it. Even so, she wasn't giving up.

'I will say it again: this woman is mute. I offered her my protection as we both go in search of a witch to heal us. And I mean to keep my word.'

'We've been watching this one. We know who she is.' The woman almost spat the words. Her cold, angry eyes fell on Ashe. 'She may have chosen silence, but she is a witch for all that, and she owes us – so much, so many – an *army*. If she can't raise our army from the death she sent them to, she'll die – slowly.'

Ashe hadn't dared hope for survivors.

'You make a habit of keeping company with witches.'

Ashe couldn't see the man, but memory supplied a face – not her memory. Brede's breath escaped in a hiss: a sound of anger and pain. *Madoc*, again.

Madoc smiled.

'I did not think to see you again. Devnet was convinced you had died, not the witch.'

Ashe strained her neck to see Brede, regardless of the knife a few inches from her face. All she could see was the hand that tightened round the hilt of Brede's knife, knuckles whitening. Such beautiful hands – a scar starting just below Brede's middle finger stood stark and sharp against her skin.

'Last time we met I took a witch from you. I shall do it again,' Madoc said.

Brede gathered herself for what must come – this time she *would* kill him.

Guida moved swiftly, pulling free of restraint, wheeling, front legs flailing. A hand grabbed Ashe away and held her still, as she tried to follow Brede, terrified that she was to be abandoned after all.

The horse staggered.

Brede threw herself awkwardly out from under the falling body, losing her knife, falling because her legs would not hold her. She landed heavily, knocking the breath out of her; one ankle pinned beneath Guida's jerking body. She gritted her teeth against the pain and utter vulnerability. A long knife pressed against her throat, black with Guida's blood.

Brede pulled her head back and squinted at the blade.

Assassin? she thought in surprise, recognising the double-edged blade.

'We want the witch, not you,' the assassin said. 'We want our blood price.'

'On the other hand,' Madoc said softly, 'it would be a simple matter to kill you too.'

Brede stared up the length of metal at the woman, nursing a strange certainty that no blade would touch her this time.

Ashe tore the bag of gold from around her neck and threw it at the assassin's feet. She didn't move: it was scooped up by another woman and weighed in her hand.

'Is that all it costs to buy you? You can't buy us back our families, our loved ones. We want you.'

They closed around her, all but the woman standing over Brede. The assassin frowned at Brede, puzzled by her calm, then abruptly stepped away, wrenching the longsword from Brede's pack, passing it to Madoc. Brede's eyes followed that blade, knowing that Madoc would recognise it. The assassin picked up the fallen knife. Her sneer was eloquent.

'Witch love,' she spat.

Brede lay where she had fallen, the woman's words finally filtering through the shock of seeing Madoc handling the Dowry blade.

Finally Brede realised that Ashe was the Songspinner hired for the battle, the witch hired to drag *her* back to the city to starve, all for the sake of a well forged sword, a sword now in Madoc's grasp. Madoc still gazed at the blade, astonished, and said nothing to his comrades.

Ashe was hustled away held by each arm and forced to run. She stumbled, trying to turn, to see what had become of Brede.

Brede forced her foot out from under Guida, ignoring the spasm that seized her as she wrenched herself free. She contorted her reluctant body until she could reach the saddle pack, and her remaining knife. She didn't think about whether what she did was wise, she only knew that she couldn't live with the contempt of those rebels, who thought her so little threat they would turn their backs.

She felt better with the blade in her hand; the tremor of rage lessened. She pushed to her feet and shouted after them,

'You've not finished with me yet.'

Ashe heard that shout, and recognised the insane anger behind it. So did the man who had her arm. He laughed, and took a step away, to give himself room to draw his sword.

Ashe swung round trying to loosen his hold on her and saw Brede staggering after them, her knife in her hand.

Madoc stepped back towards Brede, all too willing to finish her, but the woman who had taken the gold called him back.

'No, we want them to know we have the witch, leave that mad woman to tell them,' she said.

Madoc recognised the sense of that, and now that he stopped to think, he scorned to fight a cripple.

Brede called out, 'Come on you bastard, let's see you take another witch from me.'

Ashe cursed silently, knowing the cause of her persistence. That spell, still binding the sword to her.

You see what happens, clinging to power that you don't deserve, she told herself, *putting others in danger.*

But Brede no longer had the sword, so why? Abruptly, Ashe saw double again. She saw a younger version of Brede, fuller, fresher, whole and sound; the longsword clasped in both hands and the same terrible look on her face.

Ashe's lungs filled and a voice rang through the forest.

No Brede, no.

It came from Ashe's mouth, but it was not her voice. A knife stroke of fear went through her.

Brede faltered. She slowed and that look slipped from her face. Half afraid to speak, she whispered, 'Sorcha?'

Oh, sweet Goddess, Ashe thought in despair. *No. Not Sorcha; I am Ashe.*

Brede stared at her. Ashe stared back.

Brede. A wave of warmth and longing shook Ashe.

Stay back, this is not the way, that voice called, taking her useless vocal chords and bending them to a stranger's will. She sang: a small swift song and they were all motionless.

Ashe reached out and took back Brede's weapons, took back her gold, then threw it on the ground in sudden fury, spilling yellow coin in the dirt.

Brede was as motionless as the others, lost in horror, confounded. Another song sprang unbidden to Ashe's lips. There was crashing in the undergrowth and the attackers' horses came to her. Ashe pushed the sword and knife into Brede's arms and mounted one of the horses with a skill she didn't truly possess.

Brede cradled the greatsword against her, obscurely relieved that it had not stayed in Madoc's grasp after all. She glanced up at Ashe and her eyes were full of distrust.

'You are not Sorcha.'

Ashe shook her head. Brede limped heavily away. She stripped her gear from the dead horse, pausing to caress the tattoo on her bloody neck. She skirted around Ashe to haul herself up onto the horse she chose to take Guida's part, a stalwart black gelding with a trusting eye.

'What about them?' she asked, her thoughts on Madoc, held helpless, and the opportunity to kill him. Her heart curdled and she was relieved and furious in equal measure when Ashe shook her head. Ashe could not allow any more people to be cut down while she held them helpless. She sang briefly, setting the remaining horses loose, sending them far away from their riders.

Ashe turned her horse sharply, kicking his sides hard, and left them all as far behind as she could. Sorcha's song would not hold them long. Brede followed. They rode hard until the horses tired. At last Ashe slowed her winded horse to a walk, and Brede asked, 'What happened?'

Ashe sought for an answer, and found Sorcha. An incoherent jumble of thoughts battered her; she could make no more sense of it than one, overriding, desperate, un-thought-out need: *Keep her safe.*

Ashe swayed on the horse, unsteady, reeling under the onslaught of Sorcha's determination. More than a plea, more than a command. There was no question of choice. Brede reached out and touched her arm, seeking an explanation, seeking, half against her will, to touch Sorcha.

And Sorcha drifted away, and Ashe had no words, no hope of words. She squeezed Brede's hand gently. She was herself again. Tired, sore, not entirely in control of the horse she rode, and shaking with ill-suppressed fear. Quickly, before she could change her mind, Ashe reached for the hilt of the sword, and laid her fingers against it, then pulled her hand back as though she held some invisible coating between her fingers. She could not allow Brede to put herself at risk again, the spell drawing the sword, and its bearer, to her must end. She formed the words in her mind, picturing the pattern of the notes, her throat involuntarily shaping what would have been the sounds. So nearly the song – she pulled that non-existent layer away again, and felt the spell lift away. She blinked, astonished that it had worked.

Brede sighed. 'She's gone?' she asked, not daring to hope otherwise.

Ashe nodded. That was one thing of which she was certain. A germ of understanding was left behind in the dark place in her mind that Sorcha had briefly inhabited: Brede's need for healing was no more physical than her own, and if she wished it, their healing could be mutual.

Ashe had not let go of Brede's hand. Gently she raised it to her lips. She had no words for what she wanted to say, but she believed that Brede would understand.

Brede was too alarmed by what had happened to want to analyse it. They had made excellent time on their stolen horses. And how was it that in their headlong rush they had come the right way? A suspicion as to the answer stopped her thinking.

'If you want to, we can push the horses and get you home by nightfall,' she offered.

Ashe hesitated, not wanting to arrive exhausted when she was uncertain of her welcome. She shook her head.

Brede shrugged and encouraged the horse into a gentle walk. They would not get much further before nightfall at this pace, but at least it was the right direction.

Later, with a fire made and food eaten, Brede couldn't pretend to herself that what had happened was normal. Every time she looked at Ashe, she expected her to speak with Sorcha's voice, and dreaded it. Every time she asked herself why, she felt the burden of loss in her heart, felt the talisman she carried tied into her undershirt, its light weight bouncing against her ribs, a second heart beat. Her hand constantly strayed to the sword, remembering the look on Madoc's face as he held that hilt – awe, and greed. Now that he knew she was still alive, that she still bore the sword, he would not turn away, he would follow. Brede couldn't sleep.

Ashe was afraid to close her eyes. More than the horror of the battlefield stalked her now. She searched her mind compulsively, looking for traces of Sorcha. She stared at the faint glimmer of Brede's wards and wanted, desperately, to talk to her, to tell her exactly what she had done, and why. What was the use? Even if she could tell her, would Brede understand, or care? Had she not made up her mind already? But if she had, why was she still here?

Ashe shifted again; the twisting horror running through her limbs, shaking her with disgust. Those generals had been glad at the violence of that uncontrolled, frightened, frightening rabble. But for all that, it was her fault; she gave them the opportunity. She was too distraught to cry, her guilt crushing even that comfort. She was sure that Brede would understand that at least, would recognise the grinding sense of loss.

Brede watched Ashe as she by turns stirred restlessly and was rigidly still. She distrusted her for what she had done, and for what she was, and for what she was not.

Ashe watched Brede as she checked the horses, stirred the embers of the fire and added some more wood. Brede kicked the embers together, watching Ashe watching her. She didn't know how to hold a one-sided conversation with this woman. She didn't know what to think of her. Maeve would call her a monster – perhaps she was – but she seemed so young, so – vulnerable. Brede remembered the feel of Ashe's lips against her knuckles – that wasn't an act of vulnerability. Brede considered Ashe. *Young?* Who was to say? She brushed her knuckles uncertainly, suddenly angry. Ashe turned her back on Brede, feeling uncomfortable under her gaze.

Brede crouched beside her, a tentative hand on her shoulder.

'I thought we were stopping for the night to rest, but you aren't sleeping, and neither am I. Would you rather go on?'

Ashe shook her head.

Brede forced herself more upright. Slowly she made the signs for what she wanted to ask, watching her own fingers, thinking how to ask that aloud.

'Is it true, what Madoc's crew say about you?'

Ashe gazed at her face, wondering how many times she must admit it. She nodded stiffly; and waited, straining for the sense of Brede's voice, rather than her words, but she said nothing.

Brede considered her own hands, still raised to communicate, and wondered what point there was in asking why, what use there was in judging Ashe's motives or condemning her actions. She remembered Sorcha raising blooded hands to her, asking for help that she had refused to give. Brede covered her face, trying to blot out that thought. Her outraged words of anger at Ashe filtered back into her mind:

Why didn't you just kill yourself?

She matched those words against her horror at Sorcha's actions, her disgust at Ashe's, and sighed in regret.

'Was that why?' Brede asked, returning her gaze to Ashe's tense waiting, and pressing her fingers against her own throat.

Ashe jerked her head in an awkward nod and her trembling became an uncontrollable shudder.

Brede reached out to still the shuddering but Ashe flinched away from her touch.

'There were times when Sorcha needed comfort and I wouldn't give it, because I thought what she had done was – inexcusable,' Brede said softly. Ashe listened to the tremor in Brede's voice. Brede couldn't finish that thought; she wasn't sure where it ended, where it might lead her. She reached out again. This time Ashe accepted that embrace with gratitude and relief, closing her mind to the complications of Brede's half-expressed doubt.

Chapter Forty-Seven

Brede followed Ashe's lead up through the town. She could have found their destination herself; the stark tower of the keep was obvious from miles away, but Ashe needed to be first, this had been her home. Whether it still was, rested with her kin. Neither of them was optimistic. Brede could not help but think how this homecoming would have been for Sorcha, with a no-voice hand-mate in tow, and was grateful that at least she was nothing more to Ashe than a chance companion.

Close to, the keep was less intimidating. There was an air of decay about the walls; many of the windows were shuttered, unused. The cobbles under the gateway needed weeding. But the neglect did not stretch to their entrance going unnoticed.

The unexpected clatter of hooves on the cobbles brought many a head up, many an eye strayed to a window.

Islean sensed this, but hesitated over whether to join the general migration to the windows. She opened her mind to the noises from the courtyard, whilst continuing her work. There was a disturbance there that was more than the simple arrival of strangers. She put away her papers with slow deliberation.

Her wide casement overlooked the gate. She leant against the edge of the window and peered down. She didn't see the wrongness, the strangeness, she saw only the one she had been longing for, home at last, and her heart was warmed.

It wasn't until she reached the courtyard and felt the cobbles beneath her feet that Islean realised that there was something wrong. She did not understand what it was, but she slowed her impulsive rush and approached more cautiously. She arrived quietly at Ashe's side and laid a hand on her arm, and Ashe smiled, a slow uncertain smile that frightened Islean. This was not her confident, warm, charming Ashe. There was a grey tightness to the skin about her eyes, a stillness in her face that made Islean's heart lurch with dread. She opened her mouth to speak, and her words failed her. Instinctively she sensed that the silence in her friend went far deeper than her own lack of words.

Ashe saw the colour draining from Islean's face, and dropped her bag, so as to have her hands free, so that she could speak – and realised that Islean would not understand, and that she had no idea how to shape her meaning. Brede's face was closed, her mind firmly elsewhere, locked into some private anxiety. Ashe opened her arms to Islean and embraced her friend, gently at first, as though afraid to touch her, then more strongly, feeling intently every point of contact; feeling the hum of power in her, feeling the distress in Islean's tight muscles and resisting bones; feeling loss. She drew away from Islean, looking at her, searching.

Islean felt the loss, the spark that wasn't there.

'What has happened to you?' she asked, hardly daring to break the silence between them.

Ashe raised her hands, but couldn't complete the gesture. The magnitude of what had happened couldn't be contained by the slight movement of her fingers that might shape it.

Brede watched the strained reunion from the back of her horse. She wasn't sure she could get down without falling on the cobbles. She didn't want to disturb the meeting of these two with her ungainliness, but now, Ashe needed her.

'She has taken her voice.'

She shaped the words on her fingers for Ashe, reiterating the lesson, making her learn the signs. There was no way to say it that would be gentle, that would ease Islean into understanding. It was not as though she hadn't guessed.

But Islean had hoped, irrationally, that she was mistaken, that Ashe was merely ill, or too tired for speech. She had hoped, against all the evidence of her senses. Still she denied it.

'No.'

Islean's voice took on an all too familiar obstinacy. Brede had heard it before – *If I say it is not so, it will cease to be so.*

'Yes,' Brede answered her patiently.

Islean's shoulders slumped, and she clung to Ashe, to stop herself from falling.

Ashe's face froze. She would not fold under Islean's distress. There was no going back. She couldn't remember a time when this barrier of silence hadn't been there. She tried, but only the most fleeting glimpse of her carefree love for the woman she held could wind beneath her defences. Islean was a stranger. She glanced beyond her, and saw Aneira, the Elder. Ashe gave Islean a gentle shake.

Islean wiped her face. She didn't care that she was behaving foolishly. She had loved Ashe once, and she didn't think she could love her now, not as she had become. That was, for the moment, more important than the fact that Aneira was staring at her as though she was the one to have ridden home on a horse, voiceless.

'I think we need to deal with this at once,' Aneira said, conscious of the many eyes on her. She glanced at Brede with distaste.

'You speak for Ashe?' she asked.

Brede smiled at the tone, and inclined her head, acknowledging her role, accepting Ashe's name. Aneira nodded, impatient, almost embarrassed.

'You may accompany her,' she said ungraciously.

Aneira turned on her heel, and stalked to the double doors at the far side of the courtyard. They burst open at her command. Brede wasn't impressed. Ashe held out her hand to Brede, asking her if she would go with her. Brede nodded, beckoning her closer. She rubbed her aching leg. Ashe held the horse still, ready to grab Brede if she needed steadying.

Brede swung her legs down, trying to control the force with which she hit the ground. The cobbles twisted her foot at the vital moment. She winced at the stabbing pain, but managed to stay upright. Ashe's hand rested for a second against her arm, not supporting, merely acknowledging.

Islean saw that touch, that slight brush of finger and sleeve. She saw that part of the silence in Ashe was for her alone, that her heart was closed against her. She wondered if Ashe had prepared herself against the rejection she knew must come, or whether they have lost each other inadvertently. Islean glared at Brede. Why did Ashe touch her so, a no-voice? Well, and what was Ashe now? She shuddered. Islean pulled her shoulders back, examined her state of mind, and followed the Elder into the council room.

Brede's fingers interlaced with Ashe's, offering support. Ashe returned the pressure, and followed the woman she used to love into the darkness of the chamber.

It was harder to stand there than she had thought it would be. Ashe gazed around the room. It was barely a quarter full. She had hoped to come home to understanding of her choice, to acceptance, but she had also imagined the worst. She had lain awake fearing the look that had swept into Islean's eyes. Islean, of all of them. At least she had been spared open council. She could not have borne to have them all there, the journeyers, the apprentices, the townspeople, even the children – that she was being given the grace of only the Songspinners themselves was a relief, and was also terrible.

Aneira cleared her throat. Ashe heard it. That hesitation comforted her. Even Aneira didn't know what to say. The doors closed softly behind the last of the women gathered to hear, to see what she had to say. There weren't many. Saraid, Melva, Ceridwen, Islean and of course, Aneira. So few. Of course they would be harsh. Ashe didn't understand how she had thought they would be anything else.

Aneira spoke: 'Ashe has no voice. She has a – companion who will speak for her. We will listen to what she has to say about this. When she has spoken we will consult as to what we must do.'

The Elder glanced around, collecting their full attention, their assent. She nodded to Brede.

'You may speak.'

Brede brushed aside her anger. She must speak well. She knew what it was to be cast out from her kin. She had been rehearsing this ever since they entered the town, and she saw that tower and its lack of compromise.

'Your sister, Ashe, has done something she – now – understands to be evil. She has killed an entire army.' Brede hesitated, still unable to imagine that act, and uncertain as to why she had not condemned Ashe for it. 'With the weapons you taught her to use.' She glanced at the faces of the women about her, and remembered why she was protecting Ashe from their censure.

'You taught Ashe to believe in herself, you taught her how to kill, and that she was correct to use her power so. She has found that to be wrong. She has been rash – I don't know her exact reasoning, she can't tell me – but she'll never be able to injure or kill with her voice again.'

'Is that all you have to say?'

'For now,' Brede replied with as much dignity as she could muster, knowing already that she had failed.

Aneira inclined her head, waiting to hear who would speak first.

Melva stood. She was old, but she stood straight, and her voice didn't quaver.

'Ashe is right to condemn her actions. She should not have used her powers in the way she did. But she was wrong to devise her own punishment. We can't afford the loss of even one voice. That should have overridden everything else.'

Ceridwen didn't wait for the older woman to seat herself.

'Whatever Ashe did, she should not have thrown away her voice. A warrior wouldn't throw away a sword because it had cut down the wrong person, not while it was still needed for the protection of others.'

Brede was aware of eyes glancing at her, sweeping the length of metal that she used to take the weight from her injured leg, now resting beside her as she used her hands to speak to Ashe. She ought not to have brought that blade into their hall.

Saraid shook her head. She put a quieting hand on Ceridwen's arm.

'We are not warriors. We should be clear what we condemn. For myself, I think Ashe's judgement has been at fault. She has been concerned only with her weaknesses, not her strengths. She made no attempt to put right what she had done. Instead she put away her power to do anything. And in so doing, we have lost a powerful, wonderful voice. A voice second only to Sorcha's. We should be grieving that loss, certainly; but we should also be considering why it is Ashe has returned to us, voiceless as she is.'

Brede heard, and didn't hear, what was said.

A voice second only to Sorcha's.

She looked sadly at Ashe, shaping the words for her, so that she might learn them. Not just any voice, then, but an extraordinary voice. No wonder they were so bitter, no wonder Melva asked why she had bothered returning.

And then the secondary meaning bit. They did not know, as Ashe had not known, that Sorcha was dead. Brede quailed, wondered how to tell them, even as her hands moved, spelling her thought for Ashe, 'A voice second to none.'

Ashe raised her head in surprise, and Brede realised that her protest had been made out loud. She looked around the room, and tried to remember who had been speaking as she caused the startled silence. The Elder, Aneira, drew herself up.

'What do you mean, second to none?'

Brede licked her dry lips, afraid to speak again into the thickening, waiting silence. The truth that she had lived with, and tried to avoid living with, for two years, was a shocking cruelty to them; but it was too late to soften the blow. She stood, stiff with her own grief.

'Sorcha is dead.'

An intake of breath echoed around the Songspinners. Aneira's remarkable voice was shades lighter, weaker.

'Who says this?' she asked, but her voice asked far more, *Who are you to tell us this? A no-voice. How dare you even speak her name?*

Brede was used to that kind of question. She answered the intent rather than the words.

'Her companion and lover. I was with her when she died.'

For a flickering moment Brede remembered Sorcha's voice, fierce with unexpected nerves, claiming her as hand-mate, but she couldn't bring herself to voice that half-truth to these women, be they Sorcha's kin or no.

'How is it that we did not know?' Saraid asked.

She did not ask Brede, she asked the others. Accusing, disbelieving: How did they let this happen? How did Sorcha let it happen?

Aneira shook her head.

'We must not let this sudden grief cloud the issue before us. Our immediate concern must be Ashe.'

Concern? Brede snorted. She didn't think that Aneira was concerned for Ashe, but for herself.

'Ashe has done us untold damage in the eyes of the world by her rash actions. She has done us far worse injury, struck us right to the heart by casting aside a unique gift, a voice second to none.'

Aneira's voice caught.

Brede, signing this automatically for Ashe, saw the words, and separated the tone. She couldn't allow this. She sighed, and struggled once more to her feet. Aneira frowned angrily.

'You may not speak.'

Brede smiled, allowing the tone to wash over her, still steadily shaping the words with her hands.

'I shall speak,' she said quietly.

Ashe's mouth quirked into a half smile, a nervous twitch of the muscles. She was afraid of what Brede would do. Brede accepted that anxious twitch, but would not be silent.

'You've thought no further than your own hurt. I see the way you look at me, at Ashe. I see the *no-voice* you don't quite say. But I have a voice, I will speak, and you will listen. Ashe has no voice, but I can give her one. I can teach her the songs of silence, I will teach her such songs to spin on her fingers that you will be speechless.

'I don't believe you are grieving the loss of her voice, I think you are angry that she has punished herself. She has stolen your retribution. What could you possibly do to her that is worse than what she has done to herself?

'Ashe has not thrown down her sword, she has cut off her sword arm. There can be no going back for her; and you've nothing but bitterness for her. All you can say is *no-voice*, and tell her what damage she does you. Not one of you will look at the damage she has done herself, nor will you think of what she asks of you, a way to learn to feed herself, now that she has but one hand. You'll not accept your responsibility for her actions. Foolish she is, and arrogant, like her sisters, too full of pride to admit when she is wrong.'

Brede knew she still had not persuaded them. The silence was curdling with unspoken resentment of her intrusion. She glanced uneasily at Ashe, and a sudden certainty about her took root. Ashe was as young as she seemed, she hadn't grown that carapace of self-worth these other women had. Perhaps that was the root of problem.

'Will none of you look at her youth, and pity her? Can't you see how she was deceived by the pride you bred in her? Look at her, Songspinners, see what you've wrought. Why give her a sword if you don't intend her to use it? That was the path you set her on with your teaching, do you now condemn her for following your instruction? She has made her choice, and you haven't the right to gainsay it.'

Brede's voice shook, and her leg was afire with protesting muscles as she finished. She stared wildly about her, unsure of the effect of her words, or where they came from; afraid that perhaps Sorcha had spoken through her, giving her this unexpected eloquence. She was too angry to care what the truth of the matter was. Their faces were closed to her. Brede recognised that look and her heart went out to Ashe, who had no kin, as Brede had none.

'Are you finished?' Aneira asked. She would not be put at fault by a no-voice who knew nothing of their ways, of their vows; vows which Ashe had broken, intentionally or otherwise.

'Are you finished?' Aneira asked again, her voice trembling, despite her years of learnt control.

Brede nodded, unable to force another word out. She turned, walking as firmly as she could to the door. She stared at the wood for a second, anger and humiliation seething in her blood, then she threw up her hands in the sign for *open*. The door swung open gently. Brede stepped through and smiled, a small, cheap victory that one, but perhaps they would not be so swift to call her *no-voice* again, even in their minds.

Out in the courtyard, Brede didn't know where to go, what to do, so she made her way to the stables, where she buried her face in the mane of her horse. It was not used to her yet, nor was it accustomed to being used as a comforter, and stepped smartly sideways, away from her. Brede swore at the beast, and thumped it gently on the shoulder. More used to this kind of behaviour, the horse edged back up, and allowed her to lean against him.

None of this had been how Brede imagined. She had allowed her own purpose to be waylaid by Ashe's needs. She was abruptly furious, not with the witches, but with Ashe. This was supposed to have been her resolution, an ending, and now here she was, caught up in someone else's life.

Brede inspected the horse. She could just saddle the beast, ride away, and leave them to their arguments. She had done her best to make them understand what Ashe had done. Brede knew that if she were Aneira, she would condemn. She knew it; she understood the motivation, but the injustice rankled. She couldn't ride away, not yet. There was unfinished business of her own, and there would be no space in the Songspinners' minds for her, until they had finished with Ashe, and so she must stay beside Ashe, waiting her time.

Brede sensed rather than heard movement behind her, and turned swiftly, ready for a blow, but there was no hand raised against her. It was only then that she realised that she had walked out of the hall without the aid of the sword.

Saraid backed away, startled by the sudden movement and the angry expression.

'We need you,' she said, 'somewhat to our surprise. You seem to hold knowledge that we need, both for Ashe and for Sorcha. You must forgive our lack of hospitality, but this day has brought us unexpected pain, and we have not recovered our usual equilibrium.'

Saraid smiled wryly, accepting the lack of grace in Brede's nod, knowing they deserved no more.

'If you will accompany me, I will arrange for you to use the bath house, it is a good way to ease the discomfort of a long ride. If you will, I need to talk to you at length about Sorcha, when you've rested and eaten.'

Diplomatic. Brede knew that she offended them, and that she smelt of deprivation, of beggary. If Saraid wanted to ease her discomfort, she could do so more effectively with her voice. Brede shrugged off her irritation. She would like to be clean. She hadn't been really clean for more than a year.

Chapter Forty-Eight

Saraid led Brede to the bathhouse, which was not how she expected it to be: no tubs, no hot water, instead wooden benches, heat, and steam, more like the sweat lodges of the plains.

Brede stripped her soiled, ruined clothing from her. She struggled with her blood-spattered boots, and was grateful they were so loose; any tighter and it would have been impossible to remove them herself. Brede hoped that the witches, now that they had remembered how to treat a guest, would find her something clean to wear. She laid her aching body down on the nearest bench. The muscles of her damaged leg trembled now that they were released from tension. She couldn't control the jumping spasms. She shifted, awkwardly, again and again, trying to find a position that stopped the ceaseless twitching.

When Ashe entered the bathhouse, she found Brede weeping. Brede turned away, trying to hide her tears, her pain, her nakedness.

Ashe considered her. A thing of bones strung together with nothing but the sinews of her will. A pattern of raised scars, some light, some deep. Scarcely a body at all, a mass of harsh experiences, etched into her living flesh.

Ashe wrapped the robe she carried about Brede's shoulders, crouching beside her, rubbing her arms gently, trying to ease her. Brede choked the tears into silence, abruptly finding them ridiculous. She covered Ashe's hand with her own. Ashe pulled away gently, and began to untie Brede's plait. Brede submitted to her attentions. It had been years since anyone unbraided her hair – the last time rose before her eyes, and it was not Ashe's fingers she felt against her neck.

Despite the heat of the steam, Brede shivered. She allowed herself to remember Sorcha's voice from Ashe's lips. There was more to this than she could begin to understand. Ashe moved away, to get water for her to wash her hair, and Brede sighed in relief. She felt hemmed in with confusion.

And when was the last time for this? Brede asked herself sternly as she rubbed soapwort into her scalp. She liked to be clean; it allowed her to think that there could be a future. She squeezed the water from her hair, combed it with her fingers. So much grey, worse than she had thought, the dirt had been hiding some of the streaks. It was not vanity that made her sigh, but fear. She sighed again, impatiently, and gave herself over to the heat.

Ashe lay on the far bench, her eyes closed, listening to Brede's breathing. She felt the cold and loneliness leaching out of her pores with the dirt. She listened to the water dripping out of Brede's hair, fast at first, then slower and slower, comforting, sleep inducing. Then it stopped. Ashe opened her eyes, staring up at the ceiling. She listened. She couldn't hear Brede's breathing.

Ashe sat up, staring, but it was only that she slept. She calmed the panic that had raced her pulse. Brede should not sleep here, but to wake her, Ashe must touch her. She hovered over Brede, not wanting to disturb her, not wanting to wake her. Very gently, she touched Brede's shoulder. The last time she woke the swordswoman that way, she had been cursed at. She was prepared for that again, but Brede did not curse. Out of her sleep, she reached for Ashe, speaking Sorcha's name. Ashe moved swiftly out of the range of her reaching; Brede would hurt less if she woke to empty air under her seeking hand.

Brede opened her eyes. Ashe sat at her feet, her short, mousy hair curling slightly on her forehead from the steam. Brede was sure she had heard Sorcha calling her name. She rubbed her eyes, angry with herself, angry with her body for the longing that made such a fool of her, playing tricks on her mind; angry with Ashe for not being Sorcha.

Ashe stared at her hands, trying to work out how to say what she needed. She held them helplessly before her, and then stretched them out to Brede. Brede forced her body into a seated position, forced the heat-induced lassitude from her limbs. Her leg cramped immediately and she gasped.

Ashe's hands found something to do – working the injured limb, forcing the cramp into subsiding, thinking the muscles straight, singing in her mind, spinning the tune with her fingers. She could feel the muscles responding, feel the pain lifting away, layer after layer; could feel it clinging to her fingers, working its way into her own bones. She pulled away sharply, and the pain was gone. Brede took hold of her fingers gently, turning her hands over, shaping them for her, into a question.

'How did you do that?'

Ashe shook her head, bewildered. She had wanted to end Brede's pain, and she had simply done what she would have always done, except she had used her hands instead of her voice. Cautiously, she shaped a question of her own, having to invent some of it, but it was clear enough what she meant, counterpointing Brede's question.

How did you open the door?

Brede shaped the sign for open. Yes, she had done that.

I will teach her such songs to spin on her fingers – had she said that?

'Intent,' Brede said aloud. 'It has nothing to do with the method at all, it takes intent.'

Ashe shook her head. This was different; she had never felt pain creeping into her when she used song to heal. This was harder, more costly.

Brede ran her hand experimentally over her leg, testing the points that normally gave her pain.

'Will it last?' she asked.

Ashe shook her head again.

Brede flexed her leg, she couldn't believe the lack of pain. She hugged Ashe to her, in unspoken thanks. Ashe felt Brede's body against her own; warm, grateful. She wrapped her arms about Brede, hugging her back, her own gratitude needing expression.

She felt the rushing of Brede's pulse, as she rested her forehead into the curve of Brede's neck; she felt the almost imperceptible tightening of her arms about her. She moved her head slightly, so that her lips brushed Brede's skin; then a fraction further, lifting her face, her mouth, confidently, to Brede's; waiting.

Brede's body remembered this; remembered what it was like to be without pain, to be hanging that second from commitment, from pleasure; remembered anticipation. Brede's mind pinned the memory, painted in the colours, the scents, and told her when, where, and with whom: Brede's body recoiled from the memory. Her mind revolted, screaming at her, *dead, dead* – but she could still be gentle.

Ashe knew, the second their lips met, that there was something wrong. There was a sadness in the touch; it was not a kiss of welcome, but of ending. She pulled away gradually, looking into Brede's face. Her eyes were clear and calm, she smiled, but there was nothing there for Ashe.

Brede turned away from the necessity of looking at Ashe. Silenced, she shaped words on her hands, explaining. Ashe covered Brede's hands with her own. She took herself away, plunging herself into the cold water in the end room grateful for the icy sting that forced her to let go her held breath, forcing her to feel. She scrambled out quickly. She wished she need not wait for Brede.

Brede buried her face in her hands, sitting cross-legged on the bench, a position she hadn't been able to take since that fall into Kendra's territory.

It is worse now, she told herself severely.

Brede picked up the robe, pulled it over her head. She picked through her belongings, rescuing Sorcha's talisman. She rebraided her hair, plaiting the row of stones into it. She fastened her belt over the robe, tucking the hem into the belt at one side, to keep her feet free of its folds.

As she walked from the bathhouse, Brede was disconcerted to see Ashe waiting for her. She followed her silently to the guest quarters.

Ashe felt rejection for the second time in a few minutes. There were two beds made up in the guest room, one for Brede, one for her. She was no longer part of the family here. Brede was more concerned that they must share the room, given what had just occurred; but there was a warm fire, and food; and she was hungry and tired, and her leg was already beginning to stiffen again. The sword had been brought. Brede wondered briefly which of the Songspinners forced herself to carry it, or whether they kept a few no-voices about for such menial tasks. Stiff or not, she didn't intend to use the sword again. She wrapped the blade in her bright green cloak, and pushed it beneath the bed, then gave her attention to the meal that lay ready.

Ashe picked at the food, Brede wolfed it. Brede slept sound and long, too tired for anything else; Ashe lay awake until the early hours, turning over her mistakes in her mind. Wearily she added to the list of her crimes. She had never before encountered difficulty such as this. Where she loved, she had been loved. Where she desired, she had been desired. But she had never had a ghost as a rival before, let alone a ghost who had taken her body and used it.

Sleep took a very long time to reach her.

And when Ashe woke, she was in her own bed, and the sweet ordinariness of the sounds about her, and the scents of home were a balm to her, allowing her to believe that she had never left, that none of it had ever happened.

She could hear a murmur of familiar voices, Saraid and Islean, beyond the door, arguing as usual.

Another layer of sleep dissolved into wakefulness and the weariness in her limbs tried to warn her, but Ashe wasn't listening. She opened her mouth to call to Islean, but no sound came –

– and then she woke.

Ashe opened her eyes. Late morning sun streamed through the window, failing to warm the cold air. She peered at the remains of the fire, cold and grey on the hearth. Her aching limbs reminded her of what she couldn't do, and what her sisters had chosen not to do. They hadn't eased her aching; they had chosen not to expend even that small effort on her behalf. They had made her alien, a *no-voice*.

Ashe wondered how long it took for bruises to heal without help, how long it would take for the anger in her heart to ease. She pushed away the bedding, put her feet to the cold floor. She flinched from the stone slabs, and tried to stretch the tiredness from her muscles. She stirred the ashes in the hearth, hoping for a remnant of heat.

Brede stirred, having been silently wakeful for an hour or more. She propped herself on one elbow, to watch her companion as she laid a new fire, and tried to light it. Brede knew better than to help, Ashe would not thank her for her assistance.

Brede did not feel well. It had been so long since she had eaten a proper meal that her guts were rebelling at the spicy food she'd eaten. She crawled out of bed, and left Ashe to her fire making, more pressing matters on her mind.

Ashe pretended not to notice that she'd gone, that she had given her no greeting. She did not persuade herself, and flung the flint across the room. It sparked against the wall; despite its refusal to do any such thing near her patiently laid kindling.

Saraid and Islean had been waiting for them to wake. They watched the no-voice leave the guest room and were about to enter when they heard the crash of the flint against the wall. Despite herself, Islean laughed. Ashe looked up from the fireplace. Saraid sighed, and muttered a few notes of song. The kindling flickered into flame and Ashe had to pull her hem away to prevent it from catching fire. She resented the ease with which Saraid lit the fire, resented that her help was needed.

Saraid ignored the expression on Ashe's face and placed the bundle of papers she carried onto the windowsill. Ashe picked them over. They were blank. Here, back in civilisation, there were people who could read. Not that the witches had much use for the skill, they relied too heavily on their voices to choose to write often, but since she had no other way to communicate with anyone but Brede, Ashe would write. Her writing was rusty, and her failure with Brede had put the possibility from her mind. She caressed the smooth creamy pages. Yes, she would write.

She smiled at Saraid, at Islean. Islean continued to look stony. It was her paper, which she could ill afford to spare for Ashe's scribbling. She was the record keeper, she wrote down the dangerous songs, that were not safe to be spoken. She had allowed only old paper, scraped clean of ancient words and music. She passed Ashe a bottle of ink, and one of her own pens.

Saraid cleared her throat. It was too easy to catch the habit of silence, it alarmed her.

'We want you to write everything, especially which song you used. Tell us how you met this Brede, and why she agreed to champion you. Everything you can think to tell us, Ashe. I can't stress the importance of this. You can take as long as you need; I have to talk to your companion about Sorcha today. You won't have her to speak for you, so you may as well use the time to explain yourself. It was thoughtless of us not to provide you with writing materials before. For this I apologise.'

Ashe took up the pen, broke the seal on the ink and with a hand that trembled slightly, wrote her first words, her first direct communication with her sisters.

She wrote *Thank you.*

The stark plainness of the words did not show the tone she wished to use, one that made it clear exactly how little she thanked them for. Brede's hands could, and did, give the tone of what she said, hesitant or emphatic, plain or dismissive. There were limitations to writing. She thought of the pain edging into her fingers as she touched Brede: most certainly there were limitations.

Ashe collected the papers carefully together, and placed them on the bed. She resealed the ink, and laid the pen beside it. Then Brede came back into the room, which at once seemed crowded. She bowed slightly to the witches.

'Good morning?' she said, making it a question. Brede flustered them; they were out of sorts, not knowing how to deal with this towering woman, this killer, this cripple. Brede enjoyed it a little; she had forgotten how intimidating she could be. Saraid responded, mindful of her duties.

'Good morning. I hope that you are rested?' She didn't give Brede time to answer. 'I need to talk to you about Sorcha, as soon as possible. Ashe won't need you today, so it would be convenient to speak to you this morning.'

As though she were a servant, to be dismissed when not of use. Brede shaped that for Ashe, even though she would not understand. It soothed her to share the thought with her. Ashe saw that it did not mean the same as the words that issued from Brede's mouth, but no more than that, her mind was elsewhere. Brede answered Saraid,

'I am at your disposal, once I've had a few words with Ashe.' Dismissing *them.* They gathered their skirts, and went. Brede wondered why they wore their clothing so long, since they were forever having to hold it out of the way. She wished she had her breeches back; she didn't care for the heaviness of the skirted robe about her legs. She felt entangled in it, even though the hem came above her ankles. She turned to Ashe, and saw the paper on the bed beside her. So, no longer needed. Brede folded her hands away under her elbows.

'And what are you to be doing this morning, whilst I spill my guts for your sisters?' Her voice trembled.

Ashe's eyes narrowed. She did not, as she might have done, merely point to the paper. She held out one hand as though it was the paper, and used a finger of the other hand to be her pen. She did it with deliberation, sarcasm almost. She tilted her head towards Brede, patiently waiting for the attempt at signing to be corrected. She was no longer angry with Brede. There were still possibilities to be explored with her.

Brede's hands moved from her elbows, she hesitated, never having written, she had no idea what the sign for writing should be. She copied Ashe's sign, nodded and followed up with a thank-you. Ashe smiled. She was not sure where they stood, the two of them, but there was still something there to work with.

Chapter Forty-Nine

Brede hunted out her tormentors, but found only Saraid waiting for her in an alcove off the hall they had used the day before. She was glad: it would be hard enough as it was, to say the things she had stored in her heart. Impossible to say to more than one person. She would have preferred to tell it to Ashe, but what would be the use of that? Failing Ashe, Saraid had at least been civil, unlike the rest of them.

Saraid was tired; the shock had worn off, now there was only depression and grief and she didn't seek information, she dreaded it. So, she was kinder than she might have been. She had found a comfortable seat for Brede, she had brought food and wine: Saraid believed she was ready for every eventuality, but she was not.

Brede sank into the chair, and realised that she hadn't prepared herself for this confrontation. She hadn't marshalled her thoughts, couldn't give a rational account. She didn't even know where to begin. She couldn't remember her first meeting with Sorcha. She had always been there, hadn't she? All she had ever needed to do was turn, to find her; but there had been a time before Sorcha, she knew it, even though she no longer recognised it.

So Brede described Sorcha: the way she looked, the way she moved, and the way she spoke. She couldn't describe her singing; she had no words for it. Saraid was drawn into her vision, seeing, hearing, feeling Sorcha through Brede. It was a strange sensation, she saw someone she knew distorted through another's perceptions, yet recognised her. She agreed, saying *Yes, she was so, that is how she would be.*

Brede heard her acknowledgement, but didn't register it, losing herself in her memories. She spun the tale on her fingers, making the space between her hands encompass her vision of the past. She pulled Saraid in with her, unwilling, unaware.

Brede didn't try to tell her story in a logical way. She started where she felt there was a beginning, said only what she wanted to say, *So it was, so it went, and now it is gone.*

Incoherent, a flow of impressions, confused with her feelings, with sideways glances at things too painful to remember, or too precious to tell.

Saraid forgot that she had asked for this telling, forgot that she wasn't a part of these happenings. She was hypnotised by the unsteady flow of words, the constant movement of the hands, as though Brede held the world captive between her fingers, weaving her reality from the fragments of memory.

At last the telling came to an end. Brede felt empty, all her resources exhausted. She wrapped herself in the silence between them, grateful for it.

Saraid stumbled from the hall. She needed time to assimilate what she had heard, to make it bearable, to confine it within something she could bring herself to think about. She needed, more than anything, to be alone.

Brede, sitting abandoned in the hall, poured herself a glass of the red wine that had sat untouched throughout her telling. She tried to convince herself that she had done what she had come for, that this episode in her life was ended and that she could start anew. She failed. She had only let go of a small part of the ghost that haunted her. She was not entirely sure that she wanted her gone, and that too must be overcome, somehow.

Ashe, sitting alone in her self-imposed silence, struggled to remember the tune that Sorcha trapped her with, to write down the notes, so that her sisters would understand. It was elusive, slipping away, disguising itself behind similar songs that deceived her, tangling in the faded markings that already stained Islean's used papers.

Saraid barred her door, and sat in turmoil. Her certainties seemed threadbare to her now. She was afraid to think too closely about what Sorcha had done, what she had died for. She was at once humbled by it and angry with Sorcha for this last supreme arrogance, and again she was angry with Brede, because it was she who had forced Sorcha into a position where those choices had become possible. How could Sorcha have loved someone so – uncouth, so brutal, so – ?

Saraid no longer wanted to think. Whether she wished it or not, the thoughts kept welling up. She tried to order her mind, tried to rationalise the whirl of potential delight and disaster that threatened to swallow her. She didn't know how to begin what should be done to resolve the tangle of Sorcha's ending; Sorcha's *not* ending. She understood now that this was what she was dealing with; she had listened between the breaths of Brede's story and rooted out the truth, unspoken by the teller. She couldn't quite encompass the idea of it.

Aneira would find it impossible to believe. She expected the world to bend to her will, to conform to her beliefs, and this would not fit into her narrow understanding of existence; but how did it fit into Sorcha's understanding? Again Saraid balked. What to do? How to stabilise it all? Saraid didn't believe it to be beyond her, but she didn't yet hold the key to the puzzle.

Brede, alone in the hall, drank herself into a state where she no longer cared what would become of her. It didn't last as long as she would have liked.

Islean came to Ashe for her written explanation. She found her one-time lover asleep in an exhausted huddle, pen still loosely held, ink still open, sheaves of paper fallen to the floor. Islean collected the papers, sealed the ink, and removed the pen from between Ashe's ink-stained fingers. She glanced at the closely written pages. No wonder she slept. She must have written without ceasing for the whole of the day. Islean held the pages to the light, and examined the music that Ashe had inscribed. Automatically, she played the tune in her head. Her blood stilled, and the faintest stirring of pity broke through her anger at Ashe. She leafed back through the pages to the start of the music.

This is the tune that summoned Sorcha, as nearly as I remember it – Ashe's cramped script told her. *Summoned Sorcha?* Islean stretched an unsteady hand to Ashe's tousled hair. *What has been going on?* She did not touch her. She needed to speak to Saraid, who knew Sorcha the best of them. She needed to ask her if this thing was possible. She needed to ask her now. There was no time to regret that she could no longer love Ashe.

Saraid saw the greyness of Islean's face, the strain in her eyes, and opened her door wider, allowing her in. Islean handed her the music, unable to think of a fitting explanation. Saraid read Ashe's heading, then skimmed the music. She reached behind her for a chair, and lowered herself into it, without taking her eyes off the sheet of paper.

Islean's urgency overruled her patience and she laid her hand on Saraid's.

'Do you understand it?'

Saraid nodded, still looking bewildered.

'I understand it, but I do not understand how it was possible, how she dared, why it worked, nor do I understand how to undo it.'

'Should we speak to Aneira?'

'No. Not yet. This is – dangerous. I want to study all that Ashe has to tell us, there may be further clues.'

Islean nodded reluctantly and left. Saraid didn't notice that she had gone. She turned back to the start of Ashe's account.

A servant of the King came to me –

Melva discovered the no-voice in a drunken stupor in the hall. Hesitating between revulsion and pity, she sighed and called to a passing youngling. With the younger woman's help, Melva managed to get Brede to the guest chamber. Their entrance, stumbling and crowding, woke Ashe, and she helped to get

Brede onto the bed. Melva squeezed Ashe's hand in passing. Ashe caught at her hand, snatched paper and almost dry pen and scratched

I owe Brede, and I cannot help her. Will you help her, for me?

Melva glanced at the unconscious no-voice. Her stupor had relaxed the pain lines on her face, the frown was less deep. She almost looked human. Melva's heart twisted. Aneira and Saraid wouldn't approve, would think her wasting her time, if they even thought about this no-voice at all. She sang a soft catch-all for pain and healing, not knowing what she was dealing with, really. Brede sighed and relaxed further. Melva nodded at Ashe.

'Between us?' she asked, embarrassed that it felt necessary to do so. Ashe nodded and gave her a quick hug.

With Melva gone, Ashe frowned. Brede had deliberately shut her out with her unconscious state. Laboriously, she undressed her, accompanied by an occasional groan from Brede. Her hand kept catching on something in Brede's hair – something that had not been there when she unbound it in the bathhouse. Ashe felt carefully, and a sudden certainty sent her to the wall bracket to reach down one of the candles. Holding the candle carefully, she let the light play on the small stones threaded on a narrow braid of hair, woven into Brede's own, but couple of shades lighter. Four small blue stones. Sorcha's: no question. Ashe stared at the stones, feeling the loss of her voice anew, a piercing fire of longing. Once she might have had hopes of inheriting the Singer stones – Brede should not hold them; they weren't trinkets, not something for a no-voice to play with. Ashe quelled that thought. She was a no-voice herself now. She need not tell anyone that the Singer stones had survived. What did it matter? They were only a symbol. Let Brede keep them.

When Brede woke, thirst drove her from the bed. She fumbled for the borrowed robes at the end of the bed, and found her bare toes grazing a pair of strange boots, left where she could tangle the blankets about them and trip. She pulled the blankets free, and considered the boots, paired, and with toes facing out from the bed, inviting her feet. Soft, low-topped things, not much use on a horse, but better than barefoot on the cold stone floors. She pushed an experimental foot into the soft leather. Not a bad fit. She lined up the other boot, and worked her injured foot gently into the folds of leather. Not bad at all, the softness of this leather did not force her foot straight, simply holding it gently secure, like a hand against the outer length of her foot, like Ashe's hand. She wondered briefly where Ashe was, and frowned. She shrugged her way into the robe, and found the water pitcher on a shelf. Thirst quenched, Brede made her way out into the courtyard, and across to the stables.

She found her stolen black gelding, and her stolen saddle, and her stolen saddlebags, and pondered. The bags were undisturbed, and full. She tipped the contents out and ran her fingers over them. A nearly empty water sack, a silk shirt, of very fine quality – too fine for her, and too short in the sleeves. Some money, not a great deal, but a few silver coins in amongst the copper. Trail food, a better belt. She hauled that twice round her waist and fastened it. Then she put the coins into a knot in her undershirt, and the food back into the saddlebag. She saddled the horse, and walked him out into the courtyard, to a mounting block. She got astride with relative ease, and settled her weight carefully, and secured her feet in the stirrups. He sidled, then stood biddable and alert. Brede shifted her weight forward slightly and he understood her. They took each other out of the gate and for a careful exploration of the citadel and its hilltop, and the surrounding streets and market squares.

Brede thought carefully as she rode: about the furtive looks, and the frankly curious stares she got from the people of this city; about the lie of the land; measuring defences, checking through routes and alleyways, mapping enemy territory; and about the manners of the horse who strode with dignity and unconcern through those narrow paved streets. He seemed to like her better this time, more willing to pay her attention, she had almost decided he needed a name by the time she had found somewhere to barter the shirt for something of lower quality, and some breeches. She flung off the blue robe, and dressed, and the woman she had traded with laughed at her evident relief.

'You're the one brought our Ashe home,' she said, folding the robe neatly and handing it back, 'and brought the news of the Songspinner.'

Brede nodded warily.

'Thank you.' The woman said softly. Brede nodded to her then forced the robe into her saddle bag and went in search of someone to barter the saddle for leather and leather working tools to make a Plains saddle, so that she could tell more precisely what her horse was about. The saddler was a man of few words, but he had an apprentice, scarce more than a child, who kept up a steady commentary, on Brede, the saddle, and the horse. Brede grinned at her, as she moved on to her opinion of Plains saddles; and how Brede would ride a horse with no saddle, and no name.

'You can tell he has no name?' Brede asked, curious. The child nodded.

'He keeps looking at you, he's waiting for you to name him.'

Brede laughed, and took the horse away to ride him bareback and with care, back to the citadel. She had him back to the stable an hour later, an hour better acquainted. As she brushed him down, he watched her constantly, turning his head to keep her in view.

'What?' she asked him softly, as she laid the brush a final time across his shoulder. She stepped back and returned his gaze until he lowered his head and pretended an itchy fetlock. Brede allowed herself a small smile. She glanced down at herself, muddy, and covered in horsehair, and set off for the bathhouse, for another session in the heat that almost comforted her aching muscles and tendons and bones. On the way back to the guest quarters, she passed Melva, who glanced boot-wards, and smiled. Brede inclined her head, gratitude for a thoughtful act, and Melva, walked on pleased at how simple a gift had the Plains woman walking straight and tall, as she ought. She was brought up sharply by that, and stopped to watch Brede go, wondering where that *as she ought* had come from.

Brede, feeling more at home, swerved from her planned route and followed her nose towards the kitchens. She hovered uncertainly in the doorway, until a sharp-faced woman glanced up and beckoned her in.

'You'll be this Brede,' she said confidently.

Brede nodded.

'I'm Morna.' She gave Brede a careful look up and down, and sucked her teeth. 'You need feeding. Can't fix hunger and malnutrition with song, I know that; you need my kind of magic. Sit.'

Brede sat. Morna chattered and mixed and put small bowls in front of her: water, soup, poached eggs and vegetables. Brede ate everything. She almost choked on the spoonful of honeycomb, Westgate Inn and Sorcha forever tied to the flavour. Morna gave her another sharp glance.

'Saraid give you a hard time?'

'I'm a guest –' Brede protested.

'I'll take that as yes. It's to be expected. They all loved Sorcha, Goddess, *I* loved Sorcha –' her mouth twisted, but she raised her head quickly, proudly. 'She was special. But *Saraid* – well.'

Brede put down the honey, kept her head down, a slow, angry, flush creeping up her neck. She raised her head at last, driven to it by Morna's silence.

'Saraid and Sorcha?'

Morna nodded.

'About three years.'

Brede shrank into herself, struggling with astonished jealousy.

'She never said a word.'

'Saraid? Why would she?'

'Why would she not? But no, I meant Sorcha –' Brede shook her head quickly. 'How could Saraid stand to not know where she was?'

Morna shook her head.

'There was a lot of talk, a lot of angry words, when Sorcha went off without telling anyone. I think she'd have enjoyed the fuss, if she'd known. But where Saraid's concerned, I don't believe her mind works like ours, nor her heart. And don't you be thinking I'm disloyal, none of us would let harm come to a one of them, but under the same roof, you notice they aren't like *us*.'

Brede sat, puzzling over being included in an 'us' she didn't know, and at how easy it was to talk of Sorcha to Morna; easier than to Saraid, but perhaps she could see a reason for that now, and no matter how easy to talk to, there were some questions she could not put to a complete stranger.

'Speaking of roofs,' she said, shifting the subject with some urgency. 'Why is this place in such poor repair?'

'I don't think they notice.'

'They'd better, trouble will follow Ashe here.'

'They know that. And don't think they haven't noticed that sword.'

'The sword?'

'Ashe told them. Goddess, even *I've* heard of the *Dowry* blade.' Brede sat in silent astonishment as Morna gazed consideringly at her. 'They know what you've brought under their poorly repaired roof. Aneira will be preparing something, and –' She stopped abruptly, brought up against an uncomfortable thought.

'And – ?'

'And they have their defences. They don't really need walls.'

'No,' Brede agreed, feeling stupid, and sickened. 'They can kill anyone they please by singing. No need for walls, except for show.'

Slowly she stood, pushing the honeycomb away from her. Morna took it wordlessly, nodded briskly at Brede's thanks.

'Come anytime you care to eat. Help yourself if I'm not here.'

Brede nodded vaguely, and stumbled up the step into the courtyard, swearing silently at the pain, and realised that it was the first time that day she had really hurt, really felt the need of her crutch. She didn't want to talk about Songspinners as 'them' any longer; especially when she had carried trouble into their hall. She limped back to the guest quarters.

Ashe sat in the window, arms hugged about her, gazing at the gathering darkness in the courtyard.

'Sorcha and Saraid?' Brede asked her.

Ashe glanced up, and nodded.

'How long ago?' Ashe spread her hands helplessly, then signed *three – four*.

'Three or four years? Were they still together when Sorcha went to Grainne?'

Ashe shrugged, she didn't know; she was already a Journeyer then, out in the world, exploring who she could become.

Brede flung herself down on her bed and brooded. Ashe turned politely towards her and waited. Brede shook her head. Ashe leant over and touched her ankle, knee, hip, lightly and tilted her head. Brede frowned as she thought about that question.

Yes, she signed at last, *better, a while.*

Ashe smiled and made the sign for witch, then old and pointed at the boots. Brede nodded, understanding.

'Melva? I thought it might be her.'

Ashe frowned impatiently and made nonsense signs at Brede until she signed what she had said. Brede sat up; it was awkward signing lying down and too reminiscent of Kendra's cave. Carefully she signed her way through an account of her day, including a less pejorative sign for Songspinner.

'I need a name for my horse,' Brede observed, after they had sat silent and still for a few minutes.

Ashe frowned, thinking. Names were beyond her signing skills for now.

Tentatively she signed, *Lost horse, friend. This horse, name friend.*

'I should call him Friend?' Brede asked.

Ashe nodded, it hadn't been her meaning, but it served.

Call me friend? Ashe signed, and her hand shook slightly.

Brede looked up from her hands sharply.

'I don't know,' she said, but her hands shaped the sign and she held it out towards Ashe. Ashe touched her fingers to Brede's, and Brede felt a spark of – something – reach across between them. She pulled her hands back, trying to hide the urgency of the movement. Ashe stared at her hand, still out-stretched, and rubbed her fingers against her thumb, puzzling at the strange sensation.

What was that? she asked.

But Brede could only shake her head, puzzled and uneasy.

Chapter Fifty

Saraid finished her third reading of Ashe's words. She sat quietly, a stillness at the centre of the turmoil in her brain. She stretched her mind, following Ashe's lead, touching Sorcha at every move, discovering her motives which were not motives at all, understanding; and beginning to see the way to unbind Sorcha's tangle.

She collected herself, and took up her own pen, drawing a hesitant line of notes, finding the strands and phrases to unmake Sorcha's song. The pattern the music held in her head was clear: like a requiem, but sufficiently unlike that she must be careful in her choices. Each note must mirror and challenge Sorcha's. It must say, *yes; this was so and this was done – but now there is an ending.*

Saraid had never had to work so hard, it took her days: Days interrupted by Aneira wanting to know what she was doing, when she couldn't take the time to explain; and days of meals left at her door to go cold, and days that stretched through nights, as she worked, trying to meld music into the pattern behind her eyes.

When at last she left her room, she was suddenly aware of hunger, a hunger that could not be denied further. She went straight to the kitchen, the melody still drifting in her mind. And in the kitchen she found Brede, eating her way steadily through one of Morna's pies.

Saraid settled herself on a stool across the great table and Morna, without being asked, put another pie and some fruit down in front of her. Saraid pulled them towards her, and ate silently for a few minutes, staring across at Brede. There was something different about her. Saraid inspected her thoughtfully, slightly less starved looking, something approaching muscle starting to show through the surprisingly good shirt she was wearing; her hair was shorter too. Brede finished her pie and engaged with the stare. Saraid blinked first.

'I've been thinking,' she said softly. 'I've been wondering why you didn't kill Madoc while you had the chance?'

'I would have, but I didn't have the chance.'

'You had him at your mercy.'

'No, *Sorcha* had him at her mercy, and mercy is what she showed.'

'The Sorcha I knew would not have done that.'

Brede raised an eyebrow.

'The Sorcha *I* knew would have killed him without thinking about it, but she is not the woman either of us knew, anymore.' Brede's voice dried, and she had to wait to continue, her voice harsh and faint. 'She is dead, and perhaps that changes her perspective.'

Saraid shook her head.

'I would kill him.'

Brede sighed and pushed herself to her feet.

'And since I didn't, you will get an opportunity. I don't understand why he hasn't come knocking at your gate already.'

'You think he will come here?'

'For Ashe.' *And the Dowry blade*, Brede thought, dread twisting in her gut.

Saraid watched Brede limp away and finished her pie, the music in her mind soured and wrong. She hadn't thought about Sorcha's – *perspective*. She hadn't thought she might have the opportunity to face one of the men responsible for her death. She gathered up more food and went back to her papers.

So when, days later, at last Saraid had her tune, and had taught her sisters their parts and they sang, and it didn't work; then Saraid doubted herself, doubted even her sanity.

She returned to her task, exhausted, depleted, unable to think any further. Melva shook her head over the papers when Saraid took them to her.

'I thought perhaps a new pair of eyes, a new ear –'

'Your design is beyond me,' Melva said softly. 'I can see the flow, I can hear that it is beautiful; the intention is there, and I can't find a fault, I don't know why it doesn't work.'

Saraid spent more days and nights without sleeping, staring sightlessly at the papers, at the walls, at the night sky; struggling with her memories of Sorcha, trying to piece together what was missing. She knew Sorcha well, had spent several years in her close company, had loved her; she ought to be able to see what was wrong. She saw only a stranger.

The activity, and its ending, did not go unnoticed by the outcasts, the no-voices. Ashe crept to the doors of the singing room, to listen and practice the words she could hear through the door, spinning them on her fingers. Instinctively, she felt that there was something so vital missing, that no amount of re-scoring and rewording would fulfil the need. Ashe wasn't proud of the spite with which she greeted the world, but there was a part of her that said: *they can't do it. They are not so clever, not so talented, not so special after all.* If only she could find a way to free herself of Sorcha's touch, of wanting Brede free of her death.

Brede noticed the silence more than anything. She had been expecting them to sing, to do something to mark Sorcha's passing, but it didn't happen. She fumed to Morna, feeling incapable of discussing it with Ashe.

'Why did she drag my memories into the open? What was the point? Was it only to satisfy her curiosity?'

'No,' Morna said firmly.

'No? Well, I did think better of her, but now this silence, and Saraid's gone into hiding.'

'She's working.'

'I can't leave until they do something. I don't know what I should be doing.'

'Ashe –'

Brede shook her head sharply. Morna frowned.

'She's lonely. You're the only one she can talk to yet. Is that so much to ask?'

'I'm teaching her as fast as she can cope with, but what use it is to her here, if no-one else learns it.'

Morna dried her hands. She flung the cloth down and signed:

Nothing more you can offer?

Brede laughed sharply, taken by surprise.

'So I'm not the only one she can talk to.'

You sign all words you speak.

'Do I?'

Yes, now.

Brede looked at her hands, raised to speak, smiled and folded one into the other, and went to find Ashe.

Once more Ashe was at the door to the singing room, her head cocked to catch the strain of music, her hand pressed hard against the wood. She started away when she saw Brede.

I miss it, she signed. Brede nodded, and taking her hand drew her away from the door, just as it was flung open, and Ceridwen stormed out, speaking over her shoulder to Islean.

'This is pointless. What can possibly be gained from yet more?'

She sidestepped hurriedly to avoid walking into Brede, glared at her and strode away. Islean took in Ashe, tear streaked, and Brede, hand outstretched, and skirted them as though they were – as though – Islean had no idea what it was, but it wasn't good. Ashe recoiled at the sight of Islean, shook her head despairingly at Brede and ran for the privacy of the guest chamber.

Brede watched her go, angry on her behalf, pitying even, knowing that she would be unwelcome if she followed, and found herself disappointed at that. Abruptly Brede wanted to be gone, to be away from the constant reminders of Sorcha that this place held, and more than that, she wanted to be away from the subtle distress of Ashe, who was a disturbance in her mind, a restlessness in her skin. She folded her arms and glared out the window, until she realised she was not alone. She turned, and found Aneira and Melva standing behind her. She nodded to them both and went after Ashe after all.

'Have I not enough to cope with?' Aneira asked fiercely.

Melva stayed silent, waiting. Aneira frowned in response.

'What do you want me to do? We're trying not to draw attention to our singing; I understand that it must be painful for Ashe to be constantly reminded of what she has – given up –'

'And has it occurred to you that Ashe thinks we are excluding her?'

'Yes.'

'So?'

Aneira shrugged.

'If you want to talk to her, I've no objection.'

Melva sighed heavily.

'I wasn't asking for permission.'

Aneira grinned suddenly, and stretched a hand to hold Melva's wrist.

'I can find something else for you to do if you're bored?'

Melva laughed. 'I will see if Islean can spare me more paper and ink.'

Brede found Ashe sobbing and incoherent, unable to sign for the need to hide her face in her hands and cover her eyes from Brede's sight.

'Soon,' Brede said, signing as she went. 'soon, you will be able to sing using sign. You are learning so fast. It took me months to get where you are now.'

Ashe shook her head and sobbed harder. She was alarmed by that speed, understanding better than Brede its cause. Each time her hands touched Brede's; it was as though she took in a part of her, as though she was communicating by touch. Brede seemed unaware of it; she didn't feel the membranes of knowledge and existence lifting from her, layers of dead skin. And yet, Ashe wanted, craved that touch, that experience, frightening though it was. She dried her eyes on her sleeve, wiped her hands on her jerkin, and held out her hands to Brede. Brede took one in each of her hands, and conscious of taking a risk, Ashe kissed the knuckles of first one then the other. Brede took an unsteady, startled breath. Sharing space and time and words, she felt suffocated by Ashe, and her wanting, which was so self-evident, so painful to them both.

'It will get better,' Brede said, hardly knowing what she meant. She squeezed one of Ashe's hands gently then let go. Ashe tied her hands together in unconscious anguish, but she nodded and resolved to put aside her anxiety and her longing, if she could find a way, and learn everything she could.

Ashe dared one experiment to ease Brede's pain: Brede had opened doors with sign, why should Ashe not heal with it? She tried in secret, Brede asleep and oblivious, darkness to hide her signs even from herself. And it did not work. She could feel the spell building, could almost see it shimmer between her hands like wards, but there was nothing to carry the spell from her fingers to Brede, no breath of song, no – Ashe let her hands fall – no touch. She couldn't do that again with the spectre of Sorcha to come between them, not yet anyway – perhaps when Saraid got her song right. Ashe sighed, impatient with Saraid but recognising the difficulty, with her own failure so raw on her fingers.

Brede was out with the horse, exploring some new quarter of the city. Ashe had offered to go with her and been courteously refused. Consequently, she was pacing the courtyard, not quite warm enough, but in too bad a mood to seek the warmth of the kitchen, when Melva walked slowly out of the main door.

'If you don't want company, you'll find the library deserted, there's no need to catch cold.'

Ashe smiled wanly. She caught sight of the paper, and sighed. What did her sisters want of her now? She signed that, absentmindedly. *What now?*

Melva grinned.

'I can guess what that was, but I'm too old to learn a new language, my dear, so if you'll humour me, and use writing, I think we could each enjoy a conversation.'

Ashe met her eyes, and smiled more warmly, then took her arm and together they walked to the library, a small alcove of cupboards and shelves off the main hall. There was a bench set into the wall, and they sat side by side with the paper between them.

'I can talk about anything,' Melva said. 'What do you want to say?'

Ashe wrote swiftly.

Brede, Sorcha, me.

'Ah, difficult.'

I hate Sorcha for using me, Ashe wrote.

'She didn't choose you, it's not personal.'

It is. She makes it impossible for me to hold Brede as I want.

'Ah, Ashe you are young, you aren't used to being thwarted.'

Am I not? Have I not lost Islean? And now Sorcha's use of me prevents me from–.

Melva put her hand over Ashe's preventing her from writing more. Ashe looked up, frowning.

'Brede deserves better than to be retaliation for Islean,' Melva said cautiously. Ashe pulled her hand and pen free.

She isn't. But how can I tell if these are my feelings or Sorcha's?

'You must really want to cut that bond.'

Ashe nodded, then wrote, and underlined;

But also to bind her again, in the coldest regions of hell.

'No, Ashe, surely you don't believe that.'

I can believe anything, now.

Melva glanced from the words to Ashe's face, tight-lipped and unhappy and wondered which of the many events of late qualified that *now*.

'And Brede?'

How can she have room in her life for another witch? After Sorcha? Most of all Sorcha? And when I spoke to her with Sorcha's voice?

Saraid put down her papers, and crawled from her bed. She felt her grip on reality slip, and she was afraid. She knew that she must make this requiem work. Her place was in question, her value to her sisters in doubt. She must make another attempt, not for Sorcha's sake, but for her own, for the few remaining Songspinners. Sorcha's mistake was a running sore to her, it must be healed.

Saraid gathered the witches together once more, and Ashe was drawn to follow again, shut out though she was. No one explained to her what was to be different this time.

The singing was gentle at first, as it had been before. The soft chanting described Sorcha, fleshing the bones of the description with memories drawn in strains of melody. Ashe found no surprise in it, but then a harsh, ruthless note hit her, bringing the hairs up on the back of her neck. She listened hard, and abruptly she realised what Saraid was trying to do. Instead of unwinding the threads of the bonds that held the shadow of Sorcha's being to life, she was trying to cut away the life that Sorcha was bound to.

Ashe froze in shock, her mind leaping ahead to anticipate the results. Her hands trembled as she deliberately shaped other words, warping the meaning, challenging the intention, fighting, word by word, note by note, for Brede's life.

Brede felt the music. It wound into her bones, seeking out Sorcha's image, her impression, anything of her, dragging her apart, trying to force her memories to give up their hold on the dead Songspinner; trying to eat away the very flesh Sorcha had touched. Without thought, without senses to inform thought, engulfed in the death that reached for her, Brede screamed. A horror too deep for words engulfed her and she cried out for help – not from Sorcha, as she would once have done – but from Ashe.

Ashe faltered, hands misplaced, meaning adrift; distracted by a wavering darkness that called weakly to her, writhing against the pull of the music she tried to thwart. The darkness struggled to take on form. Ashe recognised with a sickened horror, that this was what remained of Sorcha – this shadow. Ashe was suddenly aware of screaming. She abandoned her battle with the music, reaching out, touching the writhing darkness, her mind open to anything that it had to tell her. Without knowing how she did it, Ashe pulled Brede from that darkness, all of her, body and spirit. She found use for her hands now, not in speaking but in comforting and soothing the anguish that roared into her own bones as she touched Brede. Aware that she must somehow stop the singing, and that she couldn't do so whilst she protected Brede, she forced her mind away from that pain, reaching out for help in her own turn, reached out with her mind, seeking a mind in tune with her own, and finding one.

Islean felt the touch of an alien mind in hers, and stopped singing. She saw with other eyes, saw a mind and body in torment, heard a voice she hadn't expected to hear, Ashe's voice, screaming at her. Her sight cleared, and she clapped her hands together sharply, singing her companions to silence with swift harsh dissonance. A dreadful continuo of screaming sobs continued, out beyond the walls of the singing room.

Searing anger held her silent, shuddering with revulsion. Islean was the keeper of those songs too dangerous to be committed to memory; she should have recognised the danger behind Saraid's music. She condemned herself for not taking that responsibility to heart.

'What do we do here?' Islean whispered. 'Are we singing Sorcha through the Gate or are we tearing a living soul from its body?' She leapt to her feet, and grasped Saraid by the shoulders, wanting to shake her. 'What would you have us do? Make the same mistake that we condemn Ashe for? Dear Goddess, do you not hear what we've started?'

Saraid wavered on her feet, then nodded slowly, acknowledging her error, her responsibility. Islean let her hands fall away from her, as though the very touch would burn her, and Saraid sank down at her feet. The silence was viscous with the weight of the Songspinners' expectations, their uncertainties, waiting for Islean's lead.

Islean stepped away from Saraid and opened the door. Ashe stood before her, rigid with outrage, not yet ready to believe that Islean would put right what had been done. Islean could not quite credit that this woman, who was once her lover, who was now nothing to her, a no-voice, less than human, had spoken into her mind, and made her follow her will. *Ashe* had done this. Islean quickened to the smell of power, the fleeting wild touch of a new strength. She reached out to touch Ashe, to renew something she thought was dead, completely distracted from her purpose. Ashe pulled away, refusing her, forcing her to see the why behind the how of that unexpected burst of power.

Huddled at Ashe's feet, Brede sobbed, mirroring and outstripping Saraid's despair. Islean was sickened by the comparison. She gathered the woman to her, singing in an undertone, almost soundless, but no less vital for that. The sobbing eased and Brede drifted into unconsciousness. Islean felt the dead weight of her drag on her arms, and let Brede down gently into Ashe's embrace. She saw the care, the tenderness with which Ashe folded the unconscious woman to her, and she almost believed that it was too late to mend what she had so carelessly discarded. Almost she believed it, but her belief in herself was stronger.

Chapter Fifty-One

Brede jerked awake, and was amazed that she had woken. She gazed at her hands, astonished that flesh still covered the bones, that there was no pain. And still there was that tremor of existence that was Sorcha, untouched, wrapping her against harm.

Brede threw herself from the bed, crackling with fury. Her mind caressed the thought of Sorcha. But it was Ashe she had called for in the extremity of need. Brede wrapped herself in a cloak, feeling cold and afraid, and went in search of her.

She found Ashe sitting at the window, her hands involved in spelling out a new song, another song about which Brede had been told nothing. The secrecy alarmed her, but she admired the skill in Ashe's fingers, she faltered only rarely. The light played on Ashe's frown, concentration making her look older than she was. The blue jerkin she wore reflected sullenly on her cheek, as she stared out beyond the town, to the forest, to the bare branches, bleak with waiting for the snow to cover them.

Brede watched Ashe's hands turning, her head tilted as she listened to the music from the next room, trying to fit the signs to the rhythm. She was finding it difficult.

She had tied back her hair, but it wasn't yet long enough in front to hold tight in its bonds and a few strands had worked loose to cast shadows across her eyes.

One hand ceased its movement to push the dull mousy wisps away. Mechanically, she returned to the song. Brede couldn't hear the words through the doors, but could read them from Ashe's fingers. She had not quite dared to do so, but a repeated sign inflicted itself upon her.

Bright, Ashe's fingers said, over and over; but her mind didn't say *bright*, it said *Sorcha*.

Brede paid closer attention to the words. Another requiem. Shadows closed about her. Brede couldn't shift the movement of Ashe's hands from her sight: telling her again and again, as she tried to fit the metre of the song, that Sorcha was gone.

'Who are you trying to convince?' Brede asked. 'Sorcha?'

Ashe jerked in surprise, but the steady movement of her hands resumed at once. The music from the next room rose, then ended. Ashe's hands stilled, and she stretched them before her, still holding the last word, as though she would create something new from it. Then she sighed, and her hands fell into her lap. She smiled, a smile at odds with her half-angry concentration of a moment before.

They still try to, her hands said; *I try to add my own version.*

Brede sank down beside her, covering Ashe's hands with her own, as though to silence her.

Trying to persuade Sorcha to pass the Gate? Will you not give up? All the song making in the world is not going to free her.

Brede didn't trust her voice for this; her tongue stuck to the roof of her mouth. She made her words against Ashe's fingers, as though she were whispering. Her memory had spared her nothing, she remembered exactly what had happened and why.

We must, Ashe replied.

Brede stared out at the forest, rubbing her hands against her face. She forced her voice into working order.

'Can you do it?'

Ashe shook her head. They had the words, they even had the right tune, there was no question of that; but instinctively, she knew that there was something missing. Islean's song would not be enough to unravel Sorcha's hold on the living: on herself, on Brede.

Ashe wanted to take back that denial. Brede's grief was a cold wind. She wanted to wrap herself about Brede, to stifle that coldness, to end her mourning; something she could do no better by her caress than she could by singing. She could still see the shadow that was Sorcha wrapped about Brede. But Brede had called *her*, not Sorcha; she didn't quite dare believe it, or what might come of it.

Brede stirred herself, remembering why she had come looking for Ashe; she had a debt to pay.

'I've something of Sorcha's that I want you to have.'

Ashe looked up at her, sharply anxious.

Brede rubbed her thumb for the last time over the only thing she had left of Sorcha, and almost changed her mind, but the stones had no place in her life now. If the witches couldn't free her of her dependence on Sorcha, then she must do what she could for herself. She stretched her hand to Ashe.

The stones lay across Brede's fingers on their braid of hair, as if they were innocent trinkets. Ashe pushed Brede's hand away.

You must give them to Aneira or Islean or Melva, her hands whispered.

Brede frowned.

'Why?'

I am not a Songspinner.

Brede's hand closed over the stones.

'Yes you are,' Brede said, but she kept her hand closed over the stones. She remembered clearly that it was Islean's voice that was raised in protest while she fought for her life. She would not trust any of the other witches with her precious last gift, nor did she wish to hand it over in public.

Brede laid the stones before Islean, her hand trembling at the magnitude of letting go of this one last thing. Islean didn't attempt to touch the stones. She saw at once that she had been given the key to the puzzle. She glanced at Brede, saw her wretchedness, and another realisation came to her.

'I've been a fool,' she said, delighted with her sudden enlightenment. 'You are part of this binding after all. You, and Ashe who has spoken with Sorcha's voice. You must both be part of the unbinding.'

'I can't sing,' Brede protested, hoping that there was nothing more to be demanded, her trust in Islean already unravelling.

'No, but I see now that I've been too concerned with what has happened and what has been sung. I've lost sight of the people those things have happened to. Do you know what these stones are?'

Brede shook her head.

'These are the Singer stones. We assumed they had been lost and that we would never be able to choose one of our number for that honour again. How did you know to save them?'

'I didn't. It was all I had left.'

Islean controlled her elation. *All she had left*; but there was no way for a no-voice to keep something so vital, so precious.

'I thank you for your trust in me,' she said formally.

Her words seemed hopelessly inadequate. There would be time enough for appreciation when Brede saw the difference these stones made. She looked again, saw for the first time the braid of hair holding the stones together.

'Is that – is that Sorcha's hair?' she whispered. Brede nodded, and almost grabbed the stones back.

'That will help too,' Islean said, standing. 'Come with me now, I want to do this straight away. We must find Ashe and as many Songspinners as we can. Bring the stones, I mustn't touch them.'

Islean almost ran to the door, then realised that Brede was still standing immovable, staring at the little stones. Islean stepped back and touched her arm.

'We will only need a strand.' she said, that *all she had left* echoing into Brede's silence once more. 'Please?'

Brede nodded, clasped the stones tightly, and followed her.

Ashe saw the singing room with the eyes of a stranger, someone with no right to be there. She looked at the patient, puzzled women who had answered Islean's urgent call, not believing that they would be any more successful with this singing than they were before. Ashe allowed herself to feel superior when she heard the gasp of concern that greeted Brede's entrance, the murmur of excitement when she placed the Singer stones into the offering circle.

Brede resisted the music when it began, fighting its entrapment. Fear that she was once more to be offered up as an unwilling sacrifice held her rigid and wary, the talisman of Sorcha's hair wrapped tight round her fingers. Despite her rebellion she was caught, trapped in the web of their words, the skein of song.

The notes lifted her up and whirled her about, entangling her in the brightness and joy of the music. Her fingers tried to encompass the words, and she recognised some of them as her own – words spoken to Saraid, and to Ashe, stolen words.

She reached out for support, unable to stand against the tide of the melody. It didn't seem possible that so few voices could make so many threads of sound; they conjured Sorcha, embodied her in their music.

Brede felt the layers of darkness between herself and Sorcha stripped away and felt again the hands gripping hers, Sorcha's hands, holding her from death.

There was an imperceptible break in the song, as though they all breathed in at the same moment. Then Brede heard a tune she recognised, a song of death; heard it not from Sorcha's weak and choking throat, but from the throats of the women about her. So far they sang it, but no further, holding the tune wordlessly for a few seconds, resolving the chord, and again, the breath of silence, allowing the echoes almost to die and then, one after another, their voices spiralled down, unbinding, setting free, letting go.

It was unspeakably beautiful, and terrible.

Brede was light-headed with the very breath of it. She didn't understand the words, but she felt a loosening about her, as though a protective arm had been drawn away, felt a chill at her back.

Almost she called out to Sorcha, to call her back. Almost, but the breath she took in to mould into words, she let loose again in a sigh. It was too late to call Sorcha now.

Brede opened her eyes, aware of the speaking silence about her, the waiting; and realised that for all their powers, these women couldn't tell whether their sorcery had been effective. They didn't know whether Sorcha had gone.

Brede looked across at Ashe, who nodded slightly, clear-eyed and certain amidst the clouded uncertainty of her sisters. Together they shaped the words on their hands.

She is gone.

The silence ended, a rustling of movement, as the tension of waiting gave way to the relaxation of sudden weariness. It had been a hard spinning. Islean stepped into the offering circle, and for the first time touched the stones. Her hand barely grazed them and they rolled away from her, separated from one another, no longer bound.

Gone, Brede buried her face in her hands. *Gone finally.*

She could feel the difference in the air she breathed, but for this departure she felt no grief. Her choice; she had done with grieving.

Well then, there was a new life you were planning: time to be about it. There is nothing here for you.

Ashe sat for a long time, unable to contend with movement, feeling both emptied and replete, feeling that she had been given something precious. She searched about in her mind, trying to place her mental clutter as it should be, searching for what it was that she had gained, but it eluded her.

She was brought back to herself by Islean's voice, asking who would take up the stones. She stared across at the woman still standing within the circle, and realised what she was doing: seeking a new Songspinner. Ashe glanced quickly around, picking out those who had any hopes.

Islean had already tried and failed, the stones rolled away from her; now she stepped out of the circle, giving way to whomever wished to try. Aneira of course, and Ceridwen; and Melva, who was perhaps too old now, her voice beginning to weaken. There was no one else among them who had the power to even consider trying for the Singer stones, apart from Saraid. Ashe glances nervously at her, but Saraid had no plans to attempt this. She had no plans at all.

Brede packed her few belongings, and walked slowly back towards the singing room, hoping to encounter Ashe, hoping to at least say her farewells and to give her thanks for Ashe's part in her release. Brede was uneasy with her new freedom, feeling unexpectedly alone. She had thought the emptiness was a part of the grief, but here it still was.

Brede didn't want to enter that room again. She stood at the door, seeking out Ashe.

Ashe saw Brede waiting uncertainly at the door and stood to leave – this ceremony had no place for her, a no-voice. As she stepped past Islean, her one-time friend stayed her with a hand on her arm, holding Ashe still to watch as each in turn failed to touch the stones. Ashe tried to resist, but Islean would not allow her to leave, not until she had tried one last move: Islean pushed Ashe gently into the circle. Ashe's presence there was greeted by an angry murmur from her sisters. Pride made her pull the shreds of her dignity together in the face of their hostility, she knelt and reached towards the nearest stone. It didn't roll away from her. Ashe picked it up, and then another, and another. She hesitated, momentarily doubting that they were the same stones, but she knew them, could feel the gentle hum of them against her palm. She reached for the last stone.

Ashe held out her left hand, palm downwards, the four stones resting uneasily on the backs of her fingers. She turned a cautious circle, so that the assembled witches could see she had them all. The angry muttering was silent now, as they watched, willing her to fail, as they had failed. Ashe could feel that wishing, souring the air about her, and she believed with them, that she couldn't do this thing. But what more could she lose? Ashe tossed the Singer stones into the air.

To complete the ritual Ashe should call the stones by their names and catch them again. How should she, having no voice, do this? The Songspinners stirred, watching those stones spin upward. Ashe looked up too, and smiled, caught suddenly by certainty and triumph; she spoke their names on her fingers. The stones waited for her stumbling signs to finish, and then dropped lightly, one by one, into the palm of her hand.

Power rushed, humming, through her bones, and Ashe feared it. She wasn't ready for this; she didn't *want* this; it made a mockery of her choices. Pride had fooled her once more.

Brede saw the change in Ashe, not something she could put into words, but something – her heart twisted, and she turned away, stumbling slightly in her fearful haste to get away from the power she recognised, and had seen only once before in Ashe.

Ashe turned to Islean, but Islean raised her hand, warding off her anger. She had done nothing but guess at what choice the stones would make; hoping that Ashe would regain her voice, or at least some of her power, that she would step once more into an existence that Islean could recognise and love.

Ashe felt the tremor of power again, intoxicating, like nothing else she had ever experienced. It was as though, lizard-like, she had regrown a severed limb.

Ashe remembered Brede's analogy, telling Aneira that she had not thrown away a sword, but cut off her sword arm. Well, if she had the arm back she need not pick up a sword. She looked about her for Brede, found her gone from the doorway and found an impending loss that was far worse than a severed limb.

Brede reminded herself that she had grown used to being alone, but she still felt that strange echoing darkness inside, the almost fear; a bleakness that

389

she used to welcome as a balm to her heart. She prodded at the feeling, trying to force it to its limits. The precipice was still there, the cold howling wind trying to drag her down. She found the edge and stood on it, daring the roaring monsters of her mind to tear at her, and the wind died, and the abyss was only a few feet wide, difficult to span, but not impossible. They had not taken Sorcha from her completely with their ritual, the memories were still there, safe, precious.

Brede saddled the horse. The citadel was strangely quiet in the aftermath of the singing. The horse clattered across the weedy cobbles, and she flinched from the noise. Morna stood at the door to the kitchen. Brede nodded to her as she passed. She was glad to be out in the bustle of the town. Out here, it was safe to think about Ashe, about the sudden rush of power Brede had seen engulf her. It was safe, out among ordinary mortals, to be bitter; to be angry that after all, she was not needed, not regretted, not missed.

Ashe almost saw her go, catching only the last flicker of the horse's tail, the echo of its hooves under the gateway. The new power roared in her, swelling in her blood, tingling into her hands. She knew with an outraged certainty that if she raised those hands, if she made the sign for *stay*, Brede would not go. She watched her treacherous hands, already moving, and forced them down. Perhaps she should in truth cut off her arm. Would she so soon forget what could be accomplished by ordering a living creature to stillness? Bile rose in her throat, anger at herself outweighing even the dread that she had allowed Brede to turn her back on her once more.

She had passed some unseen barrier. She was no longer a Songspinner, she was something more, she need not rely on her voice, or any other one fragment of her self. She glared at the meaningless handful of stones in her palm. All this she had, and nothing that she wanted. Well. Ashe gathered all of that power, all of it, and focused on the stones, filling them brim full of the molten lightning that crackled through her bones.

And then she spoke.

Islean, leaving the hall behind Ashe, almost lost her footing at the top of the steps leading to the courtyard. A handful of small stones rolled away from under her feet. She recovered her balance, and recognised the stones, cracked and scorched though they were. She took in her breath to call for help, and then she saw that Ashe had left more than the stones. As she stared across the courtyard, there was a slight shimmer in the air. She looked closer, approaching carefully. Ashe had left a message; a feeling that seeped into her as the shimmer touched her. She heard a voice, one she had hoped to hear again, but the message was not so welcome.

I am not a Songspinner, Ashe's voice whispered, and the shimmering faded.

Out in the town, Ashe ran as though the Scavenger were at her heels. She knew the town, far better than Brede; she knew the alleyways, the slips, the twists, and the stairs that were impassable to a horse. Reckless in her headlong race for the town gates, she stumbled often, still unused to relying on her body to get where she wanted to go. She slipped, she fell against the townsfolk; she knocked children flying. She was past caring. Ashe had but the one aim: to reach the gate before Brede. Her feet weren't the only part of her body that she bruised. Her lungs burned and laboured, but it meant nothing, there was only the gate and the black horse approaching it.

Brede wasn't hurrying, but the horse had a good steady pace, a long gait, and she went a route unimpeded by market stalls and the press of bodies. Brede didn't notice, she was planning her best route, her hopes of employment, the chances of a change in the weather to the waiting snow; anything, so that she might ignore the shouting loneliness that crowded her. Somewhere within that wall of plans, she discovered that the Dowry blade was still beneath the bed in the Songspinners' guest chamber. For the space of a heartbeat she considered turning the horse about and going back for it; but no: it was another ghost laid.

Brede reached the gate first.

Ashe had no breath left. She leant against the gate, raging, unable to find the strength to even step through the portal. Her legs trembled violently; she wanted to fold herself into the ground and cry. Now she might have used her power, had she not abandoned it.

Reckless, her mind screamed at her, *you see what you've lost?*

Ashe pulled herself up. Brede hadn't gone far, she might still catch her.

And what then? she asked, harsh with dwindling hope, *what then?* Another silent, embarrassed denial?

But still Ashe walked, limping now, after the receding horse.

I've done with grieving, Brede told herself, wiping away tears, unable to understand why she was weeping. *I am cured of my loss.*

The stuff of sorrow no longer knit for her, there was only dragging regret; she had left behind something she needed. She pulled the horse to a stop.

The silence out here, almost into the shade of the forest edge, reminded her. *Silence:* Ashe.

Brede eased herself from the horse, landing heavily. She walked the horse around in a slow circle, loosening the cramping pain, thinking of unknotting muscles, of bones knit true and strong, thinking of Ashe's fingers forcing the pain out of her, taking it into herself.

Ashe felt her name called; felt Brede's thoughts touch her. She looked up. The dark blur ahead was a blur no longer. She could see Brede clearly, standing beside the horse, twitching the saddlecloth into place as though there were some deep significance to the way the fringes lay. Brede wouldn't look at her, not yet.

Ashe stopped walking, and Brede felt the resistance to her call, only now realising that she had called. She glanced up, puzzled. She saw the unmoving figure on the road, scarcely believing in it; sure that it was her imagination conjuring the woman, but she left off arranging the horse's gear.

Ashe resumed her weary walking. Brede saw the limping tiredness, and knew that this was real: that this was Ashe following her.

Brede held to the horse, uncertain of her balance, doubting the cautious delight that welled up in her mind. She pushed herself away from her support, found her balance secure and started to walk back towards the city, and towards Ashe.

ABOUT THE AUTHOR

Cherry Potts is a lesbian and feminist with a love for fairy tales, which burgeoned into a love for fantasy. She wrote her first story aged about eight and hasn't really stopped. She is the author of two published collections of short stories, *Mosaic of Air* (Onlywomen Press 1992, republished by Arachne Press 2013) and *Tales Told Before Cockcrow*, (Onlywomen Press 2009 out of print but available as individual e-stories from www.cutalongstory.com), and a photographic diary of a community opera, *The Blackheath Onegin* (Curved Air Press 2011). Cherry's stories have also been published in a number of anthologies from Onlywomen Press, Arachne Press and Leaf books, and in magazines and online – at *Litro*, *.Cent, Holdfast Magazine, Latchkey Tales*, and others. She is currently working on three more novels in various genres: science fiction, young adult and historical, and her next short story collection.

Stories have also been performed by actors at Liars' League in London, Leicester, Leeds and Hong Kong and at other London events, including the Literary Kitchen Festival, and Cherry has performed them herself at the Towersey Festival, Brixton Book Jam and The Story Sessions.

After a varied career in housing, IT and life coaching, Cherry now teaches creative writing at City University London as a visiting lecturer and owns Arachne Press, editing our anthologies, inventing live literature events and runs writing workshops. She sings in choirs for fun, and lives in South London with her wife Alix, and Julian, a very spoilt cat.

MORE FROM ARACHNE PRESS

www.arachnepress.com

EVENTS

Arachne Press is enthusiastic about live literature and we make an effort to present our books through readings. We showcase our work and that of others at our own occasional live literature event in south London: *The Story Sessions*, which we run like a folk club, with headliners and opportunities for the audience to join in (http://arachnepress.com/the-story-sessions/); and we ran our first all-day festival, Solstice Shorts (http://arachnepress.com/solstice-shorts/), in December 2014, followed by a shorter second Solstice Shorts Festival, Longest Night in 2015.

We are always on the lookout for other places to show off, so if you run a bookshop, a literature festival or any other kind of literature venue, get in touch, we'd love to talk to you.

WORKSHOPS

We offer writing workshops, suitable for writers' groups, literature festivals, evening classes – if you are interested, please let us know.

BOOKS

London Lies ISBN: 978-1-909208-00-1
Our first Liars' League showcase, featuring unlikely tales set in London.

Stations ISBN: 978-1-909208-01-8
A story for every station from New Cross, Crystal Palace, and West Croydon at the Southern extremes of the Overground line all the way to Highbury & Islington.

Lovers' Lies ISBN: 978-1-909208-02-5
Our second collaboration with Liars' League, bringing the freshness, wit, imagination and passion of their authors to stories of love.

Weird Lies ISBN: 978-1-909208-10-0
WINNER of the Saboteur2014 Best Anthology Award: our third Liars' League collaboration – more than twenty stories varying in style from tales not out of place in *One Thousand and One Nights* to the completely bemusing.

Mosaic of Air, Cherry Potts ISBN: 978-1-909208-03-2
Sixteen short stories from a lesbian perspective.

Solstice Shorts: Sixteen Stories about Time
ISBN: 978-1-909208-23-0
Winning stories from the first Solstice Shorts Festival competition together with a story from each of the competition judges, Robert Shearman, Anita Sethi, Alison Moore, and Imogen Robertson.

Devilskein & Dearlove, Alex Smith ISBN: 978-1-909208-15-5
Nominated for the 2015 CILIP Carnegie Medal.
Young Erin Dearlove has lost everything, and is living in a run-down apartment block in Cape Town. Then she has tea with Mr Devilskein, the demon who lives on the top floor, and opens a door into another world.

The Other Side of Sleep: Narrative Poems
ISBN: 978-1-909208-18-6
Long, narrative poems by contemporary voices, including Inua Elams, Brian Johnstone, and Kate Foley, whose title poem for the anthology was the winner of the 2014 *Second Light* Long Poem competition.

The Don't Touch Garden, Kate Foley
ISBN: 978-1-909208-19-3
A complex autobiographical collection of poems of adoption and identity, from award-winning poet Kate Foley.

All our books (except *The Other Side of Sleep* and *The Don't Touch Garden*) are also available as e-books.

follow us on Twitter @arachnepress
like us on Facebook https://www.facebook.com/ArachnePress